THICK AS THIEVES

THICK AS THIEVES

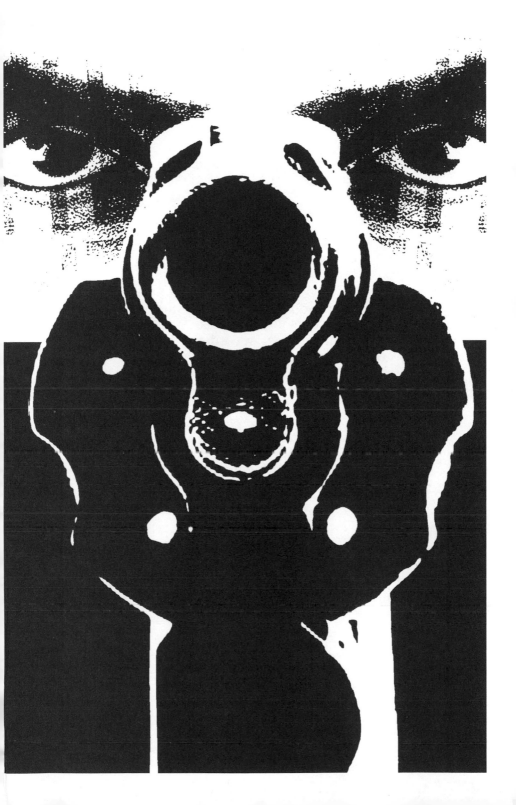

Copyright © 2008 Neil Low

ISBN: 0-9801510-1-5
978-0-9801510-1-5

Library of Congress Control Number: 2008903634
Printed in the United States of America

Editor: Don Roff
Design: Steve Montiglio
Author Photograph: Don Roff

Tigress Publishing
4831 Fauntleroy Way SW. # 103
Seattle, Washington 98116
206 683-5554

This is a work of fiction. Names, characters and incidents either are the product of the author's imagination or are used ficticiously. Any resemblence to actual persons, living or dead, business establishments, orther events or locales is entirely coincidental.

In memory of my father, Donald, and for my mother, Patricia, who exemplified the finest moral character for their seven children.

Awake early so he could deliver rolls for a local Seattle bakery, Alan Stewart listened through his opened window to a car downshifting to a lower gear, its motor whining at a high pitch, as the auto labored up the steep, cobblestone streets. Near his home, the car coasted for a second, stopped, rolled backwards, and bounced awkwardly off the curb, as if the driver were inebriated or otherwise not paying attention. A second later, the car doors opened, followed by men's voices. Alan lifted the shade for a better view of the big Packard idling in front. The large driver sat behind the wheel, white shirtsleeves, suspenders, tie, and a gray fedora, fidgeting, a handkerchief near his face. Two men, equally as large but not as well dressed, went around to the back of the car, opened a door, and pulled out his dad, who was passed out. Alan was familiar with the effects of alcohol, but he'd never seen his father in a state where he had to be carried.

The men wrapped their arms around McAlister, who was wearing a suit with a bright tie and a hat. They hoisted the dead weight between them, before dragging him toward the sidewalk, his shiny shoes scuffing across the cement as they drug him along.

1

When they reached the curb, the men stumbled with their load, and his dad's hat fell off, exposing a bloodied and swollen face. One of the men stooped awkwardly for the hat and tried replacing it on the misshapen head. Alan opened the window and cried, "Dad!"

The men looked toward the bedroom window and re-doubled their effort. When they reached the brick steps, they stopped, appearing confused. The driver said something, and the men dropped the body, right where it was, hurried back to the car, slammed the doors, and sped off.

Alan raced through the house and down the stairs. He called for his mother as he went by her room, and then he ran outside to his father, lying unceremoniously on his side, face down to the pavement. He sat next to him on the steps, still damp with morning dew. He rolled McAlister into his lap and held his head. He wasn't wearing a tie, as Alan first thought. His collar was bloodstained. There was no smell of alcohol.

Mary came onto the porch, wearing a terry cloth robe, slippers, and hair in rollers. She clutched the robe to her chest and paused for just a moment, surveying the scene below, before racing toward Alan and McAlister.

Alan put up a hand to stop her. "Call an ambulance. He's having trouble breathing."

She ran back into the house. A few moments later, joined by Alan's two brothers and his sister, she came back. "They're waking up a crew. Could be twenty minutes."

"I don't think he'll make it that long," said Alan. "Sean, you hold him, while I bring the coupe around. Mother, go back and call the police. Tell them to meet us at Providence Hospital."

Though known for her steely resolve, Mary's eyes were now wet and her lips trembled. She clasped his shoulder and spoke slowly, words carefully measured. "Keep your voice down. This was your father's business, not the neighbors' business, not police business. We don't need to be answering a lot of nosey questions from nosey people who've got no reason to know."

She squatted, taking his place. She stroked her husband's swollen face and touched the nose, tracing a new break with the tip of her finger. She picked up his hands, pulled them into her lap, and tried to rub out deep abrasions near each of his wrists, already forming bruises. Tears fell from her cheek to his. Sean, Patty-Mike, and Margaret cried, sensing the worst.

"Will he be all right?" asked Sean.

Mary didn't answer; instead, she rolled McAlister's head to the side and used the hem of her robe to dab blood trickling from his ear. She rocked rhythmically back and forth, sobbed, and said, "We'll do our grieving in private."

Alan parked his 1932 Ford coupe in front, and his two younger brothers helped him load their father into the jump seat in back. Sean asked, "Who did this to him? The men he works with?"

Alan spoke in a strained whisper. "I don't know, but someday, somewhere, there'll come a reckoning. I swear to God."

Mary squeezed her eyes shut, shook her head, and snorted contemptuously. "I'll hear none of that, Alan Stewart. Oaths have terrible power. Ya take it back."

"No disrespect to you, Mother, but I meant what I said."

"You're just as thickheaded as your father, and you see where that's got 'im. Vengeance is the prerogative of the Almighty···and not yours."

She turned to her other children. "Margaret, get a throw from the sofa and some scotch from the cabinet. Patty-Mike, you ride in the back with your father."

3

She did not have to repeat her orders.

Sean leaned close to Alan and whispered, "Dad was the most hard-boiled detective I've ever heard of, and you think you can take down whoever it was did this to him?"

Alan whispered through gritted teeth, his eyes moist, red with rage. "Some time, some place, I'll find a way!"

Alan turned over McAlister's wrists for inspection and began massaging the bruises. Sean took a close peek. "What do you supposed caused those?"

"I can't be sure, but it looks like he was bound."

Mary interrupted their reverie, dispensing directions. "Alan, this family's beholding to the union, so don't be telling the hospital who it was that brought him home. Leave the union out of it. That's what your father would want. Understood?"

Alan nodded, eyes wet and filled with fire.

"Alan, I'm counting on you."

Two years after his father's death, Alan sat in Mario's Tailor shop waiting his turn for a fitting from the family friend. Nearly finished with the customer in front of Alan, Mario took an extra moment to feel the fabric and compliment its quality. Alan had heard the routine many times, the usual flattery. He put down his magazine and watched a Packard park at the curb. The driver, a big man with a fedora, stayed put, behind the wheel. A man riding shotgun opened the back door, holding it for another man, who was followed by a fourth, a natty dresser who needed assistance. He was gravely obese, and his hair was white and tufted, rising above his pasty skin. Under his thick nose he sported a drooping mustache that was bigger than Teddy Roosevelt's, walrus-like. The other men each took a hand and tugged, gently pulling the man from the car. Then they hurried to get out of his way, deferential. The Walrus stopped and turned like the gun turret on a heavy cruiser, until he caught sight of his reflection in a window. Although it was only another ten feet to the entrance of the tailor's shop, he adjusted the hat on his head, setting it rakishly.

While the driver waited in the car, the first two held

the door to the shop for their boss. Mario greeted his guest. "Buon giorno, Signor Brinkman."

"Hey, Mario. How's business?"

"Benissimo. People tell me you send them my way. I appreciate that, and it makes the missus happy."

"I like to keep my friends happy."

"So···what is it today?"

"I have another suit needs fitting. This one's from a friend···you understand. So what could I say? He would've been insulted if I refused his generosity. Right? So I make him happy, too."

The Walrus turned toward Alan and met his gaze. "You happy, son?"

"Yes, sir."

The Walrus nodded at one of his entourage, who moved over to Alan. "Mr. Brinkman's in a hurry with important union matters to attend to. You won't mind if he moves to the head of the line?"

Alan glanced at his watch, then met the man's eyes, knowing this to be a statement, not a question.

"That won't be a problem?" the bodyguard pressed.

Alan stirred in his seat, and behind the man, Mario arched his eyebrows and coaxed him with an exaggerated, pleading nod.

"My father was a union man," Alan said with deliberate coolness. "Glad to oblige."

"Good answer," said the bodyguard.

Mario heaved a sigh of relief.

The Walrus asked, "Have we met before?"

Alan sat up straighter. "Yes, sir, a couple years back···at my father's funeral."

The other men shared puzzled looks.

Alan said, "McAlister Stewart···he was your···he was one of your men. I'm Alan Stewart."

"'Course you are," said the Walrus as he quickly waddled past the bruisers and extended a hand. He smothered Alan's hand with his flippers, a two-handed shake, following it up with a firm grip of Alan's right arm.

"You must've grown another couple of inches, but now I see the resemblance, son. It's a strong one, just like your grip. You've got Mackie's eyes, but you must have your mother's nose."

"Dad had a boxer's nose. Mine's not there, yet."

"He was a good one, no doubt. God, how I miss him." The Walrus released Alan's arm. "You've got his build, but not his mug. Do you box?"

"Mother made me quit. Said she didn't want it interfering with schooling···or the gloves marking my face."

Laughs all around. Alan sat back down.

"She's right. You got a pretty face. Keep it that way."

One of the bruisers said, "Just as well you're getting out. There's too many coloreds getting in the game now. They're taking it over. Going to ruin it."

The Walrus frowned and shook his head. "Benny's just sore because there's others putting the fix on matches he's got an interest in. He turned back to Alan. "So how's Mary getting along?"

Alan settled into his chair. "Mother's fine, Mr. Brinkman."

Mario opened the garment box and took out a new suit, uncut, fresh off a boat from Europe.

"She's a dear woman," said Brinkman. "I'm embarrassed I haven't seen her since the funeral. Does she have enough to tide her over?" he asked casually.

"She···she got a settlement check for $1,000 after Dad passed. It's been two years, and the money's gone." He made no apology for his frankness.

The Walrus scowled, and then he turned and glared at the bodyguards. They shrugged their shoulders simultaneously,

7

implying innocence, stupidity, or both. Benny spoke up. "That's standard cash out on a man who didn't retire."

The Walrus snapped, "Why wasn't I told?"

"We was following union policy. I thought you knew."

"$1,000? So what's she supposed to live on the rest of her life?"

Heads ducked and eyes avoided his glare.

"Alan, I'm sorry. I was unaware of this oversight. I'll have Vera look into it. Obviously, these knuckleheads aren't capable."

"This is a very nice suit, Signor Brinkman," said Mario, steering the conversation back to business. "Very nice material. Why don't you try the pants on first?"

The Walrus stepped into the fitting area, curtained into partitions on three sides. It provided little privacy, but it protected customers from passersby and vice versa.

Mario's eyes showed relief, and Alan worked to steel the animosity in his own, not wanting to betray his emotions. These men had some involvement in his father's murder. To what extent, he didn't know…yet, but in time, he resolved he would. It would just take more patience than he was certain he had.

The Walrus plopped on the edge of a chair, which creaked under his weight. He grunted for his henchmen to help him, and they each grabbed at the fat man's cuffs, tugging the pants over his shoes. Mario took the trousers from them, and the men helped the Walrus back to his feet, like shipyard tug boats, nudging a battleship from its berth. He was more interested in the conversation than the tailoring. "So Alan, are you still in school, or are you working?"

"I'm a relief driver for Gai's Bakery. Dad helped me get the job when I was a college freshman."

The Walrus eyed his men, and they exchanged approvals. "So you had to quit school?"

8

Alan didn't respond.

"That was the way it was for me, too. I got halfway through law school and had to pull out. I ended up getting the rest of my education from the school of hard knocks—the one with demerits, detention, and de ruler across dese knuckles," he said as he raised his thick hands for his audience's inspection. "It sounds rough, but it prepared me for the real world. I have no regrets."

Mario said, "Alan's a good boy, Signor Brinkman. His family lives on my street for many years."

The men continued dressing their boss. Alan feigned boredom but watched with fascination. As the Walrus held the pants in front of him, Alan caught a glimpse of a pearl-handled derringer pistol in a leather holster, clipped to the big man's boxer shorts.

One of the henchmen turned to check on Alan, so he faked a yawn, covered his mouth, and stretched for another magazine.

"So what are you having done, Alan?"

"Mario's going to re-cut one of my father's suits to my size."

"Special occasion?"

"It's for my twenty-first birthday··· a month away."

"Smart idea. No sense leaving it hanging in the closet. You're more trim in the waist than your father, but that'll change over time." He patted his own ample stomach.

His men waited for the Walrus to smile; then they laughed.

Mario helped him into his suit coat. The Walrus spun and admired himself in the mirror. Schoolgirl vanity.

"You ever have a new suit, Alan?"

"No, sir. Not yet."

The Walrus evaluated his image.

"So, what do you think, son?

"It's very nice, Mr. Brinkman."

The Walrus whispered something to Mario, who

glanced over at Alan and then whispered something back. Then the Walrus drew one of his henchmen close. More whispers, and the man left the store for the rear of their car. Less than a minute later, he came back with a garment box, fastened with straps. He presented the box to Alan.

"Mr. Brinkman wishes you a···Happy Birthday!"

Mario had stopped fussing long enough to watch Alan, and next to him, under his mustache, the Walrus wore a broad grin that said he was pleased with himself.

"Go ahead, try it on. It's a 44 long. Should fit a guy your size. If it doesn't, we'll try another."

Alan fought hard not to grin like a kid at Christmas. He wanted to hate this man and all of his father's friends. They may not have been the ones who killed his father—at least he and his mother didn't think so—but they had some responsibility. Instead of taking McAlister to the hospital when they should've, they'd brought him home to die. Then they ran off, no explanations, no concern, no telephone call, like schoolboys pulling a prank they hoped to escape.

"I can't accept this, Mr. Brinkman."

"Why not, son?"

"I haven't done anything to earn it."

"Think of it as a rite of passage, something your father would have given you on your twenty-first birthday, God rest his soul. But Mackie's not here, and I'd like to give it on his behalf. I loved that man. He knew what it meant to be grateful and loyal; so does your mother. I bet those qualities run deep in your family."

"This is very generous, Mr. Brinkman, but I feel like I'm taking advantage···like I'm trading on my father's memory."

"I understand, but you have to look out for yourself. When an opportunity like this comes along, you have to recognize it. Besides, you wouldn't want to hurt my feelings."

The bodyguards took this as their cue and turned square to Alan, giving him a hard glare.

Behind them, Mario gave Alan that pleading look again. He was the white knight cornered by two rooks and a bishop, but he didn't let his face betray his feelings. It was his move. He conjured up a smile, nodded his head, and unfastened the box. He pulled off the lid and set it aside. Inside was a navy blue, wool suit, with fine pin striping, and fully lined.

"This is the best there is, Alan," Mario said. "They don't make any better. Navy goes well with fair skin and blue eyes. You should be very grateful."

"Thank you, Mr. Brinkman. My mother will be pleased."

"That makes me happy, Alan," smiled the Walrus.

Taking this as their cue to relax, the men resumed helping the Walrus dress, while he basked in the attention, royalty holding court. "Tell me, Alan, is your mother still grieving?"

"Not officially, sir, but she doesn't get out much, other than spending a lot of time helping at church."

"Church? I don't remember Mary being much of a church mouse... Well, that's the past, and times change, people change. Forget I mentioned it. If church makes her happy, I'm glad for her. But tell me, does she still play the piano?"

"She's become a regular church goer," Mario cut in.

"Well, good for her. I hope while she's there she says a prayer for those of us who can't make it often as we should."

As he was leaving, the Walrus said, "Put Mr. Stewart's bill on my account, and send it round to Vera at the Union Hall."

"As you wish, Signor."

11

The Walrus turned to Alan. "Please give my best to your mother, and tell her I'd like to stop by and pay my respects. I'll call ahead, of course."

Mario stood at the window as the big car drove away, engaging in meaningless hand waving. "'Put it on my account,' he says. What account? He never pays for nothing. Signor Big Shot."

"If he doesn't pay, why do you tailor for him?"

Mario pointed toward the dressing area. "Pants first."

Alan picked up both suits and stepped around the curtain.

"It's the cost of doing business, Bambino. Overhead that don't show up on the books. It's oil for the machinery, keeps things moving. I don't charge him, so he sends favors my way, lots of business. There are plenty others I don't charge."

"Like who?"

"I don't charge the Mayor, the City Council, licensing people, tax people, or the police."

"Why not?"

"I do a good job on the mayor's suits, people ask 'who's his tailor?' and he sends them my way. Same with the City Council boys. And I have no trouble from the taxman or the licensing man, like other shops— with nosey people checking to see who I got in the back sewing for me, and if they have all the papers they need. No, siree. I got no audits and no problems at City Hall. That makes me happy, just like Signor Big Shot says. And the police let my customers be— no parking tickets. That's something I appreciate."

Mario finished chalking the first pair. "Now put on your papa's pants."

"What happens if you don't go along with the payoffs? Does the courtesy stop?"

"You betcha it does. I have a friend who owns a bar on First Avenue. The beat cops pay him a visit and ask him to play along, pay up, and make regular donations to the Police Benevolent Society, Police Ball, Pension Fund···on and on, but he tells 'em he's new to this country, got a lotsa bills and can't afford it. So the cops, they gets mad, and they start checking every customer's ID to see if they're old enough to drink in his bar, even the pensioners. The cops start running people out, telling 'em they're over-served, and then they start with tickets and code inspections. Pretty soon, nobody wants to come to his bar and his rent is due. So my friend borrows money from me, and he pays off the cops. Then, POOF! The tickets disappear like magic, and after awhile business is back and then, business gets good."

Mario finished chalking one suit coat and said, "When you walk in here you don't own a suit. Pretty soon you gonna walk out of here with a two suits!"

"Maybe my luck's changing."

"As I was saying, the police take care of my friend's problems and keep trouble away from his door. No more inspections, no more code violations. Now he's got a card room in back and stays open after hours. He's making more money than he ever dream about. He's got so much he's stashing it in the vault next door, so the government and his wife won't know. Hiding money from the government is not so bad, but I don't go for hiding from your family, but that's just me."

"Your friend keeps money in a vault?"

"Safety deposit boxes···you know."

"I've never had anything to put in one."

"Your daddy never took you to his?"

"No···least not so's I remember."

13

"I'm pretty sure he had a box in the same vault as my friend."

"Do you know the name of this place?"

"It's the one that survived the fire in⋯what was it⋯1889? Everything else burned down around it. It's now the Pioneer something or other. First and Cherry. I'll ask the beatman when he comes by. Lots of cops keep boxes there."

"Police work pays that well?"

"Police work don't, but payoffs do. And that vault's just right for them, 'cause it's so old that each box only has one key. New ones, now, take two keys, and that means you could have a someone lookin' over your shoulder. So, the old ones are better for them. You know what I mean?"

Alan nodded.

"That's one less pair of eyes you have to worry about," Mario said, shaking his head. "It's funny, you know? People pass a law nobody much care's for, and so they pay the police to turn and look the other way. Mostly it's with booze, but it's also gambling, whores, political donations, and what they call 'the blue laws.' You can bet those guys taking protection money from my friend, they got boxes there. They got to have some place that's safe."

"Looks like bullies taking advantage of the little people."

"It's not so bad. The system wouldn't be there if people didn't want it. Those who pay get something out of it, or they wouldn't do it. So it's a pretty good way of doing business⋯for now, anyway. Lot of people gets happy this way, specially people like Signor Brinkman."

"Was my father one of these happy people?"

"Alan, I like to mind my own business and not talk about what doesn't concern me."

14

"If you don't tell me about my father, who will? He didn't talk business at home, but the things I hear from other drivers and around town—"

"Your papa was a good man. He did what he had to do to put bread on your table during the hard times. You have a nice a house, just like some big-shot attorney, and your family never went hungry. You know how tough it's been to find jobs. After his boxing career, it was Signor Brinkman who took him in, like a son, and give him work in the union office. He introduced him to your mama, when there was a lot of other men waiting in line. Signor Brinkman treat him special. When they come in here together, you could see they has a special bond, not like the goons he's got now, and it looks like he likes you, too."

"You think so?"

"Look at this suit he gives you."

Mario held it for him as Alan tried it on.

"This is a bank president's suit," said Mario. "You could get yourself a table in the Rainier Club with the old-money people. But you take my advice, Bambino, and be careful with Signor Brinkman. He maybe asks you for a favor. You know?"

"There's strings attached?"

"Who knows? Maybe yes, maybe no? You just be careful, and watch out for your mama, too."

"Why my mother?"

"I don't know. He asked too many questions about her. Don't you think?"

Alan stomped on the bottom step and wiped the dirt off his shoes before opening the back door. He kicked off his work boots, left them on the landing, slid on his father's old slippers, and entered through the back door. He wore a weight-of-the-world look, tempered by a hint of pride. He climbed the inside stairs, kissed his mother on the cheek, before announcing, "Boss said I'm getting a regular route."

His mother set the roasted chicken on the table and called for the rest of the family. "That's good, Alan," she said, big smile.

"Mom, that's great! No more relief runs, a steady paycheck, and regular days off."

"But there's something more, isn't there?"

"I'm just wondering," he said as they say down at the dining room table, his brothers and sister joining them.

"Wondering what?" asked Patty-Mike.

"I was just telling Mom I got a regular run."

"That's what you been wanting, isn't it?" asked Patty-Mike.

"It is, but I'm not the senior relief man. I'm jumping ahead of two other men. It makes me wonder if Mr. Brinkman's working some magic."

Patty-Mike said, "Nothing wrong with that."

Mary said, "Don't be so sure, Patrick. When Mr.

16

Brinkman gives a favor, he expects one. If not now, later."

"Can I have your relief route?" asked Sean.

"What kind of favors?" asked Patty-Mike as their mother dished out mashed potatoes.

"Favors you don't want to return, Patrick," said Mary.

Sean asked, "Favors like Dad used to—"

Sean cut short his question when his siblings shot him hard looks. Mary set down the potatoes and said, "We'll not talk about your father's work."

"Yes, ma'am."

As Alan passed the chicken around, Margaret whispered, "Save the breast for me."

Alan, who'd already placed tongs around that piece, picked it up and placed it on Margaret's plate. Then he took another piece for himself.

"Hey. No fair," said Patty-Mike.

"It never would have made it to you," said Sean. "You're too far down the ladder, squirt."

Mary said, "You can take two pieces when it's your turn, Patrick."

As the vegetables made their way round the table, Alan said, "I see there's a new lock on the garage. Did we have another visitor?"

"We did. Looks like someone jammed the tumblers, so I had a new one put on."

"What's that? Three now?" asked Alan.

"It is," said Mary.

"We must have the most expensive garage locks in the neighborhood," said Sean. "What does someone want from our garage? Nothing in there but the Hudson, which we hardly drive, since Dad passed."

Alan asked, "Do you think they got in?"

Mary said. "I didn't check. I wouldn't know if anything were missing or not."

Margaret said, "Mother got a surprise today, Alan. Hand delivered."

His mother set down her water glass and folded her hands in her lap. She tried to suppress it, but a schoolgirl smile spread across her face. "I didn't want to spoil your good news, but I got a letter from the union, signed by Mr. George Brinkman, himself, and delivered by one of his aides."

"You mean one of his thugs?" said Patty-Mike.

"Don't interrupt, Patrick Michael. This is important, and they're not all thugs. Your father worked for Mr. Brinkman as a private detective. This wasn't one of···he was a nice man, dressed respectable···I don't know··· like an accountant. Anyway, he gave me a letter from Mr. Brinkman, which said that during a recent audit, the union found they'd made a mistake settling your father's retirement claim. To correct that error, Mr. Brinkman has certified your father's death was work-related, suffered while making emergency deliveries to a union store. This certification means that the McAlister Stewart family is entitled to survivor benefits."

Rapt attention. All stared at Mary.

"What's survivor benefits?" asked Margaret.

"Means Mother will get a pension check," said Alan.

"Is that real money?" asked Patty-Mike.

"It is," said Mary, "and there's more. The letter said that Mr. George Brinkman would like to come by Sunday afternoon and personally deliver a certified check to the family to reimburse us for payments missed over the past two years."

"Wow!" said Sean. "How much will that be?"

"The letter didn't say. I guess we won't know 'till Sunday, and while I'm at it, I expect you all to be here. Mr. Brinkman would like to meet everyone."

18

While his siblings excitedly discussed the possibilities, Alan's attention shifted toward the window and the garage.

"Alan," said Mary, "you've got that distant stare of your father's."

"I'm just trying to figure this out. This is everything we'd hoped for. It all seems to be coming together, but I don't know what to make of it."

"Grandpa Dave used to have an expression; he'd say, 'An Irishman's never content until he's wallowing in his own misery.' So, let go of what holds you back and accept the good. And in the present case, it looks like the good fairy's been remiss in her duties, and now she's making up."

"I suppose grandpa was right, but I get to wondering about the timing of things, like when will the other shoe drop—and the lock on the garage. Do you think there's something I missed?"

"I don't know who's been out there or what they're after, but I say if you find somethin,' give it to 'em. It can't be worth puttin' this family at more risk."

Alan leaned back and looked toward the garage with a scowl. "Sure. I'll give it to them."

It was mild weather for autumn in Seattle. Alan worked a half-day Saturday morning, and since he'd started early, he was home by ten. His mother and Margaret were away, church he figured, or maybe shopping. Sean and Patty-Mike were working the loading dock at Frederick & Nelson, helping the stalwart department store prepare for the holidays. Mr. Brinkman had found them jobs. It was hard but honest work. Alan figured this to be a good time to explore the garage, before Mr. Brinkman dropped by again on Sunday. The Walrus had been coming by weekly for his mother's baked chicken.

Alan opened the cupboard next to the wall phone in the kitchen, lifted a serving plate and removed the new key. Mary hid the key to the garage under a dish, but the key to the Hudson, parked inside the garage, hung on its usual hook below the telephone. He grabbed that key also and headed for the garage.

The old but sturdy structure had an alley entrance and was situated on a rise, above the house. The loft inside the garage featured a peek-a-boo view of Lake Union, a dozen or more cobblestone streets below. Constructed the same year as the house, it also had brick accents, shutters, and lead-paned windows. His father had told him its age once, but he'd forgotten. Designed to store a carriage and stable two horses under a hayloft, it was originally called a carriage house, but it had been a garage as long as Alan could remember. He had never seen it with horses, but there were a long-forgotten saddle and bridles in the loft, along with a potbelly stove that was never connected. At one time his dad had talked about fixing it up as a guesthouse, just like other neighbors had done with theirs, putting in stoves and proper toilets.

Alan opened the new lock, flipped back the sturdy hasp, and swung the garage doors wide. Usually greeted by a smell that was slightly musty, with essence of grease and oil, he caught the faint aroma of burnt tobacco. His father had occasionally smoked a pipe in the evening—but never out here, and if he had, the smell should have disappeared long ago.

Skirting the passenger side of the Hudson, his shoulder bumped the car's vent window, which was pushed open. Surprised, he opened the unlocked door and found papers pulled out of the glove box, leaving it empty. The sun visors were also turned down and the registration holder pulled off. Someone had given the car a going over, and whoever it was didn't care that anyone knew.

Alan restored the car to the exact order his mother would expect, and then he backed it out, parking at an angle just off the alley. He set out a bucket, hose, and a rag. If anyone asked, he'd tell them he was washing the car and, while he was at it, the garage windows, too. He checked around to make sure neighbors weren't watching, and then he went back inside, shutting the garage doors behind him.

Alan took a metal curtain rod next to the door, unraveled the heavy bunting, and hung it over the door.

He repeated the process on the other door and turned on the light over the workbench, before he closed the curtains over the remaining windows. The well-made curtains showed Mario's attention to detail.

Privacy assured, Alan plugged a trouble light in and dragged a sawhorse to the middle of the garage, where a large metal pan, layered with sawdust, caught oil drippings, or so it seemed. He hung the light on the sawhorse and slid the pan to the side, exposing a threadbare carpet, coated with sawdust. He tossed that aside, uncovering a wood floor. Careful not to splinter the wood, he used his pocketknife to pry up a two-by-six board, levering it high enough to get a grip with his fingers. He caught hold of the edge, worked the board loose, and tugged it and three others out of their assigned positions, then set them aside. The floorboards showed nail heads from the top, but his father had removed their business end so that the boards rested on cross joists, held in place by gravity. The snug fit of the boards made a frame on top of a metal security box, constructed under the floor.

He reached inside the box and peeled back the cover of a large canvas bag. His father's gun collection was undisturbed. It consisted of a well-oiled Thompson .45 caliber sub-machine gun with extra magazines set to the side, both the straight version and the large-capacity magazines for fifty and one hundred rounds. There were also two .45-caliber, semi-automatic pistols with extra magazines and an M-1 Garand rifle, a new prototype his father was field-testing. Alan never learned who its original owner was. The weapons were all military issue, and there were several boxes of ammunition for each, packed neatly at the bottom of the bag.

He tried to lift the bag by the straps but was surprised by the weight. He settled on dragging it from its hole. He used the trouble light to inspect the empty metal box and found nothing else inside. He emptied the bag and checked to see if there was anything lying loose in its bottom, like a key with a number on it. Nothing doing. He checked every ammo box to be sure the key wasn't hidden with the ammo. Still nothing.

When he had turned sixteen, his father showed him the weapons and took him out to the country twice a month to shoot, clean, and oil the arsenal. He learned from his father how to make earplugs with pieces torn from hankies, covered with well-chewed bubble gum. A little messy to clean up, but it worked to cut down the noise. Together they fired hundreds of rounds, and despite the gum chewing, Alan had felt very grown up. His father wanted him to be familiar with the weapons, know how to use them, should the need arise. Before the first session, McAlister said, "We'll skip the Thompson."

"Why?" Disappointment registered all over Alan's face.

"They're near useless, maybe even a liability, unless ya practice with them···a lot. Shotguns are better if you're facing a couple of mugs, but a Thompson's the welter weight champ if you're taking on a crowd, because it all comes down to who can shoot the quickest with the mostest. Being a sure shot is great, but if you can put out a lot of rounds quickly, like with a Thompson, you can make up for piss poor aim.

"They take practice, because they want to climb with recoil. And because they fire ten rounds a second, they sound like an entire gun range, where everyone's shooting at the same time. You have to get used to the noise and recoil and overcome it. You have to hold

23

the barrel down. Never shoot more than a short burst; otherwise you'll be emptying your gun into the ceiling."

Alan listened to the voice of experience, too stunned to nod his understanding.

McAlister spoke as a skilled craftsman, proud of his work and his tools. "If you have to use it, lean into it, adjust your weight forward, aim low at the knees and let the weapon work its way to the mid-section. Remember: short bursts, three shots at a time; then start over, aiming at the knees again."

Alan said, "Knees?"

"Yes, son. These guns aren't for plinking at God's little critters. They're for people, bad people, and people have knees. I'm not teaching you to hunt. I'm teaching you how to take care of business: your mama, your sister, your brothers, and yourself. I hope to heaven it never comes to that···"

Near the end of their session, McAlister took a stick and scratched a human silhouette into the side of a sand hill, which had been serving as their backdrop, twenty feet away. When he finished, he stuck the stick into the hill, next to the waist of the silhouette, where a shotgun would be held if it were a real person. From the Hudson, he removed the Thompson and dropped the rags in the trunk. And, as if reinforcing the secrecy of these forbidden lessons, he carefully scanned the dirt road and surroundings, making sure they were alone. When he appeared satisfied, he took a magazine of ammo and slid it in place. As he stepped closer to Alan, he racked a round in the chamber. His movements were smooth and practiced. He'd done this hundreds of times.

He nodded at Alan, who covered his ears, despite the earplugs. Then McAlister fired a burst of three, just like he said. POW, POW, POW! He started at the left hip

24

area of the silhouette, and the muzzle climbed, moving to center mass. He turned to Alan. "Are you ready, son?"

"But you didn't shoot at the knees?"

"No, son, I've had a lot of practice. Too much for one man." He nodded encouragement to Alan and held the weapon for him.

Alan stepped forward, and his father placed the submachine gun in his hands, making sure to keep the muzzle pointed "down range." McAlister pressed the stalk to Alan's waist and continued his tutoring. "Hold it tight with your right elbow and sight the weapon over the top of the barrel. This is point and shoot. Don't worry about aiming. You watch where the rounds land and adjust the weapon accordingly. You'll probably blink, close your eyes at first. Just like those Hollywood actors. It's natural, but we'll shoot enough rounds to get you past that."

Alan moved forward, and McAlister stepped back. Alan looked over his shoulder to his dad, who nodded once. Alan turned back to face the target, exhaled, and squeezed the trigger, firing a burst. The tommy gun climbed from the silhouette's mid-waist to high up the bank. POW, POW, POW, POW, POW, POW, POW! Alan released the trigger and felt his father's presence behind him, his warm breath landing gently on his neck, reassuringly.

"Short bursts of three, lad."

"I'm sorry, Dad. The bullets came out faster than I expected."

"They're rounds, son, and what happens is the noise and clatter makes you grab on tight, and that causes you to squeeze down hard on the trigger. You'll get used to it. Like I told you before, this one takes practice to get good at. So give it another go and focus on the trigger control. Go light, and start lower."

McAlister moved back and nodded. Alan turned to

the silhouette, fixated on the scraping's left knee. He squeezed the trigger. POW, POW, POW, POW! Holes appeared in the sand hill, near the line drawing's left knee, and finished just over its right shoulder. His father nodded, a glint in his eye.

Alan approached the silhouette to admire his accuracy. Moisture from the sand pooled in the fresh holes, and when enough of the muddy water collected, it began to ooze out of the weeping wounds, trickling down the slope.

"Try it again, and work on holding the muzzle down. After awhile, you'll get to where you can steer and direct it."

And so they repeated the exercise, going through several boxes of somebody else's ammunition. McAlister said, "Later, we'll switch over to semi-auto and fire at a target in the distance, single bursts. We won't bother with anything over fifty yards, but if you get good with this, you can probably stretch a shot out to seventy-five. I've never bothered going farther than that with the Thompson, but the Garand does a real fine job with distance, up to a couple hundred yards. I'll show you how to handle it later, but, personally, I'm not much interested in it. That kind of shooting's for hunting, sport, or war, and I'm done with all of those."

Alan sniffled, zipped the canvas bag shut, muttered an oath, shook his head, and wiped his eyes with the sleeve of his shirt. He bent over and checked inside the metal-lined hideaway. He swung the trouble light over the hole, again checking to see if he had missed anything in the shadows. No sign of a key. He put the lamp down, lifted the overlarge canvas bag by its straps, and slid it back into its bay. He set the boards back in place and tamped them down, a craftsman's fit. He slid the old carpet back on top of the boards, and set the oil catch pan back in its place.

He moved the light and sawhorse close by the workbench, trying to eliminate shadows. No sooner had he set the light in place than he found cigarette ash at the base of the heavy workbench vice. "Son of a bitch!" he muttered. It hadn't been there on his last visit, and no one in his family smoked, or so he thought. But having younger brothers, he couldn't be sure. He would have to ask them individually and hope for honesty.

He swept off the ash and ground it into the floor. Then, he searched from one end of the workbench to the other, through old coffee tins that were a catchall for nails, screws, and nuts. Still no luck. He opened a drawer underneath, and way in the back, behind assorted tools, he found a ring of keys. Encouraged, he inspected skeleton keys to unknown locks and luggage keys, but he found nothing that looked like it might fit. He wasn't even positive what a safe deposit key should look like, but he was sure none of these would qualify. He dropped them back in the drawer and closed it.

He resumed his search, now focusing on the shelf above the workbench, which was large and framed with two-by-four studs. His eye caught writing on the face of a two-by-four: "324." The numbers were written with a carpenter's pencil, years before.

"Three-two-four?" he repeated out loud.

The other end of the shelf also had writing. He held the trouble light close and read, "GPSDB," also written with a carpenter's pencil. The letters seemed too distant to be connected to the numbers on the opposite end. In fact, he guessed the letters and numbers were about three feet apart, but the size of the letters and the instrument used to write them appeared the same. He felt underneath the two-by-four and found a brad, a finishing nail, protruding from the back. He leaned under the shelf and looked up at the nail. It had no other apparent purpose, but there was no key in sight.

On top of the shelf sat an old hatbox and two suitcases. He remembered seeing them before but hadn't paid much attention. Other than the changing of the locks, his mother had discouraged him from going out to the garage after his father died. She had, however, once asked him about the guns, allowing she knew they were out there somewhere, and wondered if McAlister had shown them to him. Her questions focused more on the risk an inadvertent discovery posed to his brothers and sister, but she didn't ask specifically where the guns were stored. This was within her keeping of the family rules, her not showing interest in his father's business.

Alan moved the hatbox and suitcases down from the shelf onto the workbench. The hatbox seemed too old to be his mother's or grandmother's. It was trimmed with old-fashioned frills and satin, like something that would hold a woman's hat from the 1880s.

Under the lid, instead of finding a musty creation festooned with lace and feathers, nestled inside the plush, pink, satin lining, he found a man's hat, a black fedora.

Alan wiped his hands on his pants, eased the hat out of the box, and inspected it. It was finely crafted felt, satin-lined. The sweatband showed little, if any, wear. He'd never seen his father wear the hat. He checked it for size, took it by its crown, and carefully slid it on his head. A good fit. Like Mr. Brinkman said, he had his father's build.

He walked over to one of the horse stalls where an old cracked mirror hung. The black hat was formal, classy, and bespoke no-nonsense. It made him look like a young priest. He usually wore a snap-brim hat, like others his age, but he would ask his mother if he could have this one. It wasn't doing anyone any good locked away in the garage.

He returned to the workbench and found the snaps to the suitcases were locked, but without a pause, he opened the workbench drawer, took out the keys he'd found earlier and tried them. The first key opened the closest suitcase. A good omen? he wondered. Inside was a complete set of clothes, including two dress shirts, ties, and a full suit. The shoes were fitted with shoetrees, preserving their shape. The suit hung from a wooden hanger. He paused to feel the material, just as Mario would, and held the suit to the light. Like the fedora, he didn't remember ever seeing his father wear it.

He returned to the mirror hanging in the stable near a 1-½ inch pipe, which was similarly disjointed, connecting two wooden posts together instead of functioning as plumbing. It was high up and strong enough to hold a man's weight, should he choose to exercise, like doing chin-ups, and it was the perfect size to hold coat hangers. Alan was sure this stall served as his father's dressing room. He hung the suit on the pipe and inspected it, deciding he would try it on.

Pulling on the lapels and snugging it into place, he felt something out of place. From the breast pocket he extracted an envelope. It had some heft to it. The flap was tucked into the envelope, not sealed. He inserted the tip of his finger and flicked it open. "Son of a bitch. It's a cash stash!"

He glanced around at all the windows and doors, assuring himself he was alone. Butterflies in his stomach, once dormant, all hatched at the same time and took to flight. He took a deep breath, exhaled, and then tugged on the money, which popped out of the envelope and flopped in his hand. The stack was almost a third of an inch thick. He fanned through a corner of the pile.

They were all fifty-dollar bills. He fanned them again, a little more slowly, and guessed there were about thirty of them. He whispered to himself, "Fifteen-hundred dollars! For what? Get-away money? Were you going to leave us? Or was it for union expenses?"

He tucked the money back in the envelope and put it back in the suit coat as he'd found it. He went through all the other pockets. No key. Alan left the suit hanging, while he checked the remainder of the suitcase. There weren't any more surprises.

He closed the suitcase but did not re-fasten it. Inside the next one, he found a black, woolen overcoat, folded and alone, fit to be worn over a suit, fully lined and of comparable quality. Alan slid the coat on while walking back toward the mirror. A touch too large, it would fit better with something underneath. It bespoke gentility and went well with the hat. He tried a pose or two and shoved his hands into the coat's pockets, where he found lightweight gloves, one in each pocket. He pulled them out and tried them on. They were not lined. He closed his hands into fists and extended his index fingers. He moved them back and forth easily, as he would pulling a trigger. After examining the gloves carefully, he shoved them back deep in the pockets, and his right hand hit a small wedge of cold metal. A key!

The glove was in his way. He yanked it out of the pocket, stuffed it in his other hand, and dove back in for the key. He took the shiny treasure over to the light. The key was without markings. It hung solo on a thin string with a paper tag, which had the number 324 written on it, the same as the pencil writing on the two-by-four above his head. There was no hint as to what GPSDB represented. He stared at the letters and tried to imagine how Dashiel Hammett would solve this. All he could think of was using deduction—trial and error. Could it be: Greater Puget Sound Deposit Bank? Should be something close to that. Mario said the place had survived the Great Fire.

He bent over and reached under the shelf and hung the key on the brad, behind the letters, and when he stepped back, he couldn't see the key or tag.

Before taking off the coat, he found deep pockets sewn into the lining and vents that allowed a person to reach through the pockets without opening the coat. Near the coat's slits, on the inside, he found four deep but slender pockets. He squeezed something hard, ammo clips to the Thompson submachine gun. One was empty, and the other had two .45s remaining. He set the magazines in the bottom of the suitcase and folded the topcoat in the manner it had been, placing it on the first suitcase.

Alan paused, listening in silence, and then glanced around at the garage windows and door again. Satisfied he was alone, he checked behind the satin divider in the second suitcase. From behind the spot where shoes were kept, he felt another object, and he hurriedly pulled out another envelope, similar to the one he'd found in the suit coat. He flushed as he recognized what it was—more money. Two thousand dollars was written in pencil on the outside of the envelope. He fanned through the stack of $50s and recalculated his total. He was holding $3,500.

Alan pressed his hand against the fabric in the suitcase again and discovered another envelope. He shook his head in disbelief as he extracted a twin to the last one. It, too, had $2,000 written on it in neat lettering. He didn't have to be a full-fledged detective to recognize a woman's handwriting. He verified the

31

contents and set both envelopes in the bottom of the suitcase. The handwriting looked the same.

He went back to the suit, pulled out its envelope, and noted similar writing and dollar amount. His father must have used $500, leaving $5,500. He shook his head again and muttered, as if arguing with his father, "Roosevelt passed laws protecting banks."

Alan sat back, resting on the sawhorse, and staring vacantly at the suitcases for a moment. He figured the money was for his dad's business expenses, and the fancy clothes were special working clothes··· union business. His dad must have carried the tommy gun under his coat, and the pockets in the lining were for ammo clips.

He surveyed his found treasures, spread out on the workbench, for a few moments, deciding what to do. Then he pinched his lips and exhaled hard through his nose. Alan picked up the envelopes and felt their weight, bouncing them in his hand. It was more money than he'd ever seen, and he realized it wasn't safe there, that was for sure. He set the envelopes underneath where the key dangled. He folded the suit, pressing out any wrinkles. He saved the hat for last, having trouble parting with it. He posed in front of the mirror again, before finally taking it off and returning it to the hatbox. Done playing dress-up, he hoisted the items to the shelf and restored the garage to the condition in which he found it, parking the car back inside. He checked around one more time; then taking the envelopes and key, he left the garage.

Climbing the back steps to the house, Alan heard a car engine start up. He spun around and glanced up the alley to where a black sedan, he guessed a Ford, sat parked in front of a neighbor's garage. He could make out two shapes in the car, probably men. The driver tossed a cigarette out the window, backed the car up, turned around, and drove out the other way.

Alan slammed the palm of his hand into the stair railing, hard enough to make the wood groan. He muttered an oath.

In his bedroom, Alan pressed his nose against the window, checking up and down the street out front. Satisfied that all the parked cars belonged, he pulled down the shade and stashed his treasures in the top drawer of his bureau. A moment later, he thought better of his choice. It occurred to him that if it was the first place he thought to put it, it would also be the first place anyone would look. Someone tough enough to take down his dad and savvy enough to search his garage certainly wouldn't have scruples about searching the house. Sitting on his bed, he scanned the room for someplace safe. He lay back, hoping for inspiration, but nothing came for a couple of minutes. Then his eyes settled on the closet door, trimmed with flat one-by-four pine.

He crossed the room to the closet and checked the wood molding on the inside. It was exactly the same as the outside. He reached up and tugged on the thick wood. It wiggled but wouldn't give. With his pocketknife, he pried the nails at the top of the jamb a half-inch away from the studs.

Alan retrieved the envelopes from the bed and slid the smallest one over the molding, edgewise, until it touched bottom on the inside of the doorjamb, just above his head. Three inches of the envelope stuck out from the top, leaving it visible from inside the closet. Tucking the envelope in sideways to conceal it completely wouldn't work; he would have to tear the molding off to retrieve it. Since no one would ever look there, he decided to leave it standing up. He slid the other two envelopes in next to it, and breathed a sigh.

With the tag folded over the key, he slid it down the side of the molding closest to the wall. Snug fit. He nudged it back until just an eighth of an inch was showing. He breathed another sigh, stepped out of the closet, and kept an eye on the molding, as he backpedaled to his bed. It should work···for a while.

Sean and Patty-Mike played cribbage at the dining room table, while in the front room Alan listened to Bing Crosby on the RCA. The family quietly waited for Mr. Brinkman, who was again dropping by for Sunday dinner, which Alan's mother prepared with Margaret's help. As a distraction, Alan toyed with his father's neglected pipe collection, which sat on the table next to a pedestal ashtray.

Margaret, who was taking a break from the kitchen, stood sentry at the front window. "Mr. Brinkman's here."

Alan waited to open the front door for their guest. At the curb, below, one of his loyal goons helped the Walrus out of the Packard. They started toward the steps. Then the Walrus said something, and the large man accompanying him stopped and waited for a moment, before walking back to the car. Mr. Brinkman took the steps in stride, no hesitation, no faltering.

Alan chuckled and turned to Margaret. "Did you see him take the stairs?"

"He's a lot spryer than he lets on."

"Tell Mother our company is here."

35

After dinner, Margaret excused herself to begin the clearing and cleaning, and Mary gave Sean and Patty-Mike the look, tilting her head toward the kitchen. The young men left the room to help their sister and stay out of the way. Mr. Brinkman got up from the dining table with Mary and Alan so they could visit in the front room.

Alan settled into his father's chair, while Brinkman sat at one end of the sofa. From a silver tray, Mary poured each a glass of sherry from a bottle the Walrus had brought. The bottle's cap lacked the required Washington State liquor stamp.

"Tuesday will be your first election," the Walrus said. "Have you made up your mind, Alan?"

Alan waited for his mother's approving nod.

"The family's always voted Democratic, because Dad liked Roosevelt. I figure I'll vote the Democratic ticket."

"Smart idea, son, and that means for City Council you'll be voting for Jack Hardin?"

"That's my plan."

"Jack's a friend, and the union needs more Democrats like him, but there are some who feel the Republican slate would've gotten us through the Depression in half the time. And they're worried FDR will get us into Britain's war by agitating the Japanese."

"Is there a danger of that?"

"No, son, they're dead wrong. FDR's kept us out of war, and he's fixing the economy as well. Wendell Wilkie certainly couldn't do it, and I don't think there's a man alive, crippled or not, could have done a better job than FDR. People forget it was the Republican's fat cat, Hoover, who got us in this mess. He and Wilkie are cut from the same bolt of cloth: rich kids with no political experience. Wouldn't know a good day's work if it bit them on the···"

Brinkman turned to Mrs. Stewart. "I beg your pardon, Mary. I get a little carried away with politics."

She smiled indulgently at the Walrus, nodding for the men to continue.

"No, sir, what our country needs is FDR to keep fixing what the Republicans broke. He's a great man, a great American, and so is Jack Hardin."

"I agree, sir."

Mary topped off their glasses.

"I'm thinking you'd be just the man to help the union on Election Day with your vote, Alan. If you're agreeable to my proposition, I'll have your bakery assign you as union steward for the day, and the union'll pay your salary. I'm sure the relief driver, who backfills, would also appreciate additional work. Does that sound okay to you?"

"Sounds great to me," Alan said, this time without looking to his mother.

"We'll make it a special day for you. I'll come around with my car about 7:30 and pick you up. After we vote, we can go out for breakfast. How's that?"

Alan smiled broadly and nodded. The Walrus turned toward his hostess. "Is that all right with you, Mary?"

"Yes, George."

"So, Alan, we want to get out all the votes we can. Dave Beck is doing the same over at the Teamsters."

"I'm glad I can help, sir," Alan said.

"Say, I've just had another idea. We have supporters, lifelong Democrats, who may have trouble getting to the poles: pensioners with disabilities, people with car trouble, some in wheelchairs like Mr. Roosevelt—God bless him—solid Americans. We've always provided a free taxi service for them, so to speak. After I vote, I send my car around for people who need a ride. It

37

helps the union. It's for a worthy cause. Would you be willing to drive some of these needy people? Might be five or ten over the course of the day, and I'll pay you two dollars a piece—on top of your shop steward pay—for every registered voter you take to the polls. Does that sound okay?"

"I'd be glad to help."

"It's good to have you on the team, son. With your enthusiasm and smarts, I can see you've got a bright future."

<<<<<<<<<<<<<<<<<<<<<<<<<<<<<<<<<<<<<<<<<<<<<<<<<<<<<<<<<

After Mr. Brinkman's driver whisked him away, Alan approached his mother. "I'd like to take the Hudson out for a spin, burn off some of the old gas before it gets stale. I'll take Margaret and give her a tour of town."

"That's very sweet. Do you want to take Sean and Patty-Mike along?"

"No, ma'am, just Margaret. Give her a chance to get out and for us to catch up."

Margaret waited in the bricked alley for Alan to back the car out of the garage. Two years his junior, she was athletic and a bit of a tomboy, having played tennis at school. She bounced on her tiptoes, not from the cold, but from the excitement of getting out of the house and driving around town with her brother. With luck, somebody would see her and ask about it tomorrow.

She climbed in the front seat, and they pulled out of the alley and dropped down the cobblestone streets to the rust-colored brick streets, and then to Eastlake Avenue, one of the first streets in Seattle to have its bricks covered with blacktop. People marveled at

39

how this innovation made their car rides smoother, and experts predicted it would prolong the life of automobiles.

Alan and Margaret followed Eastlake south, past the shipyard and the tall chimneys of the coal-burning electric plant, toward downtown, passing a trolley car along the way. Margaret peeked at the riders to see if there was anyone she'd recognize, but there wasn't. They took Fairview Avenue around the south tip of Lake Union and turned onto Westlake Avenue, which cut across the other avenues diagonally, pointing directly to the heart of the city. They lazily circled through the brightly lit streets, driving past the grand theaters with colorful marquees: The Orpheum, The Seventh Avenue, The Coliseum, The Fifth Avenue, The Music Box, and The Liberty. They worked their way over to Third Avenue and took it all the way down to Yesler Street. Alan said, as if it just had occurred to him, "Keep an eye out for a building that has the initials GPSDB in its name."

She repeated the letters back to make sure she had them right and asked, "Just the initials?"

"No, silly, those are the first letters of its name. I just don't know what the rest of the name is."

"No clue at all?"

"I'm pretty sure it's some kind of bank, or vault, or investment house···something like that."

"Why are you looking for it?"

"It's a favor for Mario. He has a friend who owes him money, and he wants to find out where he keeps it. I'm playing detective for him, and you can be the secretary. But that means you can't talk about it to anyone."

"I'd rather be a detective."

Alan rolled his eyes. "Sure. Why not? I'll pay two dollars for your time."

"Two dollars? That's more than I make for a whole day baby-sitting."

"So you'll get two bucks and have no diapers to change. We find it tonight, and I'll buy ice cream."

"Sign me on."

They crawled south, down streets lined with four and six-story brick buildings, built on top of the burned-out ruins of early Seattle, decimated by the great fire of 1889. Advertisements painted on the high walls hawked cigars, cheap rooms, and hardware and clothing for the Alaska Gold Rush, some forty years before. They looped around to First Avenue and headed back north.

"Any more clues?" she asked.

"Mario said something about it being a survivor of the Great Fire. I don't know much about that, but I think it took place west of Third Avenue and burned all the way down to the water, south through Pioneer Square, and maybe as far north as Madison."

"Did you try looking in the phone book?"

"Two problems with that: I'm not really sure of the name, and I didn't want anyone seeing me doing it. Besides, this is more fun; it's like what real detectives do, and I promised Mario I'd keep this quiet."

"But you're telling me?"

"Just you, Margie. You're now part of my agency."

She smiled broadly and giggled.

They crossed Yesler heading north, approaching James Street. The light turned against them, forcing them to stop, even though no traffic was coming. While idling, Margaret startled him as she pointed across to a building wedged in between several others. She read its name, "Great Pioneer Savings Deposit Bank. I've found it!"

Alan jokingly slapped his forehead, checked over his shoulder. "How'd I miss it? I'll drive up and come back around so we can get the address and check their hours."

"Looks like I'm the better detective. You owe me $2.00 and ice cream."

Over ice cream, Margaret said, "Mother was crying the other day."

Alan said, "About Dad?"

"I don't think so. She found a letter in the mailbox that didn't have a stamp or return address. I know, because I checked later."

Alan stopped eating and rested his chin on his hands. "Do you know what the letter said?"

"She crumpled and burned it in the fireplace. There wasn't much left, just the envelope."

"Is it still there?"

"No, we've burned several logs since then, but if it helps, she did mutter something about 'not having the key,' or something close to that. I asked her what was going on, but you know her and her secrets. She snapped that it wasn't my concern. And when I asked her who the letter was from, she said it wasn't signed, but···she knows···like she recognized the handwriting."

"Why do you think that?"

"Well, there's something else, goes back to right after Dad died, maybe a week or so later. I heard her crying in her room then, so I opened the door to check on her. She was going through a box where she kept mementos, things she never shows us. She pulled out some pictures, tore them up, and threw them on the floor. I let her be, but then later I checked the trash···"

"You are quite the little detective."

"Mom calls me a snoop, but···I pieced one of them together, best I could, and it was of her and another man, not Dad."

Alan's mouth dropped open. "What?"

"I didn't recognize who it was. He had a light colored hat pulled low, stylish, expensive. It wasn't anyone I knew, but they were arm and arm, and behind them was a car with a police siren."

"A policeman?"

"I don't know, but they were standing in front of a police car, just like all the pictures of the Stewart clan—you know how they always pose in front of their cars—like it's a status symbol thing. This looked just like that."

"Did you keep the picture?"

"Too risky."

Alan paused in front of the mirror by the front door
and adjusted his father's fedora. He pulled on the overcoat
he'd found with it. He'd told his mother about the hat
and coat—but not about the suit, the money, or key. He
wanted to find out more about them, first. Wearing his
delivery clothes, he had stopped by the vault yesterday,
while on a break, gone inside, and inquired about renting
a box. The staff paid little attention to him. He'd taken
some paperwork home that he planned to read later.

Mary showed mild interest in the hat and coat.
First, she shook her head and looked away, but after
a moment, she said, "I never saw those, so they don't
have memories for me. Go ahead, it's supposed to rain."
Despite giving permission, she still seemed distant.

Alan stepped onto the large porch and shoved his
hands in the pockets, digging for gloves. Brinkman's
Packard backed into a space next to the curb. The large
driver climbed out, snapping his overcoat's collar up
to block the rain, and hurried around the back of the
car. He turned toward the steps to greet his passenger
and froze in his tracks.

"Jesus Christ, Mackie!" he gasped. He stepped back
as if he was going to pivot and run. "Holy shit, Mackie!"

Then, using his hand to help shield his eyes from the rain, he took a cautious peek at Alan and stopped his flight. He squinted and stared hard at the young man's face through the rain drops.

"Mackie?"

"No, sir. I'm Alan Stewart. His son."

"Of course, I should've known. Haven't seen you since you were a little squirt. You gave me a hell of a start, kid. I thought you was your daddy comin' back to life. Damn near gave me a heart attack." The big man thumped his chest with the flat of his hand.

"I didn't mean to scare you."

"But you did, kid. From silhouette, you look just like your old man in his prime. Is that his coat and hat?"

"Yes, sir."

"Don't need to call me sir. I'm Vic. Vic Morrison. Friend of your daddy, private detective, and personal assistant to Mr. Brinkman—at your service." He stuck out his over-sized paw, with knuckles like Kenworth lug nuts. Alan stepped down, met his grip, and shook firmly.

Vic slowly let go of Alan's hand, grinned, and patted his chest again. "So···did Mackie mention me?"

"Dad never talked union business at home. He kept his work life separate."

"Say, Mr. B tells me you were a champion boxer, like your daddy."

Alan laughed, embarrassed. "Golden Gloves. Amateur stuff. I didn't get that far."

Vic chewed on that a minute and said, "Whoa, you scared me good, Champ."

Vic opened the back door for Alan, who bent down to slide into the backseat, but he found a surprise waiting there. Instead of a wool suit covering the thick legs of the Walrus, he found a knockout blonde with killer legs. She moved them to the side to make room for the new passenger. Behind Alan, the big man laughed heartily as he patted Alan's shoulder affectionately. "That there is Miss Alice Mahoney. Alice, this here is Mr. Alan Stewart."

The two shook hands while Vic went on with background information that neither acknowledged. So Vic repeated himself. "I said, 'Alan's daddy used to work for Mr. Brinkman.' We did some P.I. work together, and he was a personal friend. He and me was very tight."

Alan stared into the green eyes of the beauty, through a veil that hung from the brim of her hat to the bridge of her nose, giving her a coquettish look. He tried to break eye contact, to be polite, but he couldn't. She, too, held his gaze and smiled warmly.

"I'm Alan."

"Yes, I heard, and I'm Alice."

Vic said, "Alice works for Mr. Brinkman in the office. He couldn't make it today, and told me to convey his regrets. He asked Alice if she wouldn't mind coming along and voting with you. It'll be her first time, too. She just got naturalized and registered in time."

"Naturalized? Was I supposed to do that?"

"No, not unless you were born out of country like me," she said. "I'm from Canada···Vancouver, actually. Uncle George offered me a job in his office, and he helped me become a US citizen in time to vote."

"Mr. Brinkman has a way of making things happen," said Alan. "It's my first election, too."

Vic drove them to the polling place without asking directions and parked outside a grade school with twin forty-eight-star US flags hanging by the front doors. A paper sign over the door said, "Vote Here." The three got in line. There was a big turnout; all eager to vote.

46

A number of volunteers moved about in the crowd, acting official. Vic said, "This line's gonna slow us down. I hope it isn't like this at all the polls."

The three chatted as the line inched forward. Vic told Alice and Alan what he heard at union headquarters about the Republicans sending out letters alerting voters that there would be line checkers at the polls this year. Vic raised his voice so others could hear. "I don't like people prying into my affairs. It's just the way I am, and I think it's un-American what they're doing. If one of them snoops comes up to me, I'm going to tell them to mind their own damn business, if they know what's good for 'em. They ain't got any authority here, and they're just trying to scare off patriotic voters."

A few people around him turned toward his authoritative voice and nodded. There would be trouble if partisans messed with this line.

Vic let Alice and Alan go ahead of him. They went to separate tables and signed in. Vic consulted his notes, greeted an elderly volunteer at a table with his booming voice, signed in, headed off to his own empty booth, and snapped the curtain closed behind him.

When the three were done, they met at the back of the auditorium. On the way to the car, they passed the nurse's office. Vic tipped his hat to the picture of a Red Cross nurse on the wall, urging people to donate blood for the war in Europe. Addressing the picture, he smirked. "Didn't hurt a bit."

His humor was lost on the other two.

Vic held the car door for Alice, while Alan hurried around to the other side and let himself in. As Alice adjusted her weight in her seat, her dress rode high, exposing calf muscles, dancer's legs. Alan made an effort to look away but worried she might have caught him leering. He asked her about the office work, just as Vic came around from the trunk with an ice bucket and champagne. Vic leaned in and set the bucket and glasses on the seat. He took the bottle and popped the cork outside the car. Then he poured the young adults each a drink and handed them a glass.

"Compliments of Mr. Brinkman."

The two faced each other, toasted their glasses, and took a sip. Vic climbed back in the driver's seat and poured himself a taste. He toasted the new voters. When they lowered their glasses, he topped them off and put his away. He proposed a toast to Jack Hardin's success. This was followed by toasts to Mr. Roosevelt, Mr. Brinkman, Charles Lindbergh, Jack Dempsey, Babe Ruth, Lou Gherig, the Washington Huskies, the Fighting Irish, and many others. Alan lost track, and Vic kept the champagne flowing for his guests, while Alice hung onto Alan's every word and laughed at all his jokes. Before they left the parking lot, they had uncorked a second bottle, and Alan already felt giddy, well on his way to getting smashed.

Vic drove for a few minutes and stopped at a brick apartment house on Boren Avenue, where the brick street started to climb First Hill, which commanded a view of the city and its waterfront below them. "Wait while I check on our voters, see if they're ready."

After pouring more champagne, Alan sat back and found Alice sitting closer. Their knees touched, and her skirt had worked its way north, sliding over her knees. She caught him staring, and before he could turn away, she said, "I'm sorry, but for some reason my skirt seems to have a mind of its own." She made an effort to tug it down, but it didn't move. "I hope you don't mind."

"Not at all," he said, trying to sound debonair.

About ten minutes later, Vic came back to the car. "I got some bad news, kids."

They turned to his voice.

"Seems Mrs. Tate has taken ill, and she had to go back to the hospital last night. I spoke with the manager, who said she left a note."

Vic produced a piece of paper and read it aloud,

"'Dear Mr. Brinkman,

Sorry I won't be able to vote tomorrow, but I had to return to Providence Hospital for more work on my legs. If there is some way you can do it for me, I would appreciate your casting my vote. I think this council race is very important for us, for this city, and for the union. I think every Democrat's vote should be heard. Don't you?'

"And she adds on the bottom···"

"'To whom it may concern: Mr. Brinkman and/or his representative has my permission to cast my vote in my stead.'

"And it's signed, 'Mrs. Lilith Applegate.' Ain't that sweet?"

"So what can we do?" asked Alice.

"I don't know," said Vic. "Wait. There's a P.S. on the bottom, and it says,

'My husband, Herman will be with me all day while I'm in surgery and recovery. He would like someone to vote as his proxy also.'

"And it's signed, 'Herman Applegate.' That throws a monkey wrench in the old political machinery. Now what are we going to do? They'll be gone all day and will miss voting. That's two votes the Democratic Party loses. You kids got any ideas?"

49

Alice looked at Alan, furrowed brow and pouty lip. Then she turned back to their tour guide. "I've got an idea, Vic. Mrs. Applegate said something about authorizing an agent for Mr. Brinkman to vote for her. Since I work in his office that could be me. Don't you think?"

Vic furrowed his brow, set his jaw, and put his mind to work. "I don't see why not."

"I think it would be patriotic to make sure all the votes get counted. Don't you, Alan?" asked Alice.

Alan's tongue felt thick and his words slurred, but he felt very patriotic. "Absolutely."

Vic said, "I'm not quite sure how this will work, 'cause they'll have you sign in. You kids saw that, and now those nosey Republicans are snooping about, trying to scare people off. 'Till now, I've never had anyone check my ID."

The two others watched, hoping Vic would come up with a solution.

"While I'm thinking of it, I've never seen no place on the sign-in sheets for proxy signatures, and I've voted every election for twenty-years or more."

"Well, since we have Mrs. Applegate's permission," said Alice, "couldn't I just sign for her? If anyone asks, I'll just show them her note, show them it was all right."

"You're a very smart lady, Miss Alice. I see why Mr. Brinkman has you in the front office," said Vic.

"And since Mr. Tate also gave his permission for someone to vote for him, couldn't one of you do it?" she asked.

"Well, I don't see why not," said Vic. "I work for Mr. Brinkman, so that would be all right for me, but I think I'm way too old to pass for your husband."

Alan said, "Well, I'm working for Mr. Brinkman. So technically I'm one of his agents. That means I could do the voting for Mr. Applegate."

50

"Now you're thinking, Alan. You got your daddy's smarts, too. I could drive you both to the polls, you sign in together, you vote, and we get back on schedule, helping the democratic process along. And if anyone gets nosey with you, I'll flash them my persuasive smile and tell them to mind their own business."

Alan raised his glass and toasted. "To Vic's persuasive smile."

"Cheers," said Alice.

"Alan," said Vic, "do us a favor, Champ, and tend to the champagne while I drive."

Vic found the shortest route to this polling place, too, going further up Boren Avenue to the crest of First Hill, which now loomed over the downtown. After a few turns, Alan lost track of where they were. His companion now rested her hand in his, like it had always belonged there. Vic parked the car near the front entrance, adorned with more flags and with more volunteers assisting, all doing their patriotic duty. Alan and Alice walked arm and arm, and moved through the line. This line was shorter than the first one.

Alice steered them to a table to sign in. She went first, he followed. He bent over slightly and signed Mr. Herman Applegate with a flourish. She waited for him to finish, took his arm, and gave him a squeeze. Volunteers smiled at the couple, the epitome of young Republicans and every bit the cute couple.

Alan and Alice didn't see Vic when they came out of their voting booth, but he soon caught up with them in the parking lot. He apologized and said he had gone to find a payphone, which took some effort to locate.

Vic consulted his notes, and they all got back in the car, Alan holding the door for Alice this time. No one seemed to mind the rain. Vic drove toward downtown,

51

stopping in front of another brick apartment building. "You kids just go ahead and visit. I won't be gone long." Vic got out, ignored the pouring rain, and danced around large puddles.

While he was gone, Alice told Alan about growing up in Canada. She was born in Toronto and moved to the Vancouver area when she was six. Her family lived out in Surry. She worked for a liquor distributor until Brinkman hired her away, giving her career a boost in the States.

Vic returned after a few minutes and said, "I got more bad news. We was to pick-up Mr. and Mrs. Sherman, but when I checked on them, she was near passed out. She said her husband got rough with her last night, while they were tipping back a few. Somebody called the cops, Fred got a little lippy, and before you know it, they hauled him off to the gray bar hotel."

Alice said, "The where?"

"Gray bar⋯you know⋯jail. You ain't ever heard it called that? 'Course you haven't, you being a young lady and all. Anyway, old Fred is incapacitated, so to speak, and so is Mabel. There's no way to clean her up and get her to the polls on time. And what makes it worse is I've got a list of others for us to pick up, and I don't know how we're going to get to 'em all."

"Will she sign a note saying it's okay for us to vote for her?" asked Alice.

"I asked her, but she's too far gone to write something you could read, and we're losing time."

"If legibility's the problem, why don't I write the note for her, like I'm her stenographer, and then you can take it back to her to sign."

Alice pulled some paper from a briefcase, which Alan hadn't noticed before. She used Mrs. Applegate's letter as a guide and completed a note authorizing proxy, giving it to Vic.

Before very long, Vic returned with a grim expression on his face. He said, "I'm sorry, kids, but she's passed out cold, and now we're so far behind, I don't think we'll get to everybody on our list."

"If she's that far gone, I guess I could sign···on her behalf," said Alice. "It would be the right thing to do."

"Well then, Champ, would you be willing to sign for Mr. Sherman?" asked Vic.

"Be glad to."

Alan lost track of the number of times they voted that day. The polling places blurred together in a champagne haze, and all the volunteers looked much the same. At the last place, a school with a granite entrance, Alice's shoe slid on a wet step, causing her to lose her balance and fall toward him. Despite the alcohol, his reactions were quick enough to catch her and steady himself before they both fell.

"How clumsy of me," she said. She clutched both his arms, looked up to his face, and gazed into his eyes. She raked a tooth across her lower lip, tugging it slightly backward into her mouth, where she licked it before letting it spring back toward him.

Alan took off his fedora recklessly, leaned toward her, and kissed her hard. She kissed him back. When they came up for air, she pushed herself back but still held his arms, steadying herself.

"Oh, my···Shame on you, Alan Stewart···Taking advantage of me." Her delivery was slow and measured. There was no trace of regret. Her smile was wide, welcoming. Her lips were still apart, still offering a tempting void.

"My apologies, but I couldn't let that pass."

She started to chew at her lip again, but she never lost contact with his eyes. She tilted her head. "You're not going to kiss me again like that, are you?"

"This time I won't be so rough."

He grabbed her chin and steered it toward his mouth. He pulled her body close and flattened it against his, while holding his hat behind her waist with his other hand. He ignored the pounding raindrops, splashing off his bare head. She lifted the veil out of her way and stood on her toes so she could reach his mouth. As they were finishing their kiss, a flashbulb popped nearby. They turned to the sound and found a photographer had just snapped their picture. A man in a hat and trench coat said, "My editor wants to run some pictures of people voting in tomorrow's paper. You don't mind, do you?"

"Of course not," said Alice.

"May I get your names for the caption?"

"Certainly. I'm Mabel Sherman, and this is my husband, Fred."

A little unsteady on his feet, Alan beamed as he swayed, grinning stupidly but not caring.

"Great. I can't promise you anything, but you two make a great looking couple. I think the paper may run your picture with our story on elections: Love Birds Celebrate the Elections."

Vic was late again, and while waiting, Alice took Alan's hands and interwove her fingers with his. "This may sound silly, but I feel like I've known you forever. You remind me of···I don't know···family."

He said, "That was quick thinking about the names. I forgot who we're supposed to be. We wouldn't want any problems from the people working the polls."

"If the Shermans see the picture, I'm sure they won't mind."

◇◇

Between store deliveries, the day following the elections, a sobered up Alan Stewart bought a copy of the morning paper and scanned the election results. The front page showed Roosevelt won his third term. No surprise. Wendell Wilkie was gracious in defeat. Alan dug deeper into the paper to find the local returns. Under the picture of a romantic couple voting at a First Hill elementary school, he saw that Jack Hardin had won a position on the City Council. Great! It was a close race with a whisker-thin margin, but his opponent had conceded, sure that a few absentee ballots would not change the results.

Alan returned to the top of the page with the happy couple and read the caption: Love Birds Celebrate the Election. It took a moment to register. Then his eyes bulged wide and his eyebrows arched. She looks... Whoa! HE LOOKS FAMILIAR! What the hell? Alan sat on the running board of his delivery truck and read the caption, "Mabel and Fred Sherman celebrate voting."

The wheels in his brain churned painfully. He wondered if his mother or Margaret would recognize him. What about the Republican volunteers at the polling places? Would they complain? Would there be an investigation? He lowered the newspaper and stared off into the distance, not sure how many times he voted. Fred Sherman was the last name he was certain of using. He remembered they were running behind, but they had all agreed to do their part to help. Getting out the vote was their patriotic duty.

He picked up the paper again and stared at the kissing couple. Her face was more visible than his, but with close inspection, he was recognizable. He did his best to replay the afternoon and evening in his head, the ghosts of which still haunted him, even while taking too many aspirins. He used his fingers to tally the votes and settled for twelve for him and twelve for Alice. He recalled Vic's voting again when they'd gotten to around five or six, but he had no idea how many times he'd voted in between all the phone calls.

Alan climbed back in the truck and threw the newspaper onto the passenger seat. He stared straight ahead, lost in thought. He retrieved the paper and carefully re-evaluated the picture, but this time with a dreamy smile and a hunger he couldn't define.

Vic had waited in the car while he walked Alice to her building's front door. It was some place that had "Angels" in its name. She wouldn't let him come inside, something about rules, guests, decorum, and hours. She mentioned a woman's name, someone who must be like a housemother, who stood sentry at the apartment's door.

Alice had kissed him on the cheek and said she hoped to see him again, but he didn't have her phone number and wasn't positive where she lived. Things were just a little too blurry, and he wondered if he had gone too far too fast. He did have her scarf, which she left on the backseat of the Packard. He'd stuffed that into his pocket and kept it from Vic. He'd find a time to give it back to her, on his terms.

A message was waiting when Alan returned to

the bakery at 1:30. "SEE MR. BRINKMAN. UNION HEADQUARTERS. FORTHWITH."

Alan followed the trolley lines above him and skirted downtown by cutting across First Hill, above the Central Business District, down Boren Avenue to Denny Way, down the Regrade to the union offices. The receptionist directed him to the waiting area outside the president's office. As soon as Vera saw him approach, her eyes widened and her brows flickered. She settled down to the confident smile of a woman sure of herself, deservedly so. "Have a seat, Mr. Stewart. Mr. Brinkman will be with you shortly."

Alan's eyes drifted around the office, and he caught Vera in an awkward attempt to conceal that she was staring. She cleared her throat and started going through papers on her desk. His eyes focused on the room past her, but he couldn't find Alice in the mix of people processing paperwork. After a few minutes, Vic Morrison came out of Brinkman's office and extended his hand. "Good to see ya, Champ."

Vera got up as Vic and Alan shook hands. She interrupted the two. "I'm sorry for staring, but you look so much like your father." She stepped forward, smiling sadly, and patted Alan's forearm.

"So I've been told···except for the nose."

She released his arm, and her eyes glistened as they lingered on him. "I miss him···" Her voice trailed off.

Alan followed Vic inside the big office, and the Walrus met him near the door. "How's the city's newest voter?" He took Alan's hand and smothered it inside his.

"Just fine, sir," Alan said, embarrassed at the attention. He was hoping to find an ally in the room. The two goons from Mario's shop stood in the background. The Walrus gave a subtle head tilt toward the door, and they slid out. Then the Walrus stepped aside, revealing an attractive woman sitting in front of his desk. "No doubt you remember my niece Alice?"

"Yes, sir." He grinned wide. "A pleasure to see you again."

The Walrus waddled around his large desk and plopped in the high-back leather chair. "I'd like to thank you both for your assistance with the voting yesterday. It was a great day for America and a better day for the union."

The Walrus focused on Alan. "I regret I wasn't able to join you as I'd intended. I trust Alice provided good company?"

"Oh, yes, sir."

"Very good, then, but I must confess my concerns. Vic briefed me on the events of the day." With an almost imperceptible head move, he acknowledged his driver, standing next to his desk with his hat in his hand and his head bowed. "It appears the three of you were involved in, it pains me to say, voter irregularities." He opened the morning paper to their picture and spread the page out on his desk. "Vic tells me there was a problem picking up some of our loyal voters. Is that right?"

Alice spoke for them both. "Yes, Uncle George, but I can explain."

"That won't be necessary, dear. I think I have the gist of the story from Vic. The Applegates were at the hospital, and then the Shermans had legal problems." He picked up the newspaper and read the caption, "'Mable and Fred Sherman celebrate voting.'" He held the picture at arms' length. "Kind of looks like you two, doesn't it?"

"Yes, sir," said Alan.

Alice nodded.

"Vic tells me you got behind schedule, so he called ahead and got permission from the others for you to vote in their stead. Is that about right?"

Alan and Alice exchanged glances but didn't answer.

"And you never actually drove any of our fine citizens to the polls. Is that right?"

Their heads hung low.

"So how many times did you each vote yesterday?"

Alan said, "Counting for myself, I think it was twelve, sir."

Alice said, "That's about what I come up with."

The Walrus turned toward Vic. "And what about you, Mr. Chaperone?"

"Maybe six or eight, Mr. B. I'm not sure either. I was just trying to help folks perform their civic duty."

"I can understand these young folks not knowing the rules, but Vic, you should know better. You may have meant well, but this is what they call voter fraud, and it's a felony. This is not what I had in mind when I sent you out there. What are we going to do?"

Alan turned to Alice. Her green eyes got bigger, and there was no answer from the big man, leaning against the wall.

"Vic, I'm worried about these young people, and I think you let them down. You let us all down."

"I'm sorry, boss."

"'Sorry' isn't going to soothe the wrath of those whiney, do-gooder Republicans you bamboozled. If they find out about this, they're going to be sore, and it won't keep you out of McNeil Island Penitentiary. This is serious business. Could be as many as twelve felony counts, each, against these young people, and six or more against you. Do you understand the danger here?"

Heads drooped, shoulders sagged.

"Then here's your picture in the morning rag. Even though you had the presence of mind to give them a different name, somebody may recognize one or the both of you. Does that concern anybody but me?"

The Walrus let the gravity of the situation settle on them.

"Okay, Vic, here's what I want you to do. Call our friends at the paper and do some sniffing around. Find out if anyone's making a stink about the picture and it not being the Shermans. What do they look like anyway?"

"I don't know···older···mid-sixties, maybe."

The Walrus scowled.

"If there's any hoopla, convince the photographer to print a retraction. He can say he dropped his notes in the rain and couldn't read them. Fifty bucks ought to help his memory. There's more, if you need it."

"Yes, boss." Vic bowed his head slightly toward the guests and left the room to work on his new task.

"Nothing to worry about," the Walrus said. "Vic is very persuasive, and I think he can plug any leaks in this old boat. Bottom line: your heart was in the right place. You did a good thing for the union and for this country. I'm proud of you both. You showed me you think well on your feet, and most importantly, you helped Jack Hardin get elected. I'm no math wizard, but the margin of victory just may boil down to the votes you cast."

The young pair sat up straighter, more hopeful.

"And that reminds me. I said I would pay you $2 for every vote you brought in for Jack. Of course I had no idea you would be casting them yourselves, but a deal is a deal. And I'm not a man to go back on his word."

The Walrus opened his desk drawer and pulled out an envelope, sliding it to the center of his desk. It was similar to the ones Alan had found in his father's belongings: plain manila with a dollar amount in a woman's handwriting. He read it upside down. Instead of the $ symbol, the word "dollar" was written in cursive.

The Walrus said, "Two times twelve is $24 apiece. Here's fifty. Why don't I give it to Alan and let him break it. Is that okay with you, Alice?"

"Certainly."

"And while I'm at it⋯" the Walrus paused as he pulled out an identical envelope from his desk, sliding it alongside the other. "Here's another fifty for you to go out to dinner—celebrate the election. I feel bad about all this hoopla and want to make it up to you. I didn't intend to come down hard on you. I only spoke up because I'm worried about your welfare; I'm looking out for you. I wouldn't want to see either of you getting into legal trouble. Somehow, I feel this is all my fault, and that's exactly the slant the newsies would take if they got wind of it. It could lead to another series of stories, all bad for the union."

Alan shook his head. It wasn't the Walrus's fault.

"Now, you two need to promise me you won't discuss this irregularity with anyone outside this room. Seattle isn't like Chicago where they 'vote early, vote often,' and no one cares. People in the Northwest get grouchy about their politics and voting properly. You're too young to remember, but there was a shooting, must have been twenty-some years back, with the Wobblies, a radical political bunch from around here. They got somebody's hackles up, and it led to trouble. It started down here and ended up in Everett with a couple people shot, but that's getting far afield...Later on, their president got himself lynched in Wyoming or Montana, I forget which.

"Now, there's no need to worry about Vic, because he works for me, but you don't want to give the wrong people something to hold over your head. That's never a good idea. So we'll just keep this our little secret. Understood?"

More nods, enthusiastic this time.

The Walrus read the paper again.

"Looks like you kids know how to have a good time without advice from me." The Walrus got out of his chair, lifted the envelopes, and lumbered around the desk. He handed them to Alan and shook his hand.

"All right, son. If anything comes up, I have people who owe me favors. They can make trouble go away. I'll look out for you. Now you two go have a good time. I'll have Vic stop by your place with the car and drive you around tonight. No need to worry about parking and driving after you've had a few drinks."

That night, Alan climbed in the front seat with Vic. They hadn't covered more than a few miles when he confided to the big man: "My family's never been much for going out to dinner, so I really don't know any restaurants. You recommend any?"

"Sure···if you like Italian, there's a good one near Alice's place, right on Madison, called Vito's. Ever hear of it?"

"I've driven by there, but like I said, we don't get out much."

"Lots of movers and shakers from the Mayor's office, City Council, and whatnot eat there. Food's good. They're famous for their veal. Drinks are better, and they leave you alone. By the way, I got you some flowers for Alice." Vic held up a bouquet of pink roses.

"There's a guy down at the Pike Place Market who's always good for flowers—cheap, too. He's got all kinds of exotic stuff he grows in his own hothouse. You can count on him having something fresh year round."

Vic eased over to the curb in front of a well-established brick building with terracotta accents. "She's in 411. I'll wait here. Take all the time you need, Champ."

In the lobby, a matronly woman sized Alan up. "Who're you here to see?"

63

"Alice Mahoney in 411."

"Really? Is she expecting you?"

"Yes, ma'am."

She scrutinized him from head to toe, conspicuously. She was the woman Alice warned about, and she was sending a message about decorum. "I haven't seen you before." She sat back at her telephone console and pulled a wire, one of many, and stuck its jack into a socket on a switchboard. Then she pushed a buzzer. Alan could hear a phone ringing through the manager's handset. She glanced sideways at him. "Whom shall I say is calling?"

"Alan, I'm Alan Stewart."

The manager leaned forward and spoke into a mouthpiece, sharing this information with the person on the other end of the wire. She lowered the handset. "She'll be down for you in a minute. And just so you know, we don't allow visitors after 10 on weeknights, 11 on Saturdays."

"We're going out for dinner and a movie."

"Just have her back by 10. That's when our doors lock, and there might not be anyone to open the door for her. Most of our tenants are nurses, and when they're off shift they need their sleep. We don't tolerate a lot of coming and going, especially late at night, doors opening and closing, people talking in the hallways, long goodbyes, and such. It disturbs the other tenants."

"Yes, ma'am, I understand. My mother would be expecting me before that. Since Dad passed, she counts on me as the breadwinner. I have to be at my job by 4:30."

The matron's eyes brightened. "What movie are you going to see?"

"Gary Cooper in The Westerner. It's playing at the Star Theater."

"Very nice. Just have her back on time. By the way, if she doesn't like the flowers, you can always leave them with me. Roses are my favorite. You must have a lot of pull to get them out of season···on an honest man's salary."

After finishing his deliveries, Alan skipped the usual goodbyes to the other deliverymen and rushed outside to his coupe. He drove toward Lake Washington, took the backstreets down the slope of the hill to the tree-lined boulevard that ran close to the edge of the water, and turned into a small park on the beach. He took a suitcase full of clothes into the bathhouse. The beach was closed to swimmers, but the restrooms were open. He made quick work of changing, putting on his father's suit, tie, and hat.

A little after two, he stood at the entrance of the Great Pioneer Safe Deposit Bank, fingering the key in his pocket. He neither knew the vault's protocol for access to its inner sanctum nor if opening a box leased in another person's name was a crime. One of the men at work told him a little about deposit boxes, not much more than Mario had already told him. He confirmed that the old-fashioned ones, which were losing favor during the era of modernization, used one key, while newer ones required two, which meant a security guard or officer of the bank had to assist with the unlocking.

As another customer exited, Alan removed the key from his pocket, took a breath, entered the bank and approached a receptionist. "I'd like to visit my box," he said, holding out his key.

"Certainly. I'll just need you to sign in first."

She wrote information down in a ledger, and then asked him to sign by his box number. She went through a card file, looked at his name and said, "Oh, Mr. Stewart. I see the rent on your box is due, would you like to take care of that today?"

"That's one of the reasons I'm here."

"George will escort you to the vault, and I'll fill out the necessary paperwork." While writing, she played with a button on her blouse with her freehand. "Would you want the box another five years, Mr. Stewart?"

"That'd be swell."

She handed him back his key and somehow managed to squeeze his hand. He sauntered over to an elderly security guard, who pushed thick glasses back to the bridge of his nose. Alan glanced back at the receptionist and found her watching him. Caught in the act, she held his gaze a moment and smiled. Do I all of a sudden look like Robert Taylor? Must be the hat and coat.

George peered through his glasses, set down his magazine, and greeted him. "We haven't seen you in awhile, sir."

Alan paused. "I've been busy, George, and haven't had any reason to come in."

As they walked down the stairs, George relied heavily on the rail. "I remember when I was a young man. Back before the fire and the rebuilding, the downstairs here used to be at street level. Wish it were that way now."

Alan walked ahead, and as he neared the bottom, the open vault door came into view. To his relief, the boxes required only one key. He turned back to George and said, "I remember the way, George. I can make it from here."

George stopped on the steps. "You don't want a private room then?"

Alan paused and shook his head. George nodded and waved him on. "Just remember to lock your box and take the key out when you're done. You'd be surprised how many people leave keys hanging in their boxes. It's not a security box if nobody practices security."

"Thanks. I'll remember."

Alan stepped cautiously into the vault and scanned the boxes on both sides of the narrow room. Smaller boxes were on top, while the larger boxes were nearer the floor. Number 324 was a small box located on the right side, just about eye level. The box was smaller than he imagined. He wondered what could be in there that was drawing so much attention.

He slid the key in the lock, half expecting that it wouldn't work, but the tumblers turned and gave way. Swiss precision. He withdrew the drawer. It was solid but not weighty. He set it on a nearby table and took a deep breath, letting the air out slowly, wondering if he really wanted to see what his father kept hidden from his family. Alan glanced again toward the door, took another breath, and pulled back the hinged lid.

Although he had tried to steel himself for what he would find, imagining the best and the worst cases, he still wasn't prepared. It was immensely overwhelming. After glimpsing the contents, he fell back against a wall of similar boxes and spread out his hands to hold his weight, bracing himself, so his knees wouldn't give out. He stared in disbelief at what his eyes told him had to be true. It was CASH! A thick slab of it. There were envelopes, just like the ones he found in the garage and seen on Brinkman's desk: same writing, similar amounts. Other cash was formed into a brick and wedged in the back of the box. He tried to fight the wave of giddiness and ignore the recurring butterflies. It took him a moment to calculate, but he estimated the pile was nearly $12,000.

Under the envelopes he found the title to his parents' house. They owned it free and clear. Poking through the box, he found a soft brown leather pouch with the words "Holy Rosary" stenciled in gold.

A rosary? We're not Catholics. Dad always said we were Irish—but Ulster Irish—Orange Men—sons of Scots.

Inside the pouch was another safety deposit box key with a tag on a string, number 502. Alan cautiously closed the lid on his father's box, making sure it didn't slam noisily. Then he slid it over on the table, and walked back toward the entrance to the vault, listening carefully. There was no hint of George, and no traffic coming his way. He went back and scanned the racks, finding number 502 in the large drawer section, third from the end of its row. He slid the key in and tugged on the drawer. It was much heavier than the first. He carried it over to the table and set it next to the first box. He closed his eyes, lifted the lid back part way, and peeked inside.

Again, his knees nearly buckled, and he put a hand down to steady himself. CASH! A cinderblock of greenbacks.

The bones and cartilage in his knees had been replaced by jelly. He had no idea how much money was boxed up in front of him, but it was a small fortune. It would take more time than he had to count it all. He pulled out a wad and scanned it: US currency in mixed denominations. He stared at the stack, which seemed different from what he was used to seeing. The colors were different and the money older. He set it back in place and examined the other items in the box. There were newspaper clippings from the mid-1930s, now yellow with age. They all seemed to be about the Lindbergh kidnapping: The Crime of the Century, as he remembered hearing. Some clippings were from 1932, the time of the kidnapping and murder, and then more from 1934 and 1935, celebrating the arrest of Bruno Richard Hauptmann, a German immigrant.

Hauptmann's trial had been well covered. Parts of the newspaper were underlined, and notes were written in the margins. Hauptmann protested his innocence and implicated a man named Isidor Fisch, saying the gold certificates found in his garage were among "important papers" he was holding for Fisch, while he was out of the country.

A margin note read, "Fisch applied for passport the day Lindbergh baby was found."

Hauptmann told police he discovered the money only after a heavy rain caused a leak in his roof, which soaked Fisch's shoebox, exposing its contents. He explained that since Fisch owed him $7,000, he took what he felt was fair, even though Roosevelt had recalled gold certificates to prevent Americans from hoarding gold. Hauptmann assumed he was in trouble for spending the certificates, not for having the Lindbergh ransom. Authorities tracked the spending of the ransom in the New York area to Hauptmann's home in the Bronx, where they found another $14,000 in mixed denominations hidden in the walls of his garage. Hauptmann hadn't bothered to tell the police about this stash of money, which was all traceable ransom.

Fisch had "returned to Germany by steamer," and "his family stated to reporters that he had died of tuberculosis." Some family came to the trial "to refute Hauptmann's aspersions on Fisch's good name."

Alan held up the old green and red money to the light. "Gold Certificates! Son of a bitch! Tell me this isn't the ransom!" His stomach went crazy with the queasy feeling.

The neatly written margin notes, which appeared to be in a woman's cursive said, "NYPD told Lt. Frantz that Fisch paid for his ocean transport in gold certificates— ransom money. Info suppressed during trial."

Another article said Hauptmann spurned an offer of $90,000 and the chance to save his life if he'd only confess to the kidnapping, but Hauptmann maintained his innocence all the way to the end." His steadfastness resulted in his execution in the electric chair, and of the $50,000 ransom, police had recovered another $5,100 before they latched on to Hauptmann. "Just over $30,300 in gold certificates was still unaccounted for···"

At the bottom of the page was another handwritten note. This one was printed in upper case, like a man might do. "No Jew in his right mind would sneak back to Germany with Hitler waiting. Seattle's as far from New York as you get without leaving the USA. Look for the new Jew in town."

At the top of the clipping was more. "ISIDOR FISCH," was written in upper case, and in red pencil, the "I," "O," and "R" were lined out, leaving "SID." Similarly, the "C" was crossed out of the last name, and an "E" and "R" were added, making the name "FISHER."

Alan took a couple of hundred from the small box, enough to renew the lease and pay for expenses. He started to put the clippings back into number 502 when he saw two more items at the bottom of the box: a US Passport and a black leather wallet. The passport contained a picture of a swarthy complected man: Isidor Fisch! Alan muttered an oath, then quickly glanced around, ready to apologize. He paused for a moment, sensing he may have heard something outside. With both boxes on the table, now wasn't the time to check. He gave it a few more seconds to be sure, and then he returned to inspecting the box.

On the back of the passport were stamps that didn't mean anything to him. He compared the picture with the one in the newspaper articles. It looked like the same man.

The wallet contained a Washington driver's license in Sid Fisher's name. He threw the wallet back in the box and shut the lid.

"Mr. Stewart?" asked a voice outside the vault.

Alan froze for a second but then realized the voice was coming from up on the steps.

"I don't mean to disturb you, sir. Just thought I should tell you we'll be closing soon, and Sally was wondering if you'd have time to pay for your box."

"I'll be right up."

Alan re-opened the box and thumbed through the news clippings. He found another margin note. "Frantz will give 30% fees, but he wants the headlines. Don't trust him."

After putting the last box in its port, Alan bounded up the stairs. He dangled the key for George. "I didn't forget." At Sally's desk, he said, "I forgot to ask about my other box. Would you tell me how much is owed on 502?"

Sally checked the card file. "This one still has a year-and-a-half left on its lease, Mr. Stewart. Did you want to renew it now with the other?"

Alan sat in his coupe outside the vault and contemplated what he'd found. Number 324 was obviously his parents' deposit box, so he had no concerns with its contents. He would tell his mother about the money and deed at some point, but he didn't know what to do about the other box. Inside 502 was evidence from the "Crime of the Century" and money he knew he couldn't keep. The ransom belonged to the Charles Lindbergh family, to The Lone Eagle. Keeping it would be more than a crime, it'd be an unpardonable sin. A guy who kept what belonged to the nation's hero would rot in hell forever, along with Hauptmann.

Alan wasn't sure how to make this wrong a right. He couldn't go to the police, according to the scribbles on the newspapers. "Don't trust Lt. Frantz." Why was that? Who is he, and who wrote the notes—in two different handwritings. Most importantly, he wondered if this is what led to the killing of his father and the burglary of the family garage. And like his mother said, "Find whatever it is and give it back." There must have been a reason why his father didn't do just that?

Alan generally confided in his sister, even though Margaret was two years his junior. He was smart, did well in school when he applied himself, had a year's worth of college credits, but he knew she was smarter. He was embarrassed to remember that it was she who'd taught him, when he was six, how to pump with his legs when he first rode on a swing set without a parent pushing. But this problem was a bit out of her league; it was well out of his.

Alan drove his coupe through downtown and parked in front of Mario's shop. He opened the shop door, which shook the bell attached to the frame. The old tailor with curly white hair sat stooped shouldered in a chair, stitching pant cuffs by hand. He did a double take on Alan.

"Holy cow, Alan, you give me a scare! I remember your papa walking through the door in this hat and coat."

"You should. You did some special tailoring—with the liner."

Mario blinked his olive black eyes, puzzled.

"The inside pockets···the deep ones. Dad used to carry his union tools in them."

"I just do the sewing. Your papa never says what he wants to put in the pockets."

Slumping deep in a chair, Alan tugged the brim of his hat low, so his blue-gray eyes were almost hidden.

Mario asked, "You got something on your mind, Bambino?"

Alan drew his leg up and crossed it, resting his ankle on his opposite knee. His foot danced rhythmically, and he grabbed it to keep it steady. "Dad ever talk about the Lindbergh kidnapping with you?"

Mario peered over his cheaters and then went back to his sewing. "Everybody talk about it. It was big news: 'The Crime of the Century' they call it."

"Did he have a special interest···more than most?"

"Well···he admires Mr. Lindbergh a lot···and his

74

wife. They are a wonderful couple and the louts that takes and kills their bambino should be···you know··· he thought the electric chair was too good for them."

"'Them?' So he thought others were involved?"

Mario stopped sewing. "There was a lot of··· theories, whispers. First, people thought it was the mobs···you know, like Al Capone. Then here comes Capone offering his own $10,000 for a reward, if they let him out of prison that is, so he could find who did this thing. Believe it or not, the people in charge was thinking about this offer, until they wise up to Capone not coming back.

"Another theory was that the doctor fellow, the one who was the go-between with the kidnappers···Dr. Jafsie···he might be the mastermind.

"Other theories say how nobody was s'pose to know the Lindberghs would be in their new home that weekend, so the nurse or housekeeper must be the ones."

"What'd Dad think?"

Mario started sewing again. "There's a one theory your papa likes. This guy they caught, Bruno Hauptmann, says his arrest was all a mistake. He says some guy left him a box of papers that turns out to be the ransom."

"Was that Isidor Fisch?"

Sewing stopped. "Yeah···that's about right."

"How about Sid Fisher? Does that sound about right?"

Mario winced, and put an index finger in front of his lips, blowing a "shhh," while shaking his head, a pained expression on his face. He got up slowly and shuffled to the door behind him, opened it, and said to someone in the back, "I'm leaving early. Something's come up."

Mario returned to the front, flipped the sign over to "CLOSED," and dropped the blinds.

"Let's get some dinner. We take your car, and you

drive me home."

"What about your car?"

"Angela's working in the back with a helper. She'll drive home." He waved for his guest to follow him out and locked up behind them. They climbed in the young man's coupe, and Alan asked, "Where to?"

"North on Aurora, 'cross the bridge, toward Greenlake. You drive, we talk. Then we eat at Chef Luigi's. No one bothers us there, and that's good, because I got a feeling you got yourself into the wrong poker game."

Mario stared out the car window at the houseboats and sailboats down below them on Lake Union. He didn't make a peep until they neared the bridge. "So, what you been up to, Bambino? Why all the questions about things that should be forgotten?"

"I've been doing some digging, and when I found this coat and hat, it had ammo magazines in the pockets, which I'm sure you made. Those fit a submachine gun Dad showed me a long time back."

Mario creased his brow for a moment and half-scowled, like he tasted something bitter. "I'm listening."

"I did some more investigating and found newspaper clippings, lot of stuff about the Lindbergh kidnapping."

"What? Are you some big-time detective now?"

Alan smirked. "Could be. I read Isidor Fisch's name—scrawled next to Sid Fisher."

"That all there was?"

"Another note said Fisch might've fled to Seattle, and it also said, 'Don't trust Lt. H. Frantz.' Frantz offered a finder's fee, if he got the headlines."

Mario stared out the side window, focusing on nothing, and then he started nodding rhythmically, keeping time to an inner drum. "That's most of it, and you got it pretty right—'specially the part about Frantz."

"Did he kill my dad?"

"And what you going to do if I tell you? He's a big-shot police lieutenant. He can make a lot of trouble for a lot of people. That police corruption we talked about before, that's him. Frantz is in the thick of it, got his hand in everybody's pocket. He changes the rules when it suits him, and that makes him dangerous. Signor Brinkman and that guy at the Teamsters is the only ones around town not scared of him."

"So it was him?"

"That's the talk, but I can't be sure. The man who was with your papa that night would be the one to say."

"Who would that be?"

"Too much knowing is one thing, but too much talking gets you a one-way ride in a boat, and there's a lot of water around here. Seattle's practically an island. You know what I'm trying to say?"

The conversation took its toll on Mario, because the Italian accent he'd worked so hard to lose over the years had come charging back.

Alan said, "You're saying what you always say: You don't like to mind other people's business?"

"That's right. You got a problem with that?"

"But, Mario, this is my business."

"It's also the business of the people who's involved, and they want to keep it just between them."

"I think you're saying, 'Frantz is a dangerous S.O.B.'"

"That's about all I'll say."

Alan shook his head, disappointed. He shifted gears and sped up. "So, how does Fisch play into this?"

"I like to mind⋯" Mario caught himself and glared at Alan. "Okay, smarty pants, this much I'll tell you, but remember, I only listen. I don't go asking questions, like you're doing. But I'm thinking it was Frantz who wanted to talk to your papa about Fisch."

They turned off at the exit to the lawn bowling center, north of the Woodland Park Zoo, and parked in a slot. "So, what do you know about Sid Fisher? Dad ever tell you about him?"

Mario pulled two cigars out of his pocket and offered one to Alan, who shook him off.

Mario put one away and licked his cigar, wetting the outside of the leaf. He bit off the tail and lit the other end. He rolled down the window to let out the smoke. After a pause he said, "It was back in '32, middle of the year. A man comes to my shop and says he's a looking for work. Worst time of the Depression, you remember? Lotta men looking for work. So, he's wearing a nice coat with fur trim, he say he makes himself. I'm impressed with his work. It's almost as good as mine. He says he work with fur, leather, or suit coats. I say, 'Maybe sometime down the road.' Now, I get along good with Jews, that's not the problem, but I don't have extra work. So, I tell him maybe he should try working for my friend at Arctic Furs on Pike Street."

Mario talked and blew smoke out the window. "So he gets the job and works hard and keeps quiet. Mind his own business. I send extra work his way, and he remembers.

"By the way, I think I send him your papa's coat to add those pockets."

Alan felt the need to examine the coat he was wearing. He started to open it, then shook his head. He knew what the pockets looked like.

"Vic, Mackie, Signor Brinkman, everybody end up having their coats worked on by him, even the cops. They bring the coats to me. I do the measuring, the fitting, and send them to Sid to finish. The beatmen bring in their blouses and topcoats for me to work on, and he the one who fix them up. He sew in pockets for their saps and flasks, and he put leather trim on the pockets to keep them from wearing down so fast. I think he might be the first one to add the trim like that, at least around here, and now all the shops do it. I get the credit for it, but it was his idea. His work.

"So, Vera, over at Brinkman's, got a fur coat that need some fixing, and I'm too busy···well, actually that wasn't how it was. Truth is, she's a too hot to handle. She got a body that'd make a monsignor forget his vows, and my wife···you know Angela···she gets jealous. She don't like me measuring women, 'specially ones that's a nice like that, so I send her down to Sid, telling her he'll fix her up."

"Did Vera have a thing for my dad?"

Mario stopped blowing smoke and turned to face Alan. "I'm not one who likes minding other people's business. I'm already telling you too much that isn't so healthy to know."

"So···she did."

"Okay, Signor Smarty Pants, this much I tell you. Back before you was a little bambino, back when your parents meet, your mama and Vera worked together for Signor Brinkman."

"Mom never told me that."

"See. I'm blabbing about a whole bunch of stuff your mama may have wants no one should know. Now I'm a sitting here singing like a soprano."

"You can't stop now."

"Sure I can, but I won't. Something's telling me you gotta know some of this stuff. I'm not telling you everything, and I hope I'm right."

80

Alan didn't respond.

"Ai, ai, yi, yi, yi⋯Should be no surprise that Signor Brinkman makes a lot of money during Prohibition. The union was just his hobby, at first. He got more interested during the '30s. That's when bakeries and dry cleaners burn down around town and the dockworkers was on strike. Lotta rough stuff happen, and he was one who came out on top. Then things settled down. But during Prohibition, if people wanted good booze, not bathtub gin that'd make you go blind, they'd go to Brinkman, who get the real stuff from Canada. He has a lot of connections up there. He owns a big boat he used to run up and down Puget Sound. He paid the cops off and they leave him alone. He also the man who finance a lot of the gin joints, the speakeasies. We call them 'the speaks' back then.

"One of the cops he deal with is Frantz. I think he was a sergeant then. They called him 'Hungry Harry,' because he's always looking for the money.

"Your mama was a piano player at one of those speaks, with a lotta guys hanging around. Brinkman take an interest in her and gives her a job—"

"I knew there was something she wasn't telling..."

"'Scuse me?"

"I came home from deliveries one day. Everyone else was out. When I walked past the garage, I thought the radio was on loud, playing old ragtime, really fast. When I opened the back door, it got louder. When I went inside, it was Mom, playing fast and strong. I watched her for a few moments, but then she seemed to know I was there. She stopped, dropped the cover over the keys, and walked away, like I wasn't there. So, I tried to get her to play more, but she shook her head in her 'don't ask me again' way. That's the only time I ever

81

heard her play anything fun. Everything else is Gershwin···"

"She was quite a player and still could be if she wants, but don't bring it up. And don't tell her I'm blabbing my big mouth about her old days."

"I won't."

"So, she ended up working for Brinkman in his other business, and that's how she meets your papa. Problem was, they were both seeing other people. Your papa was seeing Vera, but when your mama shows up, Vera was···left behind. I think she always carries a crush for your papa."

"I thought so."

"Now are you done with Sid Fisher, or do you want to hear the rest of that too?"

"Sure···I just had to find out about Vera."

"Now, don't interrupt no more, or I'll change my mind. And as I say, I send Vera over to Sid a few years back. I can't be sure when it was. Sid like what he sees with Vera, as do all men. She used to be a dancer in burlesque, you know, before Brinkman gives her an office job. She's got brains as well as a big bust. Now, Sid, he's no Robert Taylor or Valentino in the looks department, but that don't stop him from trying. I give him credit for that. But Vera's not taken with him. So, he starts bragging how he's not just some tailor, like that's something to be ashamed of, but he's got money he saves from the stock market. He tells her he'd like to spend some on her. This goes on until she finally goes out with him. I don't know, maybe she gets bored with Brinkman.

"Sid runs up a bill at a fancy restaurant and has to dig deep in his wallet. He takes out a fifty, and the maitre d' has to approve it, because it's a gold certificate. So Vera remembers this.

"Later, she brags to your papa about the fancy

dinner. She tells him she's got another date with this nice man. I don't know···maybe she's trying to make someone jealous."

Alan slumped in his seat and pulled his hat lower.

"So, they talking about the money, and they work their way 'round to the Lindbergh kidnapping. Vera kept clippings about the trial that she packed away when she moved apartments. She's going to look through them when she gets the chance."

Alan pushed his hat back up and his eyes widened.

Mario said, "So Mackie tell her to find out if this boyfriend of hers got more of this old money. Now, Vera knows how to talk to men, get them to talk, especially when booze is flowing. I tell you, Bambino, more guys get in trouble with booze and broads, and that was Sid's problem."

"Sounds like you liked him?"

"I didn't know him that well. He keep to himself. Mind his own business when I knew him, but he was okay···if you forget about that other business···

"Anyway, they have another fancy evening, and she start working her magic, asking him about that money. He tells her he pick up some here and there and has it stashed away with stocks and bonds and stuff, because it's good as gold. So, she gets a feeling, and when he drops her off, she starts digging out newspaper clippings. She shows your papa what she's got. They read how Isidor Fisch is buried in Germany, but your papa likes to see that kind o' thing for himself. He don't like taking somebody's word on stuff that important. He figures the right amount of money can help people disappear.

"So, your papa don't have no use for Lieutenant Frantz—that goes way back with them, but he have other friends who're detectives. He ask somebody

83

what they know about the Lindbergh matter, and that somebody tell him there's something the prosecutor doesn't tell at the trial, which he should have. The detective say Harry has his own ideas about Fisch, his maybe showing up in Seattle. The police was checking the Jewish community and getting nowhere. Jews have taken a lot of abuse over the years and know not to help authorities find one of their own. So, the detective wants to know why your papa is asking these questions, and he just tell him he was trying to impress some dame with a fascination for the case."

Alan rolled his eyes, pulled his hat back down, and turned toward the window.

"Mackie and Vera got an idea they working on, but first, they better find where Sid keeps his stash, because if Harry get there first, the money's as good as gone. The Lindberghs wouldn't never see a dime."

"But, if that money is still around, is it any good?" Alan asked.

"Sure, you betcha it is. Just like Sid said. It's a good investment. You spend a little at a time and nobody notices. If you like to travel, take it to Canada and spend it all. Nobody up there cares.

"So, Vera works on Sid. He ask her to come to his apartment. She play along, keep him interested. She says she wouldn't mind stopping by for drinks. So, Sid gets his place ready. He buys champagne, caviar, lox, cheeses: all that fancy stuff. He acting like a rich man. They start drinking, and he start putting his hands all over her body. She tell him what really make her sexy is rolling around naked in money; maybe they could do it together. So, BAM, just like that, he goes to his bedroom, and he's gone maybe a minute. Then he comes to the door with the lights out and says, 'I got a

84

surprise for you.' She goes dancing up to his door, and he takes her by the hand and leads her inside.

"She squeezes up next to him and says, 'This is exciting, but I can't see anything.'

"He leads her over to his bed and tells her sit down. So she puts her hand down and feels paper, lot of it. She's sure it's money, and she squeals.

"He asks, 'Would you like to see, and she says, 'Of course.'

"He tells her to get naked and then he'll turn on a light.

"She asks him to help her out of her clothes, and he's all over her with his hands. He's pulling her bra off and pulling her panties···you know···maybe I'm saying too much about this sexy stuff. I think I'm giving you more information than you need."

"Where did you hear it?" asked Alan. "It sounds like you were there."

Mario blew out more cigar smoke and finally smiled. "Your papa tells me some, another friend tells me more, and I s'pose I could imagine being there myself. Would be nice to see that."

Alan finally creased a smile.

Mario went on. "It seems Vera couldn't wait to tell your papa. She says Sid turns on the light, and she's rolling around on the money, just like that."

"So···does she···does he—"

"Make amore? I don't know. She tells your papa that Sid have a big one when he got excited···huge I think she says, but again, she might've been playing with somebody about that. You can never tell with women. You know what I mean?"

Alan rubbed his chin and nodded, like of course he knew.

"At some point, some of the money makes its way into her garments···at's a nice way to put it. She says she took some samples, but···you know···he might have

85

showed his gratitude to her. I could see this happening. No matter; she's got some of the money, and she shows it to your papa.

"It's the gold notes, just like they thought. So, he has an idea how to find out if it's the ransom. The authorities sent out a quarter-million pamphlets with serial numbers. I never see one of those pamphlets, but I hear about them. Mackie calls his detective friend and asks if he has a pamphlet. He does. Mackie asks if he can have one for a girl, make her happy. It takes a little time, but the guy gives it to him. Then they compare the numbers—and BINGO!

"So now your papa, who's a private detective··· remember? He says he's gonna figure a way to get the money, get a confession, and get the names of everybody who did this thing, before Hungry Harry sticks his nose in and screws everything up."

"Did you say, 'Everybody?'"

"I did."

"So he thought more than Hauptman and Fisch were involved?"

Mario stubbed out his cigar. "Hey, I thought we was going to eat. We can finish the rest of this over pasta and vino. I think I've told you the worst, and I don't know so much. There may be some holes in what I said, but you just don't want to get any new ones in your head."

Luigi greeted Mario like a long lost relative. Introductions were made to Alan, and Luigi gave him a hug as well. He showed them to a table with plenty of privacy. Before they had their coats off, a waiter began pouring from a bottle of Italian red.

Mario ordered entrees for the both of them and then resumed his story. "We was talking about others who didn't get caught, at least that's what some think. This is the area I don't know much about. I only guess, because your papa didn't tell me, and like I tell you, I don't like to stick my nose in where it don't belong. So, this is just me guessing, but if the police come a knocking on my door, I don't know nothing."

"Understood."

"So after they're sure the money is ransom, Mackie gets Vic, who's known to be very persuasive. You know?"

Alan nodded, while munching on breadsticks.

"Anyway, that's about the time—"

"Was Vic with my Dad the night he was killed?"

"Ai, ai, yi, yi. You're a quick one, Signor Detective, but don't go telling him I say anything."

"Don't worry."

"Where was I? Sid? That's right···he doesn't show up for work. No one sees him again."

"Do you know what happened?" asked Alan.

"I don't go prying, because···let's say this other man and your papa have something to do with this disappearance, which is kind of fitting when you think about it, the kidnapper getting kidnapped and all. Anyway, they're not going to tell nobody, because if the police find out, they could still face the gallows. You know?"

Mario stopped to sip his wine, and he continued to hold the glass near his face, while the waiter placed their food on the table. Alan dug in, and Mario studied him for a moment. "You never tell me why all the questions about this kidnapping and Sid?"

Alan pulled a twenty-dollar gold certificate from his wallet and laid it flat on the table in front of Mario.

"Madonna mia! What have you got there?" Mario covered the bill and looked around.

"Take a peek."

"I saw it."

"It's a gold certificate."

"I know, Bambino. Put it away." Mario glanced around furtively, gulped more wine, and dribbled some out of his mouth. He wiped his face quickly with a napkin and leaned closer. "That's cursed money, I tell you. People have got killed over it—the Lindbergh's bambino, Signor Hauptmann, Sid Fisher, your papa, and maybe more I don't know about. You don't wanna be next. I know I don't."

"I just wanted you to see it. I don't have anyone else I can talk to about this."

Mario put out his hand, palm pushed back, like a school crossing guard. "Let me guess, and just nod or shake your head—don't say nothing."

Alan nodded.

"You found···some···of the money?"

Alan nods, then shakes his head.

"Ai, ai, ai, yi, yi. I'm no good at games. You found what···more of this?"

Alan smiled conspiratorially, his hooded eyes meeting Mario's wide-eyes.

"You found all the money that looks like what you show me?"

Alan shrugged his shoulders, face of innocence.

"Madonna mia!" Mario sat forward and looked around again. "Did you find other···things···maybe belong to Sid?"

Alan grinned apologetically.

Mario put up the stop sign again. "We'll talk in the car."

After spumoni, Alan bought their dinners with regular money, from his father's safety deposit box. Driving a leisurely pace back toward Eastlake, Mario chewed on another cigar and blew smoke out the window. When he was ready, he got around to talking. "Don't tell me where you found it, but how much you got there?"

"I'm thinking···about $30,000."

"Ai, ai, yi, yi, yi. So, they found it—just like they figured. I never heard how it finished up. Sid must have been the one, just like your papa was saying. Makes sense."

"But, what am I going to do with it?"

"You're not going to keep it?"

"It belongs to Colonel Lindbergh. Besides, it scares me."

"I'm glad you see it this way, because it scares the piss out of me!"

"What would Dad've done?"

89

"Why do you ask?"

"It wasn't in our family's box. He'd set it aside, like he didn't want it touching our things."

"Thinking back, now, it seems he couldn't have had it all that long. Last I heard, they was a thinking about talking to Sid. A couple days later, Sid's gone, and it seems that right after—maybe a couple days later, your papa gets killed. It got crazy then. I think it was all the same week. He was right to worry."

"Mario, what kind of man was my father?"

"You don't know?"

"Well, I know he was a good provider, especially considering these last years. We didn't go hungry when others did, and I know he loved us···but···he wasn't a churchgoer."

"That's true of you, too, from what I hear now. It's true of a lotta men. Doesn't make them or you bad."

"I got a feeling about his 'union business,' and I'm sure Dad was more enforcer than detective."

"So, knowing what kind of man your papa was will make it easier for you to decide what kind you should be?"

"It seems it'd help."

"I can't tell you what to think, but, yes, your papa was a good man. He did stuff that needed doing. When people forget their promises, like who they owe money to and how much, your papa reminds them. I never hear of him going after someone who didn't need it."

"What about Vera?"

"They used to see each other a lot, sure," Mario said with a conciliatory nod, "and she would've liked to keep it that way. But now you got a lovely family that lives in my neighborhood."

"Did he see Vera on the side?"

"People talk about lotta stuff, but it don't mean nothing,"

Mario said with an edge to his voice. "Personally, I think Vera likes for people to talk. She don't want nobody forgetting her."

Alan stared at a green traffic light, listening.

"The light's changed, Bambino."

Alan shook his head and continued driving. They were nearing their homes on Capitol Hill.

"Take this for what it's worth," said Mario, "the money's no good. It should go back where it belongs. It's blood money with an evil spell that brings bad luck to those who shouldn't have it. You let the money sit for now. Then you think up a plan, but don't let that include Hungry Harry or any of his goons. You should maybe not involve Signor Brinkman either. Your papa was right about not trusting people. If you can't think of a way to give it back to Lindy, then maybe you should give it to a church. Doing good with it should kill the curse."

"What about Vic?"

"What about him?"

"Whatever I end up doing, I can't do it alone. Can he be trusted?"

"I···ai, ai, yi, yi, yi···I don't know. He might've been with your papa when they find the money, but··· too much of that—it's practically a fortune—it does strange things to people. I say you're best not to talk to no one."

"Even mother?"

"She wouldn't do nothing to hurt you, but you don't want to put her in a position that could hurt her. If she knows about it, she's in danger. I say she's better off not knowing. 'Cause, if it is Harry, there's no one who can go against him and protect her. After all, Bambino, he's the police and a big shot, too."

At 9:30 am, Mrs. Jeepers jumped on Alan's bed and

woke him up, as she began meowing, softly walking across the backs of his legs. Alan stirred and thought about the past couple of days and the joy of sleeping in late. After a moment, he rolled to his side, grabbed the cat and pulled her near for a snuggle and a scratch behind her ears. Nestled close, she sounded like a warplane fresh from the assembly line, down at Boeing Field. "Say, who let you in, anyway? I thought I closed the door."

He tossed the covers back, gently set Mrs. Jeepers down, yawned fiercely, and stretched his hands out, spanning the width of the polished cherry headboard. Alan opened the shade farther to let in enough light so he could dress without wasting electricity. Although his family hadn't suffered the financial woes others had, they still conserved, and he did his part to help.

Nearby, Alan's freshman college texts sat stacked on the floor next to the dresser. He should have re-sold them when he left school, but he was a hoarder, had trouble letting things go. Leaving school wasn't a clean break. His father had proclaimed that Alan had all the education the family could afford, more than he needed, and far beyond his own. "Real education comes from real world experiences," he said.

Hanging on a coat tree above the books, next to his dresser, were his gold-colored boxing gloves, and on his dresser were two small trophy cups, from 1935 and '36. Next to them was a framed picture of his father, McAlister, in boxing shorts, striking a menacing pose during his own championship days. The black and white glossy did little to enhance Mackie's strawberry-blonde hair and steel blue eyes, Scottish traits Alan had inherited.

Mackie's tough guy persona disappeared when he used to discuss Alan's achievements in the ring. His cheeks glowed red and his eyes sparkled with pride. As formidable as father and son were at boxing, they were no match in an argument with his mother. The last trophy came with a broken nose—his. When the swelling subsided, it left Alan with slight thickening to the bridge of his nose. Alan didn't figure it was all that noticeable, but Mary thought otherwise. She scolded him and his father. "I want him to learn there are more ways to solving problems than resorting to fisticuffs and violence."

McAlister had taken the position that boxing would help Alan "become a man, cut his momma's apron strings, get over his shyness, teach him to protect himself, and build his confidence." Boxing was one of the few areas he and his father had found a common ground. In a rare moment of male touching, right after his final match, McAlister hugged Alan, squeezing him by the shoulders. "You showed me something, lad. The first three-and-a-half rounds were your opponent's. When he knocked ya down in the fourth, you didn't have to get up. Most wouldn't. A smart man might've figured it wasn't his day, but you stuck around long enough to club him senseless in the seventh. A man needs to step into it when the odds don't favor him. No one's gonna do it for you. You gotta give it your best—all the piss and vinegar you can muster. Take your loss or celebrate your win, but don't ever quit. If he fights dirty and the ref ain't stepping in to stop it, you take matters into your own hands. You understand me, lad?"

Alan unconsciously rubbed the ridge of his nose, tracing it with his finger, remembering. Slowly, the trace of a grin worked its way onto his face, a rare occurrence since Mackie's passing. While his dad had complained his son didn't have the necessary venom in him, his mother worried he did. She wanted her oldest to study music, play the piano, become a scholar. He should make his living with his mind—like an accountant or an attorney. McAlister's concerns, on the other hand, were about toughness, steely silence, endurance, and grit.

Next to the trophies, Alan kept a large collection of his father's detective magazines, most notably the Black Mask, which featured stories by Dashiell Hammett and Raymond Chandler. Mary disapproved. She called them pulp rags. Said they were tawdry, common, and glamorized violence, but McAlister had successfully argued that detective work, his line of work, was an honorable profession, nothing of which to be ashamed.

When he delivered the magazines to Alan's room late one evening, McAlister sat for a moment and reminisced about actually meeting Mr. Hammett. Both detectives shared a distaste for the Pinkerton Agency. Hammett confided how the Pinkertons had offered him a chunk of cash to kill Mr. Frank Little, the head of the Industrial Workers of the World, while he was in Butte, Montana. Hammett refused the offer, and soon after a band of masked thugs took Little outside and lynched him. Nothing was for sure, but those in-the-know believed the hangmen were Pinkerton men. Hammett knew there were limitations on what he was willing to sell. He was "all right" in McAlister's book.

Above Alan's mirror, he had pinned a poster of Charles Lindbergh, commemorating the Lone Eagle's solo crossing of the Atlantic. Keeping with Alan's hero motif, he had made a balsa wood model of Lindbergh's plane, the Spirit of St. Louis. Alan picked up the delicately detailed replica, turning it over to catch the faint light to better examine his work. Perhaps it was time to pass the Spirit on to the next in line, his brother Sean, also an admirer of the great aviator.

Stepping up to the dresser, Alan should have stepped cleanly on the polished wooden floor, but, instead, his weight came down full on a rabbit's foot, a mottled chunk of fur on a key chain, linked to an open fingernail clipper, which Mrs. Jeepers had dragged into his room. Afraid he'd stepped on the cat, and more surprised than injured, Alan lurched forward, bumping into the dresser. His hand with the Lindbergh plane smacked into a glass covered, embroidered hanging, knocking it from its hook. In his effort to catch the decorative piece, he stabbed out his free hand, just catching the frame as it landed on the dresser, hard enough to crack the glass.

Alan blinked long and hard, letting out a minced oath—one that would have drawn Mary's wrath if she heard it. Alan released a measured sigh, set down his undamaged plane, and turned back to the embroidery and its glass, held precariously in his other hand. The frame was constructed around bleached white fabric emblazoned with the words of The Golden Rule. His sister, Margaret, under his mother's tutelage, had made it for him. Maybe she thought he needed a reminder. His close inspection showed that the glass was broken but the frame was fine. He'd stop at a hardware store on his way home and pick up replacement glass— that wasn't a problem—the problem was the cut to his thumb, which had dribbled blood inside the glass, right on top of "Do Unto Others."

He shook his head. Before he left the house, he would have to apologize to his sister and ask if she could—

Slowly his eyes focused on the pants draped over the chair. His wallet lay open, sitting on top of his trousers, along with a yellow receipt. "What the hell?"

He snapped up his wallet, examined the sales slip. It was for a $17.80 home delivery of oil. He opened his wallet and thumbed through his greenbacks. It's gone!

He hurriedly climbed into his clothes and slid into his slippers. He wondered if there was a chance the gold certificate was still in the house and maybe···

He walked downstairs to the smell of bacon, eggs, and hash browns, and to the sounds of Margaret fussing in the kitchen.

"Morning, sleepyhead, I made you breakfast," she said.

He held the heating oil receipt at his side and ran his fingers through his hair.

"Mr. Farrell came by at eight, and since you came in late last night, I didn't want to wake you. Mother's not here, and Mr. Farrell said he couldn't give us the discount if he had to charge it to our account. So I paid him with a twenty from your wallet. He said the money was old but the bank would still take it."

Alan stared at the receipt again and tossed it on the counter, while Mrs. Jeepers caught up to him and started circling through his legs, demanding more of his attention. He bent over and picked up the cat, settling it in the crook of his arm. "Breakfast smells good, Margie."

"I saved us the carrying charges, but you don't look happy."

"That was a gold certificate. They don't make them anymore. I was fixing to save that one."

"Was it valuable?

"Don't worry about it."

"I'm sorry. Can you find another one?"

"I'm sure I can."

◇◇◇

During dinner the following evening, Margaret asked
for a ride to the Greenlake Public Library. Alan
volunteered. Given that Greenlake was several times
farther away from home than their Capitol Hill branch,
he figured Margaret might be meeting a boy. Any
doubts he had were removed, during the ride, when
she said she'd be able to find her way home.

Alan said, "I'm in no hurry. I'll wait for you over in
Periodicals. Come get me when you're ready."

She sat back and eyed him evenly, not responding.

He grinned teasingly. "Don't worry. I won't tell
anyone. If you finish early and want to 'find your way
home,' just let me know."

She smiled back at him, impishly. "You're sweet."

Alan hadn't been to this branch before, so he asked
one of the librarians for a quick tutorial on how their
system worked, where they kept their magazines and
old newspapers. Miss Leadley, a heavy woman who
could pass for Santa's wife, sat at her desk, wearing a
print dress and sweater, behind a sign that demanded
QUIET. Her reading glasses dangled from a gold chain,
draped across her matronly bosom. Her thick ankles
matched her full arms and wrists, but her eyes were quick

and her mind razor-sharp. "What are you researching?"

"It's not really research," he said. "I've heard different stories about the Lindbergh kidnapping, and I thought I'd read up on it."

"Oh, 'the Crime of the Century,'" she said. Her eyes sparkled. "I'm sure I've seen everything in print about it. It really should be called 'the Trial of the Century,' because of all the hubbub. For pictures, you'll want to look at LIFE magazine, and then for stories, I personally recommend reading anything you can find by Adela Rogers St. John. She's writing screenplays now, but she was quite the girl reporter."

Miss Leadley led Alan over to where the magazines were kept, and she helped him find ones related to the trial. Without asking if he needed more help, she sat down in a chair next to Alan, filling it entirely. She laid the magazine out on the table in front of her, and when she flipped it open to a picture of Isidor Fisch's grave marker, Alan asked, "Do the police think more people were involved than just Hauptmann?"

The librarian beamed and leaned toward him conspiratorially. "Well, you know the Lindberghs were building their home in New Jersey. It was to be a big place on a huge tract of property. It had a landing strip built for Colonel Lindbergh's airplane. The house had several rooms, but it wasn't finished. And, you know, on the night the baby was stolen, the Lindberghs weren't supposed to be there." She sat up straight and raised an arched brow. "But since the baby was sick, they decided to stay over.

"Now, you must ask, who knows that? An immigrant carpenter who lives in the Bronx? Well, I don't think so. Did this Mr. Hauptmann carry a three-piece ladder with him just in case he found the Lindberghs staying overnight in their new home? I don't know about you, but I don't think so," she whispered. "And of all the rooms in the house, how would this Mr. Hauptmann know in which one the baby would be sleeping? Lucky guess? Personally, I don't think so. Now, did he put the ladder up to every room until he found the one with the baby? I doubt that either. And did he stick a tall, shaky ladder in the muddy ground and climb high up without anybody holding it steady for him? I certainly wouldn't. So once again, I don't think so. What I think is somebody who works inside the Lindbergh house said things she shouldn't have. Maybe not on purpose, but she told somebody, who told this Hauptmann person. You know how that goes."

"What about Isidor Fisch?"

Miss Leadley squirmed excitedly in her chair. "Here's what I think—"

Behind the nearby book stacks, the sound of giggling interrupted them. Miss Leadley turned her head toward the noise, put her finger in front of her pursed lips, and loudly blew, "Shhhhh!"

When the room returned to order, Leadley resumed her narrative. "One of the women who worked for the family went out on her nights off···you know··· to socialize. This was during Prohibition, so it wasn't 'acceptable behavior' for a young lady to imbibe, especially without an escort. They called women who did this 'loose.' I'm not so sure I care for that expression, but anyway, this poor soul was Violet Sharpe. The story is that she was at the roadhouse with friends when the baby was kidnapped. But she didn't want to tell the police. Can you blame her?

"People later said she didn't want Mrs. Lindbergh to find out where she'd been, because she would fire

100

her. The police asked her a lot of questions, and when they said they were going to come back to talk to her again, she swallowed cyanide and killed herself."

Alan asked, "Where'd she get the cyanide?"

"It was in the silver polish. Apparently, the Lindberghs must have insisted that their silver always stayed polished, even while—"

Again, whispers and giggling interrupted them. Miss Leadley again turned and blew another "Shhhh," even louder than the first time. She turned back to Alan with a scowl. "Young love birds come here all the time and treat this like it was a dance hall."

Miss Leadley picked up the magazine and shook it for emphasis. "But, as I was saying, when Violet learns the police are coming, she goes upstairs, takes the poison, and is dead within minutes. Poor thing. But after she died, her friends who were with her at the roadhouse came forward and vouched for her—for that night, anyway.

"And you probably heard that there was a lot that didn't sort itself out well during the trial. A number of people wanted to be witnesses for the prosecution. If I remember, there were several different taxi drivers who said it was them who gave Mr. Hauptmann a ride to the ransom pickup, and a great many townspeople—too many if you ask me—who said they saw Hauptmann around town and on the road near the Lindbergh house. Who pays attention to things like that? It's sad. You can't be sure which ones were actually telling the truth, which ones were willing to lie to help the Lindberghs, or which ones just wanted to get their name in the newspapers."

Behind the stacks, a woman's voice said, "Stop it, Bradley," and then she giggled again. Miss Leadley used both hands to lift herself from the chair, and while scowling, she walked partway down a nearby aisle, stopped, moved some books aside and peered through to the next aisle. "Young man and young lady, I've talked to you before about this. If it happens again, I will have to ask you to leave. You are disrupting the other patrons."

The young voices returned something that sounded like an apology, and then their footsteps grew louder as the approached where Alan was sitting. Rounding the corner first was Margaret, with her hand over her mouth, suppressing laughter. A young man, equally guilty, whom Alan hadn't met before, followed her. Margaret stopped abruptly, without signaling her need to change course, and the young man ran into her. She rolled her eyes in exasperation.

Alan rose immediately from his chair and eyed the young couple, evaluating.

Margaret tried to glance away, but her friend nodded impatiently, encouraging her to continue walking. Margie put up a hand to his chest to stop him, then faced her brother. She spoke, keeping her voice low. "Alan, I'd like you to meet Bradley. Bradley, this is my brother, Alan." The young men shook hands, while Miss Leadley walked up behind, stopped, folded her heavy arms, and began tapping her foot, like an umpire waiting to break-up a coach's meeting at the pitcher's mound.

Margaret peeked behind her and then said to Alan with a pleading look the others couldn't see. "I have a ride home." She didn't have to say, "Please."

"Wait up for me. I want to talk," he said.

Margaret forced a smile and while walking past his table, glanced down at the magazines that were lying open. When the couple left her area, Miss Leadley walked back with a knitted brow. Alan rubbed his nose and said, "I apologize for that. Since our father passed, it's been left to me to keep the reins on my brothers, but Margie's always been the one to keep me in check."

Alan hung his coat and hat on a hook in the hallway, before walking out to the living room and stairs. Margaret sat waiting for him on the bottom step, her arms wrapped around her legs, curled up under a bathrobe. "Mother's in her room, reading."

"Should I disturb her?" Alan asked.

"Please don't."

Without saying a word, Alan tilted his head and nodded toward the sofa in the front room, away from the steps. Margaret followed him over and sat down at the other end, again pulling her legs up toward her chest and wrapped her arms around them. "Has Mother met your young man?"

Margaret closed her eyes while shaking her head.

"It would be proper for you to tell her. Then invite him over for dinner."

"You're not upset?"

"I thought about it on the way home, and I figure you're entitled to a life. Mother can't keep us locked up in here forever, but you should be the one to tell her. And you'll have to be prepared to answer her questions: where's he from, how'd you meet him, what's he do, what's his family like, and has he got a

104

future? As for me, I only want to know if he ever hurts you—in anyway at all."

"Oh, he's so sweet; he never would."

"Long as he remembers that."

She rolled her legs under her and sat on them, and her smile radiated relief. Then just as fast, it changed to one of puzzlement. "I saw magazines about Lindbergh on the table; what were you researching?"

Alan leaned away and braced his chin with his hand, while he evaluated his sister. She waited him out, and he gave in. "I've always had an interest in the Lone Eagle and the kidnapping, so I decided to read up."

"You could have asked me, I wrote a term paper on it my sophomore year."

Alan's brow furrowed and his mouth opened slightly.

Margaret asked, "Would this have anything to do with the twenty dollar bill I took from your wallet?"

Alan's mouth started to move, like he was running in place, nothing came out. He leaned forward and rubbed both hands through his hair. "It could."

"If you have more, I can check their serial numbers. Dad got me a list from a friend at the police department. I used it in my report."

Alan fumbled a moment for the right words. "When was that?"

"Two, maybe three years ago."

"What else did he tell you? Did he mention any other names as suspects?"

"He thought others were involved and that the police only caught one of them, but I don't remember names, except for some of the staff, like the nurse and housekeeper."

"How about Isidor Fisch?"

"Hauptmann blamed him."

"Did Dad say anything about him?"

"Nothing special, other than that he wouldn't be surprised if the guy faked his death and turned up somewhere. He said that kind of thing happens every couple of years in the insurance fraud rackets."

Alan reached into his father's pipe smoking stand, picked out a pipe, and started inspecting it.

"There's more you're not telling, isn't there?" she asked.

"I know I can trust you to keep secrets, Margie, but this is one you can't tell. It might have something to do with Dad getting killed, and the same could happen to us if we're not careful."

By the time Alan finished bringing Margie up to speed, it was nearly 11:30, much too late for a man who delivered bakery goods at 4:30 in the morning. "I've got to hit the sack, or it'll take the whole family to get me up in the morning, but there's one more thing I've been thinking about."

Margaret nodded, encouraging him to go on.

"There's more than enough money for you to go to school," he said.

This time it was Margaret's turn to fumble for words. "You mean it? What will Mother say? Won't she want you to finish first?"

"There's some things I got to finish before I go back. Besides, you're the smart one, you should go first."

"What if Mother says, 'No?'"

"Then I'll pay your way out of my salary. She won't need it now to run the household. So start thinking about what courses you want to take, and you might be able to get in next quarter."

After finishing his bakery deliveries, Alan punched the time clock and headed for the parking lot and his Ford coupe. Parked next to it was the shiny Packard he now recognized. Vic stepped out casually and greeted him. "Thought I'd drop by for a visit, Champ. Do some catching up, if you don't mind?"

"Catching up on what?" Alan asked cooly.

"I thought you and me could zip on down to Chinatown and have lunch, my treat, and we could talk about···Hey, I'm no good at beating around the bush. It's about Mackie. I think it's time I tell you things maybe you should know."

"Things only him and you know?"

"Could be."

"Is it healthier for me to know or not?"

"You're Mackie's kid. He and me served in the war together. I'd only tell you if I thought it might do you good. You interested?"

"I'm interested."

"Hop in. We'll use Mr. B's gas."

Vic took Jackson Street down the hill, past the crowded streets in Japantown, further west to Chinatown. Vic tried to make small chat about Alice, but Alan wasn't budging.

"You like dim sum, Champ?"

"Don't know what that is."

"Chinese dumplings and steamed shrimp balls."

"Didn't know shrimp had balls."

"I see you got your daddy's humor, but trust me, this stuff is good."

Vic led Alan to a busy Chinese restaurant with an unrecognizable name. This part of town was not on the delivering route for white bread and rolls, nor for milk and cheese, for that matter. The sidewalks were lively and the streets hummed with cars and people who looked and talked differently than those he grew up with. Outside, the signs had strange writings, many were painted red with gold lettering, and every other building had a fresh fruit and vegetable stand on the sidewalk in front, with Chinese customers haggling prices in a rapid-fire language. Next to the restaurant was a steamy window which displayed cooked meats coated in bright red barbecue sauce, along with poultry that had its feet tied together, hanging from hooks. Behind the glass, a butcher in a stained apron chopped pork and wrapped it for customers' takeout.

The waiters greeted Vic warmly, while they treated Alan indifferently. The owner, an elderly Chinese man, waved, and then a hostess escorted the pair to a table, squawked something to others, and then waiters started toward their table, bringing chopsticks for Vic and a fork for Alan. The waiter handled the fork as if it were a strange appliance that had fallen from the sky. More than one of the waiters and some of the customers glanced at Alan, evaluating. He wondered if it was the shape of his eyes or maybe the resemblance.

A waitress came by pushing a cart stacked high

with steaming woven baskets of food, and when she picked them up and started moving them around, Vic pointed at the dishes, calling them strange names the waitress understood. After she set seven or eight selections on the table, he said, "That's all for now."

Alan asked, "You speak Chinese?"

"I've picked up some words over the years."

Alan's eyebrows arched, eyes widened, and he grinned, impressed.

Vic said, "It's not a big deal. Despite my education, which ain't much, I got an ear for how people talk."

"You speak anything else? Italian?"

"Some Spanish···Latin···German···a little French. You learn as you go. You've probably learned some, too, if you think about it."

"Your accent's different. I guessed you're from the East Coast."

"In a way···Pennsylvania Dutch."

Vic showed Alan how to take the burn out of the hot mustard, cutting it with soy sauce, while adding spicy oil to the brew. "Be careful with this stuff. Keep the mustard side up and away from your tongue as long as you can."

"If it's that bad, why do you eat it?"

Vic laughed. "I like living dangerously." Then he quickly squeezed Alan's shoulder, before patting him on the back. "I'm teasing. No, seriously, it adds a lot. You just don't want it to overpower the flavor. You want it to hit the taste buds in the back, which handle strong flavors, like beer and this here mustard. You don't want it to touch the taste buds in front, which prefer sweet flavors, like wine and dessert."

Alan nodded impatiently, his mouth already watering, ready to eat.

Vic gave the waiter a request, mostly in Chinese. When the waiter returned and opened a bottle of plum wine, Vic poured them both a glass.

"Try this, it's sweet. You sip it and use those taste buds you got up front."

Alan picked up his glass. Vic held his out for a toast. "To your old man, may he rest in peace." They clinked glasses and sipped.

Alan raised his eyebrows, nodded, and said, "Oooh! This is good. It's sweet all right, but it's got a kick."

"Thought you'd like it. Now, being up front with you, Champ, me and Mr. B were down visiting his safety deposit box this morning, when an old friend comes by to visit and says Mackie was down a couple of days before, visiting his box."

Alan stopped to catch his breath.

"Imagine my surprise!" said Vic.

"George?"

"It don't matter who told me, but I figure it was you who was there. And you was down in the vault for quite awhile."

"Lots of people have safety deposit boxes."

"True. Mr. Brinkman's got his there, I got mine there, lot of city politicos and beat cops got boxes there. Your daddy had two boxes."

Alan bit into a meatball, the sauce burned. He gasped, coughed, and reached for the wine.

"Mustard side up, Champ."

"OOOOooohhh! Ow! I forgot."

Vic poured more wine. "No problem. Just makes you look like a cherry boy."

"A what?"

"Somebody whose cherry ain't popped yet—a virgin. Not to worry. I'm just teasing."

Some of the waiters were covering their mouths

and laughing. Vic scowled in their direction, and they bowed, deferential.

"How d'you know there's two boxes?"

"I could have been bluffing, but your reaction just confirmed it. The truth is, I was with him the day he got number two."

Alan met his gaze. "And you know what's in it?"

"Stuff that used to belong to some lowlife who don't need it no more."

"That could describe a lot of—"

"It describes somebody who was supposed to be dead and buried in a country far away, but miraculously, his baby-killing ass ends up in our neck of the woods."

"I think we're talking about the same guy."

"Good. Now what do you plan on doing with what you found? And by the way, I ain't surprised you found it. You're a sharp one; could be as sharp as your daddy."

"I'm not sure yet, but the money's cursed…and it doesn't belong to me or my family."

"Good answer, Champ."

"It belongs to the Lindberghs."

"That's what Mackie and I figured."

"So, what did you plan to do with the ransom? Why didn't you just give it back?"

"We planned to take it to the Lindberghs, but we didn't know how we was going to do it. So, when Monday come, we put it in that box until we could come up with a plan, but then your daddy was killed— that same god-awful night. "

"What do you make of that?"

"I passed it off as coincidence, but most detectives I know think there's no such thing as coincidence. Personally, I've seen it two or three times, but it usually means I didn't dig deep enough to get to the truth. But as far as not giving the money back right away, we didn't really have a chance. And then there were some problems, a police lieutenant in particular, we had to work around. We didn't have such good luck with him. Mackie, in particular, had history with him—bad blood that goes back before we started working together. Mackie wasn't about to give him anything to help his career or political aspirations. He was stubborn like that. Besides, there was complications when it came to explaining a few things, which we were sure they would ask."

"Like what?"

"Like how come a certain individual, who was originally in possession of the dough, is no longer in the company of the living, you might say. How would we explain having the ransom without having that little baby killer?"

Alan glanced around the restaurant. No one was paying attention. "We're talking Sid Fisher here, aren't we?"

Vic nodded.

"Will you tell me what happened?"

"Depends."

"On what?"

"You keeping your mouth sealed shut, just like a priest in the confessional."

"I'm not going to yap."

"There's danger and maybe a curse all right, and all that goes with that could be wrapped up in a crook hiding behind a police shield. Lt. Frantz and his buddies makes me and your daddy look like altar boys, which we were once, but next to him we're practically saints."

"Dad was an altar boy?"

"So he told me."

Alan stopped chewing and stared at a wall, distant gaze.

Vic interrupted the silence. "So eat up, and we'll talk outside. The people here don't trust the police and won't go yakking, but you can never be sure who speaks English and when they might trade information for a favor."

They finished the food, a second bottle of wine, and went out to the car. Vic worked at his teeth with a toothpick, digging at wedged sinew. "How much you know, Champ? Where should I start?"

"I know about the Lindbergh kidnapping, the ransom, and Fisch showing up in Seattle, and there were notes on the newspaper clippings."

"Okay, what else?"

"Somehow you figured Fisch changed his name to Fisher and was working at Arctic Furs."

"Good. Anything else?"

Alan thought for a moment he'd said too much. Mario had told him that last bit. "No, that's about it, but I found his passport and wallet in the vault box."

"You look through the wallet?"

"Just a quick peek."

"That's okay. We left his receipts from work, but he had a phone number we needed to remove—just in case—otherwise, we left it the way we found it."

Alan took a deep breath, relieved.

"I can take it from there··· Back in late '37···give or take a few months, a close friend found where Mr. Fisch lived, gave us a tip, so to speak, and told us the

114

ransom money was in a safe in his room. Over the next few months, we was pretty sure he was our man, but we wanted to be positive. So we let ourselves in and took a look around. We find the safe, but he's got a pretty good lock on it. So I yanked it off the wall using a tire wrench I carried with me, but I can't get it open. I could have carried it out to work on later, sure, but we're not yeggs. We was more interested in talking with Mr. Fisch, see what he had to say about things.

"So, Fisch gets home late. We put the arm on him and tell him he'd be wise to keep his mouth shut. He was about to scream like a sissy, but your daddy stuffed a rag in his mouth and taped it shut. We tied him up with rope, hands behind his back, and then I point to the safe. He shakes his head, like I'm asking him if he wants cream in his coffee or a pastry to go with it. This irritates me, so I smack him alongside the head to get his attention, his eyes bulge wide, and he tries to scream again.

"Your daddy takes out a couple pair of men's hose from a drawer, ties them together, and binds his legs. We sit him down, and I ask him, nice like, if he wants to find out what a broken kneecap feels like. He shakes his head like a bee's trying to get in his ear. So, I say, 'Good. Then tell me where the key is.' He shakes his head some more and closes his eyes, like he's bracing for it.

"So···WHACK, I hit him across his right knee with the wrench, and he about passes out. I give him a minute to come around, but his eyes are filled with tears and his nose is running like a snow melt. I ask him again where the key is and if he wants to know what two broken kneecaps feel like. He shakes his head, like that damn bee's making a hive in his ear, so I give him another crack on the right knee. This time, he passes out or fakes it, and Mackie has to keep him from falling over.

"So, does this bother you? Me telling you what we was doing?"

"No···of course, I wished···never mind. I'm fine."

"So I'm yelling at him, calling him all kinds of Jew things. I repeat my request for the key, and he still shakes me off. Guy had more steel than a lot of men I've had to persuade. He didn't want to give it up. So I ask him if he'd like to see how it feels to kneel on the tire iron with two broken knees, and he wets himself. It wasn't a pretty picture, but we wasn't going to let him off scot-free···let him keep on living the high life, after killing the little Lindbergh baby. It just wasn't right.

"Mackie goes to grab him by the scruff of his neck, and he comes up with a handful of cheap chain···the kind that ain't real jewelry. The chain breaks off his skinny little neck, and a key lands right in front of us.

"No need to guess. It was the key to the wall safe. Divine providence had plopped it in front of us and saved this miserable weasel more suffering.

"So, you can see the fight's gone from Sid. We unfasten the lock, open the safe, and find his stash. Tucked next to the money is his passport, which you already know's got his real name. So I double-bag two pillowcases and start loading money, but then we realize there's a lot more money than we figured he'd have. It wasn't all ransom. I don't know where he got it all, maybe it was his life's savings, but another twenty grand was thrown in the mix. So, we figured Sid wasn't going to need it where he was going—waiting in line to get his ass electric-fried in Jersey—so we thought we better take it along with us and figure what to do with it later."

"You weren't going to keep it?"

"Wasn't ours to keep, and just to clarify things: We collect debts and persuade people to do what's right, sure, but we don't steal. Mr. B does all right by us. Know what I mean?"

"I didn't mean to insult—"

"No offense taken. I just thought I should explain. Lot of people think we're gangsters, yeggs, or Pinkerton thugs, but that's not us. We're private detectives, and at most we'd take ten percent in finders' fees, standard cut, but as I was saying, I put the legit money in a separate pillow case, scooped the passport, and grabbed his wallet from his pants. So, Sid is thinking he's just got robbed by some heavyweights and now the worst's over, but···the night's just begun for him. He's got explaining to do.

"We put his overcoat on him and take him out the back way, and since everybody's in bed, no one notices," Vic chuckled. "Least wise, no one thought enough about it to call the police.

Vic stopped his narrative and stared at Alan to make his point. "What I'm telling you now, you can never repeat. You understand?"

"Absolutely."

"'Cause what happens next ain't pretty, and I'm not about to go to the gallows in Walla Walla over it."

"I got it."

"Okay then. Me and Mackie drove Sid down to the marina and Mr. B's boat. We had to drag him between us, 'cause his knees were swollen like sewer pipes. Now, Mr. B ain't involved in this business; this was something we was freelancing, but we borrowed his boat, nonetheless. We figured on taking Sid for a little ride so we could talk without being disturbed···you know what I mean?"

Alan didn't respond, but continued to stare at Vic, mouth slightly agape.

"So we tied him to a chair, set the yacht loose, and motored out to the middle of Lake Washington. So, I'm fixing drinks, and I find Sid's come around, crying, moaning. He's facing a wall of pictures, and who's there, behind me, naked in all her glory?"

Alan shrugs.

"Picture of···the woman who steered us to him. POW! There's a glossy of her right there in her birthday suit, up on stage, tassles twirling from each teat. DAMN! We screwed up. He might've recognized her, and then what?

"We was going to have to figure out some way of covering that mistake, but it turns out the worst came later."

"It gets worse?"

"For Sid, but I'll get to that. First, we wanted to talk to him about his transgressions—the kidnapping and his baby-killing secret life. Up to this point, he thinks we're just crooks, but when I tell him we're interested in what he knows about the Lindbergh baby, his eyes go wide. This time for terror, not pain. I say, 'Isidor Fisch, I'm Detective Morrison and this here's Detective Stewart.' It was a little stretch, making him think we was the police, but I ain't worried.

"He tries to say something, so Mackie tears off the tape. 'I'm not Isidor,' he says, and I say, 'Wrongo, Sid. I got your passport right here.'

"He gives the 'I'm screwed look,' and then after a second, he says, 'What if I am?'

"So I say, 'Means big trouble, because the authorities in New Jersey fried the man you framed.'

"'I didn't frame him,' he says. 'The police and prosecutor proved he did it.'

"'That's because you planted ransom on him,' says Mackie. 'You left him with enough dough so the cops would forget about you. All they wanted was a scapegoat.'

"'Lies!' said the little bugger.

"'No, not lies,' said Mackie. 'You used some of the ransom to buy a steamer ticket to Germany, then faked your death.'

119

"'Lies! I never faked my death.'

"'Then someone did it for you. I saw your tombstone in the newspapers,' says Mackie.

"'It wasn't me.'

"'Family, friends, rabbi? I don't give a shit. Point is, someone swore you keeled over from tuberculosis and was planted in Germany. Then, miraculously, you rise from the dead and end up in Seattle. How'd that happen?'

"'I got nothing to say. I want a lawyer.'

"'For what?' I says. 'You going to write out your will, you little Jew—'

"So there I was calling him names again, getting all worked up. He made us mad with that lawyer stuff, the little whiner. So we grabbed rope, tied him to his chair, lifted him over the gunwale, and set him on that little platform they got behind the boat."

"I don't know what a gunwale is," said Alan.

"It's the low wall on a boat that protects a deck from the water. Mr. B's got a place on his boat you can step through to the loading platform. It came in real handy during Prohibition, but now, Sid's strapped to this chair, so we had to lift him over it."

"Got it."

"Now, Mackie asks him if he'd like to take a dip in the lake, freshen up a bit. Sid starts screaming he don't know how to swim, and Mackie says, 'I said, "Dip," not "swim."' Then he pushes him off, and Sid sinks underwater. We give him a five count and bring him back up, so his head's above water, and I wrapped the line around a cleat on the gunwale.

"He yells, 'I'll talk. Take me out. I'll talk.'

"We say, 'Talk now, or the next dip's longer.'

"He screams, 'I'm freezing···what do you want to know?'

120

"Mackie asks him, 'Who planned it?'

"He sees we mean business and says, 'We both did.'

"'Who's we?'

"'Richard and I.'

"'You mean Bruno Hauptmann?'

"'Of course, who else!'

"'Don't get lippy, Sid. How'd you know the Lindberghs would be home that night?'

"'A woman told me.'

"'What woman?'

"'A woman who worked for the family. I don't know her name.'

"'How'd you meet her?'

"'Pure chance. After I had checked out the Lindbergh's property, I stopped by the roadhouse for a drink. A lot of people were excited about their new neighbors, and then I heard this woman talking about working for them. So, I bought her a couple drinks.'

"'What's her name?'

"'I never got it···please take me out of the water. I'm freezing.'

"So we reach over the platform, grab the chair, and pull him up, but I leave the rope tied to the cleat. He wants a blanket, we find one, and wrap it around him. Then we say, 'You're up, as long as you're talking.'

"'What do you want to know?'

"'Everything, but let's start with the broad again. What was her job with the Lindberghs?'

"'She was an au pair or maid of some kind.'

"'Don't make me pull teeth, because I got pliers, and I'm good at it. What'd she tell you? Did you tell her what you were up to?'

"'She didn't know anything. She was a friendly person who liked to talk about what she did. I just showed interest in her and she gabbed away. She wanted to show she was somebody. She drew a floor plan on a napkin, showed me all the rooms, where she sleeps, and she says, "This one is the nursery." Just like that. I didn't ask her.'

"Was that the same night as the kidnapping?'

"Of course not, it was earlier. I asked her when she would be back in town again; told her I'd buy her another drink. She liked that, and told me about the coming weekend, but she said she never knew if they'd stay over. When they did, she'd come to town. Richard and I took a chance. So, when she showed up with some friends at the roadhouse, I tipped my hat to her, is all I did, like saying I see you're busy and maybe buy you a drink next time. Then Richard and I went out to the house.'

"And what happened there?'

"You read the papers, what's left to tell?'

"Details."

"We drove to the place where they found···the baby's body, a clearing about six kilometers away. You could see the house from there, but we need to drive closer. We get as near as we could without drawing attention. We watched the house. When the light went off in the nursery, we knew it was time to move. We both carried parts of the ladder, and Richard put it together in the yard. You know, if they had a dog, we wouldn't have gotten close, but···Richard put the ladder against the house, and I held it, while he climbed. He went through the window, and I climbed up behind him. So, he hands me the baby, and I start to climb down, slow, careful. It was harder than you think to hold the baby while climbing down. Richard thought he was such a clever carpenter, but his ladder was junk. It wasn't my fault!'

"'Never said it was.'

"'But, people will blame me.'

"'They've already fried Hauptmann for it. What happened next?'

"'I'm not even half way down the ladder, when, instead of waiting—like he's supposed to—Richard climbs on the ladder. He told me later he heard someone coming, but I don't think that was true. He just got frightened, and because of that he makes the ladder bounce, and I lose my grip. I almost fall over backwards. So I grab with both hands to catch my balance, and I drop—'

"'The baby?'

"'That's right, but you see, it wasn't my fault. I'm not the terrible carpenter or the man who changes plans when he gets scared. If Richard had just···been more patient, my plan would've worked, and the baby would've been safe. If someone comes, he was to stall and maybe hold them, give me enough time to get away, forget his junk ladder, and then run through the house to get out. No one would stop him, but no, he changed the plan because he was afraid. If he'd been more disciplined, then everything would've been all right, and the stupid police would have lost interest in some rich man losing his money.'

"'Sid, Colonel Lindbergh ain't just some rich man people lose interest in, he's the Lone Eagle. And it wasn't about "losing the money," you killed Charles Lindbergh the Third. The Eaglet.'

"'It was a mistake. It wasn't supposed to happen. The baby took a terrible fall, and I was very upset. Richard is only worried about the money, and so he climbs down the ladder very fast. When he gets near me, the weight is too much, and the ladder breaks, of course.

The fool. We both fall, but we don't hit the ladder like the baby. And we are men, so the fall doesn't hurt us as much. What was he thinking? It was only about the money⋯and he's the one who lands on...'

"'What? He landed on the—'

"'Yes, he landed on top of the baby, but I don't think this is what killed him. I read the papers, and they said it was a blow to the head, like Richard deliberately broke the baby's head, because he is a blood-thirsty German who knows nothing better than killing. The papers were full of anti-German talk. That's why they call him "Bruno," because it sounds more German. Nobody else in America called him Bruno. Everybody called him "Richard," until he was arrested.'

"So Mackie asks, 'Why Lindy's family? There're plenty of rich people out there, why them?'

"'He was picked because he's a eugenicist, but Hauptmann doesn't care about that, he just wants the money.'

"Mackie says, 'A what?"

"'He and Henry Ford preached about the purity of the European race. They both stirred up hatred for Jews. Ford was worse, but Lindbergh was accessible."

"I was just about to ask him who else was in on choosing Lindy, when Mackie says, 'You don't sound one bit remorseful, Sid. You're making all kinds of excuses, but you ain't said you're sorry once,' and he pushes Sid's chair off the back of the boat. Sid screams as he hits the water, and then the rope swings the chair to the side of the boat. He ends up near the propellers, but the engines are just idling loudly, and we're not going anywhere—but they're making a lot of noise.

"Then, all of a sudden, a searchlight shines on the boat and a loudspeaker booms at us: 'Ahoy on the Mighty Bee!' And then their big lamp finds us and lights us up, while we're still standing on the stern.

"Wouldn't you know it? Just when you don't need them, the police show up in a harbor boat."

"What'd you do?"

"They say something like, 'Lay to,' or 'Come about,' you know, sailor talk for 'stop whatever you're doing.' We freeze, and they give us a look over while they move closer. They can see us, but we can't see them, because of the light. They ask us what we're doing, and your daddy says, 'A fender came loose and got wrapped around one of the screws. We just finished clearing it.'

"They say, 'We heard screaming,' and Mackie says, 'We were just encouraging the rope... You know how it is. We got it loose.'

"Guy on the boat says for us to test our engines, and they'd standby to see if we're seaworthy. They shine the light on the stern and tell me to test one screw, then the other. Mackie nods his head and gives them a thumbs up, and they turn the light away, checking the rest of the yacht. They call out something about it being a nice boat, and then they motored away.

"So, as soon as they leave, I jumped down from the pilot's chair and run back to help Mackie, because Sid's been under awhile, and as soon as I get there, I see we got a problem."

Vic took off his hat and rubbed his scalp. Alan said, "What problem?"

"The water was blood red, like we were sitting on top of a shark feeding frenzy. We knew something was wrong with Sid. So we grabbed the line from the cleat, but it had run out a few feet. We pulled it back to the stern and jerked hard to pull Sid up. He bobbed to the surface all right, like a steelhead jumping at a fly, and what we saw would have made anybody puke."

Vic scrunched his face into a wicked frown and shook his head. "Sid's head was chopped like an axe splitting a watermelon, all the way to his shoulders. He got sucked into the screws, and there was nothing we could do but get rid of the body. So, we figure the weight of the chair would take him to the bottom, but we don't want to drop him there, just in case something happens later and the police remember seeing us, so we troll him behind the boat, like he was bait for chum salmon, all the way to the far end of the lake. Meanwhile, we're looking for something to weigh him down to make sure he never comes up."

"What'd you use?"

"Mr. B had one of those engine-order telegraphs, but his ain't connected to nothing important, it's just a big hunk of brass so he can pretend he's ordering people around. So we borrowed it and tied it to Sid's lap, and when we pushed him off that loading platform, he went down so fast there was hardly a bubble.

"You know, just thinking about it still gets me. If I was a whiner like Sid, I'd put the blame on the police for their bad timing, but I'm a man of the world. So I take responsibility for this—"

He searched for the right word.

"Accident?" asked Alan.

"I was thinking 'screw-up,' but 'accident' works.

"On the way back, Mackie starts needling me about the way I felt. He'd poured me four fingers of Mr. B's good scotch, but I couldn't touch it. My stomach was raw. Other than the war, it ain't like I killed a lot of people, and those I did had it coming. And most people would agree Sid got what he had coming. And as I think about it, it's almost like God said, 'I had enough of you, Sid, you slimy worm. It's time you feed the fishes,' and we helped

Him with His plan, unwitting accomplices, so to speak."

"How many people've you killed, Vic?"

"Too many⋯but not that many, and this is the only one I'm telling you about, for now anyways. It wouldn't be in my best interest to blab my life story. I told you about this 'cause you had a need to know, and maybe I needed to get it off my chest.

"As I was saying, Mackie says to me, 'I know this'll eat on you, so do yourself a favor—if you feel really bad—go confess to a priest. Just don't mention my name, Sid's name, and don't say where the body is.' Your dad was a real character."

"I know where the ransom is, but what'd you do with the rest—Sid's money?" asked Alan.

"We had some expenses to take care of, like buying Mr. B a new engine-order thing and replacing the chair. So, since your daddy passed away so quickly, it was left to me. I put the rest in a Christmas fund, a thousand bucks here and there." Vic finally began to smile. "I didn't want to give too much to any one place, because a big cash donation like that draws attention, and it's quite tempting for those running the show to want to pocket some. So it was my church, your mama's church, St. Vinnie DePaul, and the Union Gospel Mission. Smaller amounts to families I could see was on hard times. I got to tell you, giving away someone else's money made me feel a lot better, and it made a lot of people's crummy lives a lot better. You could've dressed me in a red suit and nightcap that year, because I felt just like Santa Claus, except for the part about killing Sid and missing your daddy."

Vic drove Alan back to the bakery to pick up his car.

Turning into the lot he said, "My advice: Leave the money where it is, for now, and don't mention it to anyone. You don't want Hungry Harry or any of his crew sniffing around. If you find they are, get hold of me quick."

"Would you go up against the police, Vic?"

"Why do you ask? You're not thinking about it, are you?"

"I'm just asking, 'cause if you have, that might explain···Forget I asked."

"I don't think of Harry as the police. He's not exactly their best representative. Know what I mean? And the goons he's got doing his heavy lifting? They're ex-cops who should've never been cops in the first place. Back before Civil Service, cops got their jobs and promotions by buying them or as political favors. Harry's days are numbered, but of course that means the same for the likes of me.

"But to answer your question, if needs be, I'd take Harry down, especially considering what he did to Mackie. We ain't gone up against the cops before, if that's what you're asking, so it'd be a first. All those cops who got killed during Prohibition? That wasn't

128

none of us. Mr. B worked out our differences with cash, top of the line liquor, and a free pass to a brothel—sometimes all three."

"Vic, somebody's been coming around snooping in our garage, and I'm thinking it wasn't you."

"When'd this happen?"

"Couple times over the past year. Someone worked over the padlock the other day and got past it."

Vic folded his hands and leaned forward. "That could of been some of Harry's boys, alright, but it's not like them be so delicate, picking a lock. If they wanted in, they'd bribe a judge for a search warrant or just break the door down and tell you to bill the City. It might've just been the paperboy or a sneak thief. You mind me asking what you got in there?"

"Dad's Hudson, some of his work clothes, tools…"

Vic looked Alan in the eye, like a father getting ready to explain one of the guarded secrets to manhood. "Glad you brought that subject up, 'cause it seems the union misplaced some of its hardware. I'm thinking of a piece built by Mr. Thompson in a machine gun factory. We don't have as much use for it as we once did, but in the wrong hands, it would be very dangerous, if you catch my meaning. I'd be most interested in taking it out of circulation, and I would be prepared to offer $500 in finder's fee.

"The other item was built by a Mr. Garand, and it's almost as dangerous. He calls it an M-1. It's a prototype and a twin to one I keep here in the trunk, under a blanket. I'd like to get it back, and I'm prepared to pay $300 for it."

"We could use the money. I'll take a look around and let you know."

"So, you know what I'm talking about?"

"Yeah. Dad took me out in the hills and let me get a feel for them. When we were done, he put them back in the trunk, but they're not there now."

"That's my Mackie. Looking out for his family. I hope he showed you good, and one more thing, Champ."

"Sure."

"Hide that vault key good, and keep an eye out for things that look out of place, like maybe somebody watching the house, a car tailing you, that kind of thing. Know what I mean?"

22

$\diamond$

Monday morning, a clerk at Seattle Trust and Savings worked through deposits, tabulating last weeks receipts from Dan Farrell's Home Oil Delivery. Recounting the cash, one bill stood out because it was different than the others. Instead of "Federal Reserve Note" across the top, this one said "United States Note," and it had significantly more red ink in the engravings on either side of the president. She first mixed it in with the other cash, but then she stopped counting and pushed the stack of money to the side. She searched a desk drawer for an old pamphlet buried under papers. She flipped it open and scanned through it for the first time in years. It listed the recorded serial numbers of gold certificates missing in the Lindbergh kidnapping.

She took the twenty out of the stack and compared its serial number to those in the pamphlet. Within thirty seconds, she found a match.

She called a supervisor over to confirm that the numbers agreed. He was unsure what they were supposed to do next. She said, "I've got the phone number of a police detective. I'll call him."

By 11 am, two of Hungry Harry's goons were paying a visit to Dan Farrell, but he was out of the office, making deliveries. They waited outside until he returned at 12:30 for lunch and to refill his truck. The detectives played it low key.

Farrell asked, "Was there a problem with the money?"

"Nothing to worry about," said the one with the limp. "Roosevelt ordered the gold certificates turned in eight years ago, so the Feds wanted us to check if somebody was hoarding them."

"I'd be surprised. The Stewarts are a nice family. Times were tough for them for a spell, but it seems like they've gotten back on their feet. I don't think you have to worry about them hoarding gold certificates."

"Was it the missus who gave you the twenty?"

"No, she wasn't home. Margaret fetched it from one of her brothers. I think it was Alan. He's been the breadwinner for the past two years, no pun intended."

"I don't get it."

"He works for a bakery."

"I get it now. Which one?"

"Gai's."

"The one on South Jackson?"

"That's the one. He makes morning deliveries."

"Okay, then, but just keep this to yourself. Don't go talking it around. We don't want to embarrass him or his family."

"Sure thing."

Alan left work at 1:30, driving down Jackson to Rainier Avenue, up Boren and across First Hill, following the trolley lines over bricked streets, looking down on the city with the waterfront at its base, getting a reverse view of the city's developing skyline. He turned right onto Madison and headed away from downtown to a branch of the National Bank of Commerce, where his family did their regular banking. He turned into the parking lot, paying little attention to the car that followed and the two men who tumbled from it. One was tall, angular, and walked with a gimp. He wore his hat low on his forehead. The other was thick and stocky, like a castrated steer. He wore his hat back on his head, exposing his full face and fat neck.

Alan stepped up to a service counter to fill out a deposit slip, and he hardly noticed the pair as they hurried inside, stopping abruptly, and taking their bearings. The two men were about to head toward a service desk, when a security guard greeted them with a loud voice. "May I help you, officers?"

The two men tried to shake the security guard off, saying something to him. He cupped his ear and turned his head to the side. "It's okay, I used to be in

133

the business. Spotted you the moment you···"

Alan finished his deposit slip and got in line for a teller. While waiting, he found a window that provided a reflection of the two cops behind him. They could pass for Laurel and Hardy, without the laughs. While one kept an eye on him, the other left with the security guard and walked over to a receptionist's desk. After a moment, she pointed in the direction of the safety deposit boxes. More questions were asked, and her demeanor changed. She shook her head, and then she crossed her arms and sat back in her chair, as if insulted by something he said.

"Next, please."

The line had moved, and it was Alan's turn.

"No cash back, Mr. Stewart?" asked the clerk.

"Not this week, thank you."

She took his check, gave him his receipt, and he started for the door, ignoring the two detectives. He touched the brim of his hat and nodded to the security guard, passing him on the way out. He quickly climbed into his coupe and adjusted the mirror to watch the comedy duo quickstep it to their car, a black Ford sedan, like thousands of others. The tall one slowed the detectives down with a gimp leg that caused him to grimace in pain, but Alan didn't wait for them to catch up. He turned his coupe onto East Madison Street and headed west. The sedan waited only a moment before pulling out after him. It's not time to worry yet. They could be headed back to their office.

Alan turned north on Boren and started down toward Pike Street. From there he turned right, heading east again, this time climbing back up the hill to Summit Avenue, where he turned right, heading farther up First Hill. He turned east again and made a pass by the

134

Knights of Columbus hall on East Union Street, where he had learned to box as a kid. He looked in the mirrors and saw the same car behind him with the same two silhouettes in the front. He turned and dropped down a side street to Pike and headed west, back toward downtown and Boren Avenue. He checked the mirrors again. Time to worry; the tail is on.

Alan calculated that Harry's crew knew about the gold certificate, and that meant the instant tail must know where he lived as well as where he worked. There was no sense making a run for home, and besides, his little coupe wasn't about to beat a police car in a race. When Boren Avenue met Denny Way, Alan turned west, dropping down the hill toward the Regrade and the union hall. As he reached the bottom at Westlake Avenue, the light turned yellow. Alan hit the brakes like he was going to stop, and then at the last second, he let up, popped the clutch, and gunned the engine, pushing the old Ford through the intersection against the light.

Horns honked, but now he could put some distance between his coupe and the tail, maybe even make another light. He checked the rearview mirror. Laurel and Hardy weren't waiting their turn. They found a hole in the cross traffic and ran the light, dead red. Horns honked and tires squealed. They were coming after him.

A couple blocks later, Alan turned off Denny, pulled into a stall, killed the engine, grabbed the keys. He raced for the front door of the union hall, and the cops' car stopped abruptly, screeching its tires in the middle of the street. The baby bull got out and hurried his way. The man reached inside his coat and was about to say something, but Alan spun away and pushed open the front door, not waiting to find out what was so urgent.

Once inside, Alan sidestepped the counter and rushed down the hallway toward Vera. A few heads turned, puzzled, but no one said anything. Alan rounded the corner as the fat detective stopped outside the glass door and waited for his partner.

Vera stood quickly to greet him. Alan said, "I need to see Vic right away."

"Is everything all right?"

"I've got···an emergency he knows about."

She leaned into the rail that separated them and touched his arm. "Have a seat, hon, and I'll get him. He's with Mr. Brinkman."

Unhurried, she entered the Walrus's office and shut the door. Alan scanned the large, open room located behind for a glimpse of Alice, but his search was interrupted by the sound of raised voices in the outer office. Vic was the first to emerge, and he stopped and evaluated the offices, focusing particularly on the glass front door, like a Grizzly scenting the air. "How you doing, Champ?"

Alan leaned over the rail, trying to keep his voice low. "That tail you warned me about, followed me here." He motioned with his head to the front.

Vic started for the front, stopped, and said, "Wait here and tell Mr. B what's going on. I'll be right back."

Vic left, and a moment later, the Walrus came out with Vera. Alan didn't get much past "Hungry Harry's men," when the voices in the front office got louder.

Brinkman said, "Stand so you can hear what's going on, but don't show your face."

Brinkman nodded at Vera, and then he lumbered out to the front, heading toward the angry voices around the corner. Vera glided through the rail's gate, took Alan's hand and pulled it close to her. She exhaled and her warmth flowed gently across him, soothingly. Without conscious thought, he instinctively moved closer to her protective glow. She radiated a nurturing quality and smiled confidently. "You heard Mr. Brinkman. Let's get closer."

They stopped short of the front office and listened. One of the cops said, "We don't need a warrant. This is what the courts call 'hot pursuit!'"

"There's no 'pursuit' in my offices," said Brinkman in a clear, authoritative voice.

"And you two aren't welcome here—on any account," said Vic.

"We could arrest you both for obstruction of justice," said one of the cops.

"Any arrest you two ever made was never about justice. Besides, you've been retired. You can't arrest nobody," said Vic.

"Sure we can. We got extended officers' commissions, signed by the big Chief, himself. We're retired honorably."

"Well, I think a couple of phone calls can undo that miscarriage of justice," said Brinkman. "I'll start with my friends at the newspapers, warm them up with dirt on you two and Harry Frantz, and then I'll take the Chief out to lunch. Before long, he'll see it my way. I'm confident of it."

The two cronies were at a loss for words, so Vic seized the moment. "What's this all about?"

"We were told to locate this kid—"

"You mean 'young detective?" asked Vic.

"Detective? Sure, that's it. Lt. Frantz wants to speak with your young detective, Alan Stewart."

"About what?" asked Vic.

"Now, we're not at liberty to discuss that with you. Let's just call it routine questioning."

"I've seen your routine questioning," said Vic. "How come you didn't stop by his home, instead of chasing him around town? Didn't you want witnesses?"

"We were going to talk to him there, but he made his play. So we followed him here."

"Is it your intent to make an arrest?" asked Brinkman.

"No, we just want to take him downtown for a talk. Give him a chance to meet the lieutenant."

"He's represented by Morris Riebman, our attorney, and you're not taking him anywhere unless he's formally charged, or you present a proper writ or warrant," said Brinkman, confidently.

His response met stunned silence.

"Until then, Mr. Stewart will be under my care, and I will consider any attempt on your part to usurp the legal process a personal insult to me. And you can be assured I will convey my displeasure to the Chief, the City Council, and the Mayor, among others. Am I clear, gentlemen?" asked Brinkman.

"We get the point, but Harry's not going to be happy."

"That's your lookout," said Vic.

"I'm just warning you, because it's going to be yours."

After the doors closed, the front office was quiet for a moment. Alan glanced down at his arm. Vera was still holding it tightly, tucked under her breast where it was comfortable, but it was time to remove it. Vera drew his other hand close and patted the tops of both, reluctant to let them go. Vic and the Walrus's voices grew louder as they came back around the corner.

Brinkman said, "Let's talk in my office."

Brinkman led the way, and Vic slowed to let Alan walk in the middle. Nearing Vera's desk, she peeled off from the group and resumed her position as the boss's gatekeeper. Before entering the big office, Alan quickly scoured the worker bees' desks again and caught a glimpse of Alice. She flashed him a smile, and he paused for just a second, tugged at the brim of his hat, and nodded in her direction.

Back inside his office, Brinkman waddled around his oversized desk and flopped into his custom made chair. In a sidebar with Vic, he asked, "Where's Benny and Ralph? What am I paying them for?"

"They're running errands, Boss."

Brinkman frowned, something went unsaid, and then he formally greeted Alan. "Vic was just bringing me up to speed. All this business about Bruno Hauptmann and the mysterious Mr. Fisch—this isn't the union's concern. But you, young man, you're a member in good standing, and what happens to you is our concern. I'm not about to let these poor excuses for police officers kidnap you out of my office and perpetuate a travesty of justice.

139

"Excuse me for speechifying, but I hang around too many politicians, pick up their bad habits. Let's get right to the point. Tell me what got those two birds on your tail."

Behind the Walrus, Vic nodded his okay.

"It was a stupid mistake, sir, mostly my fault. Someone in the family paid for the oil delivery with a gold certificate—from my wallet. Lindbergh's money."

In the background, Vic scrunched his eyes shut, a painful look.

Alan paused and then went on. "That was Saturday, and now, today, I'm being followed from work."

"Hungry Harry's a crooked cop, but that doesn't mean he's stupid," said Brinkman. "I'd guess he's cast his net wide and has a lot of innocent people helping him take in information. Somebody tipped him, but there's nothing we can do about that. We have to look out for your future, son.

"What do you think, Vic?" asked Brinkman.

"I think we need to provide protection till this cools down, Mr. B."

"What makes you think it's going to cool?" asked Brinkman. "This could be long term. Hungry Harry wants the ransom, and he wants the headlines. I see two problems with that. One, the rightful owners will lose most of their dough along the way, but they're already living with that; and two, it just might come out that people we know broke the law dealing with a mysterious person who's now gone missing. That might not sit so well with a headline-grabbing prosecutor who's out to break the back of this union. You catch my drift?"

Vic and Alan nodded.

"Vic's right, son. You need protection for the next couple of weeks. I'll have Ralph drive you to work and pick you up when you're done. While you're at work, you'll break-in a back-up driver of our choosing, so you'll always have company. I'll square that with your company. And one more thing: You ever think about carrying a piece?"

"No, sir."

"Vic tells me your daddy taught you how to shoot, and I'm going to guess he did a damn fine job."

"He wanted me to be able to protect the family."

"Your dad had a good head on his shoulders. I hope it never comes to shooting, but I agree, you should be prepared."

Brinkman addressed Vic. "Give young Stewart something to carry, and go fix him up with a proper gun permit. If there's a problem, give me a call and I'll talk to the Chief. I don't think Frantz and his men will try anything under their boss's nose."

Vic took Alan down the hall to his private office, which was surprisingly comfortable and clean, not at all what Alan expected. Chinese watercolors adorned the walls, and a glass display case featured a collection of Asian figurines. On the edge of his desk sat a hand-carved chess set, again done in an Asian motif, with jade colored figurines instead of the black pieces. The green pieces seemed to have the advantage in this game. Alan stepped close to admire it.

"Your daddy and I used to play, when we found free time," Vic told him. "I could never beat him. I haven't touched it since that night. It was my move, and I had green."

Alan spread his arms and rested them on the edge of the desk. He bent over to examine the details of the warriors more closely.

Nearby, Vic opened a factory box and extracted a new .45 caliber from the brown, waxed packing, and he held it up for inspection. "Is this what Mackie taught you to shoot with?"

Alan nodded. He took the Colt from Vic and worked the slide. "Yeah, this is the one. I can almost hear him saying, 'Know you're backdrop, what's behind where you're shooting; then it's all trigger control and sight alignment.'"

Vic passed Alan a box of ammunition and watched him load the magazine. "That's the important thing. Of course, the other thing is—"

"Keep your weapon pointed down range."

"That's right. Only problem we got here is there's no range for you to point down, and I don't want you shooting up my stuff. I use the corner when I'm racking a round, 'cause the outside wall's brick."

In the corner, Alan inserted the magazine and racked a round. Then he extracted the magazine and added a round to replace the one he had loaded, before re-inserting the magazine in the weapon.

"That's it, Champ. You've passed your test, but before you get to carry it, you need a CCW permit. So I'll hold the piece till then. Okay?"

Alan handed Vic the semi-automatic, grip first.

"It's late; we still have time to get you a license today, but we need to hurry."

Vic parked just off Yesler Way, and together they entered the triangle-shaped building, police headquarters. Vic said, "Put on your poker face and act like you belong. I don't think anyone will bother us. They're smart enough to stick to their own rule: 'A dog don't squat in his own yard if it can help it.' The crooked ones are not about to make a mess in front of the honest cops, getting doo on shiny shoes."

Alan checked out the recruiting posters, while Vic led him toward a counter with a sign that read, "Concealed Weapons Permits." Vic slid a form to Alan and handed him a pen. "When it gets to 'reason for application,' just say that you make deliveries, carry a lot of money."

After a few minutes, Alan finished the form and presented it to the clerk, working behind a plaque that read, "Robert." The clerk scanned the paperwork and nodded. "That'll be two dollars, and we'll need to take your fingerprints. Then it'll take another three days to run a check on your name and get approval. Should be ready by noon on Thursday."

"My friend's in a hurry, Robert, and you look like a man who gets things done around here. Alan's one of our union drivers, and he's had a bit of a problem in the colored part of town, where he makes deliveries."

"He works the colored area?" A look of sympathy.

"He does," said Vic, who palmed a ten spot and slid it across the counter. "The union would appreciate any assistance you could provide and anything you could do to speed up this process."

The clerk made sure no one was watching and slid his hand out to meet Vic's. "I think I could move his application up in the pile, and we could get it done tomorrow by four."

Vic's hand dove into a pocket and slid across the counter again. The corner of a twenty stuck out from under his big paw as it greased its way into Robert's hand. The clerk glanced back over his shoulder, again. "Let's roll the prints now. Then come back at twenty past. The office closes at five, and the boss leaves five minutes after. I have work to finish up, off the clock. If no one's around, I'll let you in."

Vic nodded. "Will it have an official signature?"

"The official rubber stamp. I have the keys to where it's kept."

By five-thirty, Alan was walking out of police headquarters with a permit authorizing him to carry a concealed firearm.

Alan checked the time. "I've got to call home. Mother's probably holding dinner and wondering where I am."

"You still check in with your mother?"

"It's not so much I check in, but since I live under her roof, she asks that I give her a call, as a courtesy, so she knows when to expect me and when not to worry."

"I was just teasing, Champ. Probably a little jealous, too. I never had apron strings to keep me close to home. Mein verlust. Keep as close as you can, long as you can, despite what anyone tells you."

"Your what?"

"Verlust. Sorry, it's an old German expression for 'my loss.' I picked it up somewhere."

Driving through rush hour traffic, Alan sighed heavily, letting out a loud rush of air.

"What's on your mind, Champ?"

"I want to hear about the night my father was killed, Vic, but I don't know how to bring it up."

"You just did."

"I suppose I did, but I understand it might be as painful for you as it is for me."

"So, you're saying your willing to wait me out?"

"Not really."

"You need to be more direct, Champ, otherwise, it could take you forever to find out important stuff. Being direct isn't always pleasant, but you have to be, to be a detective."

They stopped for a cop directing traffic through the intersection at 3rd and Pike, waiting their turn. Vic squeezed his eyes shut for a long moment, like he was having a tooth pulled. When he opened them again, they had a thousand-yard stare. "Yeah, sure. Where should I start? How much do you know?"

The cop waved them through, and Vic put the car in gear.

Alan said, "I just figured he was with you, since you two worked together, and it happened the night he made the deposit at the vault. That's about it."

"You're a natural for this kind of work, Champ," said Vic, as he slowed for a mid-block jaywalker. "You figured right. We were on the milk run, which is normally our Friday bonus job, but since we was busy with Sid on Friday, we had to postpone the run till Monday. At any rate, we ended up running into Hungry Harry and his crew. In fact, it was the two goons who're shagging your ass now, Hoff and Schneider. They was on the job then, not working private for Frantz, like now." Vic shook his head and grimaced. "Seems like my troubles always involve people with German names, now, but that's not my point." Vic reached up, scratched his head, and continued. "My point is—they were the ones who put the 'cuffs on Mackie and ran him out of the bar to see Frantz."

"Why handcuffs? Was he under arrest?" Alan's voice was edgy.

"They wanted to take him in for questioning, about Isidor Fisch and the money."

"What led them to Dad?"

"You remember what I told you about Sid, the baby killer? Well, you'd have thought nobody would miss him, but the fur place where he works calls in a missing person report the next morning—a Saturday. Who would've figured someone would miss this worm so quickly? By Monday, he still doesn't show up, so the blue suits do a little investigating. I'm surprised the cops got on it that quick. They go up to his apartment

146

on Queen Anne to check his welfare. Well, of course, they find his safe's been torn off the wall and the contents emptied. So it's a big deal, and they call in their safe-cracking and missing-person detectives."

Alan sat rigid with clenched fists, his knuckles white. As the story progressed, he started banging his right hand into the side of the door, rhythmically keeping time to an inner tempo.

Vic paused to watch him for a moment. "Now a lot of guys skipped out on families during the Thirties, but Sid had no bills, no starving family, nobody he was running from, or so it seemed. Add in the busted safe, and the dick gets suspicious. So he becomes more cautious, realizing he might be working a crime scene, or he just might've been looking for discarded valuables, before housekeeping came in and stole what's left. Whatever the reason, he checks inside a suit pocket, and it's got a label with Sid's real name. The dick puts two and two together, and pretty soon the police are all abuzz. Then one of them tells about Mackie calling and asking for a pamphlet with ransom money numbers.

"Hungry Harry gets the word and tells everyone to put a lid on the info—not tell any of their stooges at the newspapers, that kind of thing. Then zap, pow, Harry and his crew come looking for us, Mackie in particular. They caught up with us that night at the Kasbah, and Frantz's crew took off with Mackie in tow. I'm not sure why they did the beating there, instead of headquarters, but maybe Frantz had worries about who'd find out. They worked him over with blackjacks before I could get to him." Vic paused a moment to rub an eye. "One found the soft spot on his temple and crushed it."

147

Alan's hand thumping on the door grew louder, more rapid, breaking the skin on his knuckles. He continued to stare straight ahead, his eyes wide, showing a lot of red.

"Looking back," Vic continued, "I think it was a screw-up on their part. Either that or your daddy gave them more than they could handle, even with his hands 'cuffed, 'cause they got nothing from him."

The thumping stopped. "Was he still handcuffed when you got outside?"

"The damage was already done. They'd taken 'em off, as I remember."

"Why didn't they go after you?" Alan's voice was firm.

"That's a fair question; I've given it some thought. I'm thinking at first it was divide and conquer, but··· who am I kidding?" The big man shook his large head. "Now, you can never repeat this, never bring it up by accident in a conversation, 'cause it's going to hurt someone very close to you···"

Alan rubbed his eyes, smoothed his eyebrows, and faced Vic, mouth open slightly, eyes puzzled. "Yeah, sure."

"The bad history they had, your daddy and Harry, it's mostly about—your mother," he said reverently. "She was—"

"Harry's girl?"

It was Vic's turn to look stunned. "You know?"

"Not really, but some pieces just came together all of a sudden. Mother in a picture, with a police car in the background, behind the man, but I couldn't guess who. She got rid of the picture after Dad died. That's all."

Vic processed the information and scratched at his nose. "She played piano in one of 'the speaks,' a joint Mr. B had an interest in. He eventually offered her a legit job in the office, and that's where she met

Mackie, right after he left the boxing ring. Mr. B has helped a lot of people that way. So, obviously, Harry wasn't happy about loosing Mary. Now, your daddy may never have walked the straight and narrow, but he never pretended otherwise, hiding behind a badge, something honest. I don't know if that was the difference, but she made her choice and was happy with Mackie.

"Now, from what I hear, Harry ran into Mackie one night, probably around the time your parents was engaged. He was all liquored up, took off his badge, and called your daddy outside. Big mistake for Harry. Despite his finger gouging, scratching, spitting, and dirty play—then, again, maybe it was because of that—Mackie gave him a real working over. Took a couple of months for Harry to heal properly, and there's been bad blood ever since. There was even talk of charging your dad with a crime, 'cause as a professional boxer, his hands was weapons, that kind of thing. The prosecutor didn't buy it, but that part could've been Mr. B stepping in with his open wallet."

Alan sat speechless, dazed.

"Now, you understand bringing this up would upset your mother to no end. She blames herself for Mackie's death, thinks it was really 'cause of her, which may be partly true. So, you got to let that be, pretend you never heard it."

After a few moments, letting it sink in, Alan asked, "What's Harry look like?"

Vic rolled his head back and forth, side to side, while he thought. "He's not a bad looking man, but a little oily for me. He's what they used to call a fop, a guy who overdresses for every occasion."

"Wears a fancy hat?"

"That's his signature. He likes the attention, wants to be a star."

Alan sat back and gazed through the car's window, staring emptily at storefronts they passed.

Vic said, "There's more to why they haven't come after me that you should know. I'm thinking after Harry and his men killed your daddy, they was worried about explaining things if two guys went down hard—the same night. I doubt their consciences were getting to them, 'cause they got the greed sickness, which numbs emotions. So, I think it was a practical decision. They got nowhere with Mackie and probably figured it'd be just as rough with me, and another screw-up would completely erase the trail to the money and the front page for Harry···but you can never be too sure. I sleep with my Colt under my pillow, in case they come a-calling."

Alan's door thumping started up again. "Why's Frantz so interested in headlines?"

"Maybe he's got aspirations for political office."

"Why didn't you just turn the bastards in?" Alan's anger was near the surface, in danger of boiling over.

"Who to? What'd I see? When I got out there, I saw your daddy lying against the running board of a car. I know what they did, but the three of them would swear some drunk raced out of the lot after running your daddy down, and it was too dark for them to get the license plate. They'd call it a hit and run accident, and, if pressed, they could probably find a misplaced report that's got it all in writing. They'd swear he was still alive when I scooped him up, without waiting for the ambulance—like I should've. You know, malarkey like that. It'd be my word against theirs. So, who do you think the prosecutor'd believe?"

Alan glared distantly, unfocused, grinding his teeth.

"If I can give you a little advice···something I've learned from experience. There's a saying about 'what goes around, comes around.' I'm sure you've heard it. It means those sons-of-bitches will get theirs soon enough. You just have to be patient."

Alan sighed heavily. "I won't be happy until it happens, and I want to be the one who makes sure they get theirs."

"I'm sorry to be the bearer of bad news, but if you don't mind me changing the subject, Champ, there's something else I wanted to ask?"

"Go ahead. Shoot."

"If you're interested in making some extra dough this weekend, I could use company on the 'milk run' Friday. Benny wants the night off."

Alan scratched at his non-existent beard, thinking for a moment. "What's it involve?"

"Rent collection from places that owe the union dough. We call it the 'milk run' because it's never any trouble. Your job would be to keep me company, drive if I get too tipsy. I take care of the clients. There won't be any persuading. We're moving away from flexing muscles as we go legit. The job pays fifty scoots."

"For a night's work? I'm interested."

"I'll come for you around six, and you'll want to keep this just between us. I don't think your mother or Mr. B would like it."

"Vic, I'm twenty-one. I make my own decisions."

"I know how that goes, Champ, but like you was saying before about living with the family. Discussing those decisions can get noisy."

"I'll see you Friday."

When they reached the union offices, Vic said, "Drive your car home; I'll follow. Tomorrow, Ralph will give you a ride. Also, you'll need to stay away from Alice for a few days, until we can figure something out."

Alan froze.

"Word gets around. You might've meant to keep it quiet, but someone in the office heard you've been to a couple of movies...a little hand-holding, polite stuff, but nothing that would get your picture in the papers again." Vic smiled knowingly. "Just don't put her in the middle. Call her, but don't lead Hungry Harry to her doorstep."

Early Friday evening, Hoff and Schneider joined Lt. Harry Frantz in his windowed office, which was one of the larger ones in police headquarters. Its prized view scanned over the top of the roofs in Pioneer Square, down Yesler Way, all the way to the harbor and waterfront. Frantz had decorated his office with his own furniture, polished wood, shiny metal, and tufted leather. The quality ran deep. Behind him was what he laughingly called his "I love me wall," complete with pictures of him shaking hands with elected officials—even a Republican contender who had lost to FDR. Near the middle of his collection was a picture of Frantz holding the winning salmon from a police fishing derby a few years back. That photo was next to an enlarged glossy prominently mounted in the center of the wall, seemingly holding the place of honor. It was of a young woman playing the piano in what was likely a speakeasy. Frantz was also in the picture standing next to the piano, unabashedly holding a glass of bubbly and singing to the lady.

Frantz leaned back in his high back chair, casually crossed a leg, and gazed hungrily over his steepled hands. "So, what does your German friend have to say?"

153

Schneider, the taller of the two, said, "It's still on for tonight. Vic will be alone. He won't get up to Capitol Hill and the Kasbah till later, maybe 10:00 o'clock or so. By then, he'll have had a few drinks, which works in our favor. The Kasbah's got the parking lot out back, which gives us a little room to dance with him if we want, and the owner will work with us, like he did with Mackie."

Frantz suddenly snapped a pencil in two and threw it in the garbage can. Then he sat back, closed his eyes a moment, and smoothed his hair back with the palms of his hand, as if pressing his composure back in place. "This time there'll be no screw ups. I know you have a score to settle, but I need him to be able to talk about what happened to Mr. Fisher and his safe. He can't do that if you turn his brain to mush, and we can't be sure Mackie's kid found what we want. Understood?"

Schneider and Hoff nodded heads while exchanging glances, like school children being scolded by the headmaster.

Frantz leaned forward and rested his elbows on his desk. "I've put in twenty-five stellar years with the P.D. I've solved more crimes than any man alive, but I can see my career is nearing an end."

Frantz placed his hands down on the desk, like he was about to push himself up and spring over it. "Gentlemen, I want to take the next step, and in order for me to run for public office, I need the headlines that solving the 'Crime of the Century' can only get."

The head nods continued, enthusiastic this time.

Frantz continued, "I want both of you sharp tonight. There'll be no drinking until this is over. We'll get up there about 8:30 so we⋯"

154

Vic stopped the Packard at the curb in front of the Stewart residence. Alan left Margaret standing on the porch, and he walked down to climb in the front seat to ride shotgun.

"You're a little overdressed for what we're doing," said Vic. "I should have said something."

"Sorry. I thought Dad wore this to work."

"Nah, what you're wearing is his dress-up outfit for taking Mr. B to fancy dinners, not so much everyday stuff. Mr. B wanted us to fit in, not draw attention, but don't worry, you'll be fine. You probably won't even need to get out of the car, except for when they're serving food."

"I already ate."

"My fault, again. Some of the places like to show their appreciation, because a lot of these loans is on the Q.T. These guys are only keeping their heads above water because the union made them a loan when no one else would. So, they take it as an insult if you don't partake of their largesse."

"Their what?"

"Their good fortune···their bounty, you know, like the Pilgrims thanking the Indians for letting them live in the Virginia swamp with mosquitoes."

"I know what it means. I just never expected to hear it outside of school."

"Anyway, you're looking at a nice chunk of change for a cream puff job, plus food, and drinks."

"I can always find room for a little more."

"That's the spirit. A few extra pounds wouldn't hurt you either. Just remember to try everything and make a fuss about how good it tastes."

"You sound like my mother."

"That's funny, Champ. I haven't got the pipes or the

stems she has, but the same rules apply, like eating Sunday dinner with relatives."

"When I eat with the relatives, I don't pack a Colt with extra ammo."

"Your relatives are classier than mine."

Alan grinned. Vic was a rough cut, but easy to like.

"I'm just kidding, Champ, but I'm glad you brought that up. Sometimes I leave 'the milk,' and other times I pick-up 'the empty bottles.' But as an old Boy Scout, I like to be prepared. So the Thompson's in the trunk, next to the Garand, should anything unexpected come up."

"You expecting trouble?"

"Oh, no, no, no···They're back there if an emergency comes up, and not necessarily for tonight. They're always in the trunk, in case we ever need them, is what I should've said."

"Aren't you worried that a cop might stop you for speeding and find what you've got back there?"

"I got a twenty-dollar bill clipped to the back of my driver's license. I've gone through a few of those in my day but never got a ticket, and they ain't never going in the trunk."

They stopped at four different restaurants, two of them near Pioneer Square, the south end of downtown, and two on First Avenue, up in Belltown, which was at the northern end of downtown. Vic said, "Here, Champ, you take the keys. Since you make deliveries, you probably know this town as well as I do. Next stop: Uptown, Capitol Hill. Take me to Broadway and East Pike."

When they neared the back of a Mediterranean restaurant, which fronted on Broadway, Vic had Alan

156

stop at the curb, a short distance from the parking lot. "This spot's good. It's a little ways out, but here's a safety tip for you. Always park in a different spot, even when nothing's going on. It's dangerous to be a creature of habit."

Alan started to climb out, but Vic stopped him. "The Kasbah never feeds us. So you may as well wait here. I'll just be a few minutes."

Alan slouched behind the wheel as Vic crossed the lot to the back door, knocked, waited, and then was let in. No sooner had he disappeared than a figure stepped out into the cool air, lit a cigarette, paused a moment, and went back inside. The door didn't close all the way, allowing light to leak out, like a beacon in the night.

Far off to his right side, something moved in the shadows. Silhouettes and dark figures scurried across the parking lot, like a family of raccoons crossing a street in the dead of night. Two of the shapes had strained gaits that were recognizable. Hoff and Schneider: Laurel and Hardy and one more a snappy dresser. Must be Hungry Harry. The tall one carried something under his coat. Oh shit! Shotgun! The trio reached the back door, pulled it open, and the first two entered. Hungry Harry paused a moment, looked around the parking lot, discarded his cigar, and then he went inside.

It's a set up. Alan bailed out of the car, taking the keys, but the trunk was already unlocked. He reached past the M-1, grabbing the Thompson and two back-up magazines. He shoved those in the deep pockets, then hurried cautiously into the dark shadows at the rear of the parking lot.

He cobbled together a quick plan. He searched for anyone else sitting in a car, but all were empty, parked with their noses against the darkened brick walls of a

157

closed business, except for one car, which was backed into a stall in the far corner, giving it a clear view of the restaurant's back door. The sedan was the same— or twin to the one that followed him. It might even be the same as the one he saw in his alley. No one inside. Alan took out a jackknife and stabbed the sidewall of a front tire. It collapsed quickly. Then he stood behind the car and waited, keeping an eye on the back door to the Kasbah.

A moment later, the restaurant's door slammed wide, hitting the wall with a bang, and the fat cop led his large prisoner, hands cuffed behind him, from the light into the darkness. When the tall one, who brought up the rear, cleared the door, they spun their captive to the brick wall and shoved his head into it. Then out came their saps, and the comedy team tore into Vic with vicious blows, aiming at his head and ears. The lean one tossed the shotgun to his left hand so he could swing the sap with his strong arm, while the stocky one steadied their victim.

Some of the taunts were clear, others not. "This is for breaking my knee, you big piece of—"

"This is for breaking my balls, you filthy cock—"

The third man exited the restaurant, casual, blasé, tugging on his gloves. He turned his back to the parking lot and set his weight over legs spread shoulder width, to watch the savage attack. Stoic-faced, but approving.

Alan strode forward, gliding across the parking lot, before coming to an abrupt stop, scraping gravel, his feet spread for balance, ten paces behind the scrum. "LET HIM GO!" he barked, as he racked a round in the Thompson's chamber.

The tall one was the first to scan the darkness, searching for the voice, followed by the fat man, and

158

trailed by the dandy. The two bruisers let go of Vic, who dropped to the ground on his side and immediately began rolling away from the wall. The fat one tried to focus on the backlit specter and cried, "OH, MY GOD! MACKIE!" and the fop yelled, "Jesus Christ!" as the lean one brought the shotgun into play.

POW! POW! POW! POW! POW! roared the Thompson, rapid fire. Alan let it climb the skinny thug's leg and zero in on his center mass. There was a fraction of a second pause until the roar started again, this time on the stout one, who froze and then groped stupidly for the pistol on his belt.

POW! POW! POW! POW! POW! POW! POW! The submachine gun staccato tore into his body and knocked him back into the wall, where he tripped and landed on his slumping partner.

POW! POW! POW! POW! The shots rang out again, emptying the magazine into the pile of flesh. Then the noise stopped, except for the sound of brass making dainty music, as the spent cartridges cascaded to the pavement.

The angry specter, with fire in his eyes and a wolfish grin, moved toward Hungry Harry, who'd raised his hands. "Please, Mackie, it wasn't···."

Alan's feet scraped across loose gravel on top of the pavement, as his dark shape moved toward its prey, swearing an oath under his breath. He put the tommy gun to his shoulder and took slow, deliberate aim at Harry's face—right between his eyes.

Click!

It was a faint metallic noise, but it seemed to roar as loud as the twenty-shots before it. Alan lowered the gun to his side and dropped the empty magazine, which clanged to the pavement, while at the same time he dug in his coat for a fresh one. He continued walking toward his target, narrowing the gap, as he racked fresh ammo into place.

Lt. Frantz, however, had seized the moment and reached inside his coat, pulling a small semi-automatic. As his gun cleared leather—

THUD!

"Oooppphhh!" went Frantz.

Vic dove into Harry, ramming head first into his sternum, knocking him off his feet and onto his rear, splashing into an oily mud puddle, displacing its contents. Frantz landed hard, his hand flying back, hitting the pavement, popping the gun loose, sending it spinning into the darkness. Vic dropped to his knees, groaning.

Ten feet away, with his hands locked behind him, Vic looked like a turtle on its back, having trouble righting itself. He finally rolled over to his knees and began to rise.

Harry recovered quickly from Vic's head butt, springing instantly to his feet. He spun sharply on his highly polished heels, staggered, and fled the other way, out of the parking lot, toward the street, lurching spasmodically, like a jalopy with a worn-out clutch. Alan set down the submachine gun and snatched up Harry's small weapon. He cradled the semi-automatic between his hands, took quick aim, exhaled, and squeezed off a round just as Harry reached the sidewalk. BANG! The elegant fop's stylish Stetson popped off his well-groomed head, as he dropped like a sack of silver dollars to the cement sidewalk and crawled around the corner.

Alan exhaled through flared nostrils, like an angry bull facing a menacing red cape. "Die, son-of-a-bitch."

To his side, down on one knee, Vic moaned. "Did you hit him?"

"Hope so···but don't know."

"Let him go. In a couple of minutes, he'll be the least of our worries. Get the handcuff key out of Schneider's pants."

"What's it look like?"

"Just grab all the keys you can find."

Alan rolled one of the bodies to the side and pulled out a ring of keys. "I think I've got 'em."

"Bring 'em with you. We don't have time to unlock these here, and while you're down there, check inside the fat one's coat. He's got our money. The skinny one's got my .45 in his coat pocket."

Alan found the gun and envelopes, and he stuffed them in his coat. Then he stood up and stared down at the two bodies.

"What are you doing?"

"I'm not sure···I just wanted to see—"

"We don't have time to gloat. Grab the Thompson and the magazine. Forget everything else."

While they stormed toward the big Packard, like sailors running to battle stations, the restaurant's back door flopped against the wall, once again spreading light into the darkened lot. Vic stopped and called out loudly from the darkness. "Nick, you asshole, you saw nothing, and I was never here. I'll be back to settle with you."

The door slammed shut.

Crossing the sidewalk, Alan checked to see if Frantz was down for the count; no such luck. He opened the car's trunk and slid the Thompson inside, threw Harry's semi-automatic in with it, and shut the lid. Vic groped at the door handle with his hands still behind him, but he couldn't make it work. Alan reached around him and opened the door. Vic dove inside. "Great job, Champ.

Now make tracks. Don't draw no attention."

Sirens wailed in the distance, and ahead of them sat Harry's hat, curb lane. Alan accelerated, swerved, and crushed the tan Stetson with the front tire. He checked his work with the side mirror as he drove up to the red light.

Vic said, "Keep an eye out for Frantz. He's dangerous. He may have a back-up gun or another trick up his sleeve."

Alan nodded, while scanning down the front of the building, as they drew near it.

"Take a right and let's head some place safe, like Dark Town."

"Dark Town's safe at night?"

"Sure is. I was practically raised in one. It's only guys that never been there, like that sissy gun clerk, who're afraid of it."

"Dark Town it is."

"Wait a second. You still on Broadway?"

"I am."

"The adrenalin's wearing off—pain's setting in real fast. Stay on Broadway all the way to Yesler Way. We'll work our way through Jap Town down to Chinatown. I've got just the place that can patch me up."

"Sure thing."

"Before we get there, I want these cuffs off. Find an alley with privacy."

While driving, Alan stared down at his white knuckles clutching the steering wheel, amazed at the intensity of the shaking, despite how hard he gripped the wheel. He gritted his teeth but couldn't stop the chattering. "What's going to happen to us?"

"You drive, I'll think."

A̲lan turned in an alley off Jackson Street, stopped, and opened the back door. Vic slowly sat up. "Okay, Champ, let's see those keys."

Alan leaned in the car to help his friend out of the handcuffs, but then blood from Vic's overcoat smeared onto his hands. He traced the source to Vic's swollen, misshapened face, and said, "Holy, shit, Vic! Are you all right?"

"Just get these things off me."

Alan stepped back, tried to stand erect, and focus, but his eyes rolled into his head. He bent over sharply, as if punched hard in the diaphragm, while covering his mouth with a free hand. He pushed himself away from Vic and threw-up horrifically, getting some of the regurgitation on his dangling tie, while more splattered on his shoes. He placed both hands on his knees, continuing to wretch. After several heaves, he found a moment's rest, and Vic called to him, gently. "You all right, Champ?"

Alan dabbed a handkerchief at his mouth and waved an okay, without turning around.

Vic said, "If something hard and hairy comes up,

that's you asshole, and it's time to quit."

Alan dropped his hand and it was his shoulders that heaved up and down, as he laughed at the absurdity of humor at a time like this.

Vic said, "If you can hurry it along, I'd like to get these cuffs off. They're making me claustrophobic."

Alan wiped his mouth again and put the soiled cloth away. "Sure···which key is it?"

"The smallest, skinniest thing on the ring. It's about the size of Harry's little dick···yeah, that's it."

Vic turned around and leaned his large torso forward, giving Alan a clear shot at the cuffs. He unlocked one, and then Vic sat up, pulled the cuffs around to his front, and unlocked the second one himself. Once completed, he sighed deeply and smacked Alan's legs with the cuffs, indicating for him to take them. "Put these in the trunk with the other stuff. Who knows? We may need them as evidence some day."

Alan started down the alley, unfocused.

"Say···you alright? asked Vic.

"I'm light-headed and my mind's pinging—you know—like a car motor that won't shut off when it should."

"I know that feeling. It comes at times like this. It ain't ever easy killing a man, no matter how much he deserved it. Hope you don't have to get used to this."

"How'd this happen, Vic? Couple of days ago, my life was rolling along in third gear, I'm seeing a great gal, I'm smiling for the first time in years, and now··· I'm a god-forsaken murderer. I'm no better than···I'm going to be a wanted man. J. Edgar Hoover is going to be out looking for me. I just shot three men, all cops, killing two. What kind of man does a thing like that?"

"A damn fine one, if you're asking me. They wasn't

holding back. If you hadn't stepped in when you did," Vic shook his head at the thought. "Come Monday, I'd be buried next to your daddy, up at Mt. Pleasant."

Vic climbed in the front with Alan and directed him to a parking garage he had access to. They parked and locked the car, then stepped through an adjacent door to the sidewalk. Vic flipped up his collar and pulled down his hat. They walked a block filled with pain before Vic pointed to an unmarked door with peeling paint, one like many on South King Street. They stopped, and blood dripped from Vic's nose and splashed on the wet sidewalk. Vic wiped his nose with his hand and rapped on the door with his large knuckles. After a moment, a woman's voice answered in Chinese. Vic responded in kind, and the door opened for them.

A heavyset woman with gray hair pulled back in a bun, dressed in brightly-colored silk and slippers, greeted the two. She drew her hands to her mouth, and fussed over Vic. She called up the stairs, excitedly giving orders. The soft patter of feet could be heard above. A young woman, also clad in silk, but not as brightly colored as the older woman's, came down to greet them, bringing a towel. She started dabbing Vic's wounded face, but he took the towel from her and held it to his ear, while he lumbered up the steps to a reception area.

The heavy woman made sure doors were closed, while they went past the one that led to a parallel hallway and secret rooms, a relic of the days when Asians had to smuggle their own kind into the country. She led Vic into a room with a bathtub, and a pretty young woman was already filling it with steaming hot water. The two women worked together, helping Vic out of his hat, coat, and clothes.

Vic said, "Unless you want to watch me strip down, Champ, go next door and take yourself a bath. Wash away the night. I'll see you in an hour."

Vic said to the older woman, "Anything he wants is on me. Bring him plum wine and a girl to scrub his back. Make that two girls, two bottles."

Vic called the old woman Big Mama, and she grinned wide, showing a number of golden teeth. She nodded to Vic and sized Alan up quickly before she shuffled away, leaving the young woman to help Vic out of his outer clothes. Big Mama's slippers slapped gently on the floor and the noise faded the farther she went down the hallway. Within a few moments, a small man of similar age to the old woman entered the room, carrying a tray of potions and a stack of folded towels, antiseptically white. He greeted Vic with a casual tone. His face betrayed no emotions.

Vic said, "Just relax and let them do their job, Champ. Nothing happens here unless you want it. They even do your laundry while you're soaking."

The older woman came back and gave instructions to her young helper, who smiled shyly at the suddenly weary, young man standing with hands shoved deep in his pockets. She tugged one of his hands free, taking it into hers, and led him away.

Her delicate hands were smooth as porcelain and perfectly manicured. They moved assuredly, with grace, as she adjusted the water flow and tested its temperature. She busily worked around Alan, never making eye contact with him, until the business of filling the tub was under control, and then she stole a brief glimpse, barely longer than the blink of an eye.

166

She was very shy or deferential—maybe both. Then, as she had with Vic, she encouraged him out of his hat and coat and hung them on a brass hook. She said something, but it was neither Chinese nor what he understood as English. She repeated the words as she lifted his coat to hang on the peg.

He guessed her intent and said, "Heavy."

She tried to repeat the same word but missed.

A trace of a smile crossed his lips. He took off his tie, tucked it in his coat pocket, and leaned his exhausted body back against a wooden chair. He never took his eyes off her. She was exquisite, magically exotic. Her long, dark hair fell softly around the smooth skin of her thin neck. Her features were small and delicate, with just a hint of rouge color to her cheeks. When she squatted to take off his shoes, she wrinkled her nose but then quickly smiled. She opened a cabinet and took out a small laundry bag, inverting it, and pushing the inside of the fabric out to grab hold of his shoes, while making sure none of the vomited remnants got on her. She cinched the drawstring on the bag, and when she was done said, "Shoe shine."

Alan nodded. She went back to remove his socks, and her hair draped onto his pant legs. With effort, she helped him out of his suit pants, and as she hung the clothing, she said something, rubbing the fabric. He had trouble understanding her heavy accent, but he understood she was admiring the material.

She took an unlabeled brown bottle from a cupboard, uncorked it, and poured its fluid into the running water. The tub soon filled with bubbles, and a strange but pleasant aroma filled the room, a flower he couldn't name.

In a detached daze, he watched her remove the rest

167

of his clothing. She put his shirt, socks, and underwear into a cotton bag and turned to him. "Wash laundry?"

He understood her this time. "Sure," he said with an exaggerated nod, hoping the non-verbal cues would erase any doubts.

She lifted his arm, encouraged his naked body from the chair, and led him to the bath. He put a toe in, withdrew it, and said, "Hot."

She bowed and encouraged him to try again.

He submerged his foot and found he could stand the heat, so he brought the other leg over the rim and settled in, sitting back into the warmth, and craving oblivion. He forced himself to not think about the shooting, which only happened a half-hour before. The effort required for him not to think, drained his energy. His muscles were tight everywhere, and they throbbed with weariness. His jaw remained clenched hard enough to make his teeth hurt, but in a moment she was kneeling outside the tub, behind him, rubbing his neck and probing his shoulders.

"You like?"

He groaned a noise that passed for yes.

She worked her way down his back, into the water, and his tension started to ease. Soon, he closed his eyes and started moaning, guttural tones of pleasure, catlike, sounds he didn't know he had in him. What shooting?

She pushed him forward, and he bent at the waist and grabbed his knees. Before he realized what it was, he felt one foot and then the other massaging his buttocks. He twisted just a little and caught a glimpse, over his shoulder, of her naked body, her pubic mound inches from his face, as she slid into the tub behind him. The tension shattered and the fog began lifting. She grasped and kneaded the muscles on his back and upper arms, sliding her knees along his sides and under his arms. She worked her hands around to his chest and eased him backward and down, so his head came to rest on her bosoms. She started rubbing his temples and forehead, cradling his head, while cooing to him in a language he didn't understand.

While caressing his forehead, she said, "Name···" She smiled and nodded enthusiastically as she said something. Her pronunciation was heavily accented, difficult to understand, so he repeated what he thought she said. "Poppy?"

"Yes," she said with an encouraging smile.

He repeated her name, puzzling over it. "Oh, yes. Like the flower."

Following a soft knock at the door, another woman in a silk robe entered, carrying a tray with a bottle and glasses. In a moment, she set them on a small table. She poured him a glassful and handed it to him. He sat back and took a hearty sip, hungry to return to the spot he was just in.

As he settled, the wine server dropped her robe, casual about her nakedness. She leaned over and reached in the water, where she found his right foot. She lifted it toward her and started working its sole with both her hands, pulling and pushing on toes and tendons, one foot and then the other. She swung both of her legs over and sat on the edge of the tub. She grabbed his foot, again, and pulled it to her chest, resting it there, between her breasts, and then she worked the muscles on each leg in its turn.

The new masseuse said, "My name is Rose."

She was easier to understand. He acknowledged her with a nod.

He set the stem of his wine glass on the edge of the

169

tub. It was near empty. Rose called out to the walls, and the old woman entered the room this time, poured more wine, and handed him back his glass. She spoke to the young women, smiled at him, bowed slightly, and left. Rose stood up, turned around, and sat down in front of him, pushing his legs to the side. She slid back and placed his free arm over her shoulder, across her breasts, into her lap. She lay back on his chest and cooed the same song as Poppy.

After drinking more wine, Vic's voice boomed through the wall. "How you doing, Champ?"

Alan eyed the girls. They giggled.

"I'm fine," he said loudly.

"Great, kid, take your time. Are you going back for seconds?"

More laughter.

"Sure," Alan said.

The girls squealed. Rose said something to Poppy, who reached around and started stroking his chest with a light touch. Rose lifted his hand, moved it to her breasts, and helped him trace the circle of her nipples with his fingertips. His muscles stiffened.

She said, "You cherry boy?"

"What···no."

She spoke to Poppy, and he caught "cherry boy" among their Chinese. The girls giggled, happy at their discovery.

Rose said, "It okay. No one say what happens here. You come here cherry boy, but you not leave that way."

Rose sat up and slid back, bumping into his hardened penis. She turned on her side and worked her hand up his thighs to between his legs. She caressed his erection and said something to her friend. She responded with a long coo, and the two giggled again.

She said, "Stand up."

His eyes were rolling back into his head, but he found his way to his feet. She led him out of the tub with a gentle tug, never letting go of him. He sat back on the tub, gripping the edges and bracing himself. Rose was joined by her partner on his other flank. She poured warm oil into her hands, and the two women traded places. Poppy worked the warm, scented oil into every cell and pubic hair of his scrotum, inching her way along to his erect penis. They both stood next to him, holding him steady while rubbing their breasts against his upper arms.

Soon he ejaculated a heated flow, to the delight of the women. Poppy kept working her magic until his body began twitching spasmodically, and he begged her to stop. But she wouldn't. When he was completely spent, Rose wiped him clean with a white towel. Then she said, "You feel better now. You get back in tub and rest."

He stepped back in the water and grabbed Poppy's hand, dragging her in with him. She giggled with delight and resumed her position in the back, and then he took Rose's hand and had her join them. She returned to her earlier position and buried her head in his chest hair. She listened to his heart, while Poppy sang a soft, high, delicate song, which made him imagine angels.

"You rest now. You like?"

"Very much."

Alan lost track of time and the amount of wine he consumed. His chest hair, which was still filling in, fascinated Poppy, and she raked her fingernails through it, tracing it down to his pubics. He was near dozing off, when there was a short, hard rap on the door. Without waiting for a reply, Vic stepped in, wearing a robe and a towel wrapped around his head, hiding most of his battered face. "Okay, Champ, time for a chat. You hungry?"

"I could eat—."

"Great. Grab a robe, and we'll talk in the kitchen."

Alan took a towel, stood up and wrapped it around his waist.

"No sense in being modest now, kid. Everyone's seen it."

Alan chuckled as he walked over to a hook, dropped the towel, and grabbed a robe. "It's a habit."

"Just teasing you, Champ. I can't get over how much you look like your dad."

"You've seen him naked?"

"Of course. I told you we go way back."

Alan glanced back at the young women sitting in the large tub. He spoke slowly and exaggerated his enunciation. "Don't leave."

Vic asked, "You like them?"

"Sure do."

"I've got us a room with two big beds, but we need to talk first, without extra ears. Most of them don't speak the lingo, but I'm not chancing who does and who don't. The stakes are too high. Are you worried about calling home?"

Alan rolled his head to the side, apologetic but didn't answer.

"Well don't. I called Vera, and she'll take care of things. She'll call Mr. B and your home, but no one else. She'll let Mary know you're all right, without saying too much. Is that all right?"

"Sure." Alan paused to evaluate his decision, and then he leaned a little toward Vic and sniffed around him. "What's that smell?"

"Yak Jow⋯something like that."

"Smells like yak piss."

"You've smelled a lot of yak piss?"

They both laughed, as they neared the kitchen. Alan asked, "What is this place?"

"It's a brothel in the back end of a Chinese hotel. It ain't got a name. I call it Vic's Ritz. Big Mama rents a couple of suites—half a floor, and she's converted the rooms to her purpose."

"Did it come with a kitchen?"

"Nah, they added this so they can all eat together."

"What? Like a family?"

"Yeah, that's right. It's not so much they're saving money by not going out; the real reason is it keeps the help from wandering off. The girls are under contract, so to speak. Kind of like indentured servants. Big Mama paid their families for the girls, and now they're over here to work off the debt. After they do, they get to

173

stay in the country, and then they can get an outside job, usually at a restaurant, and start bringing their family over."

"Their families sold them?"

"Now, don't get judgmental on them. Things are different where they're from. Girls are treated like property⋯but not quite that. It's a sacrifice, and the girls do it to help the family. It's a way for the family to survive. It's the good of the many over the good of the few."

"How long does it take them to work off the debt?"

"About seven years, or until the bloom starts falling off the blossom."

They took a seat at the table, and the little man with the potions went to work, frying food on a gas stove full of woks.

Alan said, "Do other customers eat here?"

"Nah. I'm not married, so I'm a regular. Lilly's the closest thing I got to family. I'll introduce you to her when we get to our room. Don't go telling anyone, but I'm only putting in a few more years, and then I'm going to buy out her contract and take her home. Or maybe we'll buy an island a thousand miles from nobody, if the Japanese haven't scooped 'em all up."

They both stared off in the distance, each lost in a dream, until Alan sniffed the air. "What's he cooking?"

"Chef's surprise. Whatever he gives us will be good, and we'll be grateful."

"Understood."

"So, I got some ideas about tonight, but I need you to fill in the blanks. Start with what happened after I left the car."

"After you went inside, the man who opened the door stepped outside and lit a cigarette. When he went

174

back in, he left the door ajar. Two seconds pass, and then Laurel and Hardy and Hungry Harry cross the lot and disappear inside. The tall one had a shotgun sticking out below his coat, so I knew it was a set up."

"What next?"

"I went over to their car, flattened a tire—"

"Why'd you do that?"

"Slow them down, in case I needed more time."

"You think good on your feet, kid. Then what?"

"Then Laurel and Hardy dragged you through the door, smashed your head into the wall, and began whacking you with saps."

"All right···I got the rest."

The herbologist/cook took on the role of waiter and served-up their food: fried rice, chow mein, sautéed vegetables, and garlic chicken. The two warriors dug in.

Vic said, "You did real good with the tommy gun. Your dad teach you that?"

"We shot a few rounds."

"I'm thankful. Once again, Mackie saves my butt, this time from the grave. But what was that you was saying about 'a reckoning?'"

"When was that?"

"When you was pointing the tommy gun at Hungry Harry's face."

"I don't remember that···I just remember looking at the two black holes, one on either side of his nose."

"It don't matter. No one can ever remember everything that happens when the bullets are flying, but if I can offer a word of advice? You had Hoff and Schneider on the first go-round. I understand you had a score to settle, but the rest was gratuitous, wasted ammo. So, you didn't have it when you needed it. Harry could have greased us both, at that point. Now, I'm not figuring something like this is ever gonna happen again, but always keep track of the ammo you shoot··· and practice doing tactical reloads."

"Practice what?"

"Tactical reloads. Don't wait till you run out of ammo before you reload; instead, drop a magazine that's running low, and insert a fresh one when there's a lull in the action."

"Makes sense. We never practiced doing that—never thought there'd ever be a reason to—but what I really had in mind was dropping that bastard with a stock blast to his chops, like Daniel Boone swinging his empty musket, but you got there first."

"Yeah, and I don't care what the head-shrinkers say, knocking him down felt good. He surprised me, though, how fast he bounced back up and took to the heel and toe, but you got off a pretty good shot with his piece. You think you hit him?"

"I gave it my best···and then I drove over his hat. I think my aim was better with the tire."

"As far as I'm concerned, Champ, you batted a 1000. Too bad he got away. I hate leaving things unfinished, but we can live with it."

"What do you figure we're in for?"

"We're gonna have to read the morning rag to find out how Harry reported it to the press. They got two retired bulls dead in a heap behind Nick's place. It looks bad from every angle. Nick set me up, but at this point he's probably gonna deny everything to the real police. Fact, he's probably packing his bags and heading off to his homeland, because he knows what I'm gonna do to him. So, I figure he's not about to tell the legit police of the set-up."

"You think Nick was out to get you?"

"Oh, no way. What I been thinking is my partner, Benny, takes the night off and thinks I'm working alone. From what you said, Nick gives the signal, and then Harry checks around to be sure no one's tagging along after me. No···it looks like they were out to take me down, get to me first, because now they're sure you've got the money stashed somewhere: garage, house, safety deposit box, or a coffee can buried in your backyard. So, if they dust me, they still got you for later. Nah···I think the finger's pointing right at Benny's fat head for this."

"Why Benny?"

"Could've been that Harry made him a sweet offer, and Benny could've been inclined to hear it. See, Benny used to be Mr. B's favorite, until your daddy and I got together. He used to have the milk run with another guy, who's moved on, and he was sore about losing the extra dough—and a lot sorer about getting stepped over by someone with an eighth-grade education."

"You think he might have set Dad up?"

"At the time, it seemed to be just piss poor luck, our bumping into Harry's crew, but stacked up against tonight, the two look the same."

"What do you do now?"

"As for me? Benny's got some explaining to do. As for the police? Frantz'll have to cover his tracks. He's got two of his hard hitters down for a ten count, and there must be somebody in the police brass that'll want to hear Harry's explanation."

"Will they come after you and me?"

"Less you than me. Harry has no idea you was there. You heard them shout your daddy's name. Harry's probably thinking it was The Ghost of Christmas Past come back to haunt him, gunning down his crew. So,

177

what's he tell the Homicide dicks? 'It was this guy we beat to death who's come back to haunt us, shoot the hell out of Hoff and Schneider, shoot at me, and save dear old Vic's lard butt?' They'd lock him in the loony bin at Harborview Hospital."

Alan managed a grin.

"So it all boils down to what Hungry Harry says, and a lot of that depends on how bad he got hit. If he's leaking blood, he's gonna have to stick around, and he'll come up with some cockamamie story that makes him a hero. In the meantime, I say we hold up here. Sunday, we read the papers and find out what's up. Then I check with Vera to find out if the police have been nosing around your house or the union hall. Does that work for you?"

"It does, but can I squeeze in a phone call to Alice and my family?"

"If you was a full-time detective, those close to you would know there'd be times you'd be incommunicado. 'Cause if you start calling people right after something like this goes down and you're holed up, people will start connecting the dots—both the ones you love and the ones you don't."

Alan rubbed his hands through his wet hair, disappointed.

"Unless Alice was expecting your call tonight, I say you don't call her and say there's nothing to worry about, because that's just going to start her worrying. You know what I mean? You're best off waiting until tomorrow.

"As far as calling family, it's pretty much the same deal. Let Vera take care of it. She'll arrange a telegram from Portland through Western Union. It'll leave a record of us being out of town. It'll let your mother know you're alive but not available for a chat, which is still going to upset her, but she knows how to handle that. It's up to you what you tell her later—less is better—but she won't like knowing you was with me. Otherwise, I say we don't come up for air for three days."

Alan let out a deep sigh of resignation.

"And just a suggestion, Champ—when you see Alice, don't mention this place. Just say we hid out at the Sorrento."

"Got it."

"And a little more advice?"

"Sure."

"Use a rubber. There's no sense in getting these girls 'in the family way,' adding more problems to their lives.

His waking was slow and gentle, and Alan enjoyed a moment of peace. Nearby, a heart beat faintly, a little faster than his. The smells here were different from those at home, but all the same they were comforting. The fragrance from the oils in his bath lingered in his hair and on his skin, and they blended with the scent of a woman. He rolled his head to the side and peered over his shoulder. She was lying on his pillow, watching him. Poppy. He nuzzled where her chin met her neck, and she spoke something in Chinese he recognized as a greeting. "Sleep long time."

"Yes, I feel great."

He grabbed her around the waist. She squirmed and giggled.

Outside the room was the sound of movement, followed by a crisp knock at the door. Vic opened it halfway and stuck his head inside. "I see you're awake, and if you're looking for a clock, it's a little after eleven."

"No kidding? I don't ever remember sleeping this late."

"You was making a lot of noise, keeping us all awake."

Alan sat up against some pillows with Poppy close to him. Vic plopped the morning paper on the bed.

180

Bold headlines proclaimed: "Off-Broadway Massacre at the Kasbah," followed by a smaller heading: "2 Retired Cops Gunned Down in Hail of Gunfire." Below was a picture of a man with a head bandage. The caption read, "Police Lt. Harold Frantz is treated near the scene of last night's shooting. He and two retired detectives were ambushed while on a stakeout at the Kasbah Restaurant."

Vic said, "There's more pictures on page three."

Alan opened the paper and saw detectives with serious scowls staring at feet sticking out from underneath a blanket, behind the restaurant. His mouth went slack.

"It wasn't just a bad dream, Champ. Those two killed your daddy and who knows how many others. I was next. You did a good thing, but you're going to feel like shit anyway. Had my first kill during the war, and I know it'll get to you. So, remember when you're second-guessing yourself, wondering what demons you set loose, your daddy would've been proud. Now, if you want to be left alone for a while, I'll keep Rose and Poppy out of your hair."

Alan continued staring at the pictures.

"I'll check on you in a little while. There's more we need to discuss."

Vic motioned for Poppy to leave, but Alan reached out for her. "She can stay."

181

Three hours later, Alan emerged from his cave, hungry. He passed the old man in the hallway and greeted the young women playing a game with tiles. He picked Rose out of the group and asked, "Where's Vic?"

Vic came out of a room where a radio was playing a Frank Sinatra tune. "Hey, Champ, you hungry?"

"Always."

Vic spoke in fractured Chinese to Little Papa, and the three went to the kitchen. The old man led the way, his slippers scuffing and slapping on the bare wood. Vic carried a newspaper tucked under his arm. He whispered, "What you're feeling will go on for awhile, in fact, it might get worse before it gets better."

"I must be a monster, Vic, 'cause mostly I feel good about last night. That ain't right, is it? I should feel ashamed, disgusted with myself, but that feeling only lasts for a few ticks off the old clock. Then it's back to feeling good again, like winning the Golden Gloves with a knockout, only this was a heck-of-a-lot better."

"Don't beat yourself up. It's going to be whipsaw with your emotions for awhile, but I gotta tell you: I'm damn glad you chopped them bastards in two. That was nothing to be ashamed of and plenty to be proud of. Lot of men older than you would've cut and run. I saw it during the war. You just found yourself in a position to dish out justice when nobody else was holding them shit birds accountable. Guys like you can look the devil in the eye and not back down, while others wet themselves."

"You don't know how brave I was; you didn't check my skivvies."

"I'm sure···I had Mama check your laundry."

They both laughed.

At a table, Vic plopped down his copy of the paper. "I didn't want to bother for yours. Anyway, Old Harry was his usual glib self. I'm telling ya, he could have a future as a politician."

Vic read excerpts aloud:

"'Police Lieutenant Harold Frantz told reporters he received word late yesterday from a confidential informant that a Vancouver robbery team was targeting the Kasbah Restaurant and Lounge, a popular spot on Broadway. With overtime money curtailed, the lieutenant encouraged two retired detectives to volunteer. Pending notification of next of kin, authorities have not yet released their identities.

"'The trio of officers, armed with their personally owned handguns, encountered the would-be robbers behind The Kasbah, where the massacre occurred. In the moments preceding the gun battle, the detectives made the fateful decision to split up to pursue the robbers. While two detectives chased the suspects through the establishment, Lt. Frantz circled around the building in an attempt to head them off. He said, "I figured the boys and I would trap them out back, but we were out-gunned."

"'The chase led the officers into an ambush, orchestrated by machinegun-wielding accomplices who cut down the detectives in a hail of gunfire. Undaunted, Lieutenant Frantz charged the killers' position in a futile attempt to save his companions, firing his handgun several times. He said, 'I think I got off four or five shots,' but he was repelled by superior firepower, sustaining a head wound. A bullet dazed the lieutenant, knocking him to the pavement. While he lay unconscious, the robbers, who may have mistaken him for dead, stole his handgun and fled the scene. They are believed to be driving a vehicle with British Columbia plates.'

"This guy's got some stones," said Vic. "I'm tempted to believe his version."

"Yeah, maybe we should go help the police find these killers."

Vic smirked and shook his head.

"So, why the Canadian connection?" asked Alan. "And how come he left your name out of it?"

"It's cleaner his way. First of all, he's gotten over figuring you was a ghost from his past, but he doesn't know who you are. Eventually, he'll figure out the family resemblance and check your family tree. Second, he doesn't sic the real cops on me, 'cause he doesn't know what may come out of my mouth, and he might risk losing the Lindbergh money. It's better for him that I either stay free or end up dead. There's no middle ground."

Alan eyed Vic and thought for a moment. "Is this the end, for now?"

"I don't know. We may settle on an uneasy truce. I been listening to the radio, and they just keep repeating the headlines. So we'll read the final edition and see

184

what's changed. If it's a rehash of the same story, I say we stay another day, then surface tomorrow. I want to find out what the cops are really doing, 'cause the rules change when cops get killed—even crooked ones. Right now, I don't know who I could trust at the PD for a straight story."

"What about your buddy Nick at The Kasbah?"

"I've gotta talk to him, if he ain't split town already, that is. In the meantime, you won't mind another night in my Ritz?"

"Are you kidding? I love this place."

"I figured you might, but remember to keep it to yourself. This place is low key. Their customers are mostly Asian, and they've never been busted. But if the word gets out, sure as not, some snot-nosed fraternity boys will come down here, get drunk, raise hell, and spoil it. They'll bring more buddies, bring the cops, bring diseases, and bring up the prices."

"Speaking of···how much is this costing?"

"Don't worry about a thing, Champ, I've got it covered."

"I was hoping you'd say that, because I'm feeling the need for another bath, but I really need to make a call home. Mother'll be out, so I'll talk to Margie, find out how bad things are. She's level-headed and won't say nothing."

"All right, Champ. Take one of the girls on a grocery run. Go about four blocks out, like down to the Bush Hotel on Jackson, in case the police or feds are running a wire tap on your house—or from the payphones around here, for that matter. Then be sure to keep your call brief, and absolutely don't say nothing you don't want nobody repeating in a court of law some day."

Late Sunday afternoon, Lily and Poppy escorted their men to the bottom of the stairs, stopping just inside the door to give them long hugs and kisses.

Poppy said, "You come back soon, please?"

"I come back and stay long time," said Alan.

Big Mama opened the street door a crack and peeked out. Then she stepped outside and made sure no one was watching. She called back to the pair, waiting a few steps up, "You go now, be safe, and come back."

Vic and Alan stepped out onto the sidewalk and started back toward the garage, much lighter on their feet than when they parked. Alan fixed his eyes on the brothel's door, burning its memory in his mind. Big Mama had already disappeared inside. The door transformed into another anonymous slab of poorly painted wood, like many on the block, concealing the wonderment inside. Outside, Chinese people scurried about, celebrating a day with their families. The two Caucasians drew scant attention.

Alan said, "Must be some magic to the old man's potions. Your face almost looks normal."

"Yeah, I'm back to my old, beautiful self."

"I think you got the 'old' right."

They laughed.

They retrieved the car, and Alan asked, "If I wanted to visit Poppy on my own, what would it run me?"

"You like her, don't you? Was she your first?"

Alan stopped in his tracks, his jaw dropped, almost hitting his chest, and his eyebrows scrunched forward like a Neanderthal's. Vic stopped a pace or two ahead and waited. Alan scowled. "I thought Mama's place kept its secrets."

"The people do, but the walls are thin." Vic smiled. "Not to worry, though. I think your momma and daddy raised you right."

Alan's face was fully crimson. He didn't reply.

Vic said, "She's a sweet gal and may turn out to be a perfect fit, but she's going to have cultural ties and demands you ain't ever dreamed about."

"Hey, I'm not thinking of buying an island with her. I'd just like another weekend—"

"Okay, that's fair, but I'm telling you she's got feelings, too. If you just want to drop in and see her regular like, that's one thing, but if you start telling her she's your girl and you're going to start having babies and stuff, that's another thing. In some ways, she's very savvy, but in others, she's a rare flower that needs constant attention."

"I get it."

"Good."

"So···how much?"

"One American dollar for a short time, two if it goes over an hour, three for the bath, and ten for all night."

Alan was doing the math.

"That takes care of Big Mama but doesn't give your girl anything for herself, so be sure to tip her big. If she likes you, and I'm sure she does, she might refuse the tip, but leave it on the pillow, just the same. She's got family at home that are going through a war, and they need all the help she can send."

"So what's the password to the door?"

"Don't be so eager."

They were driving north on Broadway Avenue from James Street, on the crest of First Hill. Alan asked, "Where we heading?"

"I was wondering when you'd ask. You got Poppy on the brain."

"We're going back to the—"

"Scene of the crime. Yeah, that's right. I just want to pay a visit to Nick the Greek."

"Won't the cops still be there, looking to see who drives by?"

"I doubt it. The coroner's carted away the dead, and the cops would've released the crime scene Friday night or Saturday morning, 'cause there wouldn't be much for them to process. You scared?"

"I'd be lying if I said no."

"I thought as much, but I didn't bring you up here for a therapy session. I just want to see Nick before I talk with Benny. Know what I mean?"

The clock neared six, and Vic made a U-turn and parked just south of the restaurant on Broadway. From the trunk, he retrieved a tire iron, tucking it inside his coat.

Alan said, "I thought you said you weren't going to hurt him?"

"I'm not planning to, but like I said, I'm one who likes to be prepared."

"You're a regular Boy Scout."

"Yeah, I was, and while were at it, why don't you

188

wear your hat low and leave your coat in the car, in case someone recognizes the get up. We also don't want them connecting the dots."

Outside the restaurant, they waited for customers to leave. When Nick showed the last one out and started back toward the register, Vic and Alan opened the door.

Without looking up, Nick said, "I'm sorry, we're clos—"

"You got time for two coffees. Right, Nick?" said Vic.

Nick's mouth was agape, his stare frozen.

"Two coffees for your friends. Right, Nick?"

Nick tried to act nonchalant, but it didn't work. "Vic, what a surprise!"

"I bet, you little worm. We need to talk in private. You got some explaining to do."

Nick's eyes flitted around, frantic, from Vic to Alan and back.

"Settle down, Nick. I just want to talk. You try anything fancy, and the Champ will take care of you, like the others."

Alan set his feet square with his shoulders, and his eyes blazed hard, James Cagney like, from under the brim that otherwise kept his face in shadow. Vic said, "You give it to me straight, Nick, and I won't hurt you. You give me a song and dance, and it's gonna get painful in here. I can just feel it."

"What about him?" he said, pointing a thumb toward Alan.

Vic sized up his partner and said, "He's still pretty sore about what happened here on Friday, but I think I can work with him. He'll take his finger off the trigger if I ask him nice. Won't you, Champ?"

Alan sighed big and noisy, blinked once.

189

Three of the waitresses walked to the door with their coats over their arms, turned to Nick and waved good night. They were edgy. Nick waved back said, "They're detectives. This is police business."

The three appeared to accept what he was saying and left the building. Vic escorted Nick back to the entry to lock the door. Nick looked warily at him.

Vic said, "I didn't want you getting lost along the way."

Nick didn't appreciate the humor.

When they returned, they took seats on opposite sides of a table. Alan grabbed a nearby chair, angled it to face the action, and sat with arms folded.

"Spill it, Nick. Why the set-up?"

Nick's expression changed from that of the frantic jackrabbit to a beaten dog. His head slumped, and his eyebrows pinched high in the middle and sagged pathetically at the edges. "Vic, I'm truly sorry. I didn't know what the cops had in mind. I didn't know they were going to snatch you up and beat you. Honest."

Vic folded his hands and laced them together on top of the table, as if he were praying in the back of church. He spoke slow and deliberately. "So, just what did you know, Nick?"

Nick spoke rapid-fire, eager. "One of Frantz's men called. Said he heard you were coming by Friday night. He asked if that was so, and I said, 'Maybe so. Vic likes to stop by every so often to say hello, have a drink, or maybe even a bite to eat.' Then he says—"

"He knew I was coming?"

"Sure."

"How?"

"I didn't tell him, if that's what you're asking."

"That's what I'm asking."

"I don't know. He knew. He just wanted me to confirm—"

190

"Did he know the time?"

"Not at all. He wanted me to tell him. So, I said you usually come after eleven, sometimes a little earlier and sometimes—"

"I got it, but I ain't got why you held the door and gave him a signal."

Nick's eyes darted around the room, searching for a clear shot at an exit. The jackrabbit inside his head seemed to want to bust out again. Then his eyes slowed down and searched their faces, ricocheting back and forth between Vic and Alan. Their cornered prey crossed and uncrossed his feet under the table. While waiting for him to settle down, Vic dropped his hands under the table and slowly slid the tire iron out of his coat, gripping it in his strong hand.

Nick said, "Lieutenant Frantz shows up just before ten. He starts out nice enough, says he wants to talk to you about something he's investigating, something he wasn't 'at liberty to discuss.' 'Police business,' he called it. But I told him you and I were friends from way back, and I didn't like the way this was going down, him rousting you in my premises and all. He says 'Not to worry, Nick.' They would take it outside and keep it clean, if I would just let them know when you showed up. You know···come out, light a cigarette, and leave the door open. That way the place don't get mentioned in any police reports, it doesn't get busted up, the liquor boys and Internal Revenue don't come checking my books."

"Is something wrong with your books?"

"What? Oh, Jeez···Vic, old friend, you know the restaurant business. We all got problems with our books."

"Tell me about it."

"Now wait···I'm not holding nothing back from Mr.

Brinkman. It's just that···some accounting is done in my head."

Vic brought his hand out from under the table and used the wrench end of the tire iron to push his hat back on his head.

Nick let out a high-pitched squeak and his eyes bulged, showing large areas of white, which made his pupils look that much smaller. Alan took Vic's cue and leaned forward in his chair, scowling at the cornered prey.

"Well, just a little bit," said Nick, his voice climbing two octaves. "Everyone takes a little off the top, kickbacks from the bartenders, waitresses, and liquor distributor···you know, but nothing off the net sales. Those have been strictly legit."

Vic took the pointy end of the tire iron and scratched an itch behind his ear. "So, what you're telling me is, you're not ripping off Mr. Brinkman, just everyone else."

"Exactly."

Vic slowly moved the iron back under the table.

"And you don't see that as a problem?"

"Everyone does—"

CRACK.

"Ow! Ow! Ow! Oh, Goddamn, that hurts." Nick slumped over and grabbed his leg with both hands, protecting his knee.

"That's for screwing with the little people, Nick, and don't take the Lord's name in vain."

"Ow···Jesus, I'm sorry."

"You're only sorry because I don't put up with your crap, Nick. Now as far as you screwing with me, you ain't off the hook just yet. I'm holding the rest of your punishment in abeyance, as judges say, until I can check out your story, and if you been straight with me, we're square. But if you been screwing with me like

192

you been screwing with your hired help, I'm not going to give you a little love tap, I'm going to break both your knees, make you kneel on the tire iron, and recite the entire rosary. You understand?"

"I don't know the rosary."

"You will before we're done."

"I understand what you're saying, Vic. I'm sorry, but I told you the truth. I swear."

"Maybe you did, but it was late in coming, Nick. I see your fingers ain't broke···yet. You know how to dial a phone. You should've called me right after the cops phoned you, or if nothing else, given me a heads-up when I got to your door."

"It won't ever happen again. I promise."

"Put some ice on your knee."

Back inside the car, Alan asked, "Did you break his knee?"

"Nah, It'll swell up and be sore as hell, but it's not broken. I wanted to send him a message, not cripple him. He needs to make a living. It'll hurt like hell for a couple days, then bother him for awhile, but he'll get over it. Besides, it's good for our business; shows others that we're paying attention, not getting soft in the head. While he's hurting, he'll whine about it, look for sympathy, and the word spreads. It's a funny thing, 'cause it always seems like after I get physical with somebody, all the others who got loans start cleaning up their books real fast."

"So···where to now?"

"You in a hurry to get home?"

"I've got so much explaining to do—."

"I want to pay Benny a visit, see what he has to

say, and I'd rather do it away from the office. No sense upsetting the ladies."

"I'm new at all this, but I say we get to the bottom of it. I don't want to be looking over my shoulder, wondering if he's going to set me up next."

"You got a good head on your shoulders, Champ. You're already thinking like a detective."

~~~~~~

They drove to the foot of the Denny Regrade, below Queen Anne Hill, where years ago engineers pressure washed much of the grade Seattle was built on into Elliott Bay, thus giving the Regrade its nickname. Well-established homes and other buildings were torn down or moved to new locations to make way for progress, giving the north end of the city a face lift by tearing down its hill. Benny's apartment was located a couple of blocks from the armory.

Vic suggested Alan wait outside near a corner of the building, so he could watch the side and back, just in case Vic flushed Benny from his apartment. Vic entered the lock-out by holding the door open for an elderly resident, helping her inside. He carried her bags into her first floor flat, and when she offered him a tip, he shook his head and tipped his hat. He took the stairs to Benny's upper floor, caught his breath, and knocked loud, angrily.

"Who's there?" barked a voice from inside.

"It's Vic. Open up."

Scurrying noises interrupted the pregnant silence, heading frantically to the back of the unit.

Outside, above where Alan was standing, a large

shape noisily clambered out a window to the wrought iron fire escape. The big man hurried without caution, thundering down the metal steps. When he reached the bottom landing, he pushed the ladder loose, and it clanged down, near to the ground. He hurried down the slippery rungs, lost his grip, and fell the last five feet, turning an ankle, dislocating his ring finger, and landing on his backside on the unforgiving sidewalk. He cursed, winced in pain, and tried to climb to his feet and limp away. Two steps into his flight, he stopped suddenly, frozen in fear, as a specter that emerged from the shadows confronted him, machine gun protruding below a long coat.

"Mackie! Jesus Christus!" he muttered with an accent. Benny backed up, raised his hands to surrender, and then knelt down on the sidewalk, lowering his head but keeping his hands outstretched. "Nicht schieben!"

Alan stepped out of the shadows and walked toward the cowering man, a repentant sinner, crouched like a praying mantis. Suddenly, Benny lurched forward, before Alan could move out of harm's way. Alan rocked in place, regained his balance, and laid the barrel of the tommy gun across the man's massive backside, ready to squeeze the trigger, as Benny hugged his legs, crying. "Don't kill me, Mackie. I didn't mean for it to happen."

Alan lowered his voice an octave. "Get in the car."

It took a moment for his command to sink in. Then Benny released his grip and inched backed slowly, cowering, while he struggled to get to his feet. His eyes darted frantically about, but he avoided making contact with Alan, who stood with feet planted shoulder-width apart. Finally, Benny saw the car and started hopping toward it, just as Vic came thundering around the corner, then slowed to a stop.

Benny climbed in the back, and Vic patted Alan on the shoulder. "Nice job, Champ." He handed Alan the keys. "You get a promotion to driver."

Alan whispered, "He muttered something I couldn't understand...I think it was German. Then he apologized for setting me up."

"Is that right?" Vic nodded slowly, more to himself than Alan. He climbed in the car and sat next to the remorseful Benny. Alan put the Thompson away, sliding it alongside the Garand in the trunk, and then drove in silence for a few moments. He stopped at the next traffic light and twisted the mirror away from Benny so he could watch Vic for cues.

Benny was first to break the thick silence. "Vic, I'm sorry. I had no choice."

The steel tire iron cut viciously through the air. CRACK!

"OW, ow, ow, ow, ouch! Jesus Christ! You broke my knee!"

"Don't take the Lord's name in vain, or I'll break your other knee, you louse."

"Oh, God···oh, oh, okay, okay, okay! Son-of-a-bitch!"

"Did you just call me a son-of a bitch?"

"No, no, no, Vic. It wasn't meant for you. Oh, mercy."

"Was it meant for Mackie?" he asked, catching Alan's eye in the mirror.

"No, no, no, no. Course not. I'm just in a lot of pain."

"Benny Hile. You've got some Latin in your name, Benedict...Benedictus···it means something good, but I can't remember. It's been too long since I was an altar boy. In your case I think it means: Good for Nothing."

"Oh, God. I think I'm going to be sick."

"Don't get sick in Mr. B's car."

"Haben sie gnade, Victor."

"Speak English."

"Okay. I had no choice."

"Sure you did. We all have choices. Sometimes we don't make the best ones, and in your case, you made very bad ones."

"What are you going to do to me?"

"Haven't decided yet, Benny. We need to discuss your···culpability."

"I hate it when you use big words. I know you, and it means you're getting ready to do something serious."

"Don't get ahead of me, Benny. Like I said, 'I haven't decided, yet.'"

They drove in silence for a few minutes, and then Benny said, "I don't get this, Mackie. I carried you to the steps the night the cops caved in your head. I went to your funeral, but here you are, fresh as new, risen from the dead."

"'From thence he shall come to judge the living,'" said Vic.

"It's you, but there's something different···"

They circled around the base of Queen Anne Hill, ending up on Westlake Avenue, which bordered Lake Union and was home to houseboats and marinas. Alan slowed the car and waited for a signal from Vic. It came, at last, in the form of a nod. Alan steered into a marina's lot and parked in a stall close to the gate.

Benny said, "I can't walk."

"Not a problem, Benny. Mackie will bring over one of those cargo carts, won't ya? We'll give you a ride."

Alan returned with the cart, and they poured their invalid into it, rolling him through the gate, and out onto the dock, like he was gear they'd stow for a fishing trip.

"What are you going to do to me?"

"Other than talking, I haven't decided, but now ain't the time to piss me off."

When they reached the Mighty Bee's gangway, Vic motioned for Alan to lead the way. Then he turned to Benny. "You got to take the last few steps yourself." He tilted the cart forward, and Benny tumbled out, grabbing the rails of the gangway, leaning on them hard.

"Oh, God, that hurts. I feel like I'm walking the plank."

199

"I don't know if it'll come to that. Just get moving before we draw a crowd."

Benny pulled himself up the gangway, grasping both sides of the railings, struggling and moaning all the way up to the first deck. Vic followed him, and once onboard, he unlocked the cabin. Alan quietly worked his way to the shadows, near the pictures on the wall, and Vic took hold of one of Benny's arms and helped him to a chair, one that was newer and didn't quite match the others.

"Sit there, shit bird, and don't move."

Vic went into Brinkman's bar, poured three fingers of whiskey into a glass, and handed it to Benny. He leaned in close and whispered instructions to Alan, before climbing into the captain's chair and starting the engines. After casting off lines, Alan jumped back on board, and Vic worked the yacht out of its slip into Lake Union. He steered the big boat toward the Montlake Cut, one end of another engineering marvel that shaped Seattle's landmasses. It connected the saltwater of Puget Sound on the western end to the freshwaters of Lake Union and Lake Washington on the eastern end.

Vic called down to Alan. "Come on up, Champ."

While Alan climbed the steps to the bridge, he tried to keep an eye on their guest, who between sips of scotch, shut his eyes, grimaced, and rolled his head in slow circles. "What about Benny?" he asked.

"What about him? I broke his kneecap to cut down on his mobility. About the best he could do is throw himself over the side, but I doubt he can swim. Here, you take the helm until we're out in the lake, away from prying eyes. Keep to the right side of the channel until you're out in the big lake." Vic dropped back down to the main cabin, leaving Alan at the helm.

Vic went to the bar, refreshed his drink and Benny's, too, while Alan got used to the controls. The drone of the big engines drowned out the conversation below him, but by using the reflection off the front window, Alan caught the images of the big men in the back of the yacht. Vic handed their captive a drink, and the two men touched glasses, toasting something, which sounded foreign, but he couldn't tell. Benny had rolled up his pants to massage his swollen knee and was tugging at his sock. Vic slouched back in his chair nearby and stared past him, out the stern. He scratched his chin with thick fingers and watched the wake of the big boat, lost in thought.

When Alan figured they were far enough out in the lake, he cut the engines, descended the ladder, and moved back into the shadows. Vic slid his chair opposite Benny's, took out the tire iron, and rested it on his lap.

"There's no need to hit me, Vic. I'll talk."

"I appreciate your cooperation, Benjamin "

"Vic, big words again. You're scaring me."

"Oh yeah, Benny, my mistake. Okay, I'll say it so you can understand: quit stalling. Spill. Now, does that make you less afraid?"

"Where do you want me to start?"

"The beginning is always a good place. I hate conversations that start in the middle."

"Okay," said Benny. In no hurry to move things along, he took a swig of scotch and caught his breath. Vic waited him out, now generous with his patience.

"It was the middle of last week, Frantz and his boys paid me a visit. Said they was going to send me away on a beef, if I didn't help them out."

"What kind of beef?"

"Is it important I tell?"

"Yeah, Benny, it is. You know how I feel about honesty."

"Okay, but I know how you feel about pornography, too."

"I'm okay with naked···wait a minute. What kind of porn?"

"The kind you don't like."

"Boy porn or kiddy porn?"

"Let's just say···they was young."

Vic's chest heaved. He let out a deep sigh. The vein in his neck throbbed.

"How young?"

"Young enough to get me sent away."

Vic swung the tire iron with a fierce backhand. CRACK!

"OW, OW, OW, Ouch! Goddam that hurts!"

"You sicko!"

"Jesus, I'm sorry, Vic. I said you wouldn't like it."

"What'd I say about taking the Lord's name in vain?" Vic raised his arm again but held it in mid air.

"Please. No more. I beg you."

"You sold me out because you couldn't lay off naked kids?"

"It wasn't new stuff. It was from a few years back. Stuff I was trying to get rid of. Harry said the statute of limitations still hadn't worn out. Said I'd get ten years, and they'd make sure I wore a pervert jacket. You know what that does to a guy in the joint."

"Explain the porn."

Benny tried to pivot in his seat to see Alan, who was standing next to the wall of pictures.

"Back when we were running hooch from Canada, I became buddies with our supplier in Vancouver. He and I were checking out strippers one night and the talk got around to photos of naked women: no pasties, no G-strings, and who had the best rack—guy talk. So he tells me about some broad he's got glossies of, somewhere in his stash of Swedish porn. He takes me to his place to show me. He's got lots of stuff, and then he says I can have the whole box if I want. So, I says, 'Why not?'"

"Go on."

"Unbeknownst to me, he had all kinds of pictures, which I didn't check out until I got back stateside. After I found out, I knew I should've ditched them, but then I thought⋯instead of dumping it, I could make a little profit. Who's it hurting? The deeds are done, the pictures taken. It wasn't like I could undo what happened to those kids when the real pervs took their pictures⋯but⋯I let them set a while in the box, almost forgot about them. Then, wouldn't you know, when I try to sell them, the first guy I contact happens to be a vice cop. So, just like that, I get arrested, and before I know it, I'm talking to Harry."

"Why Harry?"

"I don't know. Somehow it came up I worked at the union office with you and Mackie."

"D'you bring it up?"

"He already knew. He's got his fingers into everything and knows what's going on. So he starts asking questions about what you two been up to⋯ feeling me out. He asked if you two came into some money, a stash of old notes."

"What'd you tell him?"

"What was to tell? You two ran special errands for Mr. B, some that nobody knew about, and once in awhile you were off on your own. So, how would I know?"

"You didn't know about the gold notes we found?"

Benny raised his burly head and tried to look Vic in the eye, puzzled. "What notes?"

"Gold notes, Benny."

"I don't understand."

"Okay, maybe you don't. Mackie and me found a stash that Hungry Harry was crazy to find."

"All I know is he wanted to talk to you. Told me he would make the kiddie beef go away if I gave him stuff on you two."

"What kind of stuff?"

"He wanted to know what you were doing and when you were doing it."

"And?"

"I told him about the milk run, and that's when he··· say, I still don't get it. How come we had an open-casket funeral for Mackie, and he's standing right behind me? Is this the Second Coming?"

Vic looked over Benny's shoulder to the shadow. "Step into the light, Champ. Take your hat off so he can see your face."

Alan stepped around Benny and stood next to Vic. He doffed his hat and smoothed his hair. Benny's eyes worked their way up, from the shoes to the face.

"Son-of-a-bitch. You're not Mackie!"

"I'm his son. I'm Alan Stewart."

Vic laughed hard.

Benny did a double-take on Alan.

Vic laughed more. Benny tried to laugh with his host, but it didn't work for him.

"Well, I'll be damned," said Benny.

"You probably are," said Vic.

"You guys sure had me going. I couldn't figure— and what's more, Harry thinks you're Mackie."

"How do you know that?"

204

Pained expression—the I-said-too-much look.

"He came a calling, Saturday. He had a new hat sitting on top of a big old bandage. Said you shot him and killed his boys. Is that right?"

Alan put his hat back on and pulled the brim low. Edgar G. Robinson-tough.

Benny sized him up again. "Apple don't fall far from the tree." He shook his head once, puffed his cheeks out, exhaled, and continued. "I thought he'd lost too much cranial fluid, but he says it was Mackie who gunned down Hoff and Schneider, and he wanted to know how that could be. Then when I fell off the fire escape and saw you, I figured he was right." He indicated at Alan with the tilt of his head. Benny tried to laugh again, but it was impotent.

"What else did he want?"

"He accused me of double-crossing him."

"Who was with him?"

"Two boys. Phil Arnam and some guy from his office, who I guess got a sudden promotion. I didn't catch his name. It wasn't a social call."

"That wasn't the story he gave the newspapers."

"Yeah, he said he wasn't about to play that card to the newsies, and he told me to keep it between us."

"What else you keeping between you?"

"Nothing. He just put the squeeze on me about you and Mackie, wanting to know where you might hole up."

"What about the Champ?" Vic said as he motioned toward Alan.

"He don't know about him, and what's he going to do? Hang out at Mt. Pleasant Cemetery to see if Mackie slips back in his grave?"

"Where'd you tell him I might be?"

"I didn't."

"Sure you did."

"Well···it was a guess, because I didn't know."

"What was your guess?"

"I said, 'Try Chinatown.'"

CRACK! Fierce backhand, caught Benny's left hand sitting on top of his right knee.

Benny gasped for air, tried to scream out the pain, but nothing came. After a moment, he squeaked out a sob and muttered. Tears leaked down his cheeks. He held the bear claw out and tried to shake away the pain.

Vic got up, walked to a cabinet, and took out a role of light rope. He set it down, next to his captive. "It just don't stop with you. Not only do you give up Mackie, you sold me out twice, and when that still don't work, you tell him where he can find me—a third time!"

Vic fashioned a loop in the rope and reached for Benny's arm. Just as his hand was about to grasp hold, Benny snatched Vic's arm and jerked hard, pulling him off balance, down on top of him, while sneaking something from his sock.

Alan yelled, "Knife!" and Vic wrenched his body, just as Benny grunted and swung a hard thrust toward Vic's thick neck, but his would-be victim sacrificed his upper arm to save himself. The stabbing blow caught Vic hard in his upper left arm, just under his shoulder, going through the triceps at an upward angle, knife tip sticking out the back of his coat.

Before Vic could scream in pain—BANG!

A bullet from Alan's .45, pressed close, rocked the back of Benny's skull, tearing through it, and exiting out the bottom of his jaw. Vic tumbled to the floor and landed hard on his right side. He lay helplessly wounded, directly in front of the dead man, still sitting in the chair, frozen in time. After a long, pregnant moment, Benny's head flopped to his chest, his arms followed suit, dropping down and dangling at his sides. Then blood began to drain from the hole under his jaw onto his white shirt, staining his collar. Although he was dead, his knife remained buried to the hilt in the big man's upper arm, while Vic continued to lay on his side, at his would-be killer's feet, his eyes painfully squeezed shut.

Alan kept his gun trained on Benny, checking for signs of life, and then he stared at the gun, as if wondering how it leapt into his hand so fast. He holstered the .45 and stepped quickly around the chair to help his fallen friend. "Vic! You all right?"

Vic groaned loudly, rolled on the floor, sighed sickenly, and begrudgingly opened his eyes. He put an arm down and slowly pushed himself to a sitting position, leaning back against the bulkhead. "Ah, saints above," he muttered, as if disgusted at himself. "I'm stuck like a pig, and if that ain't bad enough, your bullet got me, too."

Alan looked at the knife sticking out of Vic's upper arm and saw blood, oozing out a hole, staining the fabric on the front shoulder area of his suit.

"Jeez, I'm sorry, Vic."

"Don't worry about me, Champ," he said encouragingly. "You saved my bacon again. If you hadn't warned me···I don't know. I think he would've tore out my throat. You did good. You didn't have time to check your backdrop."

Vic rolled to a knee and stood up, staggering, unsteady.

Alan said, "Here, let me pull it out."

"No!" snapped Vic.

Alan recoiled, eyes wide.

"We don't want to do that yet," said Vic. "I don't

207

know how close it is to an artery. You pull out the knife now, and it could be like that Dutch kid taking his finger out of the dike. All hell could bust loose."

"I didn't know."

"'Course not. It's not like you been in the war."

Vic craned his neck, eyed the stiletto menacingly, and shook his head. "Should have figured that Teutonic worm would have a trick or two up his sleeve...or down his sock. Now, what you can do is push the button on this gizmo, and then fold the knife down to the side, so it's not sticking out. Then we'll wrap it with something to keep it from flopping around, making it worse."

"What about the bullet?"

"It hit my shoulder, and I'm guessing it's stuck to the bone."

"I'm sorry, Vic."

"Hey, given a choice between what you did and what he might've, I'll take the bullet."

"I'll turn the boat around and head back—"

"No, no, no. We got to take care of Benny first. We can't just leave him in the Mighty Bee. Someone might find him, or he'd stink up the place, before we could get back to him. My wounds can wait."

"So, what's the plan?"

"First, we take care of you, Champ. What with the boat rocking and all, you're looking awful green. If you're going to lose your dinner, do it over the side."

Several minutes later, Alan came back in the cabin, pasty-faced and unsteady on his feet. He took a towel from the bar and wiped his chin.

Vic said, "When you're up to it, tie him to the chair. Then we take the boat up-lake, and we'll drop him near where Sid Fisher's carcass is snagging fishing lures. But before that, we check clothing for name tags, laundry marks."

"Got it."

"You okay?"

"I'll be fine."

"Be sure to check his underwear too, and then we'll make sure everything is tidied up, meaning no blood spatters and such. We do that before we put this baby back in its slip. I hate to put the housecleaning on you, but you'll have to do most of the work and everything heavy. I'll steer the boat for now and come down when it's time to toss him overboard."

It took them close to an hour to find the right spot in the lake, to circle around and dispose of Benny. His large body became annoyingly buoyant. Despite being tied to the steel chair, Benny refused to sink on command. So Vic coached Alan on marlinspike seamanship and had him push the body away from the boat with a long spar, only to have him tug it back, hooking Benny by his coat collar. Alan had to yank hard on the collar, tearing its seam, releasing trapped air, which had kept Benny floating, dangerously resembling a channel buoy clad in tweed.

Benny disappeared beneath the surface, leaving a thin trail of bubbles. Vic said, "There's a closet below the galley that has cleaning supplies. If you wouldn't mind?"

"I'll give the place a once-over."

"You're a good man, Champ. And since the worst's behind, why don't you pour us a couple of stiff ones? Scotch for me."

"You want anything in it?"

"Hell no. If I had my way, cutting good booze with mixer would be a mortal sin."

Alan busied himself in the bar, setting out glasses and selecting a choice bottle of Chivas Regal from a cabinet underneath. His eyes scanned the wall behind him, which had lots of pictures, secured by screws through wooden frames: Brinkman as a young man, Brinkman shaking hands with important people, Brinkman with a large catch of fish, and women, lots of women.

Alan thought: Trophy wall. Before long, he found Vera's picture next to a spot where another picture was missing. She was just as she'd been described—naked, except for a G-string and silver tassels twirling from each breast. Wow! She's got it going.

As he moved down the wall, the frames to his right looked fresher, while the Walrus looked older. Alan's height cast a shadow on the pictures, and he had to view some at an angle to see them better. His eyes stopped at the face of a young woman whose smile looked familiar. She had killer legs, her bare back was to the camera, and she peeked around a large fan that allowed some of her breast to show.

Alan's heart suddenly thundered like when he'd shot Benny. He stepped back to the side to get a better view, but there was no doubt. Alice!

He put his hand to the wall to steady himself.

After a long moment, Vic's voice boomed from above. "Hey, where's my drink? I need to numb the pain."

"I'll just be a minute."

Alan walked back into the galley, set down the drinks, and pulled open drawers until he found one with tools. He grabbed a screwdriver and headed toward the trophy wall. He fit the Phillips into the slot and unscrewed one side, then the other. He tucked the picture under his arm, retrieved Vic's drink, and climbed the stairs. Vic swiveled in the chair, eager to take his medicine. He reached with his good arm, and seeing Alan's gloomy face, said, "Don't worry, Champ. Should be smooth sailing from here."

Alan presented Vic with the picture. Vic frowned, shrugged his good shoulder slightly, puckered his lips, and licked them. He returned the framed glossy to Alan and returned to his view over the bow, searching for the Montlake Cut, the channel that would take them under the Montlake Bridge to their slip on Lake Union. "You weren't supposed to see that."

"So I figured."

"Don't let her past worry you. We've all got one. Fact is···you've been working on yours all weekend. It happens to the best of us. Then comes a day you want to put it behind, where it belongs, and move on, but it haunts you."

"Is hers in the past?"

"Most of it."

"Does this mean she's his girl, and I'm the world's biggest sucker?"

"Mr. B don't have what you'd call 'his girl.' Women he meets can say, 'No,' to him, but he's···charming··· knows how to be generous. Women like the special treatment: flowers, presents, and such. Who don't?"

"How many others were there like me—with the voting fraud and all?"

"You saved my butt twice this weekend, which counts for a lot, but Mr. B's still the boss. I ain't at liberty···to say···How long you known about the voting?"

"I wasn't sure till now. You just confirmed it."

"Touché, Champ, but seeing how things turned out

between us; I'm really sorry about that. I don't want it to hurt you, so I've already persuaded people that what they thought they remembered is better forgotten."

"Alice, too?"

"It ain't like that with her. She's nuts about you. Asks me everyday how you're doing and stuff. If she didn't care, she would've moved on. With her looks, there's nothing stopping her, otherwise."

"Has she done this with other guys?"

"This is what they call 'the exception to the rule.' She was encouraged to help, Election Day, but what ended up happening was···spontaneous. We couldn't have planned it to turn out the way it did. I sure ain't that smart. Mr. B maybe saw something he likes in you and hoped it would turn into something with Alice. Guy she settles down with will be a lucky man. Mr. B. don't tell me everything he's thinking, but then if he did, I couldn't tell you."

"Spontaneous?"

"Yeah. Means···"

"I know what it means, I was just thinking what Benny said when you use big words, something terrible is—"

"Those come from doing crossword puzzles. I don't have much real education. Your daddy got me hooked on the puzzles while we killed time waiting for Mr. B. But I'm intellectualizing—trying to come to terms—my point being: the part about her liking you was all on her own. You're a good-looking lad, you swept her off her feet. You know what I'm trying to say?"

Alan climbed into the co-pilot's chair and put his feet up on Brinkman's polished woodwork. "I was feeling guilty as hell about this weekend with Poppy, but I'm over that."

After they secured the Mighty Bee, Vic locked the boat and followed Alan across the gangway, along the dock, and out to the car. He had draped a hand-knitted throw over his shoulder, futilely trying to appear casual, while hiding his wounds.

Alan planted Vic in the back seat and drove them south along the lake.

"Keep just under the speed limit, Champ. No sense drawing the police."

Alan eased off the gas. "Providence Hospital?"

"No hospital. I've got a gunshot wound and a knife sticking out of me, and that means they'd have to notify the police. Which means we'd have to concoct a story to explain all this, and with our luck, it would probably be right to Hungry Harry's face, in person. No dice. Take me to Chinatown. Little Papa will fix me up again, which means you'll play house with Poppy."

"I'm fine with that, but···what about tomorrow?"

"If you're worried about going to work, I'll give you Vera's phone number. She'll broker the necessary calls to Brinkman, Western Union, your house, the bakery, and···Alice?"

Alan chewed on that for a moment. Vic waited. Finally, Alan said, "Sure, why not?"

"But be careful what you say to Vera. No sense telling her about Benny's unfortunate demise···just yet. Say we stopped by his apartment and found he'd left town. Leave it at that. Later, I'll call Mr. B, let him know we have a sudden vacancy."

"Got it."

"Say, Champ, would you be interested in filling that spot? You handle yourself real well. It pays a lot better than what you're making."

"I don't know, Vic. A lot of me is glad these three got their due, and I want to piss on their graves. But I'm still dealing with Friday night, and now you add in this image of Benny's head exploding. I just might puke some more. I don't think I'm cut out for this."

"You could say this weekend was an···aberration. We haven't had trouble like this in years. Back during Prohibition, enough cash changed hands to keep the local cops and Feds happy with their share. Then comes the Repeal, and now guys like Hungry Harry, who's got used to a grand lifestyle and can't put it down. They've turned their greed on others, trying to keep a good thing going past its time."

"Once in awhile you say something that makes me think you like cops. Other than Harry, you make excuses for them."

"I suppose you're right. In a lot of ways, we're in the same business. I do P.I. work for Mr. B, which reminds me—you take the job, and we'll get you a P.I. license and a badge. It comes in handy, but I only use mine doing work for the union. But as I was saying, I was gonna apply to be a copper after the war, when I was done moving about, but this job came open. I think I would've been a good one. What I like best is investigating things for Mr. B, like when some lowlife tries to scam the union out of a disability pension, or fakes an injury lawsuit. I like figuring things out more than flexing my muscles, and cops get to do that full time. Maybe someday, when you're old enough, you might think about it."

"Not with guys like Harry and his boys around, and it seems like there's too many of 'em."

When Alan reached Denny Way, he turned east and drove up the hill to Boren Avenue and along the ridge over-looking the city below. His route skirted downtown traffic and minimized their chances of contact with the police, while heading to Chinatown.

"Once Mama opens the door for me, park the car in the same spot as before."

"Will your stall be open?"

"Better be. I'm paying monthly for it."

When they drew within a couple blocks of the brothel, Vic said, "Circle the block one time and see if any beat cops are nearby. As big as I am and wrapped in this blanket, I'd stick out like a meatball in a bowl of rice. And I don't want the cops seeing me near Mama's place. Hamstrung this way, I can't just run off."

"Got it."

"Now, that goes for you, too. When you come back, if you see anybody watching, just keep right on going, return later."

"What's the password?"

"I'll tell Mama to have someone wait at the door for you."

"You don't trust me with it?"

"We'll talk."

Alan followed Vic's instructions, stopped at the curb, and when he started to climb out to help, Vic stopped him. "Stay behind the wheel. I can manage."

215

Vic lumbered over to the entrance, knocked, and then said something. The door opened and Mama beckoned him inside. Behind her, Lilly stood on the bottom step, her face terrified.

Alan found the garage. The stall was empty as promised. He parked and worked his way back to King Street, the brothel, and the nondescript door. He knocked and waited. Soon a woman's voice said something in Chinese. He answered, "Alan Stewart—Vic's friend."

The door inched open, and Big Mama stuck her nose out, clutched Alan's arm, and dragged him inside. Poppy was waiting for him on the second step. "You back soon," she said.

He reached for her with his strong arms, lifting her off the steps and giving her a smothering hug. He kissed the nape of her neck and smelled lavender. "I couldn't stay away from you."

"Vic hurt. You no hurt?" Her pronunciation sounded like "heart," but he got it.

"I'm fine."

She inspected his clothing, making sure, then kissed his cheek.

He set her down, and she took his hand and led him up the steps. "You like baff?"

He nodded and said, "I'd like a long bath."

"You like Rose, too?"

He shook his head. "No, just you."

She grinned big and led him to the room with the large tub. "We take baff, and then I love you long time."

He put his hand up, traffic cop fashion. "First, I need to see how Vic's doing."

Her brow furrowed and her mouth formed an O. She took his hand and said, "This way." She led him to a door with a room number on it and keyed it open. It was the false front that led to the smuggler's passageway and the parallel hallway. She led him to another door where they could hear voices. She knocked and opened the door. Asian faces in crisp medical gowns turned in their direction. The patient was in the center of the room, lying on an examination table. Lilly, who was also wearing a gown, knelt next to Vic, holding his good hand. Tears streamed down her face.

Vic waved at the new observers. "How you doing, Champ?"

"That's what I should be asking, and what's with all those pins sticking out of you?"

"It's acupuncture. It numbs the pain."

"Looks like you lost a fight with a porcupine."

Vic managed a laugh, then grimaced uncomfortably. "This stuff really works."

"You serious?"

"Completely. That plus something they gave me to drink···I'm feeling no pain...almost."

The medical equipment was a strange mixture of eastern and western items. Bottles of herbal potions sat on a counter next to metal stirrups, which had been removed from the examination table. There was a smell in the air of something worse than yak jow, along with disinfectant. Alan scrunched up his nose.

Vic said, "They perform medical procedures here on women who find themselves in a family way..."

"I get it."

"No sense mentioning what we call it. It might give certain people the hiccups."

Remnants of Vic's coat were hanging on a hook. The left sleeve was missing, and the upper chest area was stained with blood. The shirtsleeve had been cut away from Vic's arm. Vic still had the collapsed knife buried in his triceps, and he had a hole in the front of his shoulder that still leaked blood. Big Mama, who doubled as the Head Nurse, blotted it away, while Little Papa, the Lead Surgeon, prepared a probe, boiling it in hot water.

"Sorry, Vic. Looks like your suit's a goner."

"Don't be so sure. Come tomorrow, they'll have it cleaned with a new sleeve sewn on. Good as new··· better than new."

"Will it match?"

"I have no doubt."

"How about your shoulder? Good as—"

Big Mama interrupted and said, "You go now···wait."

Poppy took Alan's hand and walked him back the way they'd come. "We take bath···eat···see Vic later."

The door of the bath was already open, and from it tumbled the sound of water filling the tub. Rose clutched her kimono as she bent over the tub, pouring scented oil into the bath. A bottle of plum wine and two glasses were on a table nearby. Poppy started helping him out of his clothes, first his shoes, and then his pants. Rose took off her robe and climbed into the tub. Poppy rolled her eyes and shook her head. Her body language meant the same in both their languages: Don't make a fuss.

Alan wasn't sure what the house rules were here, but guessed: Something's going on. It must be like the union. Rose has seniority, and it's her turn for a customer.

Poppy finished prepping him for his bath and escorted him to the tub. When she let go of his hand, he grabbed her tight around the waist and squeezed her.

He took her hand again and steered it down toward his penis, which was fast becoming hard. He nuzzled her neck and whispered, "You stay."

She stared into his eyes, not as shy as when they first met, and said louder than needed, "You want two girl?"

"Yes," he said. Then he turned to Rose. "Two girls."

She nodded···obeisant, but the smile was slow in coming. Disappointment lingered on her delicate face. I'll ask Vic about this.

Rose slid back and made room for Alan. She kneaded the muscles on his back, while Poppy slipped out of her robe and paused, naked, in front of the tub. Alan admired her slender body, then reached out for her hand. Rose held her place in the tub, limiting the room for Poppy. Alan countered her move, bending over and lifting Poppy onto his lap. As he set her down, his large erection poked her, and she squealed. She put her hand under the water and pushed it out of the way, up against his lower abdomen. He set her on his legs, and then she wrapped her arms around his neck. He pressed his head next to her ear and nuzzled her neck again, tracing her jaw line around and behind her ear with the tip of his nose. He took her other hand, and steered it back toward his throbbing groin. A slow shark attack, discreet movement. Her hand brushed against it, nudging it back and forth like a pendulum, and then she grabbed it firm by the shaft, before sliding her hand to the top. She pinched its head and stroked it with a light touch. Just enough to let him know she wanted it for herself, but not enough to create a scene.

She pretended to scold. "You no cherry boy, anymore."

Somehow, Rose and Poppy came to a peaceful accord and teamed together to take care of Alan's pressing needs. They'd emptied a bottle of wine and were well into the second when Big Mama knocked at the door. Rose gave her the okay, and she opened it and entered the room. She said, "You see Vic now, please."

Alan stood up in the tub and began to climb out. Big Mama, who'd started to walk away, stopped and peeked over her shoulder, eying the naked man as he crossed the floor to get a robe. Rose and Poppy laughed, saying something to Mama, who took another eyeful and giggled, before going out the door.

In the hallway, Big Mama pointed Alan toward Vic and Lilly's regular room. When he got to the door, he could smell disinfectant mixed with unfamiliar smells. The room had been transformed and resembled a hospital recovery room. The sheets were crisp, white cotton, and the head of his bed was propped up on boards, elevating his upper body. The long needles were gone, and his arm and shoulder were wrapped in white gauze.

Vic greeted Alan with a sappy smile. His words came out in slow motion. "Hooww yoou dooin', Champ?"

"I'm fine, Vic. Sounds like you're half-way to dreamland."

"I amm in dreeammland···opium lannd?"

"Opium? Is that···safe?"

"I hhope sooo. Thhe Chineese have been using iitt forr thousaannds ooff yearrrs."

Vic stuck out his hand; it seemed to float in the air. Alan reached to catch it. Vic dropped a hard object from his big mitt into Alan's palm, the crushed .45 round recovered from his shoulder. "Souuvenierree forr yoouu."

With that, Vic nodded off, and the ever-present Lilly shooed Alan away. "He sleep now. He okay. You go."

Alan tucked the flattened bullet in the pocket of his robe and went back to find Poppy.

Late Monday morning, Vera ushered Alan into Brinkman's office. She showed him to a chair, squeezed his arm, and then excused herself. The Walrus's eyes followed her all the way to the door, which she closed behind her. Then, with a flick of his hand, he dismissed his bodyguard. "We need a few moments."

His bushy eyebrows formed a solid ridge, low on his forehead, over his gray eyes. He steepled his hands and pressed them under one of his chins. "I understand you and Victor had a busy weekend."

Alan waited to see if there were more.

"Do you want to tell me about it?"

Alan cleared his throat. "Yes, sir. Vic said to answer your questions, but said to be careful on certain points."

Brinkman reached for the humidor on his desk, opened it, and retrieved a cigar. He gestured toward the cigars, implying Alan could help himself. He prepped the cigar for a light and said, "Give me an overall rundown, starting with Friday night, but avoid details that describe anyone pulling a trigger or Vic exercising his power of persuasion. I don't want to get put in a situation where I might get called to testify in front of a grand jury with your fate in my hands. It wouldn't be fair to either of us. You understand, son?"

Alan told how Vic asked him along for the milk run with the promise of extra cash, how he waited in the car, and that he saw it all turn into an ambush. When Alan got to "tommy gun," the Walrus sat forward and spread out his arms like a maestro in front of an orchestra, using his cigar as the baton. Alan chose his words carefully and slowed when he got to Vic's beating at the hands of Schneider and Hoff.

The Walrus raised his baton and stopped the performance. "Okay, the newspapers say 'a team from Canada' chopped up the two cops with their tommy guns. Is that right?"

"Just one shooter."

"What about Lt. Frantz? What next?" The Walrus lowered the baton.

"When a···when the shooter went for Frantz, he found his magazine empty. Before he could reload, Frantz drew his piece and brought it up to point, but Vic charged him like a bull, ramming him smack in the chest and knocking him on his butt. His gun went flying. Frantz got up and ran off, but the shooter squeezed off a shot with Frantz's own gun, clipping him on the head."

The Walrus raised the baton. "Where's the gun now?"

"I've got it here." Alan retrieved the gun and handcuffs from his coat and set them on Brinkman's desk.

The Walrus looked but didn't touch. "Whose handcuffs are these?"

"These are the ones they put on Vic, inside the club."

"Oh, yes, I see···Frantz said in the newspaper he got off several shots, but you say this gun's been fired just once?"

"That's right."

223

"Then we'll want to preserve this the way it is⋯as an insurance policy of sorts, in case something comes up in the future. We can box it up and store it in a safe place." The Walrus nodded as he thought. "Okay, what next?"

"Vic had me drive to a place he knows that could fix him up."

"Chinatown?"

"Yes, sir."

"I've never been to his place, but⋯go on." The Walrus sat back in his chair.

"Vic knew he was set up. He even figured it happened the night my father⋯was killed."

The Walrus sat up again, this time tall in the saddle. His eyes glowed wide and showed white, eyebrows pinched low over his nose, rage building.

"So, Sunday night, after things settled down, Vic decides we should pay a visit to Nick the Greek, and he persuades him to tell how this all went down. Nick tells him that Hungry Harry knew he was stopping by Friday night, and he forced Nick to cooperate."

The Walrus put up the baton again. "So Vic fixed one of Nick's knees⋯I know⋯I already heard about that. His knee'll be fine, but I'm restructuring his loan⋯go on."

"Vic said everything pointed to Benny. So he wanted to pay him a visit. We went to his apartment, and Benny bails out the fire escape. That was pretty much a giveaway. When he drops off the ladder⋯he saw someone who looked like my dad. It spooked him. Benny twisted an ankle, and Vic also caught up to him. So, Benny goes for a ride, some place where people can talk."

"My yacht?" Brinkman asked in a hushed voice, as if the walls had ears.

"Yes, sir."

224

"What happened there?"

"Vic was persuading Benny to come clean, and he'd fixed Benny's knees, but Vic wasn't hearing what he wanted to hear. So he reaches down to grab Benny's arm, but Benny jerks him off balance and comes up with a switchblade from his sock. He was about to stick Benny, when I—"

The Walrus raised the baton. "Careful, son."

"Vic was alerted to the danger. He flinches and catches the knife in his upper arm, near his shoulder, instead of the throat, and then Benny takes a bullet to the back of the head."

The Walrus put both hands up to stop the performance. "It sounds like Benny went crazy with a knife and a certain person, who's yet-to-be-named, took quick action and saved Vic's behind. Is that about right?"

Alan blushed, nodded.

"Sounds like this person did the right thing, not once, but twice, this weekend, and I'm very pleased to hear it."

"Thank you, sir."

"So   if I'm following···Benny was a lowlife subversive, maybe even a filthy Red, a spy planted by the Communists or a competing union, which can be just as bad, and he was responsible for the death of one of my inner staff and the near death of another."

Alan sat back and let the Walrus process this and catch his breath.

"So, how's the patient doing?"

"If it was just the knife wound, he'd probably be back in a week."

"There's more?"

"Yes, sir···the bullet—"

"He was shot?"

"I was getting to that. It seems the bullet that went

through Benny's head ended up in Vic's shoulder."

"Oh, that's right," the Walrus conceded, dropping his baton to the desk, disregarding the agreed upon pretense to discuss the killings in the abstract. "You said Benny had Vic on top of him." The Walrus moved his hands about, like a child with clay, trying to imagine the position of the combatants. "There wasn't much in Benny's head to slow down the bullet. So how bad is it?"

Alan reached in his pocket and took out the flattened bullet. He laid it on Brinkman's desk, and the Walrus picked it up, twirled it in the light, inspecting it closely.

"It flattened out against a bone in his shoulder, but as far as we know, it didn't break anything. He's guessing he might be out of action for two or three weeks."

"I see. Well, that's going to leave us short-staffed in the office."

The Walrus scowled for a moment, and then his eyes brightened. "Seems we have an immediate opening, son. Would you be interested in my driver's position? I could use a man who's got a strong backbone and can think on his feet."

Alan blushed again. "Thank you, sir, but···I'm not sure I'm cut out for this. This wasn't at all like I expected, and I feel rotten about a lot of it. I even feel bad about enjoying the parts I do. I don't think I could do this on a regular basis."

"Nonsense, son. You'd be perfect. We haven't had trouble like this since the Repeal. I'd just need you to drive me around, do some occasional detective work, and show your pretty face when you drop me off and pick me up. It's more of a prestige thing for me having a driver, and a lark for the lucky man who snags the job. So, why not let it be you? You'll grow into it. Besides, your family could use some good luck, and if something comes up where there's a need for heavy lifting, I've got others for that."

Before he thought about what he was saying, Alan asked, "What's it pay?"

"$300 a month to start···about three times what you make hauling rolls and donuts, and unless I'm mistaken, I believe Alice would enjoy having you available to take her out to lunch."

He had to bring her up. But···is he relinquishing his claim? "Driver and detective?"

"Sure···why not? When Vic gets back, he can take you down to get your P.I. credentials."

Alan looked toward the ceiling and chewed the back of his lower lip.

"You worried what your mother will say?"

Alan nodded, blinked long and slow.

"How much does she know about this weekend?"

"Only what Vera's told her."

"Good. I think I should be the one to discuss this with her. Given what happened to your daddy, it would break her heart to know too many details. You follow me?"

"Yes, sir."

"Just leave that to me. Meanwhile, I'll have someone drop you in Chinatown, so you can baby-sit old Vic. With Lieutenant Frantz being such a loose cannon, I don't want Vic alone where he can't protect himself. Ralph will drive me to visit your mother, so she and I can work things out. That okay?"

It was a directive, not a question. Alan nodded, all the same.

"Son, I'm going to have Vera put you on the payroll as part of my staff, and my staff calls me Mister B. I'm okay with that. You don't need to call me 'sir.'"

"Yes, sir⋯Mister B."

"So how're you fixed for money, son?"

"I've got a few bucks, and I'd forgotten—I've got the milk run cash." Alan reached in his coat pocket and pulled out the envelopes of cash. There was dried blood on them and a .45 caliber hole in the bottom edge of all four. Alan looked at the envelopes and their holes like they were a revelation to him, and then said, "Frantz's men stole these from Vic, and we recovered them⋯after the shooting." He set the envelopes on the desk.

The Walrus blew smoke at the stack but didn't touch. Then he sat back in his chair, opened a drawer, and fingered through his own envelopes. He took out four manila ones with the familiar handwriting on them. "Here's $500 for your signing bonus, and another $1,500 for helping Vic this weekend. Besides the bonus, that works out to $500 a head."

"I don't know what to say."

"You could say, 'It stops here.'" The Walrus made his point, wagging his cigar through the smoke-filled air. "There's nothing more to be gained by going after Frantz, trying to even the score for your dad. Our wayward copper might eventually get accustomed to the new part in his hair and finally realize he's a lucky S.O.B., or he might come sniffing around here, wanting to find his shooter—instead of chasing him to Canada, like he told the papers. And you know that if someone takes out a police lieutenant, no matter how corrupt he is, there'll be hell to pay for the union for a long time. The entire wrath of the whole damned police department would be focused on bringing us down, and we couldn't survive that kind of pressure.

It could break us. The police would call in favors from the prosecutor, inquiry judges, and the Feds—just like they did with Al Capone. You know it was the IRS who finally brought him down. As union boss, I have an obligation to take care and ensure its longevity. I can't let this squabble risk what we've built here, even if all those sons-of-bitches had it coming. You understand my position, son?"

"Yes, sir."

"It wouldn't take much for the police department to throw its weight behind Dave Beck and his Teamsters, and that would spell the end of us. That said, your father would've been proud. I sure as hell am, but it'll be a different story for your mother."

The Walrus stood and went for his hat and coat. "Next week I'll have a talk with Frantz's boss. I'll let him know I've seen his boy's pistol, and the number of rounds in its magazine tells a different story than what he told the papers. I suspect it won't match what he told the police, either. It ends for him, too, or that pistol will find its way to the city editor at the Post-Intelligencer. That should change his tune."

Alan followed Brinkman to the front office, where Alice was standing next to Vera, pensive. When Alan appeared, she broke into a beaming smile. He'd resolved to be distant until he had time to sort things out with her, but he gave up that notion when she reached forward and squeezed his hand. She sent a tingle through his body that reverberated in every part of his being, down to his toes.

Her eager gesture was not lost on the Walrus, who paused for a moment, adjusted his hat, like he was screwing a lid on a mason jar, being careful not to cross the threads, and then he set about the business of being boss. "Vera, see that Mr. Stewart gets a ride back to where Vic is, and I want him put on our payroll, effective immediately: office staff. Call the bakery and square it with them. Tell them I'd look favorably upon it if they could work his younger brother···" The Walrus tried snapping his thick fingers, as if summoning the forgotten detail.

"Sean," Alan volunteered.

"Yes, Sean. I want Sean Stewart put into the driver rotation. Now, I've got to run an errand, and I'll have Ralph see me home."

By the time Brinkman cleared the front office, Alice pressed up against Alan. "I was so worried. Are you all right?"

"Yes, I'm—"

She held his hand close to her chest and said, "I really think we should talk. How long before you can come over?"

He tried not to look in her green eyes, tried not to like her, tried not to remember the picture he had of her in her former life, naked except for two white, feathered fans. "It might be a week, maybe two, before Vic's well enough to be on his own."

Her frown darkened the whole room.

"But maybe I can get away for a couple of hours··· in a few days."

Vera returned with car keys and interrupted. "We'll give you a ride in my car. You can catch us up on the way. I'm sure we'd both like to hear what you two were up to this weekend."

Alan furrowed his brow, as if thinking were painful.

"It's okay, Champ. I know all the stories around here, and I know enough not to dig for details when I shouldn't. I can coach you around the rock falls."

Behind the union building, Vera turned up the heater to defog the windshield on the Buick, and in back, Alice patted the seat next to her. Alan slid in close. Vera drove and took the lead. "Tell us. How's Vic doing?"

Before long, Vera steered the questions to the Friday night at the Kasbah. Alan left out the most incriminating details and tried to turn the focus to Vic's condition.

Vera took Second Avenue through town, constantly checking the mirrors, and every few blocks she made a few extra turns, while working her way south, spy-like, as if she had plenty of experience doing this sort of thing. Alan wondered if this skill came from eluding other men's wives. Alice drew Alan's arm close, comforting him as well as her. Her dress rode high, revealing her legendary legs. She pressed them against his. He fought not to ogle, but it was a battle for which he was unarmed.

Alan said, "If you can get me to Maynard Avenue and South King, I'll hoof it from there."

Vera asked, "Can you say anything about what happened last night with Benny?"

"Dangerous ground, but I'll try." Alan opened up more and recapped what Nick told them at the Kasbah, their ensuing visit to Benny's, and his admitting the betrayal of Mackie and Vic. Then he briefly described Vic's injuries, circumspectly, not admitting his part.

Vera mumbled something, sniffed loudly, and dabbed her eyes with a hanky. Alice squeezed Alan's hand tightly, like a mother leading a toddler across a busy intersection. He leaned close to her and whispered, "Do you think I'm a monster?"

"Heavens, no," she whispered sharply, almost as if

231

she were scolding him. She touched his face, trying to rub the furrow out of his brow. "Vic needed protecting, and a wrong needed righting."

"Inside, I feel wounded in a way that won't bleed or ever heal."

"I know you hurt now, darling, but I think that's a good thing··· Trouble just has a way of finding us, sometimes. You did what had to be done, and you'll have to live with the results. Put it behind you and don't look back."

Before they realized it, Vera had stopped at a curb on Maynard Avenue. Alan reached for the door handle, but Alice grabbed his shoulder and held him back. Then she tugged him close and kissed him on the mouth. He pulled his hat off, threw it on the seat, and matched her passion with his own, eager and hungry.

Vera adjusted the rearview mirror, and when Alan slowly released Alice, Vera twisted the mirror back to where it had been.

Alice whispered, "Come see me."

He searched her eyes, trying to read all he could in the rush of the moment. She held his gaze while he groped around for his hat. After he found it, he backed out of the car, stood at the curb, returning her wave as she disappeared around a corner. He'd never kissed Poppy that way. He'd never hungered for any woman like that. He tried to tell himself to be careful with her, but he wanted more.

He licked his lips and felt traces of her lipstick. He took a handkerchief from his pocket, moistened it with his tongue, and dabbed at his mouth. Dusty rose stained the white cloth in his hand. "She said, 'Darling.'" He grinned widely and tucked the keepsake cloth in his coat pocket, turned around, and started back to Vic, the brothel, and Poppy.

Walking past a darkened storefront door, Alan caught his reflection off the glass. He stopped, faced it, appraising what he saw. "All right, wise guy, which one will it be?"

Late Friday afternoon, Alan stood lost in thought at the bedroom window, hands on the sill, gazing at the street below. His hot breath steamed the cold glass. Lounging behind him on a bed, Vic said, "I'll be all right for a couple of hours. Go take care of what's bothering you."

"Nothing's bothering me."

"Really? You're not eating, you're moody, and when you're not pacing the floor, you're staring off into space. It may not be bothering you, but it's bothering Mama."

Alan continued to sulk.

"It's the picture, ain't it?"

"What picture?"

"The one you stole from the boat."

Alan didn't answer.

"I knew it. You got it bad for her, don't you?"

Alan tried to shake his head, but it was half-hearted. He took a deep breath, but it sounded more like a deep sigh.

"Ain't nothing wrong with wanting her. She's got a past, but like you, she's a good kid. If I was your age and not so damned ugly, she'd have to get herself a stick to keep me away—an ugly stick."

Alan managed a weak smile.

"Go talk to her."

"I wouldn't know where to start."

"Start with 'hello,' and see where it goes. 'Cause if you let your pride get in the way, and she slips out of your hands, you'll always wonder about what could've been. You might end up kicking yourself to death."

"How can I be sure she's not playing me···again—warming me up for another round of voting fraud?"

"I was part of that, too, remember, and we seem to have put that behind us. Besides, you being Scots-Irish and all, you have to learn how to forgive."

"I don't see the connection."

"You know what they say about Irish Alzheimer's patients?"

"Can't say I do."

"When the Irish get the affliction, they forget absolutely everything—but their grudges they never forget. You don't want to end up like that."

Alan smiled halfway.

"But, you're right," Vic said. "You can't never be sure about who's playing who. For that matter, how can Poppy be sure you ain't playing her?"

"Ouch, that hurts."

"See what I mean? It ain't easy. You got to go with your gut on this, not your pecker, not your heart; they'll steer you wrong. When you're making it with a girl, don't pay any attention to what your pecker's telling you. It might want you to blubber out how you love the dolly you're on top of or behind, but trust me, that ain't love. That's your pecker tricking you into something it don't know much about. Your dick knows what it likes for all the wrong reasons, and your heart ain't much better. It's connected directly to your head, which is full of illogic, sawdust, and illusion, all at the same time."

"I don't know if I could tell the difference. Besides, I'm no good at talking to women."

"That's two problems you got then. Experience is usually what it takes when it comes to the first problem, the love angle, but I'm not exactly Mister Elegant when it comes to pillow chatter. You wouldn't want to follow my lead on that account. I don't know what to tell you. But for love, a shortcut is when you say something···or do something···without knowing it's coming—something opposite of what you'd expect. Let's say you're discussing shortstops in the National League, and all of a sudden you can't stop kissing her with all the passion you got···or telling her while helping with chores you love her like no other···'cause you just can't help what pops out of your mouth."

"'Like no other?' I didn't pick you as a romantic, Vic."

He laughed. "Another thing, Champ, it's in the way you two kiss."

Alan grinned at his teacher, lost in thought. A moment later, he closed his eyes, shook his head, as if tossing out an uncomfortable image of Vic.

"Sex is one thing, the old in-and-out, you gotta love it, but that ain't where the real love is. If you find your lips stuck all over her face, that, as we detectives say, is a clue."

Alan stood up quick, and reached for his coat and hat. "I need to catch a cab." He raced from the room to the hallway.

Vic called after him, "Play fair."

Alan tipped the cabby and raced up the steps to the Angeline Apartments. The manager greeted him at the counter and prepared to give him the mother-hen glare. But her eyes twinkled as she scanned a paper-wrapped package that suggested chocolates. The twinkle faded and was followed by a reaction that hinted at envy. He carried a double-bouquet of flowers and proceeded directly to the counter. Before she could say anything, he handed her one of the bouquets. "You said you like these."

Through layers of heavy makeup, she flushed as pink as the roses. "Well, aren't you the perfect gentleman."

While she fussed at unwrapping the flowers, talking with her back turned, Alan raced up the four levels to Alice's apartment, taking steps two at a time. At the top, he was panting. He put his hand on the railing to rest a moment and stared out a window that faced east, fixing on the distant brick tower at Providence Hospital, while rehearsing what he'd say.

Inside Alice's apartment, the phone rang and was answered. It's the manager telling her I'm on my way. He gave her a second to hang up before he would ring the buzzer. A moment later, he pushed himself away from the railing and crossed the hallway. He put the flowers behind his back to surprise her—but then decided that would accentuate the package in his other hand, which weren't chocolates. Grow up, Stewart! He tucked the gift under his arm and out of the way, while he held the flowers extended with his other hand.

Alice opened the door, wearing a pink sweater, a pleated skirt, slip-on mules, and something he had never seen on her before—horned-rimmed glasses. "What a nice surprise!" she said, inviting him in.

He crossed her threshold, and she said, "I'll take your hat and coat."

He handed her the flowers.

"These are beautiful." She set them on the counter and opened the closet, handing Alan a hanger. She stepped to the side, caught her reflection in the mirror next to the door.

"Oh my gosh! I forgot I was wearing these. I was reading while dinner finished. Otherwise I never—"

"That's all right. They give you that school-girl look."

"I'm not sure that's an image I'm striving for."

He set the package down and entered her living room, entranced by the view from her west-facing window of the downtown and Elliot Bay. "Wow! This is spectacular. Look at all the lights. I didn't realize how great this city looks at night."

From the kitchen, she answered, "Sometimes I just stare at it for hours. There's always something going on down there."

He looked at the different landmarks, Smith Tower and Pioneer Square, just south of it. He worked his way over to Chinatown and couldn't quite make it up to Japantown. "What's that place down and to the left, with the two towers?"

She walked from the kitchen and took a look where

238

he was pointing. "Oh that's St. James Cathedral."

"Never been there. Have you?"

"Not so much when I first got here, but now I try to get there on Sundays. It's really quite beautiful."

"So, you're Catholic?" he asked.

"Off and on again. Right now, I'm on again. What about you?"

"My dad wasn't practicing anything, never talked about it, but I got the feeling he might have been ···or grew up around them—Catholics, that is. My mother used to drag us to Sunday morning services at a Presbyterian church, but now she's given up— on me. I haven't been in two years—since Dad was killed. Trouble is, I'd feel like a hypocrite. The only time I pray is when I think of his killers—for them to be delivered from their wretchedness··· What kind of prayer is that?" he asked. "So, now, I don't think I'd be welcome. If I went inside, a bolt of lightning might strike the place."

She studied his eyes. "Sometimes you just got to make that first step toward change. Otherwise, you're just marking time on the calendar, watching the days pass, never growing."

On her way back to the kitchen, she smiled, puzzled. "Wretchedness?"

He took a seat on the sofa, which gave him a view of her. "Yeah, you know···the hell-fire and brimstone stuff. It gets drummed into you."

Although they had gone to a couple of movies, he hadn't been inside her unit before, so he had an excuse to look it over, while checking for signs of the Walrus. The furniture was simple, solid, with clean lines one wouldn't tire of. I bet this cost more than you'd think. She had a large bookcase, which was full of magazines and books. Many seemed new. The walls were devoid of personal pictures, but he thought that might be a condition of her lease.

She tossed old flowers in the garbage next to the sink. Then she unwrapped the roses, added fresh water, and arranged them in the same vase. Satisfied, she stooped to smell and admire them. I could watch her all day.

He said, "The flower guy said if you crush an aspirin and mix it with water, the flowers will last longer."

"Really? I've never heard that before, but I'll give it a try."

She stopped working with the flowers and came out of the kitchen. "Can you stay for dinner? It's chicken and dumplings. I'm used to cooking for a family and never learned how to make a small batch of anything."

The rich aroma brought his appetite back to life. "I'd love to."

"If you'd like a drink, I pretty much have everything: scotch, bourbon, rum, and vodka for sure, but I'm not much into mixers. I was told people didn't mix drinks before Prohibition, but booze was so bad bartenders had to come up with ways to make it taste better. Vic says it should be a sin to mix good booze with anything."

Alan grinned at the familiar story. "I'm with Vic⋯ not that I've had that much experience. How about scotch on the rocks—if you've got ice?"

"I've got scotch, and I've got a new block of ice in the icebox. I'll knock off some chips."

"How big is the family you cooked for?"

"There were seven of us living on a farm outside Surry, which is near Vancouver. My dad and mother, me, two brothers, one sister, and Uncle Henry. I was the oldest child, so cooking fell to me while mom and dad worked the farm."

"What about your uncle?"

She looked away, out the kitchen window. "That was a long time ago. I'm sure he's passed by now. Let me get you that drink."

Sitting on the sofa near the lamp was a book turned upside down and still open, *Light in August*. He picked it up, careful not to lose her place, and looked it over. "You do a lot of reading?"

"We couldn't afford books when I was growing up, so now that I'm on my own I've been trying to make up. I love to read."

She brought his drink out and handed it to him. "Scoot over."

He slid closer to the light, and she sat down next to him. He asked, "Aren't you having anything?"

"I don't care much for alcohol. You saw what happened when we drank champagne. We voted how many times? It's too strong for me, and I saw too much of it···as a kid, but I'll have a little wine with dinner."

He let his hand slide off his lap and it touched hers as it landed on the sofa. She put her hand over his and squeezed it. It was a good fit, comfortable, like a familiar slipper. He felt large slabs of ice break free of his iceberg resolve to be tough with her. He forgot the dinner and could smell a hint of perfume and scented powder. She crossed her magnificent legs but was careful so that her skirt didn't ride up.

He said, "You're not angry I didn't call first?"

"Not at all. From what I can tell, you're in some secret place—can't just pick-up the phone anytime you feel like it."

"But you might've had plans, it being Friday night and all. I could be spoiling something."

"Well, some of the girls from the building were going down together to catch a movie around 7:30, but I can skip a turn. I'd rather enjoy your company."

Another slab of ice broke free. He shifted his weight to face her, and his left leg drew up on the cushion, touching her's. "Alice, you're a very attractive girl, and I can't help but think you might have a dozen guys lined up like beggars in a soup line, hungry for your company. You might even be seeing someone right now."

"I'm not seeing anyone, Alan. Are you···you sound like you've got something on your mind. Are you jealous?"

He stared deep in her eyes, and she held his gaze, never flinching. He was first to break contact, and she drew his hand into her lap, onto the soft wool of her skirt.

"Yes···no···I don't know···yes, I am. I don't know much about you, but I'm jealous of every guy who's ever laid an eye on you, or a hand—"

"Alan!"

"I'm sorry···my mouth doesn't seem..." He took a sip of his drink, giving himself time to collect his thoughts.

"What's Vic been telling you?"

"Nothing. He keeps his mouth shut. I just want to know more about···"

"About what?"

"You···Brinkman···Canada and what you were doing when he met you."

She dropped his hand and scooted back. Her head slumped and her eyes filled with tears.

He set down his drink and grabbed both of her hands, dragging them over to his lap. She looked away from him and the tears started flowing.

"Alice, I'm sorry. God···Alice, I'm awful sorry. I had no right to pry."

He reached in his coat pocket, took out a hanky, and held it up for her, but she didn't see it. She was sobbing now and not caring where the tears landed. He held her chin and dabbed at the tears, trying to stop the stream before they left her face and landed on her cashmere sweater. He flashed back to a time when Margaret broke her arm playing baseball with her brothers. Here, the hurt was deeper.

Between sobs, Alice started to speak. "Why···why··· did you···have to···bring···"

"Alice, I'm so sorry. I didn't mean to hurt you."

His eyes were beginning to moisten, too, and his gut burned. He wished he could take what he said back. "Alice, please, I'm sorry. You mean so much to me···like no other girl···ever."

He tugged her close to him, and she didn't help or resist. He snuggled her head into his chest, under his chin, and then he began rocking her like he had Margaret so many years before. He held her chin and lifted her face so he could look in her eyes again, but they were still closed. He started kissing her face, soft as silk, and he tasted the salt in her tears. He kissed both her eyes, her cheeks again, and then her lips.

"I'm so sorry, Alice. I didn't mean to hurt you. I never will again. I'm nuts about you and want you only for myself."

Her tears began to subside, but she still kept her eyes closed. He began rubbing her arm and patting her shoulder. "There's a monster raging inside me that's trying to rip its way out and hurt people. Besides those men, I hurt you, and I feel worse about that than anything else. It's just that when I found about Canada—I want you so bad I can't stand it."

Sobs subsided and her breathing began to resemble normal. He pressed her forehead close to his cheek.

She took a deep breath and let it out. "It's true. I

was a···showgirl for two years. Then Mr. B offered me a job." She took Alan's handkerchief from his hand and dabbed at her eyes. "I wasn't proud of what I was doing, so I jumped at his offer to come to the states, 'the land of opportunity.' As far as he and me having—"

"I don't need to know."

She thought for a minute, then said, "You sure? Because this is your only chance. I'll never mention it again."

"I won't bring it up, if you won't."

"Alan, I can't pretend it never happened. There were posters, publicity stills, and flyers with my picture on it, and there were plenty of men besides Mr. B who went up to Vancouver to see my show."

"I don't need to know. Truce?"

She sat up and looked him in the eye. Her's were still moist with tears, while the rims of his were red. "Truce," she said.

He held her gaze, and she held his. "My God, you're beautiful!"

"You're not so bad yourself, Buster."

"Buster? Who's Buster?" he teased, as he tickled her sides.

She giggled and squirmed on his lap.

"So, is Buster someone else from your past? Tell me." He tickled her more.

"Stop it, you goose!" Then she laughed squeezing her arms close, trying to knock his hands away, squirming as she did so.

"Goose? I'm a goose?"

"Yes, you're Buster the Goose."

He laughed so hard he released his grip and dropped his arms. She seized her freedom and hugged him around the neck, nestling her head in next to his chin. She caught her breath and said, "I need to check the dinner before it burns."

She slid one hand down to his chest and started to push herself away, but he pulled her back, eager to find her mouth. She kissed him back, beginning soft and tender, ending long and firmly. Then she abruptly stood up. "There. That should hold you for a while···"

He feigned a stupor, rolling his eyes back into his head. She looked at him and laughed, mocking, teasing, finally ending with "···Buster."

Alice was a practiced hand, comfortable in the kitchen. Wanting to be near her, he asked if he could help. At first, those words seemed foreign to her, but then she said, "You can open the wine on the counter. The knife and opener are next to it."

Alan studied the bottle and the corkscrew, brow furrowed. "Only wine I've ever had is plum wine, and I don't know if that counts. I've never had an occasion to open one of these. I'm sorry."

"I never had wine until I moved to the city. So··· what you'll want to do is cut the wax off with the knife. It'll come off easily. Then line up the corkscrew and twist it into the cork. When you get it in far enough to get a grip, pull it out."

"Am I supposed to sniff the wine or—"

"I think you only do that with reds. I trust this wine, but you can check the cork to see if it's dried out and made a bad seal..."

He set about the task, careful not to make a mistake. She checked his progress every few seconds. She finished setting the table. In a moment, he tugged the cork out with a resounding pop—and a thud as his arm banged into her icebox.

"Are you okay?"

He shook off the pain, grinning, embarrassed.

"It takes a little practice. Glasses are behind you in the cupboard."

He brought down two glasses and set them on the counter. He was about to pour, when she stepped next to him. "Raise the glass up to the bottle. It's less likely to spill that way."

He poured and as the wine neared the desired level, she said, "Now turn your wrist with a gentle twist to shake off the last few drops, so it won't dribble."

She took the first glass and watched him pour the second, same as hers. When finished, he picked up his glass. "Cheers," she said, and he echoed her. She took a sip, and he mimicked her movements, savoring the wine in the front of his mouth. She waited until he nodded his approval.

"I thought you might like it." She licked her lower lip.

He set his wine glass next to the scotch and reached for her hand, steering her close to him. She didn't resist. He lowered his head, and she raised her mouth to meet his. She welcomed his kiss and his probing tongue. When they stopped for a breath, she set her glass down next to his and kissed him back, nibbling at his lips. He squeezed her tight, enveloping her in a strong hug. He pressed his nose into her hair, behind her ear, and inhaled deeply, trying to capture her smell.

She whispered, "Buster Goose."

He chuckled.

"Dinner's on. You snooze, you lose."

At the small table, they sat across from each other. She dished up the food and asked, "So how's my buddy Vic?

In between bites, he said, "He's on the mend, doing really well."

After a few more bites, he slowed down to savor a dumpling and gravy. "This is good." He began to chew even more slowly, enjoying the flavors. "This is really good."

"You had doubts?"

He laughed. "No, not really."

"But what?"

"I was thinking somebody as pretty as you could get by not knowing how to cook."

"Is this going to get us back to what I used to do—"

"Oh, no. Sorry. I was trying to say that I'm very impressed···my compliments."

Her eyes had a twinkle and hinted at mischief, and then she blushed. "Can you say who's been doctoring Vic?"

He took a deep breath, weighing his response. "He's in good hands—same people as before."

"I know so little about what happened last weekend, not much more than what you told me in the car. Do you want to talk about it?"

He shook his head slowly. "I promised Vic, and I think I said too much already." He tried to avoid her scrutiny.

She moved to the chair between them and reached out to take his hand, the one holding the dinner knife. He set the utensil down.

"I know that story in the papers about what happened up on Broadway was about you. You must have been scared."

He turned away and stared out the window, but his eyes remained unfocused. They were glistening, and he was embarrassed. "I wasn't scared when it happened. I was mad—driven to do it, but then later, that's when I got scared···scared we'd get caught and scared about the terrible thing I'd done."

She wrapped her fingers in his and pressed his hand backward. She whispered close to his ear, "My poor, silly goose. You shot⋯you killed—"

"Don't say it."

"Okay, I won't, but that doesn't mean it didn't happen. You must feel awful."

"I feel like a werewolf, just after the full moon, and it's dangerous for you to be in the same room with me."

She stood up and held his head, pressing it to her chest, holding him tight. She ran her fingers through his hair and said, "You poor goose, you're not a monster."

Alan leaned his head back so she could see his face and said, "Alice, I've killed three men—in one week—and the worst part is I'm glad I did. I finally got what I had been praying two years to get, and now I'm happy I have something to feel bad about. Isn't that crazy?"

"Other than Benny, who got what he had coming, why kill the other two?"

"Because they were the ones who killed my dad. They were about to do the same to Vic. I even tried to kill another one. He was dead in my sights, but he got away."

He pressed his head back into her bosom and wrapped his arm around her waist.

"The police lieutenant?"

"Yes. Harry Frantz."

She stroked his head and kissed it. "You said they killed your father? When was this?"

"About two years ago."

"Oh⋯before I came here."

"Dad and Vic were on the milk run, same as Friday night. It was Benny who'd set them up. The cops went after Dad. This time, they were looking for Vic, because they thought he'd be alone. They didn't know I'd be riding shotgun."

249

She leaned down, and looked him squarely in the face, their noses almost touching. She spoke slowly, "Then you have nothing to be ashamed of, Alan Stewart. As I see it, three scoundrels got what they had coming, and it took a brave person to do it. Besides, you saved Vic."

He pushed his chair away from the table, making room, and she sat on his lap. "Later, I got to thinking about the other guys and if they had families···people who'd miss them like I miss my dad. Those men might not have been any worse than he was; who's to say? They were alive one moment and gone the next—all because of me. Thinking about it makes me feel rotten to the core."

He buried his head in her neck. "Do I scare you?"

"Not that much."

"I scare myself."

"But what about Frantz? Are you going after him?"

"I can't say I went after the other three. Maybe, deep down, I hoped to square it with them, but I don't remember taking this road. Now, my enemies are thrown in my path, like it's been a gift···or some Biblical temptation, and when it happened, I took care of business. I got to tell you, Alice, I feel bad it felt so good—killing them, and I'm trying to sort it all out.

"I'm afraid there'll be more retribution, maybe it'll be for me this time. I was taught it's God's business deciding who lives and who dies. I'm hoping I only did His bidding."

"As much as it bothers you, I think it's a good thing. That tells me you're not a monster."

She ran her fingers through his hair again, pushing it in and out of place, and she said, "What about Frantz? You never said..."

"I can't promise, but I'm not aiming to track him

down—kill him in cold blood, if that's what you're asking. But I don't know what'll happen if he comes after me and the opportunity stares me in the face, like with the others."

"From what you've been saying, he's not someone to mess with. I'm worried for you."

"I've already told you more than I should've. Harry doesn't know for sure who his shooter was. He saw a ghost come out of the shadows who looked like my dad."

She looked away, toward the ceiling, thought, and smiled when she got it. "Ohhh, like when I first met you, and Vic thought you—"

"A lot like that."

"Oh, that's wonderful. So, he···didn't really see···"

"No, he didn't."

She pushed away from him to arms' length and stared him in the eye. "But if he sees you around the union office—or out with Mr. B—he's sure to make the connection."

Alan nodded slowly. "I can't pretend he won't."

"So, what he told the papers about a robbery team from Canada is all a bunch of—"

"Goose droppings."

"I guess you'd know, Buster the Goose."

He leaned forward and kissed her again. Then she led him to the couch. He sat first, and she climbed in his lap. She said, "Promise me you won't deliberately let him find out it was you. A guy who thinks that well on his feet, coming up with a story like he did, he's someone to be reckoned with."

"He wasn't so scary when he was looking down the muzzle of the Thompson. It was just lucky for him the magazine went empty. Somebody who looked a lot like Vic knocked him down with a head butt, and when Harry got up, he couldn't get away fast enough. He's lucky the Canadian goose only creased his noggin."

She brushed his hair back and touched his face. "I think you were very brave, and I'm proud of you."

"That means a lot."

The slit in her skirt had ridden up, well over her knees. He slid his hand on her smooth thigh and pulled her close. She kissed his cheek. "So where'd this phantom learn to shoot like a gangster?"

"I can't be sure, but I'd say his dad taught him the basics. They might have practiced a lot···on Sundays, instead of going to church—like they should've."

His hand worked its way under a garter and started inching up her thigh to her bottom. It was further than he'd ever gone with her. She reached down and grabbed the probe, holding it in place. "Say, Buster, where do you think you're going with that hand?" She kissed his cheek.

"Hand? What hand?"

"The one getting ready to squeeze my bottom."

"Oh, that hand. It just seemed to wander off on its own. Should I retrieve it?"

"Does it like where it is?"

"Oh···very much."

"It's getting pretty fresh; does it know that?"

"I think so."

Does it like not having any of its fingers broken?"

"Yes, very much."

"Then it's got about one more minute before it gets in trouble, and it doesn't get to go any higher."

She kissed around his ears.

He held his hand in place, above her nylons on her bare leg, and he felt and squeezed the firm muscle beneath smooth skin.

She said, "Somehow I think you're cheating."

"But I'm not going any higher."

"You know, Silly Goose, I'm growing quite fond of you."

"I'm very glad. In fact, I can't think of a time when I've felt happier. I want you more than I've wanted anything in my life."

"I can tell. There's something hard pressing against me."

He chuckled, embarrassed. "I'm sorry, does it bother you?"

"I'll make an allowance, in your case, but that's as far as you go tonight."

She leaned in and placed another kiss on his lips. He responded by giving her all the passion he could, while still keeping it tender.

He didn't want to reach for his pocket watch, so he asked, "What time is it?"

"About 8:30. Do you have to get back?"

"I do, but I don't want to leave you. You make me crazy as it is, and after I leave here, I won't be able to get you out of my mind."

"I'm not sorry I make you feel that way. I'd be lying if I said otherwise."

She climbed off his lap and he stared at her legs while she adjusted her skirt, pulling the hem back down. They're spectacular.

She caught him ogling and said, "Dancer's legs. As a girl, I practiced Irish Reels by the hour. My mother taught me. It was a good way to pass time on the farm and great exercise."

As they passed by the dinner on the table, she said, "You didn't eat very much."

"We got distracted, but trust me, I loved it···every bite and every moment."

In her hall entryway, he put on his hat and coat, and she picked up the package. "Oh, was this for me? I love surprises."

253

"No!" he said, and he realized the word came out too loud. "I mean···this is for Vic. He asked me to pick it up for him···a surprise for a friend of his."

She felt the shape of the package, shook it, and said, "I wonder what it is? It feels hard, like a wooden frame. Can I peek?"

"That might cause a problem. Vic said something about it being union business, and you know how touchy they get about that. It's best we stay out of it. He told me it's fragile." She frowned, but only for a second. She handed the package back to him and opened the door.

While passing the mirror, he caught a glimpse of the lipstick traces marking his face. She said, "What would the neighbors say?" She grabbed his handkerchief, still moist with her tears, and dabbed at the dusty rose, wiping off some while blending more in, giving him rosy cheeks. She added a little spittle and rubbed more away. "There."

He took a few steps into the hallway, spun around, and stopped. "There's one more thing I got to get off my chest."

Her eyebrows dropped suddenly from raised to downfallen, her eyes showing concern.

He went back inside, closed the door again. "This doesn't change how I feel about you, because Vic was in on this, too, and I like the hell out of him."

She nodded along, her mind working.

He kept his voice low, even. "It's that whole thing with the voter fraud on election day."

Alice dropped her eyes further, looking at the floor. "Yes?"

"Not to worry, I'm over it, but I need to tell you that nothing like that can happen again. I might be young, naïve, and it may take me a little while to figure out the ways of the big city, but I won't be played for a sap by you or anybody else. I'm done with that."

She met his eyes. "It might've started out that way, but by the first glass of Champagne, I was having such a good time, I'd forgotten why—."

"It was the best day I'd had in two years, maybe longer. I just want to make sure we understand each other?"

"I think we do, Buster."

He opened the door, again, and stepped toward her, closing the distance between them. She met him half way. He held her close and kissed her firmly, but not as hard as before. She kissed him back, and he let his hand slide down to her rear, cupping one of her cheeks. She nuzzled his neck, then grabbed his hand and pressed it in place for a moment. Then she pulled it free. "Mr. Goose, I have neighbors who pay a lot of attention to what goes on around here. This is where I live. Don't give them anything to talk about."

"My apologies."

"I'm also worried about Meredith at the front desk. She's probably running a stop watch on you."

"Meredith? I think she likes me."

"She can like, but she better keep her paws off you."

He laughed.

"Come see me again, Silly Goose."

He waved and headed toward the stairs, while a door across the hall closed. He pivoted around and danced down the stairs. His feet picked up speed on every step, creating a sound like rolling thunder. As he rounded the last turn, he slowed and reminded himself to act mature, but Meredith was waiting, eyebrows raised.

"Sorry," he said. "My feet got away from me. I had to run to catch up."

Meredith tilted her head to the side, beamed a tolerant smile. "You didn't give her the present?"

"Oh···this···this is for someone else."

"You're seeing another friend?"

"Nothing like that. An old buddy asked me to pick this up—for him."

Stony face. "I see."

"Would you call me a cab, please? I'll be outside, getting some fresh air."

39

◇◇◇

The cabbie dropped Alan back in Chinatown near Seventh Avenue on South Jackson Street. Alan hadn't wandered more than half a block toward Vic's Ritz when he passed two garbage cans, set near the curb. He reversed direction, stopped next to one, and stared down at the wrapped package he'd been carrying. After a moment's pause, he furiously ripped away the paper, tearing it until he exposed the picture underneath. He studied Alice's face and back, through the protective glass. To the left of her shoulder, a stylish dedication covered a corner of the glossy: "George, you're the best. Always, Alice."

Veins near each of his temples throbbed, his eyes bulged, and his lips moved along with the words as he re-read the inscription. He exhaled through flared nostrils, clutched the frame by its side, and slammed it hard into the edge of the can, breaking glass and cracking the wood. He shook the rest of the glass into the can on top of the restaurant's discarded food. Then he delicately removed the photograph, lifting Alice free of the frame. While holding her in one hand, he pounded the frame with the other, until all the wooden pieces separated, leaving their thin brads exposed like sinew ripped from raw bone. He tossed the broken remnants on top of the refuse. He inspected the picture again, before tearing off the offending inscription from the upper corner. While holding the rest of the picture between his teeth, he tore the offensive writing until he could subdivide it no more. He sprinkled the tiny pieces on the rest of the rotting mass. Then he held what was left of the picture at arms' length, gripping the top middle with both thumbs, preparing to tear the remainder of the photo to shreds, but he stopped and slowly brought it back close to his nose. He could almost smell her presence. He inhaled deeply, confused about the achy joy she made him feel; it went deep to the pit of his stomach. After a moment, he lowered the picture, folded it carefully, and put it inside his coat pocket, near his chest.

Walking away, he took in a deep breath of Chinatown's heavily scented air and exhaled, more calm than he'd felt for a while. Across the street, a man sitting on a bench watched him curiously. It was the owner of the restaurant where he and Vic had eaten the week before. The older man sat comfortably on the rigid bench, stoic-faced, as if he neither understood what Alan was up to nor cared. Alan stopped, returned, and placed the lid back on the can, covering the mess. The observer's face creased a smile. Alan touched the brim of his hat, a mock salute, and walked away.

Alan's stomach growled fiercely as he neared the entrance to the brothel. He hadn't eaten much at Alice's, and the hunger was catching up to him. He would ask Little Papa to fix him a meal. That, a hot bath, and a bottle of plum wine would settle him down. Wait··· hot bath means···Poppy. Damn! I've got to talk to Vic.

Alan checked up and down King Street before he knocked on the old wooden door. When a woman's voice answered, he gave her Vic's name. Big Mama shooed him inside and closed the door quickly. At the top of the landing, a couple of the house girls gathered to see who their guest was. Poppy came down the steps to meet him, and Big Mama stepped past her to climb the stairs. Poppy wrapped her arms around Alan and gave him a tight hug, as if she hadn't seen him in a month. He returned the embrace and his hands slid familiarly over the back of her kimono, which felt as smooth as a second layer of skin, revealing there were no undergarments to cover her nakedness. She kissed him on his cheek and near his ear. Then she started sniffing, smelling his scent. She said, "Where been?"

"I ran an errand for Vic."

"You smell⋯pretty," she said, not sure of the words, knitted eyebrows.

"Yes, I stopped by my mother's house, and my aunt gave me a big hug."

"Ant? I don't understand?"

"She's a relative⋯like Big Mama's⋯sister."

Poppy nodded and said, "Like ai yi. I see." A moment

later, she appeared puzzled again, but then she dismissed whatever was bothering her. She bounced up the stairs, leading the way. Her kimono sashayed across her bare legs, teasing him. He thought for half-a-second about being polite and not ogling her assets, but her legs and rump were too close to his face for that to happen. She glanced behind and giggled. When she got to the top of the stairs, she opened her kimono, giving him a full frontal view, tempting him with her delicate beauty.

His eyes widened, dreamy. She said, "You like?"

She came toward him and gave him another hug. "We take bath?"

He clasped her by the shoulders to keep her at a distance. "In a little while. I need to see Vic, get some food." He used his hands to mimic eating with chopsticks.

"You eat?"

"Please, and see Vic."

She left him standing in the hallway, while she went to find Little Papa, but he hurried the opposite direction to find his confidant. Vic's door was ajar, but Alan knocked anyway, a brothel courtesy. Inside, Lilly was standing behind Vic, massaging his neck.

Vic feigned checking his watch. "Back so soon?"

"I could've stayed away longer?"

"Sure. You seen how tough it is to get in here. The house takes care of me. They'd have me whisked off into the catacombs before anyone would make it up the stairs."

Alan plopped in a chair, sighed, and stared unfocused at a Chinese watercolor on the wall.

Vic stopped Lilly's hands and motioned his head toward the door. She understood his signal and left.

Vic leaned forward and kept his voice low. "How'd it go?"

"Can we talk over dinner?"

"Of course. That's what I love about this place; if you're hungry, they feed you. They don't worry about the time."

Vic slipped a shirt on to cover his bandage, and they walked into the hallway. Passing by another room, the sounds of loud passion emanated through the thin walls. Alan shot Vic a puzzled look and shrugged his shoulders.

"You didn't think we're their only customers? It's Friday night, payday for a lotta people. This is their prime time."

"What about Poppy and Lilly?

"Lilly's out of the rotation while I'm here, and Poppy can be, if you want."

"Who's in there?" he asked, indicating the room the noise was coming from with a tilt of his head.

"I don't keep track. It's none of my business. Could be Rose, but it might be Poppy, or one of the others."

"That might make things easier, and that's what I wanted to talk about."

In the kitchen, Little Papa was soon hard at work, concocting magic in the woks. Exotic smells filled the room. Vic asked for a bottle of wine and sat back in his padded whicker chair. "You look chipper. Did anything I say help?"

"More so on the ride back, when I had time to think. I went there planning to show her the picture, but when she sat next to me on the couch, all I could think about was wanting to see her every night in that exact same spot."

"Whoa. Did you tell her that?"

"Not in so many words. First, I brought up Vancouver, and she knew where I was going. She started crying, real tears, not the fake stuff girls do when they're

261

trying to get their brother in trouble, but the open-the-floodgate, heaving-shoulders kind. She looked so hurt. I felt so mean. My guts were ripped out. If I'd had your tire iron, I would've broken both my kneecaps and gone upside my head."

Vic chuckled. "So, what'd you say to her?"

"I don't remember it all, but I dumped a bunch of stuff: how I think about her all the time, how I go nuts thinking of guys who might've—"

"How'd she take it?"

"She calmed down after a bit, but I felt like a total bastard. We ended up on the couch, me holding her, kissing her···you know."

"Nice, wasn't it?"

"After we got past the tears, I let my hand do a little exploring, but she stopped me."

"I figured she would. Fan dancing is one thing, turning tricks with the customers is another, and she didn't. Lot of guys wished she would've, but wishing don't make it so."

"Well, I'll never find out that part of her past."

"Why's that?"

"Because I told her I'd never bring it up again."

"Damn, you're smart. Now just make sure you do that. You don't want to get yourself half-in-the-bag some night, go over there, and throw old business in her face. You made a promise, stick to it. Promises don't wear down like the heels of old shoes, giving an excuse to not keep 'em anymore. Men keep their word."

Their cook interrupted, bringing over plates of food, and the two started dishing out servings.

Vic said, "I'm serious about that. You're only as good as your word. If you break your promise—even if it ain't put into some kind of contract —you'll unravel everything you got, and I can promise you what you don't know about her past ain't worth the worry."

"How much do you know?"

"Oh, no. Same rules apply to me, Champ. I've made promises I can't renege on."

"Can't do what?"

"Renege. It's from a card game. Means you can't go back on your bid and play a card out of turn···like a trump card when you shouldn't, and it applies to men of their word."

"We didn't play cards at our house. If Mom had her way, there wouldn't have been any booze, either."

"Too bad. It comes from Pinochle. Great game. I should teach it to you and the girls. Nice way to pass the time."

Alan ate like he'd been starved all week.

"You mentioned the picture," said Vic. "Is that the one from the Mighty B? Did you show it to her?"

"I changed my mind, but it didn't survive an accident on the way back."

Vic cackled, teasing. "I get the picture."

"No, you don't, I do."

They both laughed and enjoyed the meal, lost in their own thoughts. Alan broke the reverie. "What am I going to do about Poppy?"

"You've made up your mind; it's Alice you want then?"

"Like no other."

"How deep is it with you and Poppy? You been whispering mush in her ear along with everything else?"

"The sex has been great. I've got a powerful craving for it, and it's as intimate as you get with a person, which means—I can't do it here anymore."

"Before you swear it off, let me ask you another thing. How about the kissing? You and Poppy been doing that, too?"

263

"Sure, but not like with Alice; our tongues were dancing around each other's mouths—"

"So, with Alice you got great smooching but no sex; with Poppy you've got great sex, but the smooching ain't all you've been hoping for?"

"That's about it."

"I think you've got it figured out then. You don't need my help. But it's sort of funny when you think about it—the passion's in the kissing, not in the sex." Vic smiled like a Cheshire cat and nodded. Vic thought for a moment. "Ever notice how it always gets complicated with booze, broads, and dough? Those three things get more guys in trouble."

Vic picked up the bottle to pour more wine, but it was near empty. He shook out the last few drops into Alan's glass and held up the empty bottle, while speaking Chinese to Papa San. The little chef set down his wok, went to the hallway, and barked out a request. A few moments later, an attractive Chinese girl Alan hadn't seen before entered the room wearing a bright, new silk kimono, and carrying a tray with two more bottles of plum wine. She was as pretty as Poppy and maybe a little younger. She opened a new bottle and refilled each of their glasses. They both scrutinized her every move. When finished, she bent low and stepped back.

Vic said, "Thank you, Iris." Vic winked and shook his head at Alan, grinning. Alan couldn't hold his gaze. He finally closed his eyes and dropped his head. Without raising it again, he said, "This isn't going to be easy."

"Nothing worth doing comes easy. Let's go back to my room. We're going to send out for a pack of pinochle cards."

264

Monday morning Alan's mouth felt cottony and slightly bitter, but he was in no hurry to get out of bed to slake his thirst. All that changed moments later, when he heard angry shouting on the street below, where heated Asian dialects mixed with English. He arose, rolled up the shade, and drew back the curtain. A group of older men and women, some holding newspapers, yelled at young Asian men in another group, farther up the street. The words "murder" and "rape" were in English and resonated above all others, along with "Nanking," a scourge that happened a few years before.

Rose rapped on the door, came in quickly, bringing Iris and Poppy with her. They joined Alan at the window. Rose scowled and said, "Elders shout about Japanese. They invade Hainan and Indochina, and the Japanese boy say something back. I don't speak Japan—"

"East Asia for Japan!" shouted the tormentor in English.

The Japanese youth had danced to within ten feet of the Chinese, spun around, turning his back on them, playing to his friends. Like an animated choir director, he led their chant, "East Asia for Japan!"

The familiar face of the restaurant owner was

prominent among the Chinese who gathered below. He was three times the age of the Japanese boys. He broke away from his group, kicking at his tormenter. It was a martial arts move, weakened by age, but strong enough to cause the young man to falter and stumble forward. Friends reached out for the old man and tried to tug him back into their fold, but the young man sprang to his feet and punched the elder solidly in the face, knocking him to the ground. The young man's friends stepped forward.

The girls next to Alan said something fast and angrily in their language, directing it through the glass. Alan thought, Son of a bitch is a bully, and although Alan was a couple flights above the street, he'd clenched his own fists, ready to step in and help.

The young man on the street menaced with his fists raised, moving toward the elder, who was bleeding from the mouth, and the youth yelled, daring the old man to get up off his back. Then one of the other Chinese men pushed the young man backwards and the youth responded, swinging at him but missing. Meanwhile, the fallen man rolled over, from his back to his knees, while he dabbed a hanky to his mouth. As the youth spun back to face him, scowling, the elder extended his other arm with something black at the end of it.

BANG! A gun roared and nearby pigeons took to flight.

The youth buckled at the knees and clutched his stomach, stumbling backward, and then falling to the pavement. His friends froze, too stunned to move. Seconds passed as they stared at the shooter, who was now standing on both feet, gun at his side. He brought it up again, and they turned on their heels to run.

BANG! The gun barked again.

His shot hit another of them in the hip, before the

266

youth covered six feet. The wounded man hopped awkwardly for another dozen feet before he lost his balance and fell to the pavement, clutching his lower side.

As the elderly man prepared to shoot again, a man next to him clasped his arm and forced it down.

BANG! The third shot slammed into the street and skipped off the pavement into the unknown.

Rose and Iris grabbed onto Alan's arms and squeezed tight, burying their heads against his chest.

The Japanese boys scrambled away frantically, disappearing around the corner, and the Chinese quickly closed ranks. The older man's friend grabbed the shooter, gave him rapid-fire directions, and pulled him along as they ran together to the end of the block, to where they tapped on another non-descript door. In a moment, the door opened, and the men disappeared.

From the group gathered below, an older woman emerged and approached the man lying on the street, clutching his middle, trying to stem the flow of blood and somehow push it all back inside. Despite his efforts, the blood continued to pump and flow. She squawked at him, shaking the newspaper. Then she kicked him hard where his rear end met his upper leg, as if trying to dislodge his scrotum, like kicking a slug off a garden stone. One of the other women tried to pull her away, but she jerked free, stomped her feet, and spat on the young man, cursing.

Twenty feet away the other injured man was on his side, trying to drag himself away from the melee. In the distance, a siren wailed. A moment later, a beat cop rounded the corner on a full run. When he spotted the two bodies sprawled in the street, he slowed his pace and studied the crowd, as if memorizing who was there.

267

He went past the one crawling and said something to the group, looking back and forth between them and the two wounded youth. The one boy stopped crawling and pointed to the Chinese, with an accusing finger. The beat officer walked toward the first youth, who a moment before taunted with loud bravado, but now was writhing in a pool of his own blood that continued to spread in silence. He screamed in English, "I don't want to die!"

The beat cop squatted, examined the wound. He said something to the boy, who softened his wailing and began to cry. The officer stood up and approached the crowd, which now contained newer faces. When the police officer got close to the still-agitated woman, she shook her head defiantly and crossed her arms, refusing to answer whatever question he posed and started to walk away. The officer turned to someone else in the group, and then the woman who did the kicking came back, and she shook the newspaper at the police officer. She said something and pointed at the fallen boy, cursing him. She menacingly approached him again, but the officer held her back, forceful but comforting. Then he addressed the crowd. Several heads shook, while others turned away. Alan thought, Nobody saw nothing, and they're sticking to it.

Vic knocked gently and entered Alan's room, joining the others. "Quite a show!"

"Did you see your old friend drill those guys?"

"If you ask me, they had it coming. They was rubbing it in their face about what's going on in the Pacific. Lilly's concerned the Japs have taken her island, near Hainan. Course it's small enough it shouldn't have any real value to Japan, but after the Rape of Nanking, the girls are scared for their families."

Another beat officer arrived, followed by a squad

car with the wailing siren. It was fifteen minutes before the ambulance arrived, and by then the once loud youth lay stone silent. A police officer took a sheet from the ambulance crew and placed it over the body, pulling it up to cover the boy's face. The second youth, lying on his side, let out a harsh scream.

"What will happen to the shooter?" asked Alan.

"Odds are his tong's running him through the catacombs. He'll soon be on his way to Frisco···or north to Vancouver. They've also got Chinatowns."

Down on the street, the officers led two Japanese boys back to the scene. The boys crossed their arms and hugged their chests, nodding to some questions, shaking their heads at others. As the officers took notes, a dark sedan stopped in the middle of the street, north of the crime scene. Two men got out, and then one held the door for a third. Out stepped a dapper male, with a haughty manner about him.

Vic said, "Speak of the devil."

Alan said, "What's he doing up so early?"

"Hungry Harry's a glory hound, so he may have jumped the call."

The lieutenant paused for a moment and adjusted his hat, using a storefront window as a mirror.

Vic said, "Looks like he got himself a new Stetson."

"I wonder how long that one will last."

Vic chuckled and reached up and clasped the back of Alan's neck, giving him a squeeze, a playful shake.

Lt. Frantz strode over to the body on the street. He motioned toward an officer, who peeled back the sheet for him. Other officers approached the lieutenant, deferential, providing him with details. Frantz said little. The officer gestured at the crowd, shrugged, and lifted his hands, palms upward.

269

Then Frantz, who seemed unhappy with the officer's response, raised and swept his arms about him, pointing toward the surroundings, like an opera tenor acknowledging his audience. The officer followed the lieutenant's motions and gestures toward the buildings and the people at their windows. Harry scanned the windows also, until he stopped short at Vic and Alan's room.

Vic snatched hold of Alan and jerked him back. "Ach heilige scheibe!!"

"What?" asked Alan.

"Never mind. He saw us!"

Vic called for Lilly, and she came running from her room. He told her to go to the window and tell them what the fancy man in the beige fedora was doing.

She said, "He pointing to this building, telling policemen something. He look mad. One is staring up here, and now he come this way. He try to find door."

Vic said, "Ach scheibe! Grab all your stuff, Champ. Time to beat a hasty retreat."

Alan slipped on his pants and hat, and Vic ran from the room and called out a warning to Big Mama. The house sprang into action.

Inside the brothel, everyone dashed about frantically, ignoring the angry voices and pounding on the door below. Big Mama shouted to the men from the top of the steps that she'd be down in a moment. She faced her staff and gave a slow farewell bow. They stood in a line opposite her, gathered around Little Papa, and they returned her bow with equal grace. Papa reached for the handle next to him, and opened the door to the Smuggler's passage. He shooed the girls through, while holding the door for them. Vic and Alan followed the others, and once through the door, they raced down the parallel hallway, around a corner, and into another bedroom, not down the stairs to the basement, or outside, as Alan had guessed they might.

Inside the room was a stepladder, lying on the floor. Lilly and one of the other girls set it under a closed hatch in the ceiling. Lilly got Alan's attention and pointed to the hatch, making shoving motions. He got the message and led the way up the steps, pushing open the latch, raising himself into a seldom-used attic. The girls followed: Poppy, Iris, Rose, and two others, whose names Alan didn't know. Alan squatted and grabbed arms, lifting the girls up one by one, but

271

Lilly stayed behind steadying the ladder, urging Vic to go ahead.

Vic had trouble clearing the top step, because he favored his injured shoulder, instinctively protecting it. Alan leaned down below the hole, grasped Vic's good arm firmly, and tugged hard, helping hoist his large friend into the attic. Then Alan reached back for Lilly, but she had already taken down the ladder and was carrying it away. Vic called after her, but it was no use.

Vic's eyes were wild and anxious. "Why didn't she climb up? We could have pulled the ladder in after us."

Alan shrugged, and as he closed the latch, the attic darkened. The only source of light came from the large, round windows at the peaks of the four gables on the four distant ends of the building. The girls began whispering, but Rose made a hushing sound, scolding. She pointed at the men's feet and shook her head. They slipped off their shoes, tied the laces together, and carried them. Then she went through the hushing motions again, and motioned for the girls to stay put, while nodding for the men to follow her, tiptoeing across the dusty attic floor. Alan calculated they were heading back over the ceiling of the brothel. Soon, deep voices boomed below, accompanied by the sound of heavy feet running up the wooden steps. A voice demanded, "What took you so long?"

Rose stood in front of Vic and Alan. She tapped her lips with her index finger, while softly blowing a "shush" at him. Then she quickly pointed at a section of Persian carpet on the floor between stacks of boxes, which was incongruous with everything around it. She knelt and lifted up the carpet's edge, while again cautioning them not to make a sound. They peered through a vent over the top of the hallway, which ran through the brothel. Below, a uniformed police officer held Big Mama by the arm, while more feet pounded up the stairs, and then another officer and a sergeant with stripes on his upper arms entered the floor. They were followed in a moment by their scowling leader, Lieutenant Harold Frantz.

As Frantz stepped into the hallway, he took off his hat, withdrew a bright silk handkerchief from his coat pocket, and dabbed his brow and the top of his head. From their vantage point, Vic and Alan could see that Frantz had a wound that had scabbed over. Instead of the part in his hair running north and south, as it should, it crossed diagonally. The area immediate to either side of the new crease had been shaved to treat the bullet's wide trail. Vic patted Alan on the back and grinned predatorily, showing his teeth. After Frantz finished dabbing the sweat, he replaced his hat and took off his gloves.

The sergeant gave instructions to the two officers, who began checking the rooms. In a moment they came back, one of them with Lilly in tow, the other had Papa.

Frantz asked his prisoner, "Where are the others?"

Papa shrugged but said nothing. Frantz inclined his head toward the officer holding Papa's arm. The officer quickly drew his nightstick and dug it hard into the little man's ribs, causing him to bend over in pain. Big Mama shrieked, and the officer said, "The lieutenant asked you a question, Chink."

Big Mama pleaded for understanding. "He not speak English."

The officer roughly shoved Papa to the floor and turned to Mama, and Frantz said, "Same rules apply to you. Where are the others?"

She said, "Nobody here."

Frantz snapped the gloves against his leg and said, through clinched teeth, "I see that. What I want to know is where they went. Where are the people I saw up here?"

She said, "Nobody here. Just us."

Frantz said, "Don't lie to me. I saw at least three Chinese girls in one window and two white men in the other. Right over there," pointing to the room Alan and Vic had vacated. "Where'd they go?"

Mama shook her head. "You make mistake. No other people here."

Frantz struck quickly. SMACK. He hit Big Mama hard in the face, backhanding her with his gloves. He'd cracked her lower lip, and she shrieked again.

The men in the attic above clenched their fists and glared at the enemy below.

Frantz shoved her backwards and she fell to the floor next to Papa. He said to the sergeant, "Search all the rooms. Check the other side of the hallway, too, and be careful. I'm sure it's the ones who shot Hoff and Schneider. They must've hid here instead of going to Canada. Surround the building and get more officers. These killers are armed and dangerous."

The sergeant gave instructions to an officer, who went back down the stairs. Then he and the remaining officer started checking rooms, leaving Frantz alone with the prisoners.

The lieutenant turned to Lilly. "You speak English?"

"Some."

"Where's Vic?" he asked in a hushed voice.

Lilly seemed puzzled. "Bric?"

"Vic! You slant-eyed whore," he said, raising his voice again. "Don't play the dumb ass with me. He's a big, ugly, stupid ox. A blind man could spot him a mile away. I saw Vic and another man in that window," he said as he pointed to the room where Alan had slept.

She said, "I don't know a Vric."

Frantz let out a breath, looked at Big Mama, then Little Papa. Then he stabbed out an arm and grabbed Lilly by the throat, pinning her against the wall. "The name is Vic, you dumb slut. I saw him in that room, and I want to know where he's at···right goddamn now!"

She squirmed in his grasp and shook her head.

Frantz placed the hand holding the gloves over her mouth, keeping her pinned to the wall as he pushed a knee against her legs, and pulled open her robe with his free hand, exposing her naked body. He continued to hold her trapped against the wall, while he checked to make sure the other police were not around, and then he smirked, stared at her body, and ran his hand over her smooth skin, caressing a nipple, before pinching it. She squirmed in pain. Big Mama said something in Chinese, and Frantz met her gaze with a sneer.

Then Frantz turned his attention back to Lilly, and he forced his hand down between her legs, rubbing her pubic region hard. She squirmed, crossing her legs, trying to keep his fingers out.

Vic, who was on his knees peeking through the vent, sat back and pulled his .45 from his coat. He rolled his large head on his neck, reached the gun out to arm's length, and took aim on Frantz's Stetson. Alan also grabbed his rod, thinking back-up shot, and he scanned the floor for other targets. From below, Big Mama caught Alan's eye and shook her head, closing hers as she did. Alan stretched out his hand and waved it in front of Vic's face, getting his attention. Vic indexed his trigger finger, exhaled noisily, and scowled at Alan. Alan shook his head and pointed down toward

275

Big Mama, who glanced up again and shook her head, as before.

Vic brought his gun to his side, squeezing the grip tightly, while he glared at Frantz, his eyes wild with rage. Through flared nostrils he exhaled air so hot it nearly singed the hair on his knuckles.

Out of view, the sergeant's voice boomed. "Why's this door locked?"

Big Mama didn't respond.

"I said, 'Why's this door locked?' If you got a key, you better get it over here goddamn quick, or it's going down."

Big Mama got to her knees with slow, deliberate movements and stood up, shaky, tottering. She grabbed a wall for support and then disappeared from view. She said, "I never see it open. I not sure I have key. Let me check."

The sergeant pounded fiercely on the door and said, "Open up in there!" Frantz stopped his exploration of Lilly's body.

"Not fast enough, lady," said the sergeant, and then CRACK. The door shattered and the frame splintered. A second kick sent the door flying and banging off the wall. The sergeant's size-13 boots had dismantled the gate to the parallel hallway. "Hey! There ain't no room here. It's a smuggler's passage."

From under Frantz's glove, Lilly cried in pain. Frantz pushed her face away, cocked his arm, and slapped her hard. She shrieked. He pressed up against her again and dropped his hand to her bare chest, holding it there a moment and squeezing her breasts, before shoving her away. Her robe flew open, exposing her completely, as she fell backwards, landing on top of Little Papa. Frantz barked at the two of them. "We're not through yet. Come tomorrow, if you're still here,

I'm going to have Immigration send all your asses back to whatever slant-eyed country you came from."

He glared at them both, before going toward the passageway.

Vic brought his gun up to eye-level again and tried to track Frantz, but he had stepped out of view. Vic lowered his piece and rested it on his leg. Again he exhaled noisily.

Below them came the sounds of more voices in the hallway, and then there was the thunder of more footsteps and shouting on the stairway leading up to the brothel from the street. "We've got the outside covered, Lieutenant."

Frantz and the sergeant came back into view and approached Lilly and Little Papa. Lilly had covered herself, and Papa had an arm wrapped around her, trying to shield her with his body.

Frantz spoke to the sergeant. "The Chinks built false passages— mazes—so they could smuggle other slants into the country. I thought they'd all disappeared, but you can bet this passage leads to the basement and a tunnel under the street, which will take you to the catacombs. Odds are they're probably already in there and going out the back door of some gambling house or opium den."

The sergeant said, "So, what do you want us to do, Harry?"

"Take a couple of men and search this place, just in case, because it's still possible they never got out. We can't afford not to check···top to bottom."

While the noise of running feet and banging doors continued below them, Vic lowered the carpet back over the air vent and put a finger in front of his lips. He motioned to Alan and Rose, and they tiptoed over to where the other girls were gathered. He whispered, "We'll have to find somewhere to hide, just in case they figure out how to get up here."

Vic stood tall and carefully scanned the large attic, full of stored and forgotten items from before the turn of the century. "Is there another way down?"

Rose said, "I know of two ways. There's one like this at other end, and then there's big one at the front. This is place where they bring things up to keep long time."

Vic said, "It's too late to use the far one now, 'cause the cops got the building covered, but we might be able to—"

"Go through the other hatch after they've searched this end of the building," added Alan.

Vic nodded, and the women looked hopeful.

Vic said, "Problem is how will we know when they're done? We could end up dropping down right in their path. So we better find a place to hide, because they're gonna find that stairway and come up here."

Rose translated for the women, while Vic and Alan started checking for suitable places to hide.

Alan sat back on his heels and glanced up to the rafters. His eyes fixed on something big and bright. He tapped Vic's good shoulder and pointed. "There's a dragon that dancers carry in parades. We could take it down and—"

"What? Scare the crap out of them? They'd shoot us."

"I don't think so. We could string it out over the floor and hide under it···in plain sight."

Vic closed his eyes for a moment and puffed out his cheeks, as if he were blowing taps on a bugle. "We could all get under there, but nobody moves a muscle."

"I figure if they find one of us, they'll find us all. We may as well stick together," said Alan.

"Let's do it."

Vic explained the plan to Rose, and Alan approached the dragon, studying it, and figuring how to get it down from the rafters. Vic soon joined him, and Alan said, "It's tied in five places with silk strings. The knots aren't difficult, they're just out of reach."

Vic called Rose and Poppy over. He pointed at the knots and said, "You'll need to untie them, Rose. I'll lift you up, while Alan lifts Poppy."

Embarrassed, Rose started to giggle.

Vic prodded her. "Now, we haven't got much time, and we can't make no noise."

Rose inched closer to Vic, and he squatted down and wrapped his arm around her just above the knees, sat her back on his good shoulder, and stood up. He raised her more than high enough to reach the knot, and she went to work immediately. Poppy watched, giggled, and moved hesitantly toward Alan. He grabbed and lifted her in the same manner in which Vic held Rose. The two teams each worked separate knots. The other women came over and took hold of the red and gold dragon as it was handed down, leaving the silk strings dangling, dancing in a cross current of air.

Alan set Poppy down, just as the sound of voices intruded at the far end of the attic. A second later, a flashlight beam began to dash back and forth across the distant rafters. Someone was climbing the far stairs.

279

Vic lifted the head of the dragon over his head, and he started squatting, lowering himself and the dragon to the floor. Alan was close to the dragon's tail, with Iris in front of him, Poppy behind. They moved quickly to get their part of the dragon's body in place and quietly sat down on the floor, hunched forward in silence.

A distant voice loudly proclaimed, "Okay, nobody's here."

"Not funny, Raymond," said an older voice. "Sarge said that we're to check the whole building, and that's what we're doing. No shortcuts. These guys peppered Hoff and Schneider."

The voices went quiet for a few moments, but their feet continued to work their way ever closer. Footfalls moved carelessly across the wooden floor as the beat cops poked about. Their presence grew more lethal, as the searchers moved closer to the hiders.

The younger voice was louder, nearer. "Do you believe his version?"

"Hahh."

"'Hahh?' Is that a laugh or···"

"'Hahh' means it's none of my business···and it means it should be none of yours neither···you know what's good for you."

The voices were now very close, maybe twenty feet away, and Iris squeezed Alan's scrunched-up legs, drawing them to her sides. Poppy wrapped her legs tightly against his arms, while she hugged him fiercely around the waist. Her grip was of terror, not lust.

The shoes plopped heavily as they drew near, sending a vibration through the floorboards they were sitting on. The younger voice, very close by, said, "I didn't say it was my business, but his rounding up all the bulls to chase his phantoms is treading on ours. Has he ever done anything for you? He hasn't for me."

Alan and Vic peeked out through slits in the fabric. The flashlights crisscrossed the floor in front of them, one beam cutting within two feet of the dragon. Any second, they would know if their plan worked.

"Can't say he has for me either—"

"Agghh!" screamed the younger officer, his flashlight now darting everywhere and nowhere.

The senior officer trained his light on his partner.

"Get them off me!" yelled the junior, as his feet stomped about madly. "Spiders!"

The veteran moved up close. "Knock if off! These ain't spiders. They're just some kind of braided string."

Stunned silence, and then the rookie said, "Damn! I hate spiders, and this goddamn string feels like a goddamn spider web."

His partner laughed, and then the young officer lowered his flashlight beam and it crossed the face of the red dragon.

"Agghh! What the hell···" The young officer yelled again and drew his revolver.

Inside the dragon, Rose flinched and moved her leg. Vic clutched it and pinned it firmly against his side.

The veteran jumped and spun around to see what was behind him, reaching for his gun as he trained his flashlight on the dragon, studying it carefully, from head to tail, "Aaaahhh···you numbskull. It's just one of those papier-mâché-silk dragons."

"Did that thing just move?"

"No."

"You sure?"

"Nothing here's moving but your imagination and my bowels. Now put your smoke pole away before you shoot yourself in the foot."

The rookie heaved a sigh, slouched, and dropped his

arms to his side. "This place gives me the creeps. I'm done."

"You give me the creeps. Now be a nice boy and put your toy back where it belongs."

The officer holstered his revolver and directed his attention to the offending string, slapping it with his billy club, knocking it into the rafters. Their footfalls began to move away and the hiders began to breathe again, as the voices faded. The veteran said, "Park your fanny for a few minutes. We'll give it some time and have the sarge think we're up here tearing the place apart. It's either that, or we go back down and he assigns us a new spot, like the catacombs—with the sewer rats and rotting timbers. There's places in there you could get lost. We'd never see your ass again."

"Rats? I hate them worse than goddamn spiders. They carry diseases."

"Then sit your butt down and take a load off."

As the fear of discovery lessened, the hiders relaxed their muscles and their grips on one another. Poppy twisted her head to the side and pressed it against Alan's back. She squeezed him tight around his middle, and then she unbuttoned his shirt and rubbed his chest with her hands, delicately playing with his hair. He got the message but also felt a pang of guilt, because his mind had drifted away to thoughts of Alice. Now, here he was with Poppy, her comforting him again, wanting him, despite his unexplained aloofness. She didn't seem to understand his new obsession to learn Pinochle, and he didn't know how to tell her their relationship couldn't be more than what they already had. As her hand started sliding down his stomach, he grabbed it just above his pubic region, held it, and whispered, "No."

The huddled, little group listened in silence to the

distant voices, not always able to tell what was said, until the rookie asked about the morning's shooting. The other one said, "It's got something to do with what's going on with the Japs in China. You can bet on that. The kids must have pissed-off the old folks down here. Got themselves shot, probably by someone who takes care of us, and we'd just as soon not put in the pokey."

"So, we don't care one way or the other?"

"Not particularly. I'm not going to stomp around and try to figure it out. Better to let sleeping dogs lie—least as far as I'm concerned."

After a few more minutes of ruminating, the beatmen got to their feet.

"All right, I officially report the attic's been tossed. Let's go," said the senior partner.

At the top of the steps, the junior one turned and called out, "Alle, alle, oxen free."

"Grow up, would ya?" said the man of experience. "Sarge might hear you. You trying to get us in trouble?"

The rookie laughed as he thumped down the steps, making twice the noise of the larger veteran.

Later that day, Vera showed Vic and his protégé into Mr. B's office. The Walrus stepped from behind his desk. He took hold of Vic's right hand and shook it, two-handed grip, one of appreciation and encouragement. "Vic, you old dog, you've had me worried. First, you get your bell rung by Harry's crew and now this···what···a gunshot wound to your shoulder?"

Brinkman still held onto his trusted aide but leaned back to arm's length to better size him up.

"Yeah, Boss, but it ain't nothing serious. Benny was nice enough to throw hisself in the way of the bullet, slowed it down for me."

The Walrus raised his eyebrows, patted Vic's good shoulder, let go of his hand, and then did the same with Alan. "It's good to see you can be counted on, just like your daddy. You think good on your feet, son."

Since Alan had been thanked earlier in the week, he figured this time around must be for Vic's benefit.

"Vic, I'd like to get your take on what happened last weekend."

Vic was more direct in his approach than Alan and less concerned about the legal issues as he told about the Kasbah, Nick the Greek, and Benny's running off.

Vic said, "About then, that snake-in-the-grass tried to stick a knife in my neck, but the Champ warned me and splattered Benny's brains over my suit. Only trouble was the bullet that passed through Benny's noggin smacked me in the shoulder, just above where that prick stuck his knife."

The Walrus, who had sat back in his chair, steepled his hands and closed his eyes as Vic narrated his story, not interrupting. When Vic finished, he opened his eyes, and said, "Ungrateful bastard."

"A godless traitor is what he was. Now he's getting his chance to explain the kiddy porn and what a worm he is to his Maker," said Vic.

Brinkman said, "I'm not in a hurry to check out of this life, but it'd be worth standing behind Benny when St. Peter gives him the what for, snatching him up by his pants and stuffing him in the coal chute that feeds Hades' fires."

Vic laughed, and Alan joined him.

The Walrus said, "So···here we go with Lieutenant Frantz sticking his nose in again, blackmailing one of my men, turning him into a traitor, so he can bring down my organization that serves hardworking, red-blooded Americans. It's like he's got a hard-on and wants to screw this union with it. That's the crying shame of this."

"There's more, Mr. B."

"Go ahead."

"Early this morning, there was a ruckus out in front of Big Mama's. A bunch of Jap kids was gloating over what Japan's doing to China, and two of 'em got themselves shot. Looks like one died, but that's not my point. Along with the police comes Hungry Harry. None of the locals are cooperating, so Frantz tells the coppers to check the hotels nearby. Somehow he learns we was at Mama's, and he gets rough with the owners, slapping them around and such. He's threatening to sic Immigration on 'em, send 'em back to China, which is a goddamn war zone."

Vic was sitting forward in his chair, and now was holding his head in his hands, staring unfixed at the floor.

"You say Frantz knew you were there?"

"Yes, sir. Benny pointed him in the general direction, and Frantz did the rest. He wasn't shy about telling Mama he wanted a piece of my hide. He also told the beat cops who was looking for us that we was the shooters from Canada. The good news is he still ain't got a clue about the Champ, here, but that could soon disappear the next time he sees him with me."

Brinkman's glance acknowledged Alan, then he returned to Vic. "I think I got the picture. It's time for me to get on the horn with the chief of detectives, rein in our hungry lieutenant. Mike Ketchum's a no nonsense guy, and he just might be interested in the return of Harry's lost peashooter."

Brinkman rang the front desk. "Vera, get Deputy Chief Ketchum on the line. Tell Mike he and I need to talk, no spectators. Dinner's on me at the Rainier Club, and don't take 'no' for an answer."

Alan stopped the car in front of the stately, brick structure with a pitched roof. Unlike commoners who walked past the front, the ivy was permitted to encroach on the lead-paned windows that featured fancy glass cuts, showcasing the massive crystal chandeliers, which added to the exclusive club's ambience. Alan stepped to the passenger side, adjusted his brand new gray fedora, and dusted lint from his new coat. The new ensemble was Brinkman's idea. He told Alan he didn't want to chance Frantz recognizing him and linking him to Vic's rescue. Alan opened the door and extended his arm, giving the Walrus a courtesy tug, helping him to the sidewalk. Vic leaned forward to peek out briefly, but then he sat back next to a curtained window.

The Walrus stood a moment, gathering his bearings and surveying his environment. Alan soon figured that this was another performance, a chance for the Walrus to pose and remind people of his influence. His gestures were slow and eloquent, and his voice boomed louder than was necessary as he waved hellos. Then he shifted gears, lowering his voice, as he gave Alan instructions. "The hardest part, son, will be getting you through the door. Otto has standing orders not to let chauffeurs,

287

personal detectives, coloreds, or unescorted women through the front. So, once I've been greeted, park the car and fetch my billfold from Vic. I want you to go through the delivery entrance. Tell them you need to give this to me···personally. Once inside, check with the maitre d', name's Jerry. He's an arrogant fop who lives for tips. He'll bring you a sandwich and let you sit where you can watch my table. Understood?"

"Yes, sir."

When Brinkman and Alan reached the front, they paused under the awning. The doorman was handsomely dressed with a velvet and satin topcoat over his tuxedo and crisply starched white shirt. His hair was neatly trimmed and gray at the sides, while his shoes were black and highly polished. He stepped forward. "Good evening, Mr. Brinkman. The Rainier Club is eager to serve you, sir."

Otto swung the glass and brass door open and bowed slightly at the waist. Alan stopped on cue and watched the Walrus walk inside. Satisfied with Mr. B's safety, Alan hurried back to the Packard. Before he reached it, a standard-issued Ford sedan pulled up and idled while letting out its passenger. The driver, a heavy man, remained seated, adjusting his weight, like he was about to get comfortable for a long while. The tall, angular passenger with silver hair opened his own door. Like Brinkman, this man scanned the territory. His luminescent blue eyes flowed over Alan and up to the well-established building that bespoke old money. He straightened his fedora, said something to the driver, and strode slowly to the door, matching the same deliberate pace veteran cops used when pounding their beats. Alan climbed in the Packard, while the man spoke with the doorman. After a moment, Otto stepped aside and opened the door, this time with just a hint of a bow.

Alan asked, "Is that Chief Ketchum?"

Vic leaned forward in his seat. "It is, and his driver looks to be Sergeant Watkins."

"Mr. B said to park the car and fetch his billfold."

"No problem. I know the drill. Drive up the hill and around the block, and when you come back down, park in their lot, off Columbia."

"Does Mr. B trust him?"

"Ketchum ain't no saint, but he's a man of his word. He's old school, one-room schoolhouse sort, oldest of eleven. Word is, he tramped his way to Seattle in a boxcar, not to run away from his responsibilities, but to make good for his family and send money home. He brought a couple younger brothers out later, and they're now on the force. He's okay in my book."

Alan followed the directions, and then Vic leaned forward again, arm stretched over the seat. "Here's his billfold. There's only a couple of 'C' notes in here. It's just for show. You carry this in case someone asks what you're up to. Mr. B just wants you near him."

"Got it."

"Shouldn't nothing ugly happen here, but if it does, you stall for a minute, and I'll come running with Mr. Thompson and a full spool."

"You expecting trouble?"

"Not here. This here's high rollers' territory. They wouldn't let the likes of Frantz in there, not even with a search warrant, 'cause they know it'd be a phony."

"Why's that?"

"'Cause all the judges are in there having dinner. Who'd a signed it?"

At the side door, a valet gave Alan the once over,

289

saw he was clutching a billfold, and didn't bother to challenge him. Alan let himself in and picked his way through the kitchen, navigating back to the main entrance and the maitre d'.

He approached Jerry, who had just dispatched regular customers to a table with their waiter. Jerry finished his entry on the seating chart before he acknowledged Alan's presence. Without saying a word, the maitre d' frowned at Alan's hat. Then he went back to his seating chart.

Alan removed the hat, crossed his arms, forming an X, and held the chapeau in front of him, bouncing it gently on his legs.

Without looking up, Jerry said, "May I help you?"

"Mr. Brinkman asked me to bring him his billfold and wait for him···said you'd arrange a table."

Jerry snapped to attention. "Mr. Brinkman said you'd be coming, Mr. Stewart, but we didn't expect you so soon. Right this way," he said with a bow.

Jerry escorted Alan to a raised booth, draped with heavy white linen, positioned near the kitchen with a view of the whole floor. Jerry pulled the table out so Alan could slide in. "May I take your coat, sir?"

Brinkman and his guest were in a nearby booth, sitting across from each other. "No, thank you. I'd like to keep it nearby."

The maitre d' rolled his eyes, but Alan ignored him. As he stretched to pull the table in after him, Jerry stepped forward and eased it back in place. Then he picked up the napkin, which was folded into a decorative pattern, snapped it open, and set it across Alan's lap.

Chief Ketchum and the Walrus were already eating salads when water and coffee appeared at Alan's table, as if conjured by an unseen magician. Ketchum fidgeted as he sat, taking long pulls on his scotch, while Mr. B sipped his martini.

This corner of the dining room was almost empty, making it easier for Alan to listen to their conversation. He wondered how much this seating arrangement was costing Brinkman.

After the waiter brought the chief a second drink, Brinkman said, "I understand the tragedy on Broadway could have been much worse. Your man Frantz was lucky to have escaped with a head wound."

"Very fortunate," said the chief. His knuckles showed white as he clutched his glass.

"The papers say Harry got word of a robbery team in town. Is that right?"

"Greedy bastards. With the Repeal, Vancouver's become a Wild West hideout, like that one for the Hole In The Wall Gang. From up there, they sneak down to the states, find a soft spot to hit, but they ran into a buzz saw with Harry."

Two waiters interrupted. One removed the salad plates, and the other replaced them with generous portions of prime rib. Alan chewed on a steak sandwich, which was accompanied by a cup of au jus and a bowl of soup.

The chief spread horseradish on his slab of prime and cut into it with a sharpened knife.

Brinkman said, "If you give me a description of the shooters, I'll put the word out for my union men to keep an eye open. We cover the entire state. Someone may have seen something that might help, like up in Everett, Mt. Vernon, or Bellingham···"

The chief nodded and took another bite.

"Or Chinatown," added Brinkman.

Ketchum set his hands on the table and sat back against the cushion. "What do you know about Chinatown?"

"Like I said, Mike, I've got a lot of people on the street···a lot of eyes and ears."

Ketchum shook his glass and motioned to the waiter for a refill, and then asked, "What have your people heard?"

"This stays between you and me?"

"If that's the way ya want it."

"Harry's got a hard-on for one of my men, and what he says about the Kasbah is bilge water."

Ketchum eyed Brinkman and gripped his utensils hard enough to make his knuckles turn white.

"I want you to put a harness on him and rein him in," said Brinkman.

"Why should I? He's after the godless scum who gunned down Hoff and Schneider, and I'll use whatever it takes to get them. Don't forget, I worked with those two when I was coming up."

"Mike···what your good lieutenant told the papers isn't what really happened, not by a damn sight."

"I stand by Harry."

"I know you stand by him, but do you believe everything he says?"

Ketchum chewed on a piece of meat and took a sip of his scotch. "Whew. Damn fine horseradish···but as I was saying, Harry's got a reputation, I'll give ya that. But he's a helluva bull. The good people of Seattle want to feel safe when they're walking about at night. Time was when the streets were so rough the cops had to walk in groups of six. Guys like Harry changed all that. With his ways, and given a free hand, he made the streets safe so now even a lonely spinster can walk her poodle up and down Pike Street, if she likes. People don't care much for his methods now, but law and order came with a price. And we owe him a debt and have to make allowances. Sure, he's got sticky fingers, but he also helps other cops who suffer on the meager salaries the City begrudges."

"I have no problems with that, Mike. People give me gifts all the time. I understand how it works—like that suit you're wearing···and the one the Chief's got. It's the same in the Prosecutor's Office. I could go on. My point is everybody should be sharing in the wealth, and what gives me pause is when a guy gets greedy and takes seconds before everybody's had firsts. You know what I'm saying?"

Ketchum resumed eating and nodded.

"And it's when a greedy bastard sics a couple of his goons," said Brinkman, "on my personal staff of detectives, that's what gives me real heartburn."

"What are ya saying, George?"

"Harry's so crooked he couldn't piss in a urinal without getting it on the next man's shoes. There never was a robbery team from Canada. It was just him and his two thugs going after one of my boys, trying to beat his brains in. That's what got them all shot. He did the same damn thing to McAlister Stewart two years ago and got away with it."

Ketchum held up his hand to stop the Walrus. He shook his head and swallowed what he was chewing. "That's not the way I remember it. The reports from the hospital said Mackie Stewart was a drunk. Hell, his own boys found him busted up behind O'Malley's Bar on Eastlake."

"Mackie was as fine a man as you'd ever want to meet. You'd be lucky to have men like him working for you, and it was Hoff and Schneider who sapped him silly." Brinkman had raised his voice. Behind him, Alan glared over his coffee cup, his eyes predatory, focused, and his glands pumping adrenaline rage.

Brinkman continued, "One of my men had a change of heart the other day and admitted to setting Mackie up for the take-down, and he fingered Harry as the guy pressing him to do it. Your lieutenant blackmailed him with a porno charge, and last week's disaster with yet another one of my detectives happened at the same exact place with the same exact people...even the same goddamn porno charge. As you police say, it's the same M.O. Can I make that any more clear?"

"Which of your detectives?"

Brinkman ignored the question and took a sip of his martini.

Ketchum took another bite of his rib and glowered at the Walrus.

Brinkman said, "One of my personal detectives. That's all I'll say for now."

"If your detective was getting his melon split, as you say, who did the rescue work? Who did the shooting?"

Brinkman took another sip of his martini.

"You know, and you're not telling. Is that right?"

"Perhaps."

"All right, George, this isn't difficult for an old detective to figure out: It has to be another one of your detectives."

"Does it?"

"Well, it wasn't some goddamn Good Samaritan who just happened by. Was it? I saw what your shooter did to those two men. This was top-drawer, professional shooting, done with a tommy gun. Now, how many Good Samaritans you know carry them around in case they run across crooked cops in the middle of a take-down?"

"You're getting off the point, Mike. Your lieutenant has been lying to you about this."

"Can you prove it?"

"Absolutely."

Ketchum stuck his knife into his meat and scowled at Brinkman. "And how could you do that? There were no witnesses, and we have all the evidence: the magazines and shell casings. Our lab is working to get prints from them. That'll tell a story, and you'll see I'm right."

"Did you recover Harry's gun?"

"What? No···the robbers···what about his gun?" He drained his scotch and stared at the melting ice, his words starting to thicken. "Do you have it?"

Brinkman glanced up at the chandelier, taking his time, weighing his response. "I believe I could put my hands on it." He finished off his martini, smacked his lips, and signaled the waiter for another round of drinks.

"George, old friend, if you have Harry's gun, or if you know where it is and you're not giving it to us, you're obstructing a police investigation—withholding evidence."

"That's a lot of 'ifs,' Mike, but again, this is left of center, far from the point I'm making, which is: Harry, whose crew was beating hell out of one of my men, made himself out to be a hero in this fracas, firing 'several shots at the Canadians,' when his gun shows it was fired only once—and that was at him—putting a crease in that doorknob of a noggin he uses for a hat rack."

Ketchum sat back against the cushion, dabbed his brow with the napkin, and threw it on the table. "You know this for sure?"

"How many shells did you recover that'd match his gun?"

No answer.

"Check with your lab boys, but I know for a fact it was only one. Now, have I ever lied to you?"

The chief turned away and watched a waiter clear

a table, defeated. "Can't say you have."

"Well···I'm not starting now. I want you to call Harry and his dogs off my people, starting now, and if you do, I'll make sure his gun finds its way to your office."

"And what if I don't?"

"I'd rather not go that direction, but I might not be able to stop the people who've got it from delivering it to the newspapers or FBI, along with the police-issue handcuffs he hog-tied my detective with."

The drinks arrived. Ketchum grabbed his and stared into it, while he chewed at sinew caught in his teeth. "I want the gun and the handcuffs."

"And···"

"Effective immediately, I'll re-assign Harry to the City Jail as assistant commander···for career development."

"Will he leave my people alone?"

"He will if he ever wants to get out of jail."

Ketchum sloshed a large swig of scotch and smacked his lips. "This is nice stuff, nothing like Prohibition hooch."

"We made a helluva lot of money during those days," said Brinkman.

"But it was tough on the department, too. We lost nearly two-dozen officers, just in Seattle alone. Must have been another good dozen killed in the county and around Puget Sound."

"It wasn't all good, neither were they, neither were we."

"How true, but we can't continue to live in the past···and in the present, I've got a double homicide on my hands. We can add two more to the growing number of lost boys."

Brinkman finished his rib and crossed his knife and fork on his plate.

"George, we've still got a problem."

"How's that?"

"You'll have to give up one of your boys. The Chief will expect it, and the rest of the brass will demand it. I don't see any way around it."

"You know I can't do that."

"Sure you can."

Brinkman shook his head.

"I'm not asking for both your men, but I've got to have a body. Somebody's got to take the fall, because I can't just take Harry's gun and call it even. It won't sell. The boss won't care what you've done for us over the years, not with a couple of retired bulls gunned down in his city. Think how that'll look for him and play out in the papers···and with your union."

"What do you mean, 'with the union'?"

"There's no getting around it. You've already told me your boys were there, and I can promise you··· this old dog," he said, jabbing a thumb toward his own chest, "has still enough teeth left to take a nasty bite out of Harry's behind. I'll shake the story out of him. He'll roll, one way or the other, and tell what happened, who was there—"

"I need some time."

"To do what?"

"Make preparations···find a replacement···soften the blow. I don't know, Mike, but I'm not ready."

"We've got good history, George. That means something. So, I'll settle for a name, and I'll keep distance between it and the union. I don't need the body···just yet. You give me a name, and I'll give your man a two-day head start."

Brinkman studied Ketchum's face and said, "What if he outruns you?"

"It's a chance I'll take···for old time's sake. If there's a chase, it'll give the men a sense of purpose and something

297

legitimate to focus on. Hell, it'll raise morale and remind anyone else like Harry that the old ways have ended."

"You're asking me to ruin the life of one of my men, when the entire shooting was self-defense."

"George, I saw the bodies and read the autopsy reports. These two men had a combined total of twenty rounds pumped into them, and unlike the St. Valentine's Day Massacre, there weren't any rounds wasted. There was none climbing the brick wall or busting up the rafters. These shots were meant to count, and that's a killing, not a defending. There's no prosecutor or jury in the country going to call that self-defense."

Brinkman wiped his mouth and dropped his napkin on the table. "This is an entirely one-sided proposition. I give you evidence to a crime, along with one of my best men, and all that's required of you is to put restraints on your loose cannon."

"I see it as a goodwill gesture, George. You and your union will be doing the right thing, and instead of getting on the wrong side of my boss, the department will be impressed with your commitment to civility. I can see the Chief throwing a lot of support and goodwill toward the union, which needs all the help it can get, going up against the Teamsters."

"Above all else, I'm the boss, responsible for the welfare of a lot of men and their families."

"You're a good steward for your folks, George. No one says different. You do all right by them."

Brinkman made eye contact with Alan inclining his head toward the door. Alan reached for his hat and coat. Mr. B was doing the same. When the Walrus stood up, he said, "I'll have a name for you tomorrow, Mike, but the two-day clock doesn't start until then. Now get Harry off our backs."

Alan stopped the car in front of the club's entrance and hurried around to the passenger side, opening the rear door for the Walrus, who was taking his time with Ketchum, finalizing negotiations. The chief of detectives asked, "So, how's Vera doing? I haven't seen her in ages."

"Vera's fine. She keeps busy."

"Still look as good as ever?"

"That she does."

"When you send down your package, why don't you have her deliver it? If it's not a problem, I'd love to see her."

"I'll see what her schedule looks like."

Their business behind them, the two shook hands, and as Brinkman climbed into the back seat, the chief sized Alan up from head to toe and looked him square in the eye. After a moment, he shook his head and turned away. Reaching his car, he grumbled to his driver. "They're recruiting 'em young now days. This one's still wet behind the ears."

Alan drove up Fourth Avenue, and Mr. B said, "Take me to the Sorento. We'll get a couple of rooms tonight. We'll all need to get up early and have a strategy session, away from prying ears. I want both your opinions⋯Vera's, too. Tomorrow will be an exception; we'll start off with Bloody Marys, because no one's going to be happy."

299

The following morning, Vera led the way into the union's great hall, jingling the keys to the liquor cabinets and carrying a grocery bag with celery sticks and tomato juice. The men sat in silence as Vera performed for them, concocting a mix of Bloody Marys, heavy on the vodka. No one spoke until everyone had a drink and Vera joined them. As she climbed onto a stool behind Alan, her knee rubbed up against his back, but she didn't apologize or move it.

The Walrus led off, bringing Vera up to speed, explaining the basics of Ketchum's offer to silence Hungry Harry, in return for surrendering a name.

She huffed, "Where's the justice in this?"

"Justice isn't the point," said Brinkman. "Retribution is. The police want a pound of flesh for the loss of two retired coppers. Doesn't matter that they were murdering thugs. Point is—they want to balance their loss with an arrest."

Brinkman continued talking, while the others sipped drinks. Alan shivered on his first sip, and Vera said, "What's the matter, Champ? You never had a stiff one this early?"

"No, ma'am," he said innocently. "Have you?"

Behind them, the Walrus roared with laughter, leaned forward, and slapped Vic's knee. Vic joined the laughter, at Vera's expense, and laughed until tears came to his eyes. It took Alan a moment to get his own joke, and then his cheeks flushed, as he laughed nervously. From behind, Vera feigned faux rage, then smiled, nodded, and ran her fingers through Alan's hair, leaving it thoroughly mussed.

When the laughter died down, she said, "Don't call me ma'am. It makes me feel old."

He attempted to apologize to her, but that only served to re-ignite the laughter.

Brinkman took out a hanky, wiped his eyes, shook the moistened cloth, and stuffed it back in his lapel pocket. "I stayed up most of the night thinking about this, and I got some ideas. But before I pontificate, I'd like to hear other opinions."

Vic spoke first. "I thought about it, too, and I think I know what needs doing."

"What's that?" asked Brinkman.

"It's me. You gotta give me up."

"Why you?" asked Alan.

"I've done my time around here, and you're just getting started. It makes more sense—"

"But why does it have to be anybody?" asked Vera.

"Those are his terms," said Mr. B. "We don't play ball with Ketchum, then the department's going to screw with the union, force out of us what they want, and like he said, they got their ways of getting the story, one way or the other. So···they'll find out who was there, eventually, painfully."

Vic said, "If pressed, Harry'll give up my name. So there's no sense in giving 'em the Champ, because even if you do, they'd still come for me someday, if someone

301

gets a hair up his ass···sorry, Vera."

She tossed her head back and forth, indicating she wasn't offended, and then winked at Vic.

With a napkin, the Walrus dabbed at tomato juice that was coloring his mustache. When he was done, he said, "You make sense, but giving you up would be like cutting off my right arm, my strong arm. You're family, Vic. I can't bear to part with you···" Then he turned and acknowledged Alan. "Nor you, son."

Vera asked, "Can we hide Vic out for awhile, until this cools over?"

Brinkman shook his head. "It's not going to cool, and that's no way to live."

Vic crunched on his celery stick. "I can get pretty far with a two-day head start, if Ketchum keeps his word. It ain't such a bad idea, Boss. I been thinking about retiring, so to speak. This'll just move the time line up, and with Harry threatening to sic Immigration on Lilly, now's the time to make my move. I'll marry her and set off for the Orient."

"Where in the Orient?" asked Brinkman.

"Some little island, south of China. I got enough money to buy the place, but there could be Japs swarming all over."

"Sounds dangerous," said Vera.

"Probably is, but I was already thinking about moving there in a couple of years. So, I'll just move up the time schedule and get Lilly home before Immigration casts her adrift."

"You've been quiet, Alan," said the Walrus. "What are you thinking?"

"I did the shooting. So I already made up my mind I'd turn myself in, if—"

"NO!" shouted the other three.

Alan stopped and shrugged.

"What good would that do?" asked Brinkman.

"I figured it was me who caused this."

"That ain't so," said Vic. "They was using my skull to beat out jungle rhythms—like to kill me, 'cept you bailed me out. If you hadn't, I'd be dead anyway. You just delayed the inevitable, providing they don't catch me before I set sail."

Brinkman asked, "Vic, old friend, can you make it out of here in two days?"

"I believe so."

"How? Where to?"

"Canada··· for starters," said Vic.

Vera crossed her legs and folded her arms, lips puckered in a pout. Brinkman said, "Of course··· I'll have Alan drive you."

Vera asked, "Are you sure you have enough money for this? What if they don't take American greenbacks where you're going?"

"Everybody honors those," Vic said.

"Not necessarily so," said Brinkman. "There's a war going on 'cross the world. Won't be too long before we're dragged into it, despite Roosevelt's best efforts to avoid it. Greenbacks might lose favor, but if you've got gold, that's international currency."

"What about gold certificates?" asked Alan.

"Good as gold," said Brinkman.

Alan said, "I know where there's a ton of them, but they're not mine to give away."

Vera eyed him thoughtfully. "You have the ransom money, don't you?"

"I know where it is, but it rightfully belongs to the Lindberghs. I figured I'd give it back to them."

Vic said, "The Champ found the key to Mackie's

vault. The ransom was all there."

"Oh, yes," said Brinkman, as if reminded of a minor business detail.

Vera said, "I have an idea."

Brinkman waved his hand, giving her the floor.

"As the detectives who recovered it, you're entitled to ten percent finders' fees. That would be just over $3,000."

"Good start, but not enough to live forever," said Brinkman.

Alan asked, "What about swapping out the other 90 percent for greenbacks? Is there anything wrong with that?"

Vic said, "The money's jinxed. Too much blood's been spilt over it."

"Money's money, but gold certificates leave a trail," said Brinkman. "Without the government's okay, that money's still recorded and traceable. And that trail could point the FBI, the Treasury, or US Marshalls to where Vic's hiding. Then somebody'll put a fugitive detainer on him and seek an extradition so they can bring him back stateside to prosecute."

"None of that sounds good," said Vera.

"And I don't want none of it, unless the Lindberghs give their okay." Vic shook his large head.

Vera picked up the Bloody Mary mix and poured another round of drinks, and Brinkman nibbled on the edge of his celery stick like a rabbit, lost in thought. When Vera brought the fresh drinks to the table, Mr. B jabbed the celery into the ice at the bottom of his glass. He said, "We don't have any time to waste. Vera, get on the horn and call that prosecutor in New Jersey···you know the name."

"David Wilentz," said Vera. "He's the Attorney General."

"That's right," said Mr. B. "Here's a guy who became New Jersey's A.G. without ever trying a case.

304

Then a year on the job, he ends up prosecuting that Hauptmann fellow. Did a damn fine job. His very first trial was the crime of the century. Amazing man. Well, get a hold of him, and we'll see what we can do."

Vera used the telephone on the wall at the end of the bar, calling the long distance operator. After a minute or so, she cupped the receiver and said, "I've got his secretary. She told me Wilentz was busy, until I told her your detectives found the Lindbergh ransom and would like to discuss it. She said somebody would be with me in a minute."

Brinkman lumbered over to the phone and put the receiver to his ear. After a few seconds of waiting in silence, he said, "This is George Brinkman, and I'm the union president for—

"In Seattle, that's right⋯

"We're not exactly near San Francisco, no⋯

"And you are Mr. Wilentz's aide⋯James⋯

"Well, James, I wanted to speak to Mr. Wilentz about—

"Yes, I see⋯Well, James, the crux of the matter is that my detectives have recovered the missing Lindbergh ransom—

"Impossible? Actually, no⋯and no, they're not Pinkertons. They're employed by me and the union—

"Yes, I know what the Pinkertons did during the strikes, but these aren't those kind of detectives⋯ We're getting off the point⋯Listen, James, will I be able to speak to Mr⋯

"I understand. We're all busy⋯

Brinkman covered the receiver and turned to the others and said, "Someone else is coming to the phone."

"Hello, yes, we would like to discuss returning the ransom to the⋯No, we're not pushing to re-open this⋯

"No, we haven't discussed it with the newspapers. My detectives found it in the possession of a man whom we think⋯

"What do you mean the matter is closed? May I speak to—

"Impossible? And why is that?

Brinkman continued for a few more minutes and finished. "I understand. We'll take care of it."

Brinkman handed the phone back to Vera and returned to the others. "They're disclaiming the money."

"Why's that?" asked Vic.

"Someone was coaching the schmo. He said he didn't want the case re-opened. Some people have already complained that Hauptmann was a patsy, and New Jersey fried the wrong guy. He's worried the newsies would make another circus out of this, and the family has been through a lot...too much, actually."

"Well, that's what he says," said Vera, "but what about the Lindberghs? What do they say?"

"They're not going to contact them. He said they're living in Europe now, where it's safer. Imagine that. The whole European continent is torn apart by war, and he says it's safer for them over there. He says they're trying to put the ugliness behind them, and 'as a kindness to their family' they would not be re-opening this matter. Can you believe that?"

"Actually, I can," said Vera. "But what did they say to do?"

"Donate it to charity."

"Any particular one?" asked Vera.

"He said something about widows and orphans."

"Well, I know where there are plenty of those," said Vic. "The war zone—China."

The other three looked to Mr. B. "Are you okay with that, Alan?"

"Sure. Just as long as it kills the jinx."

Mr. B left the group to themselves so he could put together a severance package. Vera gave Vic a long, bon-voyage hug, dabbing tears as they streamed down her cheeks. When she let go of Vic, she turned immediately to Alan, sobbing uncontrollably. She clutched him, pulled him close, and cried on his shoulder. He didn't push her away. Her crying was disconcerting, but she smelled wonderful, classy, like he imagined Lorreta Young or Claudette Colbert.

Before long, Brinkman returned to the hall carrying a handful of manila envelopes, and Vera finally let go of Alan, going back to her barstool. Mr. B pressed the envelopes into Vic's hands and said to keep him advised of his whereabouts. The money exchange was followed by awkward man-hugs and shoulder pats. Saying goodbye wasn't easy, and it took its toll on everyone present.

Deciding it best to avoid the rest of the office staff, Vic and Alan left through a side door. Alan drove and Vic rode shotgun. Alan asked, "Where first?"

"The vault."

"I'll need to sneak home and get the key."

307

Alan retrieved the safety deposit key from his home

while everyone was away but Margaret. She only slowed him down enough to wish him luck, before Alan and Vic resumed their drive to the vault. Vic asked Alan to stop at a luggage store on Second Avenue so he could pick up a couple of large canvas grips. When they entered The Great Pioneer Savings Deposit Bank, Sally greeted them professionally. After Alan signed in, she smiled. "Oh, Mr. Stewart, I'm sorry, I didn't recognize you."

While Alan made nice with Sally, Vic visited with George. The security guard looked over his cheaters and said, "Good to see you together again. Just like old times."

Vic patted George's arm, excused himself, and signed in beneath Alan's name.

As a courtesy, or to amuse himself, George walked the pair down the steps. "Looks like you boys are fixing to move some things around. I won't get in your way, just stick to your own boxes." He beamed, apparently hoping they'd get his humor. "This place has never been robbed," he said with pride. "It even survived the great fire—"

"Thanks, George," said Vic. "We'll be all right."

George tottered his way upstairs.

Alan put his key in box 324, opened it, and extracted the key to 502. Meanwhile, Vic opened his own large box and began stuffing bricks of cash into an opened bag. Alan chuckled, thinking how they must resemble bank robbers looting a vault. He opened his bag and started filling it with the gold certificates.

Vic said, "Done," and he moved closer to Alan, who pulled out the last brick of ransom and tossed it in the bag.

Vic peered into the box and said, "What's this you got?" as he reached for Sid Fisher's wallet. "Haven't seen this in awhile." He picked it up, thought better, and tossed it back in the box. "You might want to hold onto that, Champ. Never can tell when it'll come in handy. It could be worth a fortune to a collector some day. Some guys get their rocks off dwelling on the morbid.

"And speaking of money," said Vic, as he reached into his bag and grabbed a brick of green. "Here's your father's cut of the finder's fee."

"I can't take this."

"Sure you can. You heard Vera. Ten percent finder's fee." He grabbed another brick of cash and said, "No sense my being greedy. You can have my share, because look at what you're giving me for a currency exchange. I'm coming out way ahead. I'll be spending the gold certs like a sailor on leave, buying whatever Lilly wants for her village with the Lindbergh's money, but it won't feel good unless I'm square with you."

"I don't know, Vic, you're retiring, might need it."

"Nonsense. It's the only way I'll take blood money. I want to make sure it comes clean, without that bloody curse attached. Bad money punishes the greedy."

Vic stuffed the two bricks of greenbacks in 502, while Alan stood back, hesitant, unsure. Then Vic dug in his pocket, pulled out his box key, and tossed it into

Alan's box. "The rent's paid for another seven years. If I don't come back before then, help yourself."

"What've you got in there?"

"Ain't got time to discuss it now, Champ. Our best bet is between here and Canada. Next stop: Chinatown."

Upstairs, they said their good-byes and hurried through the front door to the sidewalk. Nearing the car, Vic said, "Try not to stare, but that looks to be a standard-issue detective car across the street. Pay it no mind. Should they ask, we're just running an errand for the union."

"Got it."

After they put the bags in the back and climbed inside, Vic said, "If we head south, they'll know we're on our way to Chinatown, and they'll smoke us out at Big Mama's. So make a U-turn, take us uptown. Make a few laps around Pike and Pine, and we'll see if we can lose them in heavy traffic."

Alan checked the mirror, revved the engine, and put the car in gear. Behind them, the police car in the plain wrapper lurched into traffic. Alan turned east on Yesler and veered off Jefferson on the short block to Third Avenue. The tail car hung back a block. Alan turned north, now heading up Third.

"Just don't run any lights, give them any legit reason to stop us," said Vic. "I want to get out of here without a fight."

After they reached Pike Street, Vic gave Alan directions, making right turns and then a quick dash south through an alley. When he reached Pine, he broke through traffic and headed east to Boren, Alan's favorite cross-town route. To be sure they lost their tail, Vic directed Alan onto a side street, having him park near the hospital. For a few minutes, they sat and observed traffic passing by, focusing on drivers and passengers, particularly looking for pairs of large, well-dressed men with fedoras and overcoats, a trademark of Hungry Harry's crew.

Satisfied the immediate danger had passed, Vic said,
"Go ahead and take us down to Chinatown. Park in
my garage. Then you'll wait in the car and keep an
eye on the money. I'm thinking Harry will have a crew
surveilling Mama's, but I got to risk it to bring Lilly out."

"Why don't I go get her?"

"I don't think she'd come with anybody but me,
and Mama maybe just too bull-headed to let her go,
even with the cops hot on her footsies. She can be as
stubborn as a dowager's bowels."

Alan managed a smile. "Now there's an image I
could've lived my whole life without."

They parked in Vic's stall and checked the area
around the car. Since nobody else was in the garage,
they transferred the grips full of cash to the trunk. Vic
moved the M-1 over to the side and took the Thompson
out, loading it with the big spool. He set the gun in the
back on the floorboards and said, "Sorry, Champ, but
this is about as much a plan as I can come up with—I
should be back in ten···fifteen minutes tops. If I'm
not out in twenty, think about taking the money and
running to the union hall. But, if you hear shooting,
you might consider coming for me, and bringing Mr.

311

Thompson along. That's your call, but if you can't make it, I'll understand. You've done enough for me already."

Alan's brow creased, hangdog frown, as if offended. "I'll cover your back." He wanted to let Vic know his concerns were misplaced.

Vic flashed a smile and offered his hand. "Wish me luck."

Alan clasped the large hand, and Vic patted him on the shoulder. Then he lifted his coat collar and snapped the brim of his hat down, while exiting through the pedestrian door, next to the garage's main entrance. Alan held the door and kept an eye on Vic until he disappeared around the corner, without leaving a trace. Alan checked the time on his watch: 12:10 pm. Already? Why is it that the time flies when every second needs to count?

Ten minutes later, not knowing Vic's fate, he wished the time away. As his mind raced with what might be happening in the brothel, he paced the dirt floor, from the door to the car. While turning around at the car, something banged into the side door. He reached for his .45, just as a small figure stepped from the light into the darkness.

He moved quickly toward the figure clad in heavy garb, which was soon followed by a second shape, both carrying too much in their small hands. The person spoke hesitantly. "Alan?"

"Poppy?"

He ran toward the women and took their suitcases. Setting the bags down, he wrapped his arms around Poppy, giving her a huge hug. Then he checked to see who was with her. "Iris···good!"

Poppy put her hands out, pressing against him, cutting the reunion short. "Rose and Lilly come soon. Vic come last."

He lifted up their bags and put them in the trunk.

"Any trouble getting here?"

"No trouble."

"Anyone follow you?"

"Follow? No understand."

"Any police?"

"No see."

Alan went back to the side door, opened it a crack, and peeked outside. No movement. As he held his position, Lilly and another refugee hurried around the corner, carrying all their earthly possessions: twice what Poppy had brought.

When the women reached the door, Alan opened it, letting them in. Then he took their belongings, carried them over to the opened trunk, and stashed them inside next to the other gear. He opened a passenger door and said, "All of you sit in the back and wait. Don't make any noise—just like inside the dragon."

Rose explained to the others.

He picked up the Thompson and held it out of their way, so they could scoot by. The women stared wide-eyed at the heavy artillery, while stepping past and climbing inside. Poppy was last. He held her hand, while helping her inside, and closed the door gently after her.

The women began whispering excitedly in their native language, so Alan pressed his face to the glass, put his finger to his lips, shook his head, and blew the quiet sign, which they understood. When the noise subsided, he pushed away from the car and hurried back toward the pedestrian door, resuming his sentry position, holding his tommy gun at port arms. He checked his watch. It was 12:24. Vic's keeping to his schedule.

Alan's vigilance was rewarded. Before another minute passed, Vic came around the corner and dashed to the door. Alan quickly snapped it open, and Vic dove

313

inside. Alan shut the door sharply, and Vic nodded his thanks. "Bolt it."

Then Vic drew his piece and flattened himself against the wall and gave the quiet signal to Alan. He motioned for him to step back and take a position behind a Chinatown hearse, parked near the garage entrance.

While backing up, Alan racked a new round into the chamber, ejecting one he'd forgotten was already there. It hit the packed dirt floor with little sound. No sooner had Alan taken position than tires squealed to a stop outside on the brick street. There were desperate voices and the sound of leather-soled shoes slapping on the hard surface.

An angry voice said, "He's got to be in this block," which was followed by a hand pounding on the pedestrian door, testing the lock. Below the large sliding door, ankles, shoes, and shadows crossed back and forth. Two shadows tried to pull the door open. No luck.

The voice said, "Come on. You just need to look where the flies are gathering. That's where you'll find that piece of shit."

Another voice said, "Don't waste your time here. Check the noodle factory and some of those other doors. He may already be back in the catacombs."

The shoes moved away, and after a moment Alan relaxed his grip on the submachine gun and started to drop his guard. He lowered the gun and began to walk back around the van, but Vic shook his head vigorously and gave him the alert sign. Alan nodded his understanding and returned to his position, shrugging.

Λ moment later, the quick smacking of shoes on the sidewalk interrupted their silence, and it was soon followed by a thunderous WHAM! The pedestrian door jumped but held. One of the men outside had thrown his shoulder into it.

The voice grumbled a curse and moved off. He said, "It was worth a try, Harry⋯"

Vic got Alan's attention and pointed at his watch, and signed "Five," with his big hand, as he mouthed the words "Wait five minutes."

They held their positions for longer than Alan thought necessary, but he deferred to experience. It was Vic's call.

After a stretch of silence, Vic inched over to where Alan was standing and said, "Let's roll the car back, and when you're ready to start the engine, I'll throw the garage doors open. You slow down for me when you get to the curb, and I'll hop in."

"Got it."

Alan set the Thompson on the front seat and put the transmission in neutral. Then the two men gave the car a push out of its stall. Alan climbed in and turned the wheels so that when the car rolled to a stop it faced out.

Vic pressed his ear to the garage's main doors, listening for a moment, and then he pulled the bolt back, opening one door wide enough to stick his head outside. Satisfied, he gave a nod, and Alan started the Packard's engine and eased the car toward the exit. Vic pushed the far door to the side and tugged on the nearer one, sliding it open. Alan stopped the car with a jerk, straddling the egress. He moved the Thompson out of the way, making room for Vic.

Vic waved Alan forward, and when the car was moving, he pulled open the door and jumped in. "Move this baby!"

Alan gunned the engine and hurried toward Jackson Street, where he turned east, climbing the grade to Twelfth Avenue, seeking Boren Avenue, which would take them north of town and up to Denny Way.

Before the Packard made it up Jackson Street, one-half mile behind them, Harry and his crew drove back in front of the garage. The detectives saw the wide-open doorway and hit the brakes. Harry and one of his men climbed out, drawing their guns. The lieutenant stealthily approached the door closest to him, holding his gun in the high-ready position, while his detective did the same and hid behind the far side. Harry poked his head around and peered inside the gaping chasm. Seeing nothing, he motioned the detective and they stepped around the doors together, guns covering the parked vehicles. They entered and gave the garage the once-over, moving from car to car. One stall was empty.

Satisfied the garage was clear, Harry walked back toward the entrance, holstering his gun. While looking down, he caught the glint of something shiny in the packed dirt, next to the hearse. He bent down, picked up the .45 round, tossed it in the air, and caught it, showing his find to the detective.

They hurried back toward their car, and he yelled at the driver, "They were here!"

He climbed in the passenger seat, and the driver asked, "Where now, Boss?"

"They're on the run. Head over to the highway."

"Which one?"

"South on Highway 99··· No, wait. Make that north. With their contacts, they're going to run to Canada, not Frisco. And keep an eye out for that big Packard they always drive. Step on it; they've got a big head start. Bust red lights if you have to."

By the time Lt. Frantz and his crew reached Jackson Street, Alan and the rescue mission had crested Boren Avenue at Madison Street and were descending the hill toward Pike, on their way to Denny Way. Alan adjusted the rear-view mirror to check the passengers in the backseat. The women were huddled together, terrified. "Are you okay back there?"

"We so scared," said Lilly.

Vic said, "Don't worry your pretty head, Flower. Soon as we clear town, it'll be smooth-sailing."

Alan asked, "What happened to Brinkman's deal? That was Harry outside the garage."

"Well, technically, we're also jumping the gun, getting a running start. Mr. B ain't given Chief Ketchum a name, so our two-days, according to the rules of war, ain't begun yet. Either that or Harry's coloring outside the lines, which wouldn't surprise me. But as it stands, I ain't so sure I want to find out what his problem is."

Alan dropped down the Denny Way hill and turned north on Aurora Avenue, which was Highway 99's dressed-up name for this stretch of road.

Vic said, "Drive fast, but not too fast. You know the drill."

317

Frantz's driver, Detective Rousseau, turned west on Jackson and then north on Fourth Avenue. Frantz asked, "You sure you know where you're going?"

"Sure, Harry. We take Fourth uptown to Denny, and then we get on Aurora northbound, across the new bridge. It's a straight line, the shortest route."

Frantz rubbed his face and said, "You're going to go through about seventeen traffic lights this way, and the way our luck is going, you'll miss every damn one and run over three pedestrians, who will all be related to the mayor."

"I'll bust the ones that ain't busy."

"Make it snappy. They're probably halfway to Everett by now."

Frantz tossed and caught the bullet again. He held it to the light to inspect extractor markings on the cartridge. The detective said, "What's that you got?"

"A .45 round, and I'll bet it came from a Thompson." After letting that sink in, he said, "I'll make another wager—Vic's new muscle is with him."

"They got a machine gun?"

"It would appear so. Undoubtedly, it's the same one they used at The Kasbah."

The detective in the back chimed in. "Not to worry. We've got our own artillery." He bent over and began to pick it up.

Frantz said, "Leave it—until we need it."

Alan made good time traveling north, taking advantage of the head start. Vic did his part keeping the women calm. Alan asked, "Did you have any trouble with Big Mama?"

"Oh···heck, yeah···until I dropped five grand in front of her, gold certs, and told her she and papa better hide out somewhere, think of moving their shop···until things cool down. It got noisy, but while she was counting money, I grabbed the girls and made for the door. These four all came from the same island and want to stick together."

"Are they looking forward to going home?"

"Hard to say. Right now, they're scared. They don't know what's going on, with the war and all, but I got enough dough to take care of their whole village."

An hour-and-a-half later, Detective Rousseau asked, "How can you be sure they're heading this direction, Harry?"

"I'm sure."

"We're nearing some bump in the road called Stanwood, and I ain't seen no sign of 'em. So···how long do we keep driving? How far—"

"All the way to the border and beyond, if necessary."

"And what happens when we—"

"Just drive!" snapped Phil Arnam, the remaining regular from Frantz's crew, riding in back.

"How we doing on gas?" asked Vic.

Alan searched for the gas gauge on the dash. "Quarter tank···maybe little less."

"That won't get us to the border. Stanwood's coming up, and it's got a gas station that's friendly. It has a mom-and-pop store on the side, if the girls need anything. Stop there, we'll fill up."

"Roger, that."

Vic pointed out the station as they drew near. Alan pulled into the lot, rolled down his window, and got in line behind a local farmer with a trailer full of hay. The local had finished getting gas but lingered next to the

319

pump, apparently enjoying a social chat with the attendant. Alan raised his arm, getting ready to tap the horn, but Vic discreetly stayed his hand. "Just give them a minute."

In a few moments, the attendant acknowledged their presence and began his farewells to the local. The attendant said, "Looks like the young fella's in a bit of a hurry."

After the farmer drove off, Alan eased the big sedan up to the pump. Dressed in bib overalls, the attendant stepped to the window and said, "Welcome, folks. What can I—"

"Fill it with premium, please."

"Yes, sir, and would you like me to check your oil and wash—"

"Won't be necessary. We're in a hurry."

The attendant peeked inside the open window and started to grin a neighborly welcome to his visitors, but he cut it short. He clumsily backed away, toward the pump, with his eyebrows pinched at the middle and sagging at the edges. A frown now warped his once friendly face, like he'd found a fly in his oatmeal. His mouth moved as if he were chewing a bite of the tainted mush, feeling the need to be cautious.

Vic said, "I'm going to get the girls some bread and lunch meat. You want anything?"

"I'll have what they're having."

Vic climbed out, stretched, and checked the surrounding area. The traffic was very light, and at the rear of the car, the attendant continued to stand vigilantly, holding onto the gas nozzle, while he stared through the rear window at the girls. Vic shook his head and frowned. He focused on avoiding the numerous mud puddles, crossing the graveled lot to the store.

320

Detective Rousseau pointed to the sign on the side of the road. "We need gas, and I need to piss."

Frantz said, "Make it quick."

As they slowed to leave the highway, Frantz suddenly sat up straight, cursed, and stabbed his arm toward the steering wheel, forcing their sedan out of the gravel, back onto the road. "Don't stop. Keep going."

"What the···"

It took Rousseau a second to catch on, but less than 100 feet away, a big man walked away from the Packard gassing up at the pumps.

Rousseau brought their car back up to speed and drove past the filling station. Frantz said, "Take her down the road a stretch. Then turn off where we'll have a view of the road."

Rousseau asked, "What do we do then?"

"We wait."

Rousseau turned off at a Tack and Feed shop and wedged the plain, black sedan between a couple of pick-up trucks with hay bales stacked high. He pointed the car back toward the highway. If not for the hay bales camouflaging their location, the city slickers would have stuck out like relish on a white T-shirt.

Within five minutes, the Packard drove past, getting up to speed for the highway that cut through farmlands. Rousseau engaged his clutch and worked their car back onto the roadway, keeping his distance. Frantz said, "Give them about a mile, then pull up alongside."

"Then what?"

"Then we see what they do, and we react, accordingly."

Within three-quarters of a mile, Rousseau had closed the gap, narrowing it to within thirty yards of the Packard. Out of habit, he signaled his lane change before moving into the passing lane, drawing the detective's car up close to the refugees. In the backseat, Arnam rolled down the window and brought the nose of the Thompson up, setting it on the window's frame.

Vic opened a loaf of bread and slapped cold bologna between two pieces. The women in the back scrunched their noses, and said, "Ewwee," almost in unison. Vic grinned, turning around. Handing a sandwich to his skeptics, he momentarily froze, his eyes filled with terror. "Scharfshutze!" he yelled.

Vic dropped the sandwich in someone's lap, snapped around forward, threw his leg over Alan's, and stomped down on the brake. The big car skidded to a stop, fishtailing and plowing gravel.

Alan squeezed the steering wheel, fighting to keep the car under control, and barked, "What the hell?" The change in momentum caused the girls to fall forward, en masse, sliding off the backseat. The police car sailed past in the next lane, before its driver hit the brakes, stopping a hundred yards down the road. The girls got up and sat back in their seat, panicky, while Alan, sensing their imminent danger, spun the steering wheel and took a sharp right down a side road. He pushed the big engine through the gears, trying to put distance between them and their pursuers.

Vic said, "They're backing up and coming after us. See if you can ditch 'em."

The big car barreled down the road, tossing gravel but making little dust, thanks to a recent rain. The road came to a T, and Alan slowed to make a left turn, still trying to keep a northerly course. He shifted gears, accelerating up a grade past farmlands and dairy cows, munching on the shortened winter grass. He crested the hill and raced toward an empty hay wagon parked between the last two driveways, looming at the end of the road. One driveway went right and up a slight grade, the other left and up a small hill. Alan chose left, slowed for the turn, and then sped up the twin ruts toward the old farmhouse.

Vic brought the Thompson to port arms, took a deep breath, and closed his eyes momentarily. Alan said, "Pray us a miracle."

Vic said, "Drive past the house. Some of these have a way through their fields to the next road."

Alan skirted around a pick-up truck parked near the house. He slowed as he passed by the back steps of the house, which craved paint. A woman in an apron came out and stopped on the porch. The barn, which sported a fresh coat of red paint, was located a hundred yards ahead. It had a white wooden gate connected to its far end, which was open and led down to a pasture···he hoped. As he drove alongside the barn, Vic grabbed for the door handle. "Let me out. Then come back around when I've finished."

Once through the gate, Alan slowed to a near stop, and Vic jumped out with the tommy gun, pushing the car door shut. The Packard rumbled away, down toward the pond and the pasture. Vic wasted no time, racing across the driveway and hiding behind the corner of the barn. He peeked out from his position, while holding the Thompson down and back behind him, continuing his vigilance of the farmhouse and the drive. A moment later, the police car crested the driveway, pulling next to the house. A man had joined the woman on the porch. He was pulling up suspenders, putting on a coat, and carrying something with a long barrel, deftly managing all three tasks at once. The black sedan came to a sudden stop next to the couple. The voices were distant, but the one that mentioned "police" could be heard at a distance. The woman pointed in his direction, or that of the open gate, but did so without say anything.

The police car's engine revved, the driver engaged the clutch, and the vehicle crawled rapidly in Vic's direction. He stepped backward a few yards into the grass, away from the edge of the barn, and he leveled the muzzle of the Thompson, while listening, watching, and waiting.

Within seconds, the sound of the police car's engine grew closer, paused, and then the clutch caught again. In a moment, the nose of the car passed the side of the barn, emerging through the gate. Vic stepped forward and brought the muzzle level with the driver's door, tracking its movement. Terror erupted on the face of the man in the back seat, and he was all elbows and awkward movements as he tried to swing his own tommy gun around toward his window and bring it to bear on Vic.

Vic let go a burst at the driver. BANG! BANG! BANG!

Male voices screamed, cursed. The driver's hands went spastic.

Vic continued slogging through the wet grass toward the car, now aiming the Thompson at the rear passenger, who had worked the barrel of his tommy gun out the window. The would-be assassin looked familiar, even though absolute fear contorted his face. Vic squeezed another burst. BANG! BANG! BANG! BANG! The bullets crashed through glass, sheet metal, and flesh.

The car slowed to a near stop, pausing for a moment, like it, too, was wounded, but then it lost its battle with gravity, a relentless force that pulled it down the hill toward the pond. Vic brought the Thompson up to his shoulder and took aim on the back of the coupe. BANG! BANG! Insurance shots. He did the math.

Nine shots, two men down, but weren't there three?

He peeked around the edge of the barn and back up toward the house. Something moved at the edge of his field of vision. Harry's in the barn!

Up on the porch, the two people stood near each other and watched the show unfolding before them. Stay out of this. It's not your play.

Vic jerked around and raced toward the far corner of the barn, guessing Harry would be sneaking up on the near side, using the side next to the driveway for concealment. Inside the barn, the whinny of horses and cackle of chickens alerted the other animals to an intruder.

In the field below, Alan's view of the barn was partially obstructed by blackberries that covered the fence, but he'd heard the gunplay and then watched as the detectives' car rolled down the hill, picking up speed, until it lunged into the pond. There was no sign of Vic, up the hill. Alan put the Packard in gear and spun it around on the wet grass, finally settling the car back on the grass drive, putting it on a course leading back to the barn. Passing the pond, he slowed to examine the bullet-riddled police car, sinking into the brown water, its hot engine sending steam into the cab through the open windows. The driver was slumped forward but was still alive. His right hand held the steering wheel, while his left hand jerked about, as if its owner were swatting at wasps.

There were no signs from the passengers, and Alan figured they were down for a ten count. He didn't want to hazard a closer inspection, so he hurried up the rise toward the house on the odd chance someone was still capable of firing a gun from the sinking car.

325

Vic worked his way along the backside of the barn, having to be cautious, knowing whatever Frantz was packing was easily capable of penetrating the thin cedar siding that separated them. The windows on this side of the barn were of no help to him; they were high up the walls and thick with dirt. Near the far end of the barn was an entrance for dairy cows. He moved among several skittish Holsteins and cut one from the herd to use as a shield. He crept through the thick mud, which sucked at his dress shoes and caked on the cuffs of his suit pants. The afternoon sun broke through heavy clouds, far to the south. He was concerned the new sunshine would backlight him, so he caught his breath and pieced together a plan.

In the field below, the sound of a motor grew louder as the Packard climbed the hill toward the barn and Hungry Harry.

Nearing the barn, Alan expected to see Vic, but he was nowhere in sight. A knot quickly grew into a large, heavy ball in his stomach. He worried the big man must have also been hit in the exchange of gunfire. He scanned frantically while driving, half expecting to find Vic's body lying in the grass, but he was too worried not to check. He crested the drive and moved the car alongside the barn. Up at the house, a man now stood next to the woman, both keeping their distance. Seeing no sign of Vic, Alan stopped and parked, so he could run back and check the field behind the gate. He opened the car door and began to climb out.

BANG! BANG! BANG!

Three shots from the barn tore into the car. One zinged through the open back window and smashed into the doorframe, behind where his head had just been. He couldn't tell where the other two rounds hit, and he didn't have time to search. He ducked for cover behind the rear tire and pulled out his pistol. Inside the car, the girls screamed, sobbed, and talked fast.

He opened the backdoor and took one of the girls by the arm, pulling her out. It was Rose. He told her to call the others out after her and line up in his shadow, like goslings behind a mother goose.

Iris came out next, followed by Lilly, but no Poppy. Rose called for her, but she got no answer.

The girls huddled in a line behind Alan. He pushed the door further open with his free hand and peered inside. Poppy sat on the opposite side of the car, slumped back on the rear seat, her body slack, like a cut flower wilting in a vase without water. Her head leaned against the door, and she didn't respond to his warnings to leave.

Alan pressed the door closed and said to Rose, "It's not safe here. Take the girls behind the well."

"Where Poppy?"

"I'll take care of her," he insisted. You need to run now. Go some place safe."

Rose searched his eyes, angry, scared, and confused. He held her gaze. And then she moved into action, barking orders. The other two girls followed her away from the car, running close to the ground, while Alan covered them, pointing his pistol at the barn, praying for a target that didn't appear.

Nearing the large opening in the side of the barn, Vic heard the three shots, which weren't aimed at him. He worried for Lilly and the others. With no time to waste, he prodded an unhappy cow with the muzzle of his

Thompson, urging her through the door. He followed behind, grabbing another cow by the ear, leading her inside, keeping his head low and next to her's, while minimizing his large silhouette. The cow's eyes were wild, untrusting, and darted about, avoiding contact with his. Her nostrils flared and she billowed hot steam into the crisp air. His grip was firm, forcing her to follow his lead.

Once inside, he hurried up next to an empty horse stall and took his bearings, trying to sift out human sounds from those that belonged in the barn. During a lull in the cacophony of chickens clucking and scurrying about, a car door opened and shut, just outside the barn. Then, on the other side of stacked hay bales, horse hooves clomped rapidly, as the large animal steadied itself, paused, and then took off at a noisy gallop.

Vic clambered over the hay and called out, "He's got a horse!"

Outside, Vic's warning rang out over the pounding of the large hoofs in the barn. Seconds later, horse and rider burst from the far end of the barn, closest to the house. Frantz raced wild-eyed on the bareback of a Percheron, a line of horses bred for strength, not speed. This breed once carried knights in full armor but was now relegated to plowing fields and pulling wagons.

Alan swung his .45 to eye level, locking his right arm and supporting it with his left, as his father had taught him, but the distance was too great. He quickly lowered the gun, tucked it into its holster, and rushed back to the car, where he thumbed the trunk latch and threw up the lid. He groped for the M-1, hidden under the refugees' belongings, and found its stock. He yanked hard, and it broke free of the luggage weighing it down. As the powerful rifle cleared the trunk, a bag tumbled to the ground, trailing after it.

Alan ran to the crest of the hill, next to the house, slid to his knee, and racked a round. He flipped up the long-distance sight, wrapped the sling around his arm, and jerked it tight. He took aim on the galloping figure and tracked horse and rider as they left the driveway and crossed the road, increasing their distance. He sat back on one foot as he brought the Garand to eyelevel, sighting in on the fleeing fugitive, remembering his past, "Trigger control and sight alignment, son." He exhaled softly, blowing the warmed air across his pursed lips. He squeezed gently on the trigger, butterfly touch. This one's for Poppy.

BOOM!

The rifle roared, kicking into his shoulder, while a single shell casing ejected from the breech, flying into the air before bouncing into the wet grass. Two hundred yards away, the figure on the horse jerked, his head snapping to the side, but somehow he maintained his grip on the horse's mane and kept riding, heading into the pasture to the south.

Vic soon joined Alan, while the couple stayed back and watched the gunplay. The man set his shotgun's butt on the ground and used the business end's double-barrels as an armrest. Alan tipped his hat, politely acknowledging their hosts. The woman stared openmouthed, while her husband nodded a reply.

Vic and Alan turned back to watch Hungry Harry on the Percheron. The farmer and his wife slowly came over and stood nearby. Across the way, the big horse dug hard with powerful hind legs and climbed the rise, rider draped over its thick neck, his head bouncing uncontrollably, flopping with the horse's mane at every gallop.

"Where'd you hit him?" asked Vic.

"Not sure···maybe his shoulder. I was aiming high—didn't want to risk the horse."

The farmer said, "I appreciate that, but it looks like young Rex's gone to visit his girlfriend. Means I'll be out stud fees, but that's okay."

Vic made introductions to Albert and Mary, while the horse picked its way through the field toward some large horses pasturing on the other side of a large ditch. As Rex jumped into the water to make the crossing, Hungry Harry pitched forward and fell off, splashing into the foul runoff.

The farmer said, "That's probably as nice a shooting as I've ever seen. Was he a banker?"

"No, sir."

"Looked like a banker, and they're always in season around here. When they drove by the house, he said something about being with the law, but he's dressed like a crook, the kind that only sides with the law when they're repossessing farms."

Alan said, "He was after what didn't belong to him."

The farmer explained. "We lost three farms in South Dakota to locust, dust, and drought. Bankers had no patience for us. We moved here so our boys could work for Mr. Boeing, build airplanes for that war in Europe. Nice family, the Boeings."

Across the road in the far pasture, Harry stirred, showing life, struggled to his feet, and turned to face his assassin. Still standing in the brackish water, he reeled and caught his balance. His right hand went to his jaw and it seemed as if he were trying to yell something to them, but nothing clear came out. He pointed his finger at Alan and tapped his chest, as if indicating a new target for the marksman. He stood up straight and spread his hands wide, forming a human cross—a human target.

Alan adjusted his weight as he sat back on his heel, again taking aim. He let out another gush of air through his mouth and went quiet. Fifteen to twenty seconds passed, and he didn't take the shot. He slowly withdrew his finger from the trigger, indexing it alongside the stock. Finally, Vic asked, "You had enough?"

Alan took in another breath, exhaled hard across exposed teeth, adjusted his aim, and drove his finger back inside the trigger guard, gently resting the pad of his finger on the trigger. Across the way Rex whinnied loudly. Then without explanation, Alan shook his head, raised the barrel, lowered the stock, and removed his finger. "If it's what he wants, I'm not giving it to him."

Vic patted Alan on the shoulder. "There's been a reckoning."

Across the way, Harry dropped his arms, they flopped to his sides. Seconds later, he fell to his knees and pitched forward, landing face down on the far bank of the water. He lay motionless.

Alan inclined his head and indicated to Vic they needed to have a word. Vic caught the signal, and the two excused themselves to talk in private, back near the car. Alan said, "He shot one of the "

"Oh, God, no! Which one?"

Alan opened his mouth, but the words stuck in his throat, not wanting to come out, as if not saying it wouldn't make it so. He shook his head and wiped the corner of his eyes with his sleeve. His voice cracked as the name finally tumbled out. "Poppy." Vic stopped in his tracks. "How bad?"

"She wasn't moving."

Vic bent at the waist, as if kicked in the stones by the runaway stallion. He slowly dropped to his knees in the driveway, put his hand to the ground, shook his head, and muttered a curse in a strange language. Alan gave him a minute, stared off in the distance, and wiped a hand across his face, as if trying to erase the misery he felt.

When Vic collected himself, they walked down to the car. Alan opened the back door, which had been closest to the barn. Poppy rolled out into his arms like a rag doll. He caught and eased her out of the car, holding her snuggly to his chest, cuddling her head in the crook of his arm. The hair behind her ear was wet, matted, and reddened with blood.

Vic dropped to his knees and slid next to Alan. He ran his thick fingers gently through her sticky hair, probing for the wound, while Alan watched, puzzled. Behind them, the farmer and his wife walked up, also curious, pensive. Soon, Rose, Lilly, and Iris came running from behind the well to the car, crying in anticipation.

Vic raised his eyes anxiously to the couple and inclined his head toward the approaching refugees. Their hosts understood and intercepted the little women, gently holding them back, despite the girls' loud protestations.

Vic spoke quietly to Alan. "Run your hand here, near the base of her skull. There's an entry wound, and just a little further over you'll feel a lump. It's misshapen, but it's the bullet. Probably flattened out some going through all the metal."

Alan's fingers met Vic's in the wet hair. Vic steered Alan toward the hole, clearly the source of the bleeding. "Now follow that across to the other side, about an inch-and-a-half, and you'll···see what I mean?"

Reacting to the probing, Poppy's body suddenly jerked a short spasm and went rigid, while her arms thrashed for a second, her face wincing in pain. She groaned but didn't open her eyes. Vic and Alan exchanged a hopeful glance, both men's eyes leaping wide, and then they returned to their patient.

Vic said, "That's a good sign. It's probably better that the slug's stuck there than in her skull. 'Course that ain't for sure. Before it stopped, it might've bounced around, cracked something, or tore away at nerves. You never know with head wounds until you look inside. For now, we got to stop the bleeding and get her to a doctor."

The farmer said, "We haven't got a doc handy. Closest one is in Mount Vernon."

"We can't head back that way. There could be more who're after us," said Vic.

"Well, you folks do what you must, but I've a salve and dressing we put on the animals when they get a puncture wound. It should slow down the bleeding 'til you get where you need."

Lilly pushed past Albert, stared down at Poppy, and let out a shrill cry that pierced the farmland tranquility. The other girls anxiously joined her in wailing. Vic put up a hand, signaling them to stay back. "She'll be all right, Flower."

Anguish tortured the beauty of the women's faces. Lilly spoke sternly to Vic. "You make her better!"

Vic asked the farmer, "How long before the sheriff shows?"

"Don't know he will, but I can't be sure. No one at this end of the road's got a telephone. We live near enough to town to have a mailbox, but got no phone. Out here, a little gunfire ain't all that unusual. 'Course this was a little more than people are accustomed to···"

"Soon enough you'll have to let the authorities know about the police car in your pond. They may take you in for questioning."

"Was that a real police car?"

Vic raised his eyebrows and shoulders. "Well··· yeah. All the way from Seattle."

"Hooh! Those boys are a long way from home."

"They were a long way from the law···"

While the farmer tended to Poppy's wound on the back porch, inserting white gauze into the wound before applying a thick dollop of Vaseline mixture to hold it in place, his wife fixed sandwiches for the refugees in the kitchen. Lilly got busy making a special tea for Poppy on the wood burning stove. Vic seemed to recognize the odor from the tea, and he smiled approvingly. Lilly held the cup for Poppy, who had come around but remained in considerable pain. Lilly explained to her what had happened and what everyone was trying to do to help her.

Vic and the farmer discussed Poppy's wound and their medical strategy. They would leave the slug in place, deciding a real doctor should determine if it could be removed. Then, while Vic studied the farmer's handiwork, restlessness got to Alan. He went outside and sat on the porch, which was set high enough so he could watch traffic on the main road from town, while he twitched his ankle nervously.

Twenty minutes later, Vic carried the groggy patient out to the porch and down to the car. Alan had seen the dreamy, glazed look before. Despite her painful injury, Poppy was in another world. Alan helped Vic

335

load her into the car. With Poppy braced between Lilly and Rose, Vic assured Alan they would breeze through the border crossing. Vic folded a fifty-dollar bill in next to his driver's license, just in case.

As the guests made final preparations to leave, the family refused offers of money, even though it was obvious they were starting over in their later years. Pride was at stake, as well as rural courtesy. The farmers even extended an invitation to all their guests to "drop by again, anytime."

Driving away from the house and down toward the gravel road, Alan interrupted Vic's reverie. "Son-of-a-bitch!"

"What's wrong?" asked Vic.

"Harry's gone."

"You sure?"

"Look to where he went down. He isn't there now."

"Could've sank and drowned⋯I wish."

At the foot of the hill, Vic put up his hand, signaling for Alan to stop. He stared at where the lieutenant had fallen off the large horse. "Go on up the neighbor's drive a touch."

About a hundred feet up, Alan stopped the car and pulled the brake. Vic climbed out and tromped away into the tall grass, toward the ditch. After a moment of studying the ground, he shook his head and returned to the Packard. "The horse knocked down grass on his way to the far pasture, and there're signs Harry went through the field, heading southeast...." Vic pointed along with the directions, as he talked.

"What signs?"

"Blood and mud on grass he trampled."

"What now?"

"We don't have time to track him. By now, he's

likely found someone to take him to a hospital or call the sheriff. So, back the car up next to our friends' mailbox."

Alan didn't ask why. When he stopped the car, Vic took an envelope from his coat. He opened the mailbox, set the packet inside. Then he reached across and tapped the horn twice. While driving away, they gave the farmers a wave. Vic said, "Nice people. Don't you think?"

"Sure, Vic, but what about Harry?"

"In an hour and change, I'll be out of the country, on my way to China, and Harry'll be a memory."

"Great, and for me?"

"You've plunked him twice, but he just keeps on breathing, like a cat falling out a tree, always landing on its feet. The good thing for you is—Harry might have gotten a peek at your handsome mug, but he still don't know for sure. 'Course, it's only a matter of time 'fore he figures it out, with you looking just like your daddy and all. For now, when Mr. B has to give up names, he can tell Ketchum it was Harry's old treacherous buddy, Benny, who did the shooting—all of it—Broadway and here. Then, Benny felt so bad about double-crossing Harry, he's now decided to hide out in Canada, and he ain't ever coming back.

"Now, if Harry survives, makes it back to Seattle, how's he going to refute that? Is he going to tell Ketchum he personally knows that double-crossing SOB Benny, and he's positive it wasn't him? Not likely. My advice is when you get back to the city, read the papers and see what they got to say. Somehow, old Harry's going to make himself out a hero again, but he's still got Chief Ketchum and Mr. B to deal with."

Vic reached in his coat pocket and took out the spent M-1 shell and bounced it in his hand. Then he reached over and tucked it in Alan's coat pocket.

337

"Whenever you can, always pick up your brass. These things end up with little marks on them, and the police labs can tell what gun fired—"

Alan furrowed his brow and nodded. "I know that."

"I'm sure you do, but my point is you shouldn't leave them lying around. Also, if Harry gets wise and comes after you, he'll probably have to do it on his own, because the police won't be wanting nothing to do with it. He's just lost four members of his crew, so his ranks are a bit depleted. Guys rally 'round a winner, but Harry looks to have lost his luck. He might be flying solo for a while, but if he starts making noises like he's coming after you, just wipe this one clean of prints and send it to him anonymously, a little gift. You don't even have to pen a note; he'll get the message."

After they passed Customs at the US/Canadian Border, Vic heaved a huge sigh and relaxed in his seat. "The worst is behind, Champ. Just stay on this road. It'll take us into downtown Vancouver—where we got friends. So, no need to look so glum."

Alan continued staring distantly down the road, eyes heavy. Occasionally, he used the rearview mirror to check on the passengers in the back.

Vic silently nodded approval and peeked over his shoulder, doing the same. All the girls were pensive but a little happier, except Poppy, who slept soundly. "If you're worried about her, she'll be fine. We'll find a doc in Vancouver. They also got a Chinatown."

Alan blinked long, a silent acknowledgement, but he didn't reply. After a pause, he sighed heavily.

"Something's on your mind. Is it Poppy, or you just hate goodbyes?"

"Yeah. Her···and some things that don't add up."

"Like what?"

When he didn't reply right away, Vic waited him out, looking lazily out his window, unfocused. Finally, Alan said, "Okay, let's start with what you yelled just before you stomped on the brake."

339

Vic slowly eyed Alan, carefully appraising him, like it was the first time they'd met. Then he stared off into oblivion toward the open road, a smile creasing his face, eventually confident in his decision. "You weren't supposed to find out 'til you looked in my safety deposit box, but I suppose it can't be helped, now. Fact, it will be dangerous for you not to know.

Alan scrunched his brow, hearing of the new enigma. He stole a puzzled glance at Vic.

"Trouble is," said Vic, "I've taken countless oaths to never reveal these secrets, short of a national emergency, but the way the winds of war are blowing, it looks like we're approaching that point. My plan was to let you do some more digging on your own, find out without me saying a word."

Alan again looked at his passenger quizzically, then back to the road.

Vic said, "The word was 'scharfshutze.' It slipped out. It's German for 'sniper.'"

"Why German?"

"It's my native language, English is my second. Under stress, it comes out."

Alan's mouth sagged open, matching his lowered brows, puzzled.

"Just remember, Champ, I ain't lied to you yet, and I don't figure to start. I'm going to tell you things I never told your daddy or Mr. B, and this you got to keep your yap shut about, or it could get you, your family, and others killed. Understood?"

"Understood."

"I'm on my way to another world, but people can still reach out and find me, if properly motivated."

"I get it."

"Sid Fisher wasn't the only one changed his name.

I was born Victor Randall to a German family near the East Coast. I picked up 'Morrison' after the war, from a tombstone in a Veteran's cemetery. All I had to do was change my last name."

"I thought you said, 'Pennsylvania Dutch?'"

"Same thing. And, I was in the war with your daddy, only I was on the other side of the fence···or so it appeared."

Alan's jaw dropped another half-inch, and he had to make a quick steering correction to get the car back in its lane.

"When I enlisted in Philly, I met some people, right off, who recruited me to go back to der Heimatland to serve as a German soldier, report what I saw. I had no family to worry about, I could speak German, I didn't look too bright," Vic said with a grin. "And they figured I was good with my hands. Good enough that I ended up working around Germany's airplanes and dirigibles—perfect place for espionage. I saw some action, but I had strict orders not to shoot Americans. But I could—if I must—it was that important. That's why the first kill haunts me. He was an American boy attacking our position, and when he saw me, he saw a murdering Hun. It was kill or be killed. But···I wish to hell I could forget some things.

"So after the war, I stayed in the business, and I traveled about for these same people, did what they wanted me to. Then they sent me out here to Seattle, because of the Boeing factory and the naval shipyards. The government knew there were spies working the area—and still are. I could work either side. My job was to get close to them, which I did. Same rules applied as during the war: defensive kills only; report what you see and hear. But, for your own good, Champ, I won't tell you who're my contacts—either side of the fence, or the pond, as the British call it. I never told your dad."

"How come?"

"No need to mention it. Closest I came to telling was when we were on to Fisch, but your daddy wanted him just as bad as me. That said, our finding him was not just happenstance. My handler wanted him, too—wanted proof he was involved with Hauptmann and proof he'd been eliminated."

"Okay," said Alan thoughtfully. Indicating with nods that he needed more information to see where Vic was headed with this.

"Lucky Lindy was traveling around Europe on goodwill tours. Germany wanted badly for him to visit, which he did, and the Nazis pressed him to evaluate their airplanes, because he was a trained engineer and test pilot—a lotta people forget that. He was the most famous pilot in the world, but he only wanted to do a walkthrough. Those in charge needed his endorsement on their planes, their manufacturing techniques, and they were looking for political leverage to cower their enemies. A lot was involved—still is, and now they've used Lindy's public praise as propaganda. Now, here's where it comes together: If the Nazis could show they had taken care of Lindy's kidnapping misfortune, especially when his own country couldn't do it, he might respond favorably to them."

Alan nodded subtly.

"Now, you know what happened to old Sid—and there's only a few people beside you who do—keep that in mind. So, when Sid finally meets his demise, Lindy starts paying more attention to Germany, and then Hermann Goering presents him with the Verdienstkreuz Deutscher Adler."

"The what?"

"The German Service Medal of the Eagle."

"The one everyone wants him to give back?"

"Exactly. It's a thing of beauty, even with the Swastikas and all. I've got one, too—for my help on this, because it was that big of a deal. O' course mine was all done in secret—"

"You have a German medal?"

"Not just any medal—the Verdienstkreuz Deutscher Adler. I left it in the vault with some instructions. You can't show it or discuss it with anyone. Understood?"

"I get it."

"Just follow the instructions."

Alan nodded.

"It's kind of a hoot when you think about it," Vic said. "What with my being on the other side—"

Alan rolled his eyes and shook his head, trying to piece it all together. "You are amazing."

"Sometimes I amaze myself. I think I'm just a regular guy, but then look at my life, where I've been and what I've done. I wouldn't trade none of it. It's funny how things turn out, but as I was saying, there are very few of these out there. Lindy got his six months after Henry Ford—another Jew hater by the way, but no one makes a stink about his. They both got them before the war broke out. Soon after Lindy gets his, he inspects the Luftwaffe's newest bomber, the Junker JU-88, and he actually flew their best fighter, the Messerschmitt ME-109."

"If I follow what you're saying, you helped swing Colonel Lindbergh to Germany's side to help them with their Luftwaffe, and now they're running all over Europe, bombing the hell out of England."

"So it would seem, but that was inevitable, because the Brits focus too much of their attention on the navy, not enough on their air force—but that might change, now. And the French ain't nothing but a bunch of pacifists. They got their head in the sand. Now that they've got their teat in a wringer—again, I might add—they'll expect the good old US of A to come bail them out. And what you don't know—and need to know—is that Lindy's still an American patriot—the best we got. Sure, he's got this thing about eugenics and the Jews—"

"What is that, anyway?"

"It's something about creating a better human race with proper breeding, which means Arians and Norse only—no Jews, no Russians, and no Asians of any kind."

Again, Alan rolled his eyes.

"But, it was actually the US Military Attaché to Germany who begged Lindy to go to Germany, see what they had. Because of who Lindy is, he got VIP access to places no other American could. And he took all he learned to share with our intelligence people. Who better to see what the Germans are up to than a test pilot and engineer? Lindy knows planes. So, as it turns out, America is actually in a better position should the war come to us."

"You say 'us,' but you're not going to be here."

"Yeah, but I'll be pulling for the home team."

Alan was quiet for a long moment, and then he said, "On the Mighty B with Benny, you were speaking German, weren't you?"

"You heard that over the roar of the engines?"

"I wasn't sure until now."

"You're a sharp one, but I can't say... Let's just leave at—the USA is a lot better off with Benny gone, and I'd have more explaining to do if I stayed."

Alan tipped his hat back and scratched his head. "You got any more secrets I should know about?"

"Just remember, a whole lotta people in this country speak German, especially if you travel to the Midwest.

We used to have our own local, German newspaper when I was growing up. Then came the war, and everyone had to switch to English. Speaking Deutsch don't mean they're treugesinnte zum Heimatland—German loyalists. And remember what I said about not mentioning this to anyone. That includes around the office."

Three days after arriving in Vancouver, Alan drove back home. He crossed the border and made his first stop at the Greyhound Bus Depot in Bellingham, where he retrieved the Thompson and the M-1 Garand. Before going into Canada, Vic had helped him disassemble them for storage in an overnight locker. With Poppy needing medical attention, neither Alan nor Vic wanted to risk an encounter with Customs, which toughened up after the Repeal.

The drive home gave Alan time to think about the past couple of weeks, the men he'd killed, and the man he'd saved twice. Vic tried to convince him there had been a third saving, when Alan's mere presence flushed Frantz out of ambush in the barn, but Alan wasn't buying it. It was connected too closely to Poppy's head wound, which hurt to think about. He chose instead to rehash Vic and Lilly's wedding, and his getting to be best man.

In return for the favor, Vic gave Alan his well-worn detective badge, telling him he wouldn't need it in retirement. Alan took the prized badge from his pocket and tossed the hefty brass lightly in his hand. He rubbed a fingerprint smudge off the finish with his thumb and put it away. It was the perfect gift.

Vic had breezed through the Canadian channels, finishing the necessary paperwork for a proper wedding. His powers of persuasion worked just as well north of the border, which gave Alan hope Vic would continue to be successful once he arrived on Lilly's island.

Alan stayed with the refugees all the way to a merchant ship, making sure they'd gotten on board without interference, and he had given the other women hugs. Parting with Poppy was more painful than he could imagine. With her confined to a ship's bed, their farewell hugs were limited, awkward. Still, her tears were real and ripped at his heartstrings, forcing him to bite the inside of his lower lip in an effort to appear in control of his emotions that he didn't completely understand.

Vic stayed out of it, neither encouraging Alan to flee with them nor making it easy for him to stay behind. There wasn't a simplistic platitude to make the pain go away. For Alan, it was akin to dealing with the shootings and all the recent violence, leaving more turmoil he would have to learn to cope with, finding a place in his heart for pain.

When Alan tried to say goodbye to Vic with a proper handshake, Vic would have none of it; instead, he wrapped his arms around Alan and gave him a crushing hug. When he released his grip, he chucked Alan on the chin and wished him luck, a gesture of affection Alan was more comfortable with. Retreating up the gangway, Vic called after Alan. "Leave Harry alone. You squared it for Mackie."

Alan tipped his hat to him and returned to the car. Climbing in, he thought: What about Poppy? Is it square for her?

Several hours later, Alan stopped in traffic at the University Bridge in Seattle, where the University

District met Eastlake. The bridge was in the up position, waiting for a schooner to pass underneath through the channel, returning to its berth on Lake Union. Like other motorists in line, accustomed to the drawbridge's temporary interruptions, he got out of his car and joined them at the pedestrians' rail and watched the boat's crew tending lines and holding bumpers at the ready, as the boat passed below them. More so than those on the boat, Alan hungered for home, but at the same time, he dreaded it. His first order of business would be to make peace with his mother, assure her he was safe, she was safe, and the family was safe. As important as doing that was to him, he also hoped there was enough time left in the day to see Alice. Come Sunday, maybe she'd let him accompany her to church. He hoped it would be amenable to forgiveness and equipped with a certified lighting rod.

It was near suppertime, too late in the day for Alan to exchange the Packard for his Ford Coupe, so he drove near home, parking it in a lot at the foot of the hill behind an Eastlake market. If the police were looking for him, they would have someone watching the front of the house. Parking in the back would run the risk of the neighbors' speculating about an overnight guest, putting a strain on reputations.

Before he reached the front porch, Margaret, who seemed to sense his arrival, came out to greet him. She wasn't too embarrassed to gush over him, where his brothers were more restrained. She fussed to see what he was holding behind his back, grabbing his arms to hold him still. When she got a peek, she put her hand over her mouth, as if to quiet a squeal.

348

With his free hand, he pulled his detective badge from his pocket. She took it and inspected it, trying to rub out the same fingerprint he had worked on earlier. Her joy turned bittersweet. She said, "Dad used to have one of these. I wonder what happened to it?"

"I'd be afraid to ask Mother."

"Is this yours to keep? Are you a real detective?"

"I am."

"Then I'm sure you'll be interested in the newspaper articles I saved."

He stared into her eyes a moment, checking to see if there was more she knew but wasn't telling. She met his stare evenly with a poker face. She stepped to the side and held the front door for him, as if he were a guest. When he walked by, she said, "There's something different about you. Have you grown, and I didn't notice?"

He chuckled. "I'm tall enough."

From the dining room, Mary set down a roast on the table and stoically joined the others in the front room, stopping in front of the piano. "Margaret, would you set out another place setting? It seems we're having company."

Alan rushed to his mother, who held her ground, and he reached out to give her a hug, but she presented her cheek stiffly, for a proper kiss. She stared past him at the lake and across to Queen Anne Hill, in the distance, with the sun setting behind, but he was close enough to see tears welling up in his mother's eyes. She wasn't going to let any loose without a fight, but he had prepared for this battle. "These are for you," he said, as he brought the large bouquet from behind him. "I hope you like roses."

In the dining room, Margaret bubbled with delight, again muffling an excited screech, while Mary's eyes widened. Her mouth opened, but no words came out.

A moment later, her lower lip trembled and the tears finally broke free. She softened. She retrieved a napkin from inside her apron, while at the same time she reached for the bouquet with her other hand, clutching the flowers to her chest.

"Pink ones are my favorite."

Then she cried happy tears or ones of relief, Alan wasn't sure. He was just relieved she'd begun to get over being angry. She said, "Your father used to bring me roses when we were···it's been a long time."

She pulled Alan close and gave him a robust kiss on the cheek. She glanced down at the bag still in his hand. "And what else have you brought, young man?"

"I picked up some French wine while up in Vancouver. I thought it might go well with dinner."

Mary stared at him in silence for a moment, catching her breath as she evaluated. "No harm in trying something new. You set out whatever glasses you think are appropriate, while I put these in a vase. Then you can tell us about Canada, and we'll celebrate your safe return."

THE END

Neil Low is a captain with the Seattle Police Department and the agency's first commander of its new Ethics and Professional Responsibility Section. Other areas he has commanded include: Homicide and Violent Crimes, Internal Affairs, and Domestic Violence and Sexual Assault. He is a Vietnam veteran and a cum laude graduate of the University of Washington's Bothell campus, where he also wrote for the school's weekly newspaper, The UW Bothell Commons. A Seattle native, he now lives in Everett with his wife and three daughters.

ACKNOWLEDGEMENTS

Although writing is a lonely pursuit in which the author spends countless hours pecking away at his/her computer, the end product would not have been as polished as it should without the help of several people along the journey. I am very grateful and wish to acknowledge the many who made this come true. First and foremost I wish to thank my wife Lesley and our three daughters, Amanda, Michelle, and Meghan for their patience and acceptance of my passion. I am also immensely grateful to my University of Washington instructors, such as Rebecca Brown and Carole Glickfeld, both wonderful writers. I also wish to acknowledge my professors from the Bothell campus who generously gave of their office hours, answering questions and offering encouragement. In alphabetical order they are: Constantine Boehler, Michael Goldberg, David Goldstein, Gen McCoy, and William Seaburg. I also wish to apologize to the very charming Sarah Leadley, a UWB librarian who in no physical way resembles the librarian in my fictional tale who possesses a similar name. I also wish to acknowledge the first draft readers who eagerly read this creation in its early stages and offered critical, necessary advice. They include: Terrie Johnston, Carole Jordan, Donald Roff, Mary and David Tilbury, Dawn Todd, and my mother, Patricia Low. Special thanks goes to my chiropractor, Dr. Jeffrey Abrams, whose wonderful stories inspired some of the characters' traits. And of course none of this would have been possible without the expert help and guidance of my publisher, Kristen Morris. Again, to all of you, thank you.